BLANK PAIGE

Inklings Literary books may be purchased for educational, business, or sales promotional use.

First Inklings Literary edition published in 2023

Library of Congress Control Number: 2023910584

Griffin, Ashley.
Blank Paige/ Ashley Griffin – 1st ed.

Copyright Registration Number: TXu 2-325-372
Library of Congress Catalog Card Number:
ISBN: 979-8-9885099-0-5 (paperback) 979-8-9885099-1-2 (hardcover)

www.ashleygriffinofficial.com

BLANK PAIGE

ASHLEY GRIFFIN

For the original denizens of The Bookstore

Especially:

Case Aiken, Mark Epperson, Eddie Gutierrez, Martin Landry, Janice Landry,

Lauren Lopez & Ray Virta

(And Shadow, though I didn't know him yet.)

And,

For anyone who has ever felt like they didn't quite fit.

CONTENTS

DEAR READER

On this side of the looking glass, as it were, The Bookstore seems the stuff of dreams.

But it is no dream.

It is more real, more…important…than anything else that ever was or will be. Where everything misplaced since your childhood, both your wonderful fantasies and horrific nightmares have been lying in wait for you.

Once you have found your way there you will spend the rest of your life trying to get back. For, if you are one for whom The Bookstore is meant (and no one finds it unless they are), when you walk through its doors you will feel you are finally arriving at the place you are truly meant to be. Not necessarily safe, but right. Everyone who has been there, no matter the time or place from which they come, feels the same. The world moves ever faster as history marches onwards, but The Bookstore's steady metronome still ticks at the same speed and rhythm as it did at the dawn of creation.

The most intoxicating thing about The Bookstore is its scent. The smell of books, especially old ones, can be as potent as the siren's song of old to Odysseus. The mix of aged leather, gold stitching, thread and dust is as powerful an elixir as any magic potion. Visionaries dream of bottling it.

The scent was the first thing the girl remembered.

But I'm getting ahead of myself.

We will get to her in exactly two thousand and fourteen words.

There are employees in the Store, though they often go unnoticed, as most in the service industry do. It is a fascinating truth that an apron and a nametag are all it takes to make you invisible. Tragic, really. Since childhood Fairy Tales teach us that the seemingly least important people are often the most significant.

People ought to learn from stories.

There is a reason that person in The Bookstore, the one whose face you never looked at and whose name you can't recall knows so much about Sci-Fi or Fantasy and why they cared so deeply about helping you find just the right book. Perhaps they ended up not being quite the right person to assist you, but you'll find the perfect one eventually. Sooner or later you always find just what you need at The Bookstore.

But did you ever think how long the thing you needed had to wait for you to find it?

PROLOGUE

SOMETHING WICKED

The moment Paige came into being, dear reader, was the beginning of the end of the world.

She hadn't known that when she winked into existence, but the two men arguing in the circus knew from the start (whatever "the start" really means).

"Because of this girl, every story that ever was, or ever will be, will disappear forever. Drystan! Pay attention!"

Drystan dodged out of the way of pedestrians, clamoring for the magic on sale as they weaved in and out of the maze of tents. Dr. Nightingale pulled Drystan against the canvas of the nearest tent, grasping for the closest thing to privacy he could get. "All of them! The secret bedtime story your grandmother tells you when you're tucked into bed on a dark and stormy night, the great classics, even the ancient ones – passed down before such a thing as writing existed, will vanish out of time and space."

Drystan and Nightingale were an exercise in contrast. Lanky with baggy clothes and permanently unkempt hair, Drystan was reminiscent of The Scarecrow in "The Wonderful Wizard of Oz." He seemed to almost dance when he walked. Dr. Nightingale, however, was wizened in the manner of someone who was a rock star in his glory days but had done a complete one-eighty to become the very "man" he had once rebelled against. He was tall and wore a long, velvet coat that upon close inspection was a crosshatch of burgundies, deep golds and plums.

"Are you even listening to me?" Nightingale snapped, trying to keep the passersby from hearing. "There will be no bringing them back. This girl will destroy our world!"

"No," said Drystan as he finally locked eyes with Nightingale. He'd heard every word perfectly. "She's the key to our liberation."

"Step right up!" a barker cried. "See your secret dreams made manifest right inside!"

"Take charge of your destiny with these enchanted amulets all the way from darkest Peru!" called another.

"MUST we do this here?"

"We are not going to the teahouse."

"It's calm and quiet."

"We have different priorities." Drystan reached around to a nearby stand and plucked a flower from the display – a beautiful bluebell somewhere between the regular kind and pure crystal. Drystan held it to his ear and heard the song of fairyland echoing deep within its petals.

"You don't know what you're talking about. If something isn't done, this beloved circus of yours will be eviscerated along with everything else," Nightingale added, looking for any sort of unoccupied corner.

"Things are changing."

"Nothing changes. It can't. It can only exist or not."

"Not anymore," said Drystan. "Because of her -"

"There's an answer," Nightingale cut him off. "We just have to find it."

"Of course."

"We're leaving!" said Nightingale as a passing patron accidentally stabbed her heel into his foot, splashing a red drink all over him and Drystan in the process. She was too enchanted with her surroundings to notice. "Besides, this place is going to turn rather diabolical in a moment."

"We still have time," Drystan said, trying to hum the tune echoing from the flower. "Fancy a trip to the fortune teller?" He smiled.

"I'd rather redo my Annwn thesis from scratch."

"That the best you can offer?"

"It involved having myself disassembled, spread over the four corners of the world (and some other worlds too), and magically putting myself back together. Want me to try it on you?"

That shut Drystan up.

An acrobat on a trapeze swung down right over their heads.

Nightingale grabbed Drystan, pulling him out of the way.

"We need to have a serious conversation."

Drystan acquiesced. He put the flower back, pulled out a book from his pocket and begrudgingly opened it.

Instantly Drystan and Nightingale were standing in a beautiful, enormous bookstore. They wore the same clothes, which were now completely clean - unlike others they rarely felt the need to change for a story - the bruise on Nightingale's foot gone. But they barely registered their surroundings. Instead, Nightingale grabbed the book out of Drystan's hand, placed it back on a shelf, and walked purposefully to another section of the Store, Drystan following behind.

"We're really going to the teahouse?" Said Drystan, recognizing the path they were taking.

Nightingale didn't answer

They quickly found the Steampunk section. (Steampunk, dear reader, is a retrofuturistic subgenre of Science Fiction or Science Fantasy that utilizes technology and style from 19th-century industrial steam-powered machinery. Basically, imagine a science fiction story taking place in Victorian England). Nightingale quickly found a well-worn book with gold embossing and, looking around to make sure no one was watching, took Drystan's arm, opened the book, and instantly the unlikely companions disappeared.

A moment later they found themselves seated at the back of a Steampunk teahouse, a brandy in front of Nightingale, an absinthe for Drystan. Music from a strange band floated over, the singer scratching out:

" You could write but never edit…edit…

Try to read between the lines…the lies…the lines…"

The place was a hodgepodge of patrons. Ghosts intermixed with the living, everyone wore a combination of Victorian clothing and fantastical "technology." Practically everything in the room from the tapers to the teacups was partially made of gears and chains along with the usual materials – but all vibrant and antiqued. Burnished gold and glowing, smoky copper seemed to saturate the air.

Drystan stuck his index finger in Nightingale's drink, then slipped his finger in his mouth, savoring the taste of the brandy.

"Excellent vintage. A bit one note, but then, so is everything here," he joked.

Nightingale slid his glass to the side and, with a sour look on his face, signaled to a waitress to bring him another. She appeared almost instantaneously and quickly took Nightingale's glass before he could explain that he didn't want his cup cleared, but rather a fresh drink. Glowering, he curled his fingers and performed three intricate movements. Another brandy appeared in front of him. It wouldn't be quite as good as the one he'd just been drinking (magic can't perfectly replicate years of oak barrel aging, no matter how talented the caster, dear reader), but it was better than going through the folderol of trying to summon the woman back.

"What kind of third-rate book is this?" Drystan laughed, looking after the waitress. "Really, Ozymandias, she's not even fleshed out."

Nightingale looked back, making lazy circles with his finger to magically swill his drink. Drystan was right. The waitress appeared normal enough if you caught her out of the corner of your eye, but when you looked directly at her she seemed a bit…fuzzy. Even close up you couldn't quite make out her features. Her whole being had the appearance of an ink smudge.

"She's just a periphery character. She probably doesn't even have lines in the actual story."

"That's no excuse. Look at her! No determinant physiognomy whatsoever. Not to mention no waitress would actually be able to fill orders as quickly as she is. It's just sloppy writing."

"I'm sure she'd be happy to bring your drinks more slowly if you asked."

Drystan downed the rest of his absinthe and raised his empty glass for the waitress to see. He thought she turned to look at him but couldn't be exactly sure which of her smudges were her eyes.

"There's an explanation," said Nightingale.

"For the waitress?"

"For the girl! Stay on track!" he sighed, then got back onto the argument he'd been preparing. "Our world runs on order -"

"Maybe it's time it stopped."

"What do you mean?"

"I wish you would drop the 'wise sage' act. It's so tedious. And you don't even do it well."

"And what archetype are *you* playing? The Fool?"

"The Fool is often the truth teller."

"Or just foolish."

"Epic Comedy was revered once," Drystan sighed. "Mine was a beloved genre. But tastes change. Even in The Bookstore. They <u>change</u>." He chuckled. "The two longest suffering employees of the Store should know that. You weren't always the manager you know. And I -"

"This isn't a game."

"Everything's a game."

The waitress returned with a refill of absinthe. Drystan downed it in one. "Fine," he said, joyfully slamming down his glass. "To business. If we are facing the end of the world, what do you propose to do about it?"

"You are not to go messing with things."

"Me, specifically?"

"This is your death too."

"You and I have an understanding…"

"One that's served us <u>both</u> very well I believe," Nightingale's rage starting to bubble.

Drystan picked up a knife and playfully ran the point between his fingers.

"If fate is so absolute I can't do anything to mess with it even if I want to. Isn't that what you're always preaching? No free will?"

Drystan suddenly raised the knife and slashed it across his forearm. Nightingale winced but didn't stop him. Several patrons saw and gasped.

"You know it's more complicated than that," Nightingale said through this teeth, pulling Drystan's arm down, trying to get the attention off of them.

There was the faintest trail of redness, the lightest of scratches but otherwise Drystan's arm was completely fine. He stared at it…almost sad.

"We're the only ones…who really know," said Nightingale.

"Don't you hate it sometimes?" Drystan asked, sincerely. "Our existence?"

"Be careful with wishes. When people have a say they choose wrong."

"Speak for yourself," said Drystan.

"Have you learned nothing from the stories we care for? 'Frankenstein?' 'Animal Farm?' 'Paradise Lost' - emphasis on the LOST?"

"I learned very different lessons from those books. I won't stifle this girl's power. Not even for you. She might finally be the key to getting the Ur Book! And once we have that –"

"No, it's dangerous! <u>She's</u> dangerous!" Nightingale hissed.

"Quite right. She's a nuclear missile."

"One I'm not placing in your hands. Do you understand? End of discussion. None of your antics have brought the Ur Book and this will be no different. It's time you accept your fate."

The band started a new song:

"Why have you left me all by myself?

Why don't you come and claim me?

I'm just sitting on the shelf…"

"I hope you finally get written. I truly do," Drystan said, standing.

"At least then you'll get a spine. Now if there's nothing else, I'm going back to the circus. Maybe the fortune teller has something new to say."

"She never does. And never will. It will be 'Your future is unfolding exactly as planned' for all eternity. Won't it?"

Drystan forced a smile.

"You know, I've always been rather fond of chess," he said. "Fine then. Let the games begin."

He turned and sauntered out, calling over his shoulder:

"Get yourself a better story. Steampunk is so derivative."

The second Drystan was out of sight Nightingale got up and rushed out a back exit. He didn't bother to pay. He didn't need to. The scene would reset as soon as he left.

He had to find Paige before Drystan did.

As promised dear reader, we come to the Girl in

Three

Two

Paige stood behind the front register, her fake smile wearing thin.

"I would do anything to get out of this Store," she thought.

A customer, an entitled blonde woman in her late forties, stood in front of her. Paige already knew where the conversation was going before the woman opened her mouth.

"WHERE is the restroom?!"

Paige momentarily glanced above her and to the left where a large sign read "Restroom" with a brass hand pointing towards a flight of stairs.

"Upstairs," Paige said, as cheerfully as she could muster.

The woman looked at the staircase.

"Do these stairs go up?" She asked.

Paige's incredulity involuntarily shone across her face for the briefest instant, but she quickly suppressed it, deciding to give the woman the benefit of the doubt. Paige thought she knew what the woman meant ("Are these the stairs that go up to the restroom?") Maybe the words just didn't come out right. She had to think positive.

"Yes," said Paige, jovially. "And," she added a little joke, trying to make the woman smile, "from the right vantage point, they go down too."

The woman didn't smile. She said;

"So they DON'T go up?"

Dead serious.

This type of customer interaction was far from an anomaly.

Paige wanted to scream.

"Yes," Paige replied, slowly. "They go up."

"Thanks."

She was off. Paige dropped her smile.

"I pity the character that has to be in whatever story she writes," Paige thought.

She couldn't take this anymore.

Paige had been working in The Bookstore for weeks. Well, weeks is the closest analogy for you and me, dear reader, because time doesn't exist in the Store, at least not the way it does for us. But suffice it to say, for Paige, it felt like an eternity.

"Welcome to the wonderful world of retail," said a sultry, no nonsense voice winding its way around a stack towards Paige, an elegant smoke trail following behind. "We may be keepers of the literary canon, but don't kid yourself. It's a nice job in title only."

The voice belonged to a pencil skirt and a pair of red lips that happened to be attached to a body - like a woman out of a 1940's film noir, in color against her will. When you remembered Gwen, it was in pieces. Still, cinematic frames – her skirt and calves, her sleek, platinum hair. Never quite the whole.

"But it's retail. Don't try to fancy it up. Invisible. Lowest of the low. No union, no benefits, no wages but the promise of a brighter future."

She reached Paige and plopped against the front desk in a pose only a cartoonist could draw.

"Don't be such a downer Rose!" a voice called from a few shelves back. "Hey! If you're heading towards Gothic I got a misshelved Poe here!"

"Don't make me bust your chops Arden!" she called back.

"What'd I do?"

"My name is Gwen."

"Gwendolyn Rose Friday. But everyone calls you Rose!"

"Why?" Paige asked.

Gwen rolled her eyes. "That way all the Romance girls in the Store have flower names. It's 'too cute,'" she hissed before turning back to

Arden. "You want a knuckle sandwich? My name is Gwen!"

"Sure, Rose. So, you gonna shelve it for me?"

"No."

"Pretty please?"

"No."

"All you Romance Novel girls are the same."

"What's that supposed to mean?"

"You know."

"Don't test me Coming of Age Wallflower. I'm subgenre Crime."

"So?"

"And you can go shelve that Poe right up your -"

"Hey! You don't have to be so…mean!"

"You still wish you could date me."

He did. Everyone did. Arden sighed and walked away. Gwen turned to Paige.

"Don't let the customers get you down. I know it can be soul crushing. But with any luck you'll get a fabulous author and go on to a wonderful existence as a New Classic, while future worker bees tend to YOUR tome in this never ending hall of purgatory. I marvel it wasn't Dante's tenth circle of hell."

"I haven't gotten to Dante yet."

"You'll love him, toots."

"Thanks," said Paige. "I appreciate it."

"You want some advice?" Gwen asked, leaning over the counter. "Know your losers. If you really want to end up a classic you don't want the more…disposable genres rubbing off on you. The last thing you want is to pick up one of their tropes."

Paige's stomach dropped. She didn't know her genre, which was far more dire than it sounds, dear reader. She was the first character ever to arrive in the Store with no knowledge of it and she was shocked everyone hadn't found out by now.

"You seem like a smart cookie. And us higher genres have to stick together."

Paige wanted to say, "You don't know what my genre is!" but she held her tongue. She couldn't help feeling that Gwen was really just trying to elevate the standing of her own genre…Romance Novel didn't seem to be terribly well respected in the Store, subgenre notwithstanding.

"Take those two, for instance," Gwen continued. Paige followed her gaze.

Across the large entrance hall a petite young woman, no older than seventeen, sat on the floor next to a small stuffed rabbit. They were both placing price tags one at a time on a large stack of Danielle Steele novels.

The young woman had long, mousy dark hair, glasses, and wore a deep blue hoodie over an otherwise all-black ensemble on which a crooked nametag reading "Eleanore" was haphazardly stuck. She looked a little Goth and rather sickly – a state made more dramatic by the oxygen tank resting next to her – a breathing tube running from it to her nose. Seated, she was significantly smaller than the tank.

The Rabbit was made of velveteen and was about the length of the girl's forearm.

"Imagine, a stuffed toy as your only friend!" Gwen said to Paige, loud enough that the girl and rabbit might have heard.

Gwen put out her cigarette then flicked it perfectly into a trashcan behind the desk. She pulled a compact out of the pocket of her skirt and quickly absorbed herself in her makeup.

But Paige watched the two across the room, just able to make out their conversation.

"I should so like to be a real rabbit," The Velveteen Rabbit sighed. "It is very difficult to walk through the Store or climb up the stacks with sewn up legs that don't move very well. I don't think anyone could love a play rabbit the way they could a real one. And I do so want someone to love me in my story."

"Don't let Nightingale hear," said Eleanore.

"I know," said the Rabbit. "But it's easier for him. He is a great Fantasy Mage and I am ever so threadbare."

"Sometimes," Eleanore said, "I wish I were…real too."

"What do you mean?" Said the Rabbit. "You're a very real human girl. You've got eyes that open, and close, and don't fall off, genuine hair and no patches on you anywhere."

"I meant…well, I'm always sad, and sick…and I know I'm going to die not long after I get written…and when everyone makes fun of you for those things well, sometimes you can't help but feel like you're not the way you're supposed to be. You're…less than a girl…in a metaphoric sense."

"Oh, I see," said the Rabbit as its eye fell off.

"Here," said Eleanore as she sewed the eye back on. The Rabbit always kept a little needle and thread around its hind leg for just such an occasion.

Eleanore thought for a moment.

"Do you think we'll be real once we're written?"

"I hope so," said the Rabbit. "I hope ever so much. But still…I don't see how. I am a toy rabbit, no matter which way I look at it. So that must be what my author intended. I wish I knew more…about how it works."

Just at that moment a little bell tinkled, and the front door opened. Eleanore looked up, locking eyes for a brief moment with Paige. Paige quickly looked away, embarrassed.

"Well, look what the cat dragged in!" Gwen said, a look of awe on her face.

"Did someone call?" A cat grinned down, suddenly appearing over Paige's head.

"No, we did not," said Gwen, annoyed.

"No need to be…mad…" the Cheshire Cat mocked as it disappeared…cat first, then grin. "Get it? Mad?"

"Excuse me…"

Paige's attention snapped back to the tall, British man walking through the front door. Gwen couldn't take her eyes off of him.

"That's Richard Gainor!" she whispered.

"How can I help you?" Paige asked.

"Anything new in Fantasy?" he asked with a smile.

"He means any new characters," Gwen added. "He doesn't know it. None of the authors do. But that's the gist."

"I know," Paige whispered to Gwen. She turned back to Richard. "Have you seen 'The Inheritance Trilogy?'"

"No, I don't believe I have."

"We don't have any new Fantasy characters," Gwen whispered.

"It's on the front table," said Paige, ignoring her. "Also Madeleine L'Engle's 'Walking on Water' is really wonderful. Not many people have heard of it."

"Thanks! I'll check it out. In YA Fantasy?"

"Religion, actually." Said Paige.

"Interesting."

Gainor smiled and headed into the stacks.

"What are you doing?" Gwen chastised. "I told you, there aren't any new Fantasy characters."

"Maybe he just wanted something good to read. He's a famous author, right?"

"I should say so!"

"Well, he can't write ALL the time. Maybe -"

"You are an idiot. An author like Gainor starts wandering the stacks, every character in the Store is gonna start getting their hopes up."

"But if he's looking for new characters, I assume he's met the ones already here."

"Well, yeah…"

"So then they know he's not here for them."

"Emotions are rarely logical. Everyone wants to think that their story is important."

"Aren't they?"

"If they're written by someone like Richard Gainor they are!"

Paige had a thought.

"If we house all the books that ever have, or ever will be written, can't you just…find yours? Save all the drama?"

"You're funny. You're not Satire are you?"

Paige shook her head "no," not sure if Gwen was making fun of her or not. Or whether or not she was indeed Satire.

"If anyone's managed it they've never shared the secret. Books that haven't been written yet tend to stay…ephemeral. Especially in regard to a character that's in them – or the author who writes it. They're like… oil and water." She thought for a moment. "You know how the stacks rearrange themselves?"

"Yeah, either makes the layout magically simple or a labyrinthine nightmare."

"You'll get better at navigating. But… it's sort of like that. Authors tend to pass by books they haven't written yet. Once they recognize their character and write their book then they'll be able to see it in the Store. I think it's something like that for us too. Finding it, I mean. But Nightingale would know better than me."

Paige suddenly had a horrible thought; "What if Richard Gainor is my author and I didn't realize it? He asked for something new. I'M new. What if…because I don't know my genre…he didn't know me?"

"How'd you learn so much about literature anyway?" Said Gwen. "You haven't been here that long."

"Been reading a lot," said Paige. ("And trying get familiar with genres as fast as I can," she thought).

"So?"

"Don't you remember what you read?"

"Not THAT well. Even ones I've been in. I approve. Crime always values a good memory," Gwen smiled. "Well, welcome to the Store! It's nice to have new blood. Trust me. Eternal customer service is a tedium beyond compare."

"I'm realizing that," said Paige as a customer spilled half a milkshake on a table of books.

"That's my cue," said Gwen, picking up a stack from the "to reshelf" section behind Paige and heading out into the Store before someone could make her clean up the mess.

"See you later!" she called back. "Oh! Maybe we could go into a book sometime! Ok? It'll be a gas!" she smiled and sailed off. Paige saw her accidentally step on the Rabbit (her foot took up a good half of its body).

"Ouch!" it cried.

"Don't sit on the ground if you're so tiny. It's a hazard."

And she was gone.

Paige was about to go deal with the milkshake when the bell tinkled again.

This time a little girl walked in. She couldn't have been more than five. She had a Polaroid camera around her neck and a big smile.

"Hi!" she exclaimed, bounding over to the front desk. "I'm Adrian!"

Paige couldn't help smiling too. Genuinely, this time.

"Hi Adrian, nice to meet you. My name's Paige."

"Like a book page?"

"Yes, but with an "i" right in the middle."

She showed Adrian her nametag. She'd arrived in the Store with it, an apron, the clothes on her back and nothing else - not even any idea who she was.

"Is someone here with you?" Paige asked.

"No, my dad's getting ice cream. He doesn't like books much. But this is my favorite store!" said Adrian. "He said he'd wait." She giggled. "He's so silly. Acts like he doesn't even see the Store when I show it to him. Like it's just a game I'm making up. Mommy too. But she loves books. Last week she read five!"

That meant Adrian's parents weren't writers.

People on the outside confused Paige. She'd heard of some who never wrote a word in their life who went through books like they needed them to live, while some authors who came in the Store (no one ever came in unless they were or would be an author) seemed like they absolutely despised books. Like the milkshake woman.

"What's your favorite sort of book?" asked Paige.

Adrian suddenly got very serious. She thought for a long while, taking this as a Very Important Question.

"Different versions of fairy tales," she said as a definitive statement.

"I don't discriminate, though," she added, diplomatically, proud that she could use a word as difficult as "discriminate." "Though historical fiction and action aren't my favorite," she added. "But I just finished reading a wonderful book with a green and yellow cover…" She pulled out a little case from her back pocket. She opened it, revealing a giant stack of polaroid photos. She pulled out the top picture and looked at it. "'Pippi in the South Seas' by Astrid Lindgren," she read. She flipped the picture around to show Paige a photo of a book cover featuring an illustration of a boisterous, happy young girl with two gravity defying pigtails and a monkey, sailing atop a palm tree.

"I take pictures of the covers of all the books I love," Adrian said. "Sometimes I can remember a book cover, or a character, or a scene but I can't remember the title or the author, so I get scared I'll never be able to find the book again and it'll get lost in the stacks forever."

"I think that's a wonderful system," said Paige. "It seems you're a very advanced reader."

"I like to challenge myself," said Adrian.

"I think I know a book you might like very much," said Paige. "'Pippi in the South Seas' wasn't too hard for you?" She asked.

"I had a little trouble with 'Villa Villekula,' but my mommy helped me sound it out."

"This little girl is going to make a wonderful author," Paige thought.

Paige wasn't supposed to leave the front desk without being relieved first, but she had something special she wanted to show the little girl.

Perhaps if she knew what was to come after, she would have thought twice before being free and loose with the rules…even with something seemingly so insignificant.

"Ok," Paige thought, "let's get it right on the first try this time."

Navigating The Bookstore is a challenge even for an expert on a good day. The Store has a habit of rearranging itself - one moment its sections ordered according to chronological publishing dates, the next by historical influence. But if a character is really clever, they can influence the shelves to move exactly the way they need them to to make their commute as short as possible.

After a brief hiccup involving a detour through Math where Adrian happily found a lovely red book called "Alice in Puzzleland" with logic problems inspired by "Alice in Wonderland," (it really was too advanced for her, but she adored it nonetheless) they finally found themselves in Children's Fiction.

The Fantasy section of Children's Fiction was housed in an elegantly whimsical room with wood shelves going up about thirty feet forming, not straight rectangles, but curved, almost bouncy lines twisting every few feet into a half circle giving the appearance of a pillar made of books. About three quarters of the way up the stacks was a small balcony railing you could reach by climbing one of the golden ladders that slid around the room, letting you walk around the upper most part of the shelves and more easily examine the books. The ceiling was painted with illustrations from classic children's books (ones that have already been published in The Bookstore), such as (at this moment) "Peter and Wendy," "Snow White," and "The Little Mermaid." Nightingale had been in the store with Peter Pan long ago, before Pan was written and his illustration made it onto the ceiling.

"Annoying little brat," is how Nightingale described him.

Paige walked along the stacks, carefully looking over the author names.

Dahill…Dahir…

Dahl.

She picked up a book with a golden yellow cover featuring a little girl surrounded by a pile of books.

"Matilda," Adrian read.

"Do you know it?" Paige asked in a hushed tone. Noises seemed to be louder in the Children's section.

"No."

"You'll love it."

When they were back in the front of the store, Adrian bought "Matilda" and "Alice in Puzzleland" with money she'd saved from her allowance. She took pictures of the covers of both books with her polaroid camera and added them to her collection. She waved goodbye to Paige and made her way out of the Store, hoping her ice cream would have chocolate sprinkles. As soon as she'd left, copies of the books she'd bought reemerged on the front desk for reshelving.

Paige looked over and saw the girl with the blue hoodie, now sitting alone, still putting stickers on books. She was crying. Softly. Trying not to let anyone hear.

The spilled milkshake was gone. The table and books good as new.

There was a dirty rag next to the blue girl.

Paige walked over.

"Sorry, were you going to shelve here?" The girl asked, quickly wiping her face. "It's a pretty easy spot, I'd understand if you'd want it...I'll just go somewhere else..."

"Actually...I was hoping...we could hang out..."

The girl wasn't sure how to react.

"Aren't you hanging out with Gwen?"

"Does that exclude me from talking to you?"

"No..."

"I'm Paige."

"I know. The new genre-less girl. Oh, sorry! I didn't mean...to just call you the...new girl...um...genreless...sorry, I know you don't want that info getting around. Um...I'm Eleanore."

"Well, Eleanore, I have a feeling you know this place pretty well."

"Oh, Nightingale's much more -"

"Nightingale isn't working the floor every day. And I have no idea how you managed to clean up that mess! The books look good as new." Paige smiled, then sighed. "Plus, I have a feeling that once Gwen finds out I'm...genreless...she's not going to be so...hangy-outy....I'd rather be friends with someone who's nice. OK with my being...strange."

"Why do you think I'm nice?"

"For one thing, you called her Gwen, not Rose. Also...I heard a bit of your conversation with the Rabbit earlier...what's their name?"

"I call them Rabbit. Or Velveteen."

"And you were there when I arrived…you know I'm…genreless. And you're talking to me."

Eleanore let out just a slip of a smile.

"Aren't you scared my tropes are going to rub off on you?"

"What do you mean? Like, what Gwen said?"

"Yeah. I'm YA. Young Adult." She paused, waiting for a reaction from Paige. "Teen Drama?"

Still nothing.

"It's not a very popular genre. At least…I mean in the Store. Especially being sub, sub-genre 'sick lit'. I'm not going to be a High Classic like "Wuthering Heights," or "Great Expectations.""

"I don't see why not."

"Annoying tropes." She took a gasp of air. "Like that," she said, with a nod to her oxygen tank. "And other things."

"Well, if by tropes," said Paige, "you mean that you're kind, smart and empathetic, then I hope they do."

"Is angst girl bothering you?"

Gwen was suddenly standing over them, a new cigarette in her perfect red mouth.

"We were just chatting," said Paige. "Wanna join?"

Gwen laughed.

"And after I…" Gwen sighed. "Have fun with your social downfall," she said.

They watched Gwen walk away, shaking her head.

"Anyways," Paige continued, "I could have some terrible tropes myself."

"Oh, I doubt that," said Eleanore.

"Why?"

"Because, you're…well, you're so well spoken and brave for one! I'll never forget the way you talked to Nightingale when you arrived! I'll bet you're going to be written by one of the Brontës or…Kazuo Ishiguro."

Paige laughed.

"Thanks. I don't know the Brontës or Ishiguro yet. But I'll take your word for it. I'll bet you have an amazing author yourself."

"I doubt it."

"You all know your genres…but not your authors…?"

"No…"

"I think you're going to have to explain it…what it's like…for you…"

"What do you mean?"

"Well, I don't seem to know…I'm like…missing a sense or something."

"Oh!" Eleanore smiled. "Well, we know our genre, our personalities…but the rest…the plot, our author…we won't know those things until we're written."

"Then how do you recognize your author when they show up?"

"It's like…I think…love at first sight, I guess."

"Have you been in love?"

"No," Eleanore said a little too quickly. She pushed her glasses up on her face and blushed. "It's…how I heard it is…it's like…you just KNOW. I mean…" she thought for a moment, "you can usually narrow your author down to a degree. A Sci-Fi character isn't going to be written by Nathaniel Hawthorne, but, still…"

"I hope you don't mind my asking all this," said Paige.

"Are you kidding?! I finally get to be the expert! It's nice not to be the new girl anymore."

"YOU were the - ?"

"Yeah. Most recent arrival before you."

"Well, you seem nicer than anyone I've met."

"I can't help it," said Eleanore, almost apologetically. "I just have all this…involuntary empathy. Part of my genre." She took a deep breath. "Thank you for not making fun of the…oxygen tank in the room," she laughed.

"What is that?"

"So I can breathe. Some characters come into existence with important accessories. Apparently mine is a terminal illness."

"That's horrible."

"Oh, I won't die in the Store. No one can. But once I'm written… well…yeah, it kind of sucks. But Rabbit's sweet about it at least. Rabbit's my only, sort of, friend."

"Well, I hope now you have another," said Paige with a smile.

"Oh…yeah!" said Eleanore, letting the reality of the idea wash over her. It was a little overwhelming.

"Hey! Showing the newbie the ropes?"

"Drystan!" Eleanore smiled more broadly than Paige thought possible.

He walked over to them. Midway he slipped on nothing and went sliding across the floor, taking out a table of books in the process.

"Drystan's Epic Comedy," Eleanore whispered. "He's a bit… stumbly. But he's nice."

Eleanore got up and ran to Drystan as quickly as she could dragging her oxygen tank behind her. She helped him to his feet and set the table and books to rights.

"Oh, don't –" Drystan said.

"I'm happy to," said Eleanore.

"Excuse me, Paige? Is that right?" Said Drystan as Paige walked over.

"Yes, nice to officially meet you."

Drystan offered Paige his hand.

"Drystan!" a voice called from the balcony overhead. They looked up and saw an intense, brooding man staring down at them. Everything became instantly somber. "It's…," he said, sadly, unable to get the name out.

Drystan and Eleanore looked at each other, then, in unison, turned and made their way up the stairs, Drystan, gentlemanly carrying her oxygen tank. It was slow going as he tripped every few steps, hitting himself with the metal tank each time, Eleanore anxiously trying to tend to his wounds and obsessively offering to carry the tank herself.

Paige followed behind, feeling like a third wheel.

A motley crew of characters had assembled in a large, circular room from which dozens of stacks spoked outwards. They poked their heads from around stacks, sat on shelves - magical creatures stood next to basketball stars; a little girl sat on the shoulders of a menacing vampire;

all trying not to be too conspicuous to the two men standing in the center of the room.

A character had just found their author.

A male employee was deep in conversation with a man who looked like he'd just stepped out of a Renaissance faire.

"I believe I'm finished now actually, Mr…?" the employee said to the man.

"Will, please. All my friends call me Will," said the author.

It wasn't just their lilting British dialects, or the fact that their sensibilities seemed to stem from the same time and place. It was something in their eyes.

"Love at first sight," Eleanore whispered.

"Would you care for some tea?" Will continued. "It's rare I find such a…kindred spirit to talk to. In fact I…I haven't felt much like talking to anyone for quite a while."

"Of course."

"He's not…put off by the characters dressed differently than him?" Paige asked, looking at the customer's elaborate collar and buttoned up appearance.

"Nah," said Eleanore. " Customers tend to see the Store through the lens of whatever time they're from. Someone I was helping at the front desk once said it was so nice to be in an upgraded 'Barnes and Noble,' then five minutes later someone else said they loved how much the place reminded them of Alexandria. There's lots of ways to get the essence of something across. Maybe it's the same with our clothes too."

"My son died recently", said the customer. "Everyone keeps saying 'Put it in your art, it'll help.' I'm a writer by trade. But I…I can't find the words this time. I'm sorry, I don't know why I'm pouring my heart out to you…"

"How weary, stale, flat and unprofitable seem to be all the uses of this world?"

"Yes! Yes, that's exactly how it feels."

"I just need to turn in my things. Please, feel free to look around."

The employee turned for the first time to face the room full of hidden eyes. He smiled, then walked over and shook the hands of a few of the characters nearest him. Like a graduation.

"The readiness is all," he whispered to the assembled crowd.

Slowly he removed his apron, folded it, set it and his nametag (which read "Hamlet,") down on a table. He turned and followed William Shakespeare down the steps, across the entry hall and out through the front door stepping carefully over the threshold and finally disappearing from view.

The others stood silently, staring at the door as it swung closed, the little bell tinkling again before the door snapped shut as if a religious ceremony had just occurred.

"Someday, that will be me," thought every character watching.

Every character except Paige who, deep in her soul, knew it never would.

CHAPTER 2

...LIKE A GATSBY PARTY

"Time to CELEBRATE!" Herc yelled.

The crowd cheered, except for Paige, Eleanore and Drystan. Drystan leaned against an isolated corner of the stacks looking depressed, Eleanore stood silent, feeling very small amidst the throng and Paige, the only one who didn't know Hamlet, slowly migrated to the balcony railing, feeling like an intruder.

"Party! Party! Party!" Herc chanted, fist bumping the air getting the group riled up.

Herc was Action and his defining character trait was that he liked to smash things. He was closer to the mythological action hero genre than, say, the novelization of "The Fast and the Furious," but he was no Thor.

He had sandy blonde hair, gigantic muscles and a laugh that sounded like a bad theme park automaton. No one had high hopes for his author, and he was pitied by the more High Concept characters. But he was always good for a party.

Drystan looked like he was about to cry.

From rage.

"If I have to shelve one more new release of some stupid…I'll kill myself," he said under his breath.

"You can't kill yourself," said Gwen with a laugh, her red lips winding their way towards him. Drystan didn't smile.

"Come on joker, what's eating you?" She said, lighting a cigarette.

He didn't answer.

"You know how it works, kiddo," Gwen softened. "If you do what you're supposed to and follow the rules you'll get your happy ending. You just have to wait your turn. I know…It's been a long time…especially for you. But think how wonderful it'll be when it does happen. We're the real-life muses, sweetheart. A beautiful, immortal story all about you."

"They're not all immortal."

"Yours will be. I know it. I mean if old Hamlet ended up with Shakespeare, anything's possible, right?" She laughed. He wasn't joining in.

"Just trust fate. Like Nightingale says. If you're patient things always turn out the way they're meant to."

"What if you don't like the way they're 'meant to'?"

Gwen looked around, nervous that someone had heard. You weren't even supposed to think things like that.

"And in the meantime," Drystan continued, "you're stuck in a world where nothing. Ever. Happens. I can't…I just can't take it."

Gwen smirked.

"What?" Drystan looked livid.

"I'm sorry, doll face. It's just…you're trying to be such a rebel when …well, you're not built for it."

"You don't know anything about me," he said.

"I know everything about you. We all do. You're Epic Comedy and that means you're…well, clumsy, and silly, and sweet. You shouldn't let it upset you. It's just the way you're written. You're…a loveable fool. Besides, you know everything about me. I'm…stunningly gorgeous."

"There's more to us than that," he said with uncharacteristic intensity.

Gwen's stomach lurched. No one had ever said anything like that to her. Stunningly gorgeous was her defacto personality trait.

"I'm sure," she said, gently, trying to steer them back on track, "you probably have one of those highly artistic authors who creates completely fleshed out, three-dimensional well-rounded characters. But you're still Comedy and there's nothing you can do about it. You can't change your fate."

Drystan turned and walked away. Gwen realized she may have actually hurt his feelings and was just about to go after him when a forty-something man covered in blood, wearing a surgeon's outfit, apron, and nametag wandered out of the stacks and walked directly in front of her as he made his way to the assembled group. By the time he passed, Drystan was gone. Gwen looked after him, wondering if he'd really meant what he said.

"Hello," said the surgeon, amiably. "I'm Fred."

Everyone looked at him.

"Horror," he added.

"Sub-genre?" asked Dracula.

"Satanic Bargains."

"Thank goodness, someone to replace Hamlet on shelving duty!" said Arden.

"Head over to the office and fill out your paperwork," said Edwin Drood. "Second room on your left."

"Righty-O," Fred said and jauntily ambled off into the stacks.

"Where is Nightingale?" whispered Drood to the Raven perched next to him. "He should be here when a character leaves. More importantly when a new one shows up."

"Nevermore," the Raven cawed.

"So, are we celebrating or not?" Herc called.

"Celebrating?" Paige mouthed, catching Eleanore out of the corner of her eye.

Eleanore went to her, weaving through the throng.

"Going into a book to have an honorary goodbye party for Hamlet," she explained.

"Which book?"

"That IS the question." She smiled and leaned against her oxygen tank as if ready to watch a sporting event. "This is the fun part," she said, "watching a motley crew of genres try and decide where to go for fun. If only we had popcorn," she added, deadpan.

"None of that kiddie stuff this time," Gwen shouted, making sure she got in first. "We're goin' somewhere with hardcore moonshine, music and –"

"Now wait a minute, not too much moonshine!" a high, airy voice called out, "I'm coming too!"

"Does she have to?" Dracula replied, regarding the owner of the airy voice (Willa), speaking of her in the third person even though she was right next to him.

Willa Posey was the current resident children's book character. Children's literature was the kind of genre most characters prayed they would never have more than one representative of at a time in the Store. One could be...charming. Whimsical. Even endearing on occasion. More than that became a little hard to swallow.

Willa was that magical age of just a hair's breath away from thirteen – the age every child desperately aspires to be until they've actually reached it. But she was a REAL, old-fashioned thirteen, not the thirteen you see in films where a tiny twenty-year-old is made to look like a young teenager. She had auburn hair that she wore in pigtails (not as gravity defying as Pippi Longstocking), a smattering of freckles you could only see if the light was just right and wore a dress that looked something like a more fantastical Rebecca of Sunnybrook Farm.

"It's not like you're Mr. Party Animal," she giggled. "Why do you care so much?"

"I never get to choose the place."

"No one else considers a blood bath a good time." She paused. "Very FEW people consider a blood bath a good time. And majority rules," her singsong voice gently teased.

"I'm aware," Dracula replied, each vowel elongated. "But if I must always be the one forced to compromise my enjoyment do I have to…" (He wanted to say: "Have you around annoying me too." But he refrained.) "I already let you sit on my shoulders…Besides, last time we had a 'celebration'…" He shuddered. "I don't even want to think about the horrors of last time…"

"I thought you liked singalongs?" Said Willa. She'd chosen the last place and it involved a primarily pre-pubescent female campout complete with marshmallows, lanyard making and lots of "Kumbaya."

"I do not," Dracula replied.

"OK, Mr. Sulky Shorts," she acquiesced. "Just remember," she added, as if sharing a warm-hearted life lesson with a friend, "you're not so scary in here."

Dracula let out a small, somewhat threatening hiss, fangs exposed. Willa giggled.

"Hey!" Herc's voice pierced through the crowd. "This is perfect!" He held up a dark green book with gold stitching he'd found lying open on a shelf. "Looks like this is where Wesley disappeared to."

Paige looked at Eleanore quizzically.

"Wesley's the guy who told us about Hamlet," she said. "I wondered where he'd disappeared to."

"He sure knows how to pick 'em." Said Dorian Gray. That was high praise coming from him.

"Ooo! Pretty dresses," Willa chimed in, jumping with excitement seeing the book's cover.

"Count me out," Dracula purred. "I hate those kinds of gatherings. You always go off and have fun and I'm stuck pathetically staring at all the exposed necks I can't touch." It was true. He did have a tendency to look rather like a dog with a cone around its head when he joined in with group activities.

Willa chuckled.

"What is so funny?"

"COUNT you out? You're COUNT Dracula. You made a funny!"

Dracula turned and sulkily glided away. He thought he might go find The (Frankenstein's) Creature and they could have a good depressing wallow. Ideally in a graveyard.

"All right," said Herc, "gather 'round!"

"Sounds like fun," Paige said to Eleanore.

"Oh, you go ahead," Eleanore replied. "I have some things to get done."

"And all eternity to do them," teased Paige. "Come on! I've never been to a party. And I thought you were excited to see where they went."

"To see what they chose, not go with them. And after one, you won't be in such a rush either," said Eleanore.

"Why?"

"Oh, never mind. I'm sure you'll have better luck than I do. I really do need to catch up on some work. But you go! You deserve to get away from those crazy customers for a while."

"If you're sure…" said Paige. "If you change your mind, come find me? It'd be funner with you." She smiled.

"No, it wouldn't," Eleanore said, depressed.

Paige joined the others just as Herc opened the book. Everyone was holding onto someone who was holding on to Herc. Apparently you had to be in some way touching the person with the book in order to go in en masse.

Paige glanced down and saw a creepy pirate smiling up at her, his hand leeched on to her elbow.

"Hi, Captain Singleton," she said, reluctantly acknowledging his presence as she tried to keep from vomiting in her mouth after getting a whiff of his scent.

"Poppet," he replied, his smile never moving.

"It's Paige."

"I remember."

His smile grew.

"Yup, he was definitely not the right first person to meet when I got here," she thought. Was that right? Yes, technically third creature, first person. Of all the luck…

The moment was interrupted by a piercing horn blast. In an instant the company vanished from The Bookstore.

Eleanore went over, picked up "The Great Gatsby" and put it back in its place on the shelf (Herc would have his own copy inside the story), wondering how to best get her oxygen tank, which weighed almost as much as she did, back down the stairs without assistance. It was always a challenge.

* * *

"Ugh. The second trumpeter is sharp."

"Nah, you don't get jazz."

"HE'S SHARP."

Lights glistened everywhere and the group suddenly found themselves in a wide open space surrounded by hundreds of people.

"Ooo! I told you, pretty dress!" Willa cooed. She was now wearing a short, light yellow party dress with a ruffled skirt, white sash, white stockings and shining patent leather shoes. Her newly ringleted pigtails floated over her shoulders. She immediately took off into the throng shouting: "Shirley Temple! Shirley Temple please!"

"Willa!" Edwin yelled, running after her. "Shirley Temples weren't till the thirties! Don't disrupt...have some sense of historical accuracy!"

And they were gone.

The rest of the crew was now also dressed in book appropriate attire. Herc was squeezed into a suit that made him look like the Incredible Hulk as a sausage roll. Every time he even thought about moving he split a seam. Paige wore a gown she thought looked rather like a collection of morning dew - a kind of netting of teardrop crystals hanging over an under dress of soft, terribly pale blue that fell just barely below her knees and tied with a bow around her waist. Her hair was pulled back and partially up in loose waves and curls, held together by a diamond and silver band wrapped all the way around her head. The whole ensemble was much heavier than it looked, and that, plus this being her first experience in high heels (a lovely white deco pair), made her feel incredibly awkward. Everyone else quickly dispersed, the loud, big band music drowning out their squeals of delight. Arden grabbed a drink from off a server's gleaming silver tray.

"What is this?"

"Iced Tea," someone said with a smirk.

"Sounds nifty," he said as the server moved on.

"Arden –" Gwen tried to warn him, but he cut her off with:

"It's fine! I love iced tea!" He took a sip. Gwen shook her head and moved on.

At the center of the large, too-green lawn was a marble staircase leading up to a landing and, beyond, a great, opulent house. On the landing was a bar that offered a stunning view of the gorgeous, manicured grounds and, in the distance, a glimmering green-lighted lake. Wesley sat at the bar nursing the latest in a long series of drinks he was hurrying through, hoping they'd eventually make a dent. Turning his gaze towards the party's hub he caught a glimpse of bouncy auburn ringlets on a tiny head jumping up and down on a trampoline and a large man with buttons bursting off his suit.

"Oh come on!" he muttered. "Get your own party."

He knocked back the rest of his drink and ordered three more. If he'd wanted the rest of the Store following him into "Gatsby" he would have invited them.

Paige stayed on the outskirts of the party. She felt lonelier in the crowd than she ever had being alone in the Store. She looked around at the overwhelmingly vivacious group of people. Across the way she saw Arden trying very hard to get a cherry stem out of the bottom of his glass without using his hands.

"Don't help me!" he said to no one. "It's a right of passage." He hiccupped. "This doesn't taste like an iced tea…" he said.

"It's from Long Island," someone replied as Arden threw up into a hedge.

Suddenly a young woman (not from The Bookstore) with a short black bob and bright yellow and white dress, dancing like there was no tomorrow, spun directly into Paige knocking her, hard, into the ground.

"Ow!" Paige cried, landing elbow first onto the grass.

"I'm LILYANNE!" the girl shouted.

"I said Ow! Watch where you're going!"

"LILYANNE O'CONNOR!" the girl screamed as she downed a glass of champagne and Charlestoned back into the crowd.

Paige brushed herself off and finally made her way into the throng, weaving up to the bar where she asked for some ice and sat overlooking the water, nursing her elbow.

It was summer and slightly muggy - the stickiness made worse by the number of bodies in close proximity.

"It's hot here," she said to no one in particular.

"Yes," replied Wesley. His head didn't move, his response only out of obligation to politeness.

"You're the one who told us about Hamlet. Wesley?"

He turned. A centimeter.

"Ah," he said, looking her up and down. "Yes. You're...the new girl." Whereas Eleanore had used it as a plain descriptor, there was something condescending about the way Wesley said it.

"Yeah."

Eleanore was right, the moniker kind of sucked.

"I thought you'd be...taller..." he said. "More...dark, and diabolical...or something."

"Why?"

"You're the girl who's going to end the world."

"Excuse me?"

"Well?"

"End what world?"

"All of them."

"Says who?"

"Just Nightingale, for now."

"Not you?"

"I haven't made up my mind. But you'll be trouble, Nightingale's right about that, <u>genreless</u> newbie."

"My <u>name</u> is Paige."

He chuckled.

"Now that is grotesquely poetic."

"Why can't everyone just leave me alone?" Paige said under her breath.

"This <u>is</u> everyone leaving you alone. Enjoy it. I can't imagine it'll last much longer."

"So, some party," she said, her tone insisting they change the subject. Wesley smiled and humored her.

"It's a Gatsby party," he replied. "And there ain't no party like a Gatsby party 'cause a Gatsby party don't stop until at least two people are dead, and everyone is disillusioned with the jazz age as a whole."

"Doesn't seem like anyone got the memo."

"I beg your pardon?"

"Well the party must be long over judging by your apparent disillusionment with everyone and everything here," Paige said with a passive aggressive smile. "You look like you're ready to drop dead of boredom. But maybe you're just waiting for someone else to go first so you can make sure you've fulfilled the two-death quota." She picked up a small, soft pretzel and took a bite.

Wesley turned all the way around.

"I said it's not over until <u>everyone</u> is disillusioned with the jazz age as a whole."

"My mistake." She said, popping the rest of the pretzel into her mouth.

For the first time, Paige and Wesley got a really good look at each other.

He was handsome in the extreme. Dark, world weary. His eyes were his most arresting feature. Deep, black wells that looked like they held the ink used to write creation. And right now they blazed. His cheekbones came in second – so chiseled they might cut you. Sitting this close, Paige could see gentle lines on his face, as if the storms and winds of life had etched their mark onto him. His hair would have fallen just below his jawbone if it hadn't been slicked back in a 1920's fashion. He was fit in an accidental way – if you'd asked him he would have said that his defined muscles came from carrying the weight of the world on his shoulders, and meant it. His hands were just slightly too big, and he desperately needed to shave.

If this were a different kind of story, dear reader, this is the moment Paige would succumb to his dashing good looks, clever wit, and charm, falling in love with him the moment their eyes locked.

But she didn't. Paige wasn't that sort of character. And this isn't a Romance. No matter what may happen later, dear reader, please remember that this is not a Romance and do not treat any forthcoming incidents as heralding any episodes or endings inherent in such a genre.

Logically, Paige could appreciate that he was attractive. But that didn't attract her to him. He was self-righteously apathetic and while that might be seductive to a certain type of person, to Paige it had the diametrically opposite effect.

Not to mention, he was rude.

She picked up another pretzel. She'd never eaten anything before, and she was finding that she quite liked the taste of the little tiny things on top.

"Can I get the lady a drink?" The bartender said, smiling at Paige.

"Yes, please."

"What's your poison?"

"Um…"

"What do you like, sugar?"

"What's this?" She said pointing to the clear granules on the pretzels.

"Salt."

"I like that."

"Hmm…don't have any grapefruits for a Salty Dog…"

(Margaritas, dear reader, were unfortunately not invented until 1938. In the 1920's the only common drink with a salted rim was a Salty Dog which, if you would ever like to make, please refer to the following:

Salty Dog
- ½ cup vodka or gin
- ¾ cup fresh grapefruit juice
- Ice
- Salt (The only thing to differentiate it from a Greyhound).
- To make it non-alcoholic remove the vodka/gin. You'll be left with salty grapefruit juice on ice which, frankly, will likely taste better than salty grapefruit juice on ice + alcohol.

Go ahead and try it. This will be an interactive chapter. Don't worry, the characters will wait, even if you decide you need to go to the store and get some ingredients (that's the magic of books…). And please do not attempt to make the alcoholic version unless you are of legal age to do so or I will strongly disapprove and may not finish the story)…

"Any other drinks you like?" The bartender asked.

"I…don't know…" Paige said.

"Uh…" The bartender said, confused, but still holding on to his smile. "You don't know if you like…?"

"Any of them…?" She said glancing at the glittering array of pink, and yellow, and green, and blue and clear liquids resting in ornate bottles and glasses. "I've never had a drink. I hear good things about water…"

"Get me another bourbon. Double," said Wesley. "And a sparkling lemonade for her. Pink."

The bartender relaxed, smiled for real, and rushed off.

"First time in a book?"

"Yeah."

"I can tell."

They stared out at the lake.

"Why did you take off so fast?" Paige asked. "I didn't see you once Hamlet…"

"I'm Gothic Romance," he said.

Silence.

"Sorry, that means nothing to me."

More silence.

"I haven't gotten to that section yet," she added as justification.

"I shouldn't have to…explain…myself…to you."

"You don't have to explain yourself…just…your genre…"

"Same thing."

"I'm strange, what can I say?" said Paige. "Throw me a bone."

He sighed. "It's like playing translator for a foreign exchange student," he thought. "Why me?"

He stared at the lake for a while, hoping the question would fade.

It didn't. Paige just kept looking at him, waiting.

"I don't…do…goodbyes," he finally explained, using the fewest words possible. "Really, I'm not one for intimate personal interaction at all."

"That sounds rough."

The drinks arrived. Quickly. They tend to in books. Though not as quickly as in Nightingale's steampunk teahouse.

"Here. You'll like this. It's…girly."

Paige did like it, but, with the way he said "girly," she somehow felt like she shouldn't. She especially loved the ice cubes with mint leaves frozen into them.

"What book are we in anyway?" She asked.

"'The Great Gatsby' by F. Scott Fitzgerald."

"Ah. Hence the Gatsby Party," she said. "What's it about?" She asked dipping a pretzel into her drink.

"Lost love, a pointless narrator, and a green light (yes, that one just across the bay) that's a metaphor for the unattainable American Dream."

"What's America?" she asked.

"A country," Wesley said. "Officially founded in 1776, on the ideal that every human being is deserving of 'life, liberty and the pursuit of happiness.' Well, really every straight, cis, male, Caucasian human being. Although trans wasn't in their vocabulary then, and gay was more of a 'don't ask, don't tell' thing." He took a sip of his drink.

"What about Cheshire Cats and Velveteen Rabbits?" She asked.

"Not applicable. It's a non-anthropomorphized world. At least in this book." He took a sip. "In America you can be anything you want to be. Pull yourself up by your bootstraps, have the freedom of upward social mobility, go from rags to riches and get everything you ever wanted."

"That sounds great!"

"It does."

"Is it…not true?"

"It is enough to let the fairy tale survive."

"But you said 'Gatsby's' about it being unattainable?"

"The getting rich part is potentially attainable. The getting everything you ever wanted, not really. But that part never is, no matter what story you're in."

"So, how is that green light a metaphor for…all of that?"

"I'm a Byronic anti-hero, not an English Professor."

"You could've fooled me."

Silence.

"Are there any currently in the Store? English Professors?" She asked.

"No."

"Well then, you're the best I got."

He sighed, leaned over, and spoke in hushed tones, careful not to let anyone from the story proper hear.

"It's about a poor man named Jay Gatsby who falls in love with a woman named Daisy – a girl way above his station. Gatsby privately vows to become rich enough to win her, so he disappears, and gets insanely wealthy but in the meantime Daisy marries someone else. Gatsby builds this house, the one we are currently drinking in front of, directly across the water from where Daisy lives. That green light is the light at the end of her dock. He throws these lavish parties hoping someday she'll come, but she never does. He spends the whole book trying to steal her away from her husband. She leads him on, but he never gets her. He ends up dead in that swimming pool over there, and no one but the narrator goes to his funeral."

"All these people…and none of them go to his funeral?"

"No."

"And he never gets Daisy?"

"No."

"And it's all a big metaphor for how wealth won't make you happy?"

"Yes."

"Seems like a lot of depressing events to get you to a rather obvious conclusion."

"Gatsby? Jay Gatsby?" A lovely southern, soprano voice urgently called.

Paige turned and saw a beautiful, delicate woman with blonde bobbed hair, and a pale pink dress running up the stairs. She stopped near the bar, looking both ecstatic and distraught, turning in circles calling:

"Jay Gatsby!?"

"He's not here!" someone called. "He never comes to his own parties!"

"Really?" asked Paige, intrigued. But Wesley didn't hear. He just stared at the woman in the pink dress, who suddenly looked like she was going to cry.

A whisky smooth voice called down from the top of the stairs:

"Yes, I do. I don't let them know it, but I've never missed one. How could I... when you might turn up. It's the only reason I have them in the first place – hoping one day I'd see you." The pink lady looked up and locked eyes with the man. They ran towards each other. You could practically hear violins swell.

Wesley was all but frozen.

"Is that...? But you said she's not -" Paige started before Wesley clamped a hand over her mouth.

"Daisy...what about your husband?" Gatsby asked, nervously.

"There could never be anyone but you, Jay Gatsby. You with your... loyalty...all these years...and your...your beautiful shirts!"

He laughed and kissed her.

"We'll get married tonight! Right here! Find a preacher!"

Everyone cheered, except for those from The Bookstore. They all looked terrified.

"I thought you said they didn't end up together -" Paige mumbled through Wesley's hand.

"They don't," said Wesley. "They're...not supposed to."

The green light across the lake grew brighter, and brighter. Then, in a sudden, brilliant burst, it went out all-together, like a star extinguishing.

Paige pushed Wesley's hand off of her.

"What're you playing at?"

"Quiet! You want to tell every character here the plot of their own story?!"

"Well, it doesn't seem to matter now…"

"Not matter?! Oh, you idiot."

"What's that?"

Everyone from the Store was panicking. From frozen stillness they suddenly sprang to life and ran against the flood of people rushing to congratulate Daisy and Gatsby.

But Paige didn't panic.

She noticed something strange.

Daisy was surrounded by what at first glance appeared to be tiny, white footprints. Every time she took a step she left one behind her. But it wasn't really a footprint... A print covers something. This was as if her steps were erasing whatever they touched. The color of the cobblestones, part of a scarf Daisy caught underfoot, half a leaf…

They had all been…erased.

And then the sound came…so loud it made everyone stop in their tracks and cover their ears. A sort of giant, whirring whistle. And when it sounded, the white from Daisy's steps started swirling…expanding… seeping into the world around it. One of the staircase railings vanished right before Paige's eyes. Where Daisy first entered the scene the whiteness…the…nothingness…was growing the most rapidly – turning into a sinkhole. The louder the screaming noise got, the more the sinkhole expanded…as if the noise originated just underneath the ground.

"Gatsby" itself was being erased.

"Get to the book!" Wesley called. Paige turned and saw him running and waving to her to follow.

"What book?"

"Get to the book that brought you here! Now!" he yelled. But this time it wasn't just to Paige – it was to all the other characters from The Bookstore. Wesley pulled out his copy ready to take as many with him as he needed to, but making sure no one got left behind before he did.

Paige jumped off her stool and took off after him, sprinting as fast as she could, the whiteness blinding her as she tried to outrun it, twisting and dodging as puddles of it oozed out around her. Finally she stretched out her arm and was able to grab Wesley's hand. The Bookstore crew was running away from the eye of the storm towards the woods, where Herc was holding the copy of "The Great Gatsby" that brought the group there in the first place.

"Everyone here?" Wesley screamed over the blast.

They looked around. Everyone, including tiny Willa, the Velveteen Rabbit clutched in her hands, seemed accounted for.

"Look out!" Paige cried as a wave of nothingness rose above them like a tidal wave.

"Grab on everyone! NOW!"

Paige grabbed Wesley's arm, shut her eyes and held on for dear life.

Just as the wave was about to envelop them all, Herc opened the book –

And they were back in the Store.

CHAPTER 3

TO BE

"What the hell was that?!"

"Something bad!"

"It was nothing…"

"That was definitely something!"

"No…it was…<u>A</u> nothing…like from 'The Neverending Story.' A nothingness…that's the closest I can describe it."

"But not exactly like 'The Neverending Story…' this was more… an erasure. Like the story was literally being erased. Not that nothing existed…exactly…"

"The Nothing is as good a term as any."

The Store was panic and pandemonium with everyone shouting

at once, talking over each other, terrified. Their clothes were back to normal, and any effects of alcohol, for those who had partaken, regrettably vanished the moment they returned.

Arden stood in the corner, slightly asthmatic, slowly inching away from Natasha Rostova who, looking concerned, seemed like she might be about to go over to him. Arden was more petrified by the possibility of being touched by a girl like Natasha than of anything that had just happened.

"Daisy wasn't supposed to be there! I know that book inside and out and Daisy Buchanan never shows up unexpectedly at one of Gatsby's parties. They never get engaged, let alone married!"

"Did someone interact with the main plotline?"

"No!"

"Of course not!"

"Besides, what main plotline? Nick wasn't even at the party yet –"

"Who's Nick?"

"The narrator."

"There was a narrator?"

"I never heard a voice over…"

"That's because we weren't in the main plotline, nitwit! And even if we had been…Daisy isn't supposed to appear in that chapter at all. There was nothing TO interact with…"

Pandemonium burst forth again.

"Quiet!" a voice boomed.

The silence was immediate. Everyone turned and saw Nightingale gliding quickly towards them. His eyes flashed and locked with Paige's. She couldn't be sure if anyone else noticed, but to her the laser beam anger he was sending felt palpable.

Could this all be her fault? The beginning of the end of the world?

"Will someone <u>calmly</u> tell me what happened?" said Nightingale.

Everyone looked at each other searching for some way to explain…

"We…don't exactly know, Sir…" said the Velveteen Rabbit, who'd posed as Willa's stuffed toy (as they often did) in order to enjoy the festivities when visiting a story that didn't include anthropomorphic beings. "But it was…very frightening."

Herc looked at the book in his hands. He held it out to Nightingale as if whatever contaminated it might be contagious. Nightingale took it and moved to open the front cover.

"Don't!" Paige cried.

Nightingale looked at her like she'd lost her mind.

"Is there something you'd like to share?"

"Don't go in there, Sir…" she said, ignoring the stares from the others.

"I have no intention of doing so," Nightingale replied. "I can open a book without entering its pages."

Some of the other characters chuckled.

"I know…just…it's bad and I didn't know if –"

"I appreciate your concern," said Nightingale.

"Chapter Three," said Wesley. "Between Nick receiving the invitation and his arrival at the party."

Nightingale opened the book and flipped to the appropriate page.

The paper was corroded - holes appeared in the middle of the text. The ink itself was fading and dripping down the page. Nightingale slammed the book closed before the ink could escape and land on the floor.

Wesley explained the events, from Daisy's surprise entrance through to the appearance of the Nothing.

Nightingale carefully flipped through the final pages of the book. They were white and pristine, with clear, fresh lettering.

"Do you know what it is, Sir? This…Nothing…?" The Velveteen Rabbit asked, timidly.

"Has anything like it ever…happened before?" asked Fred. He looked so hopeful, as if this must be a, certainly scary, but commonplace speedbump.

Nightingale wrestled to find a way to avoid saying what he knew he had no choice but to admit.

"No," Paige replied, reading the answer in Nightingale's face. "It hasn't." Nightingale just looked at her, his silence confirming her statement.

"But…you know what's wrong?" Fred said urgently.

"It's her fault."

Nightingale didn't say it. Paige was never sure who did.

"What are you talking about? How's it the newbie's fault?" asked Gwen.

They couldn't keep it under wraps anymore. Paige knew it. So, rather than waiting for someone to "out" her, she said:

"I don't know my genre. There's…something wrong with me. But I'm…working on it."

"Was it your first time in a book?"

"Yes, but –"

"That's why it started falling apart!"

"She's tainted!"

"She's a virus!"

"I'm not!" Paige exclaimed, though honestly, she couldn't prove that she wasn't. "Not being…exactly sure of who I am is…a problem, I admit," she backpedaled, "but it isn't going to destroy the universe! That's just…a mean story."

"What do you mean, 'a mean story?'"

"Gossip. A rumor. A lie."

Several of the characters gasped.

"A story is anything but a lie."

"Are we lies?"

"No…that's not what I meant," Paige apologized.

"Don't attack the girl," said Giant Rimblebiffin. "After all, a story is a kind of a lie, but it is a good lie that says true things."

"You must be more careful with language," said Nightingale. "If you mean a lie, say so."

"Yes….always say what you mean…or is it 'always mean what you say?'" hissed the Cheshire Cat.

"I'm sorry," said Paige. "But I'm not going to destroy anything just because I'm a little…unfinished."

"Who all knew about this?" said Gwen.

"Rumors get around," Wesley replied.

"And no one did anything?"

"Like what? Sounds like a quirk more than…anything dire."

"She set foot in a book for the first time and the book was erased! How would you feel if that was <u>your</u> story?!"

Everyone started backing away from Paige.

"We will figure this out," said Nightingale. "There's a reason for everything. 'There is nothing lost that may be found if sought.'"

"You're not quoting at us!?"

"Quoting?!"

"That was from 'The Faerie Queen.'"

"I thought it was nice," said the Velveteen Rabbit.

"Don't try, we've read it all!"

"I would never hurt anyone," said Paige. "I swear."

"And we should just believe you? You could be…Epic Tragedy for all we know! A Tragic Villain! They're the worst! The most dangerous!"

"I'm not!"

"How do you know?"

Paige started to answer, then stopped. She didn't know. She couldn't honestly say she did. If she didn't know what she WAS, that meant she couldn't know what she WASN'T.

Her mind flickered through the ways she'd been described. "Wrong," "Dangerous," "Odd…"

No, what other people say you are isn't always the same thing as who you really are. What did she know for sure?

She cared about people. Eleanore, little Adrian…but did that really count? Everyone must care about <u>some</u> people…except a psychopath. Did psychopaths care about anyone? She'd have to do some research (if only The Bookstore contained non-fiction books! It was very challenging to verify any hard data…though even hard data changes depending on time period…). But Paige didn't think so.

OK, so it was likely she wasn't a blood psychopath. One point in her favor…but she knew it was more than that. It wasn't just caring about someone…there were people she didn't much care for, but she still didn't wish them ill. Page definitely knew that she didn't want to destroy anyone or anything and that knowledge made her happy. And Eleanore said she was nice…that had to count for something.

"I don't want to hurt anyone," Paige pronounced. "I know…you might think I might be lying, I guess, and even if I'm not, that fact doesn't make me very…distinct. But it's the truth and that's got to at least eliminate 'Diabolical Villain' doesn't it?"

"That's not enough. Not wanting to do something doesn't always keep you from doing it!"

"If we don't have a choice about our actions then…what's the point?" Paige said.

"DO we…have a choice? In who we are?" asked Arden.

"No, some things just ARE whether you like it or not. Belladonna is poisonous regardless of if it wants to be, it's just the way it's made."

"But…Jay Gatsby didn't end up with Daisy…and then he did…" said Arden, trying to fit pieces of a puzzle together. "That means however it happens…things can change."

"We can't rewrite ourselves or our stories!"

"It would be suicide even if we could! We're not authors – imagine the chaos!"

"Well…perhaps I shouldn't say it," Arden continued, emboldened, pushing his glasses up and walking forward, "but maybe some of us have things about ourselves we've never really liked that much. If I don't HAVE to be the wallflower…I'd rather not be."

"You don't know what you're talking about," Nightingale warned.

"When people choose they choose wrong."

"NO MORE QUOTING!"

"We are who we are. You can't change your personality like…like… changing your clothes when you go in a book."

"Why not?" Arden snapped. "Maybe some of us don't like the way we're being described."

Nightingale slid next to Paige, absolutely venomous.

"Do you see what you've done?!" he hissed in her ear. "Your toxicity is seeping into everything! I tried to protect you and keep this contained. And what did you do?"

"I didn't <u>do</u> anything! But maybe I should start. At least then I'd be able to take responsibility for the consequences of my actions."

"Start taking action? Your very existence is parasitic to our world."

"Get her away from me!" someone cried. "The…crazy wallflower too!"

"Wetvewn gwoidyo fioguioj ouoiu noioij shhh zun!" yelled an odd man in a space suit.

"Quinn, we're not telling you again, you don't have to wear your helmet in the store!" said Gwen.

Willa jumped up on a ladder and took his helmet off.

"It makes me feel…safer," Quinn said.

"From what?! The world is ending! A space suit isn't going to protect you!"

"Stop it!" said Willa. "We can all be polite, even if it is the end of everything…"

Quinn grabbed his helmet and slammed it back on.

"You're telling me there's no precedent for a character not knowing their genre?"

"No," said Nightingale, begrudgingly.

"Because of her, I might never be written?" Dantès exclaimed.

"The very framework of imagination might crumble," Wesley replied, "but please, think only of your story."

"As a wise man once said, 'no character is an island…'" Drystan said jovially.

"This is no time for your jokes," sniped Wesley.

"Where on earth have you been?" Gwen asked, sidling up to Drystan. He looked at her almost apologetically.

"Drystan, not the circus again!"

"I can't help it."

"You're just going to keep getting disappointed."

"Better there than 'Gatsby' it seems."

"You heard?"

"Everything."

"Have any brilliant ideas?"

"Me? The village idiot?"

"Lock her in a book!" someone shouted.

"What?!"

"That's a bit extreme."

"Maybe there's an explanation. She could be a Medical Drama patient who has amnesia."

"Amnesia wouldn't manifest until after she's written. It works the same as superpowers", said Gwen.

"Superpowers?" asked Fred.

"They're...muted..." someone explained. "Like Herc...he can carry crazy heavy books, but he can't smash the shelves to pulp like he'll probably be able to do in his story..."

"And I can't fly in the Store," Dracula moaned.

"But I can disappear..." the Cheshire Cat bragged.

"We know!"

"See? Rules are mutable!" Arden shouted.

"No, we just don't always understand the structure behind them."

"Will you all stop?! We need to contain her until we figure this out!"

Some of the characters started moving towards Paige with enough intensity that she started backing up.

"I'm a living person," she shouted, "not some pages that need to be edited!"

"You could take away our only chance for happiness." Captain Singleton growled. "And we're not gonna give you the chance!"

They were moving quicker now. Paige stumbled backwards.

"Expel her from the store!"

"That's not even possible!"

"Arden wants to test out the rules so badly…send him with her!"

"She belongs in a world of chaos, not here –"

"I invoke a council!" Paige cried.

"That only works once!" said Wesley.

"Was he a representative at my council vote?" Paige wondered.

"Council vote?! You let her have a blooming council vote?!" Singleton cried.

"I never know anything that's going on," sighed the Velveteen Rabbit.

"No! She'll infect you!" someone shouted at Singleton as he lunged out of the pack towards Paige.

Paige took off like a shot, dodging and weaving between the stacks. She was running out of breath when she turned a corner and felt a strong hand grab her arm and yank her into a dark room.

"You've been a problem from the moment you arrived," she heard Nightingale's voice in the shadows. "You can't outrun it anymore."

"How did you…get out…in front of me?"

"Shh!" Nightingale warned.

They heard Singleton round the corner and stop.

"Well, shiver me timbers. Them shark bait's quick…"

"Give it up!" someone called. He skulked his way back to the crew.

"She'll be dealt with," said Herc. "Nightingale'll see to that."

"Did everyone who went into 'Gatsby' get back safe?" Drystan asked, trying to refocus the group on something else.

"Yes. All present and accounted for, though a little worse for wear."

"Well, that's something at least."

Wesley took off his cravat and carefully wrapped it around "The Great Gatsby," as if the book was some dangerous, cursed item.

Drystan scanned the room.

"Everyone's back?" he asked, confused. "You're sure?" He paused. "Did everyone go to the party or are some folks off…shelving or -?"

"Of course not. Like anyone would be shelving at a time like this!"

"You're positive?"

"Yes! Why?"

"Then…where's Eleanore?"

CHAPTER 4

FATE

Unfortunately, dear reader, Nightingale was right - at least about one thing: Paige created chaos from the moment she arrived in the Store.

I shall explain.

Paige arrived at the bottom of a giant stack of books going up so high it was as if she was looking up through an ancient forest made of shelves, and books and paper. There was no swirling of magical dust or anything so dramatic. She simply opened her eyes and looked around, a bit disoriented, like a child who'd fallen asleep in a department store and woken up to find the place empty. But unlike that child, Paige didn't know where she was. She didn't know how she'd gotten there. She didn't have a family who'd lost her. She didn't know her name. Quite simply, though she was a fully formed person who could speak, and think and feel - she couldn't remember anything before opening her eyes.

But she didn't just sit there or wander around in a dreamy daze. She figured if she was IN someplace there must be an OUT and she ought to try and find it, especially since the place appeared to be deserted. The books were surrounded by other books, and she, being a person, felt instinctively that she ought to be surrounded by other people.

The place wasn't deserted, of course. Paige just happened to appear in the middle of Mathematical Fiction which is never the most populated section. At the moment, Gwen, Eleanore, Hamlet and the rest of them were dealing with a particularly difficult customer who didn't understand why Fan Fiction was tucked all the way in the back and not properly displayed at the front of the store like the Classics or New Releases. This customer himself happened to be the author of no less than two-thousand and nine fan fiction collections – each containing between ten to thirty individual stories, mostly about anthropomorphized Ligers and himself as Dr. Who.

That's why Paige didn't see anyone for a long time.

But someone saw her.

Two someone's, to be precise. Me (though I don't quite count), and a man whose silhouette danced like a specter along the wall as he followed her.

She passed giant atriums made entirely out of dark, rich wood with ceilings covered in Byzantine carvings. She wandered along balconies formed into arches that went down instead of up, but still she saw no exit. So she passed by spiral staircases made of antiqued copper with sides formed like lilies that ran from step to rail, rolling ladders with gold edging and ceilings painted in trompe l'oeil, still focused on her mission.

Eventually, she passed a mirror.

That made her pause because she couldn't ever remember seeing herself before.

She wore a simple, white dress that was remarkable in its unremarkableness. If it's possible for clothing to not provide any hint of a time, place or type of person likely to be wearing it, this dress succeeded to perfection. There was a utilitarian apron tied around her waist, and it looked like she had some sort of pin on the top left side of her dress.

She had light brown hair and intense hazel eyes that glinted in the light. She looked rather more like a woman than she felt. Beautiful was not the first word to describe her. Pretty - possibly second, or third. Perhaps. My favorite way to describe her is that she looked like someone painted by John Waterhouse.

Go look. You'll enjoy it. I'll wait.

Paige thought her nose was rather too long, but she didn't mind her eyes. We are all trained to have so many opinions about the way we look, it's nice to think of someone experiencing their image with no biases. Few people remember the first time they saw their reflection and realized "that's me!" What a fascinating experience. An all-around neutral one for Paige, but one I find quite beautiful.

She was just about to get back to her search when something flew out of nowhere straight towards her head. She ducked just in time, her hands frantically shielding her face. She spun around and saw a raven winging its way away through a row of books.

"Nevermore!" it cawed in a loud, decidedly annoyed tone.

"Why is a raven like a writing desk?" a voice purred above her.

Paige turned but couldn't see anyone. She looked back towards the Raven, worried it would return for another attack.

"Don't mind him. He seems to think that being able to fly automatically gives him the right of way wherever he goes, when in fact, it's just the opposite."

Paige scanned the shelves but still couldn't see where the voice was coming from.

"Up here, by the by…"

She looked up and saw an odd-looking cat with a large grin, or more like an odd-looking grin attached to a large cat, lounging on the top shelf of the nearest bookcase.

"Is that really your name?" The Cat laughed.

Paige looked down and read:

ƎƆIAꟼ

On her nametag. (She was looking at it upside down and backwards).

"Yes, I guess?" she said.

"Paige," the Cat purred.

She tried out the word and smiled. "I think it sounds nice."

"Bit on the nose," the Cat smirked, indicating the books surrounding them.

"What about my nose?"

"No. ON the nose. Your name. Considering the setting," the Cat chuckled.

"Well, no more so than yours," Paige said.

The Cat looked down. Fur was covering the top part of their nametag, so it simply read: "Cat." Paige smiled.

The Cat frowned and brushed the fur aside. The tag now read: "Cheshire Cat."

"There." It said.

"It's nice to meet you. Mr. Cheshire Cat."

"It's THE not MR." He replied.

"The Cheshire Cat?" said Paige.

"Meow."

"May I call you Cheshire? Or Cheshy? That is your first name?"

"No. It's one, unified moniker."

Paige sighed, turned and started walking the way she'd been heading before she'd encountered the mirror.

"I wouldn't go down there if I were you."

"Why?"

"That's Apocalypse Horror and zombies are not the friendliest folks even in the lightest genres. Nightingale would have my tongue for saying it, we're not supposed to judge, but I wouldn't want to run into them in a dark stack."

"Are they dangerous?"

His grin, if it was possible, widened. The effect was not comforting.

"No," he said through his immovable grin. "Even if they wanted to be…they couldn't. They're more annoying than anything else. But still…"

"Then which way should I go?" Paige asked.

"That depends a great deal on where you want to get to."

"Out of here."

"Out of here…" he chuckled. "You must be Comedy." Paige was just about to ask what was so funny when the Cat continued: "I'd advise Nightingale's office, to get your paperwork done. There is always so much paperwork."

"Where, exactly, am I…now?" she asked.

"With me."

"And we are…?"

"I should think that would be obvious."

"A bookstore."

The Cat's grin dropped slightly.

"Don't you know?" he replied. "Newbies always do."

The silhouette stepped closer. You'd forgotten about him, hadn't you, dear reader? Don't ever forget about him…

"Not A bookstore. THE Bookstore. Our home."

"Who's home?"

"The books of course."

"I'm not a book, I'm a person."

"I should think you a children's primer. You're really rather simple."

"That's rude."

"Do you know yet where you want to go? Specifically?" the Cat asked, with an odd growing excitement.

"Actually Nightingale's office...sounds like my best bet. If you could just point me in the right direction. Maybe I could ask him -"

"Oh." the Cat interrupted, looking disappointed. "I hoped you were going to say, 'I don't much really care where I get to as long as I get somewhere,' and I was going to say, 'then it doesn't really matter which way you go,' at which point I would slowly disappear until only my grin remained. That feels like the way it should go..."

"I can say it if you want...you'll have to repeat it -"

"That's alright. Can I still do my disappearing exit when we're finished?"

"Sure. So, how do I get to the office?"

"Well, every direction leads everywhere eventually," the Cat said, grooming one of his claws with his teeth.

"I've been walking in one direction for a long time..."

"Not everything is as it seems," the Cat said. His grin widening to an inhuman size. Paige started to respond, but the Cat began to fade... then disappear outright.

"That's a pretty good trick," she thought. "Terribly unhelpful Cat. But good trick."

Paige looked towards Apocalypse Horror where the stacks seemed to fade into a darker wood. Well, the section certainly seemed… interesting. And she'd take interesting over retracing her steps. So, ignoring the Cat's advice, she marched on in.

She walked for a while, the stacks getting darker, and darker around her.

"That's funny," she thought. "There aren't any windows…or lights… Shouldn't the light be the same everywhere? Where does it come from?"

Magical places are rarely practical.

She was wondering how she knew what windows were, but not her own name, when she heard another voice. This one much more sinister.

"Hello, poppet."

This was a human voice. Gruff and oozing.

At the far end of a stack Paige saw a lumpy silhouette. This, dear reader, was not the silhouette of the person following Paige. He was still watching as this new figure limped closer, till Paige could finally make out that it was a man - a hunched study in asymmetry. Though his back bore no hump, one shoulder was a good six inches above the other, an angle accentuated by the lean of his head – as if he was staring at Paige through his one good eye. His clothes looked like they'd withstood sand, saltwater and steel through sheer force of will.

He came closer…

"Can I help ya find something? Adventure caught your fancy?" he growled, toying with something sharp in his hand.

"Look at that apron," a new voice hummed. "She's no customer, Singleton."

Paige spun around and found herself face to face with a man who looked exactly how one would imagine Jack the Ripper.

"She's a newbie!" exclaimed the Pirate.

"Fresh meat!" Jack said, suddenly an inch away from her face, seemingly ready to pounce the second she tried to run. "I'll be nice. Give you a head start."

"Thank God I ran into you," Paige said, with no hint of fear. "Maybe you two will be more help. Can you tell me how to get to Nightingale's office? Practical directions, please." Singleton and Jack looked at each other, flummoxed.

"Nightingale is a person, yes? Not an actual nightingale…? I don't think I would fit in a bird's office."

"We don't get to play Spook the Newbie?" whined Jack. "You promised me next time we'd play Spook the Newbie!"

"I'm trying!" Singleton groaned. He turned to Paige. "Couldn't you run a little bit?" he asked. "Let us chase you for a while? It's just been so long with nothing to do…"

"You can't properly chase characters in stories," Jack added. "Even on the periphery. They just start screaming and there's only so far they can go staying out of the main plotline. But here there's so much room! Please? We need a bit of entertain-"

"We have a new arrival?" a charismatic voice sounded. Paige turned.

"I'm looking for a Nightingale…"

"I am Doctor Octavius Nightingale."

"She thought you were a bird!" Singleton laughed.

"Don't you have some shelving to do?" he warned.

"Oh, please no, Gov! We needs a break!"

"Couldn't we chase her for a little while?"

Nightingale gave them a look and like a shot Singleton and Jack hurried back into the stacks. Paige could hear Jack as he turned a corner –

"Wouldn't be much fun anyway. She wasn't scared at all…"

Paige saw some decaying zombies turn, grunt and waive to her from a nearby stack. She waved back.

"Come now, don't distract them," Nightingale said to Paige, adding to the zombies: "You have shelving to do too!" The zombies turned and got back to work.

Nightingale led Paige silently through the stacks until they came to a room where the shelves seemed to be made almost entirely of stained glass. There was space in between the stacks showcasing the glowing colors and designs and, right in the middle, a large, stunningly crafted wooden door.

"My office."

He handed her a pencil and clipboard with several forms.

"Finish it quickly," he said, as he disappeared, slamming the door behind him. Paige heard music coming from inside – a beautiful classical piece. Paige peaked through a small gap in the doorframe and saw Nightingale masterly playing the piano with utter focus and passion.

"Nevermore!"

Paige jumped.

There were two chairs in front of the office. In the one furthest from the door, the Raven was intently filling out his paperwork, holding his pencil in his beak. Paige sat down and saw him scratch "Raven" under "name." He quickly rounded his head towards Paige, snapped:

"NEVERMORE!"

As if admonishing her for spying. Then he quickly returned to work.

Paige turned her focus to her clipboard and the attached questionnaire, immediately finding herself on the back foot. She didn't know what to put for "Genre," so she left it blank. She'd been debating what to answer for "Place of Emergence" for a quite a while when the door swung open and Nightingale returned. He collected their forms with Paige having written nothing but her name.

"Welcome. I am Dr. Nightingale," he said, beginning a well- worn speech. "As I'm sure you have already gathered, this Bookstore is home to fictional characters like yourself who have yet to be written. We tend to the literary canon until our author arrives to claim us. You will be doing your training in Historical Fiction –"

"Nevermore!" squawked the Raven.

"Unfortunately we've found that Gothic Poetry does not provide the strongest…foundation upon which to serve the canon at large," Nightingale replied. "Don't worry, we all intermingle here. Now, third stack back, make a right. Ask for Alexander Hamilton."

"Nevermore, nevermore, nevermore" the Raven whimpered as he hopped off looking as sullen as a raven possibly can. Paige started to follow -

"You've left…everything blank?"

Paige stopped and turned back, the Raven disappearing into the stacks ahead of her.

"Are you trying to waste my time?"

"No –"

"Genre?" asked Nightingale, pencil poised, ready to fill out the form for her.

"Genre?" Paige asked tentatively.

"A category of artistic composition characterized by similarities in form, style or subject matter."

"Nicely said."

"Thank you. Yours?"

"My description wouldn't be as good."

"Your genre."

"That won't be good either."

"Why not?"

"Because I don't have one? Oh!" she had a thought. "Do I just pick one? That Cat seemed fun, what genre are they?"

The silhouette inched closer.

A weight settled over Nightingale as if a doomsday clock had just started counting down.

"Don't play games."

"I'm not…"

There was a long moment of silence. Then Nightingale forced a laugh.

"Don't tell me you're Post-Modern Socratic Allegory! That –"

"N…nope. I don't think so… Can I just go with the Raven? I'm going to lose him…"

"You can't do anything until you tell me your genre."

"Why?"

Nightingale looked around furtively, then leaned down, face to face with Paige – trying to keep an air of nonchalance, but not fooling her in the least.

"So we know how to relate to you," he said in a light, forced tone. "What universe you function within. It helps things run smoothly with so many divergent genres coexisting. But more importantly, without your genre you have no chance of finding your author. Come now. No need to be nervous. I won't think any less of you no matter what -"

"So I can't just pick one?"

"No."

Nightingale took a breath. "You haven't…told anyone else? That you…don't…know…your genre?" he said like a child forcing down brussel sprouts.

"No."

The man with the silhouette smiled.

"I am losing my patience," said Nightingale.

"Would you prefer I lie?"

"No…but I don't think you understand the consequences…what would have to be done…if what you say is true."

"Consequences?"

"Yes…the <u>problem</u> will need to be…taken care of."

"What does that mean?"

Nightingale thought.

"You'll have to be…quarantined…or if that won't…"

"Killed?!"

"Nonsense. You can't be killed…I don't think…?"

"WHAT?! Look I showed up with an apron and nametag, I'm clearly a…character…so I deserve to be here as much as anyone else."

"Says who?"

"The apron and nametag…"

He just stared at her.

"I'm afraid you'll have to come with me. Now."
The silhouette took a step out into the room.

"I demand a vote!" Paige shouted.

"A what?"

"A vote. I'm not letting my existence be determined by…I demand a democratic council."

"A novel idea," said Nightingale.

"Pun intended."

"Actually not," Nightingale replied. "How do you know…about a council?"

"Who doesn't?" she said casually. She <u>didn't</u> know, she'd just suddenly gotten the idea…but it seemed everyone here was supposed to just know magical things…why not give it a whirl and commit.

"It's been a long time since it was invoked."

Oh, thank God, she'd gotten lucky.

"But if anyone else finds out…about you…it will be pandemonium…"

"I'll keep it a secret," said a man prancing towards them. (This was the silhouette who'd been following Paige). "Forgive me, I didn't mean to eavesdrop…or is it I didn't mean to be dropping eaves?" he chuckled. Nightingale glared.

"Drystan, how long have you -?"

"We could keep it small," he said. "Only those with the most level of shoulders," he smiled. "Sharing responsibility…might be smart. That way, no matter what happens, all the blame won't fall to you."

They locked eyes.

"I'll even volunteer to represent Comedy."

Nightingale didn't budge.

"There's not much you can do," said Nightingale. "Once a council has been invoked."

Drystan just smiled, shrugged, and shuffled his feet.

"You," Nightingale said to Paige without looking at her. "Wait here."

Paige sat outside Nightingale's office for a long time while several people made their way discretely inside. She could hear fighting, lots of fists banging on tables, but the only words she could make out were: "Dangerous," "Strange," and "Wrong." Paige never knew what exactly happened in that council, but eventually Nightingale re-emerged followed by Drystan, a small girl with an oxygen tank, a tall, broody man (neither the girl or the broody man ever looked at her), and a zombie and quietly told her to seek out the Raven and Alexander Hamilton in Historical Fiction. It seemed she'd been granted a temporary reprieve and Nightingale would try to keep the lid on things long enough for Paige to sort out who exactly she was before anyone else found out the truth and started rioting in the stacks.

* * *

Now Paige was back at Nightingale's office, this time inside, where he'd pulled her to escape the mob. He plopped her in an oversized chair in front of a large, wooden desk, the door locked firmly behind them. It took her eyes a minute to adjust to the change in light, but when they did, she saw Nightingale on the opposite side of the table staring her down, exasperated.

"I'm going back in 'Gatsby,'" she declared, not waiting for Nightingale to speak. "If what happened there is somehow my fault, then I'm going back to figure out how to fix it. That'll do far more good than whatever everyone out there is…thinking about doing…I'm not going to let 'Gatsby' die!"

"You're not going anywhere."

"I know you've wanted to be rid of me from the moment I showed up but –"

"I was the deciding vote on the council…to allow you to stay."

Paige was stunned into silence.

Nightingale started pacing, though there wasn't much room. The inside of his office looked like the inside of a tree trunk. The wall closest to them was a combination of stained glass and bookshelves allowing red and golden light to stream in. The rest of the place, including all the furniture and most of the Victrola, were made of wood. It was whimsically elegant. But there wasn't a great deal of space for Nightingale to walk. It was almost comical watching him try.

"Why on earth would you vote for me to stay?"

"I believe in trusting fate. Taking it into our own hands…that way lies disaster. Fate put you here. Don't ever forget that fate is what saved you."

"You were going to kill me."

"Don't be dramatic. I said I couldn't kill you even if I wanted to. And for the record I didn't. Want to." He sighed and sat down. "But this is what I was…we can't keep something like you hidden."

"Some<u>thing</u> like me?"

"I can't protect you from that mob forever. Democracy or no."

"I don't need protecting, I need to put it right."

"Paige we don't know what this…Nothing…is. We don't know what caused it, except that it might, somehow be linked to you. You can't go barreling through, trying to fix a problem none of us understands. This is bigger than what's happening in 'Gatsby,' and rushing in and trying to patch up a story…might very well make it worse. For now we can keep it isolated…"

"And what happens to Gatsby, and Daisy and all the rest of them? Your plan is to just sit around and…wait?"

"That is often a very prudent and undervalued plan."

"I don't need your permission."

"You can't even book jump."

"How hard could it be? You just open the book, click your heels three times and say: 'There's no place like Gatsby,' right?"

"Are you serious?"

"That's not right?"

"Don't be ridiculous," Nightingale said in exasperation. "And after you thought I'd go in just by opening…you just have to open the book with the intention of going into it. It's not complicated!"

"Thanks for the tip," said Paige. She winked then jumped out of the chair, turned the lock on the door and ran straight back towards where everyone was gathered like she was on some kind of suicide mission. He was right. She hadn't known how to book jump. She did now.

"Paige!" Nightingale called after her.

She didn't stop. In her periphery she saw Wesley walking towards Nightingale's office carrying the wrapped, soon to be quarantined "Gatsby" as if it might somehow infect him. She changed her trajectory in mid stride and raced towards him, ripping the book out of his hands, discarding the wrapping, and, as carefully but quickly as she could, turned to just before the dripping page where everything was horribly wrong.

"I'll fix it, I swear", she called back. She fully opened the book and, on her first attempt, disappeared into its pages.

"Newbies aren't usually able to do that…so easily…" said a stunned Wesley to a heavily winded Nightingale who'd just caught up to the scene.

"Shit."

CHAPTER 5

THE FAULT IN OUR STARS

Paige was back in "Gatsby" – but the Nothing was gone. She looked around, confused, accidentally bumping into a young woman with black bobbed hair and a yellow and white dress.

"Sorry," Paige said, distracted.

"LILYANNE!"

"What?"

"I'm Lilyanne O'Connor!" said the girl as she danced away.

The book had reset.

Well, not reset exactly, dear reader, it was about to go to hell in a few paragraphs. But Paige reentered the story exactly where she'd entered it before which meant that the Nothing wasn't there yet, Lilyanne danced by just as she had (only this time Paige's elbow was saved another scrape), the band played the same song and the second trumpeter was once again a hair sharp. This is what the characters in the Store meant when they talked about stories never changing (not that the stories' characters realized - that's what happened when you were written). It was like an eternal groundhog day, at least when things went the way they were supposed to. But it was very much about to NOT go the way it was supposed to, and Paige had to stop it. The world was already starting to fray at the seams - plot threads were unweaving, and the edges of the scene looked blurry...like a cloud of dust hanging over the proceedings. Once Daisy showed up it would increase to a full whirlwind again. The grass and trees were no longer as vibrant...their technicolor green was fading, like the faded ink in the book Paige held. She looked down at it - her only way back to the Store. Some of the dripping ink seeped onto her hand. She didn't have long.

This time Paige didn't go to towards the party. She needed to head off Daisy before her new disastrous entrance, so she immediately started running in the opposite direction of the celebrants, across the grass – almost immediately tripping over her beaded dress and white heels.

"This is ridiculous!" Paige said, ripping her bow off and wrapping it around her copy of "Gatsby." She slung the makeshift bag over her shoulder and across her chest to better carry the book without risk of further injury or worse, loss. "You'd think you'd get some choice in what you wear," she huffed as she pulled off her heels and stockings and took off again, her skirt twisting around her legs as she ran.

The front drive was packed with cars, with valets desperately trying to figure out how to jam in more. To her left were more wild parts of the grounds…trees and fields with no other house for miles. Far to her right was the lake. There was no more grass, so she stepped, painfully, barefoot onto the gravel.

"Excuse me! Has anyone seen a blonde woman in a pink dress come this way?"

A couple valets looked up. One hiccupped.

"What're you shouting?"

"I wanted to know," said Paige urgently, while picking her way towards them as quickly as she could on the gravel, wincing in pain with every step, "if you've seen a blonde woman in a pink dress come this way in the past few minutes?"

"She thinks we remember anyone who's come by here tonight?"

"Sounds like a fool."

"That's the best thing a girl can be in this world, a beautiful little fool."

They laughed.

"Look! I found another one!"

One of the valets who was rifling through a car pulled a flask from a glove compartment. He opened it and took an enormous swig.

"I like large parties," he said. "So intimate. At small parties there isn't any privacy."

"That doesn't sound right."

"Makes perfect sense."

"So, no one's come by –?"

"Lady, we're trying to figure out how to get five hundred cars into a hundred spots. We haven't SEEN anyone."

"Except the Vice President. We saw him."

Exasperated and losing time, Paige turned and made her way back to the grass, looking around, trying to figure out how much time she had until Daisy showed up.

"How long was I talking to Wesley before -?"

Wesley…and the lake. The lake that ended in the green light on Daisy's property. The quickest…most likely way…

Paige dashed up a large, grassy hill – at full speed it took her a solid three minutes to reach the top. I know three minutes doesn't seem like a long time, dear reader, but when you're running full tilt uphill under a life or death time crunch, trust me, it does. You could pause and try it now, if you like. Run full tilt for three straight minutes (up a hill in a heavy dress if possible).

When she finally got there Paige could just see the dock below, illuminated by the moon and the green light from across the bay. She thought she saw something in the water…

And Paige took off like a shot, half running, half sliding down the other side of the hill. Her dress was mud-stained and torn by the time she reached the small wooden dock and saw a small, pink woman trying to get out of a rowboat and up a tiny ladder.

"Stop!" she managed to wheeze when she finally reached the bottom.

Daisy, spooked by Paige's sudden appearance, stumbled and the boat began to rock viciously. Paige ran forward "Ow, ow, owing" her way over the rocks, and grabbed Daisy's hand just in time to prevent the inevitable.

"Thank you!" Daisy cried. "Would you please help me off this dreadful contraption."

"No, you have to go back now or something awful will happen," Paige exclaimed a bit melodramatically. But it was all she could think to say in the urgency of the moment.

"Something awful will happen if I stay in this boat!"

"You don't understand," Paige said, "it's going to…create a lot of problems if –"

"Oh, see I never listen to anyone who tells me what to do," said Daisy with an impish smile.

Her smile didn't work on Paige who was frowning intensely.

"All I want to be," Daisy continued, "is very young always and very irresponsible and to feel that my life is my own – to live and be happy and die in my own way to please myself."

"Well that sounds rather selfish."

"And that's a bad thing? Why shouldn't I be?"

"It's…dangerous for everyone!"

"I've never cared much for everyone."

"If you don't turn around and go back home now, everyone is going to die!" The words hit Paige as she said them. It was true. People, worlds, were going to die because of her.

"My dear, this has been an entertaining conversation, but exactly how drunk are you?"

Paige let out a yell of primal frustration.

"That much?!" Daisy replied. "Well, get me some of whatever you've been sampling. But not before I see my dear Gatsby!" She pulled out a flask tucked into her garter and took a swig.

Paige didn't know what to do. She couldn't tell Daisy the truth – even if she believed it, she wouldn't care. And even if she did care… Paige wasn't supposed to mess with the story proper. She wasn't, strictly speaking, supposed to be interacting with principal characters or the main plotline at all. But the main plotline was screwed anyway, so she felt she was allowed a little license.

Then Paige saw the lake water under Daisy's boat turn white. The whirring wind picked up, becoming more and more centralized around the dock.

What could she do? She hadn't even read "Gatsby." All she knew of the story was her brief sojourn at the party, and Wesley's description.

She wished she was an author. Authors have the precious, omnipotent magic of being able to step away from a problem, think on it for as long as they need, and come back without time passing at all for the characters. But Paige wasn't an author. She was stuck inside the story, and she had to come up with a solution NOW.

"Why do you even want to be with Gatsby?" Paige asked. After all, it was a giant departure from the plot of the book. Maybe there was a clue in why Daisy had changed her mind so suddenly. "It's been years, and years and tonight you suddenly decide you can't live without him?

"Well…" Daisy said, "I can't really explain it to be honest," she realized as she said it. "But…I suppose, it's because I know he worships me, and he always will."

"But…that's…" said Paige, "he <u>worships</u> you. He has a fantasy he's built up for all this time you've been apart, and I doubt it bears much resemblance to the real you anymore. He doesn't love the person you've become. He doesn't even know you, if he ever did."

"But <u>you</u> know me?" Daisy tried to step around Paige. Paige stepped in front of her, cutting her off. Daisy was just about to give Paige a what for when the ground started cracking around them.

"We don't get earthquakes in West Egg…?"

"This isn't about me this is about you and Gatsby," Paige said, trying to distract from the rumbling. "You're just a dream to him…a fantasy you can never live up to."

How was that for applying literary symbolism, Wesley?

"Oh, but that's exactly how every woman wants a man to think of her."

"I don't," said Paige, horrified.

"It's the only power we have." Daisy paused. "Oh no," she looked at Paige sadly. "Did you grow up in one of those poor areas where they tell you your power is in educating yourself? How sad. Your parents did you a great disservice."

Paige didn't know what to say. Existing in the mecca of literature, literacy and education was sacrosanct. There may be shallow, vain characters, but even they revered the Order of Literary Canon.

All Paige finally managed was:

"I don't have any parents."

"Oh, my poor dear, an orphan is just about the worst thing you can be."

"That's...incredibly unkind."

The ground rumbled again. The leaves on the trees around them started turning completely white.

"Please, Mrs. Buchanan..."

"Don't you dare!" Daisy teased. "Mrs. Buchanan is my husband's doddering old mother. I'm –"

"Daisy!"

Across the bay Paige heard a man calling "Daisy! Daisy!" and a child crying. Daisy turned to look.

"Is that Pammy?" she said vacantly.

"It sounded like a man's voice."

"No, Pammy, my little girl."

"You have a daughter?" said Paige, incredulously.

"Oh, yes."

"You're going to...abandon your daughter?"

"She has her father and plenty of money. And a pony! It's what I need for my happiness." Daisy looked back towards her home. "Pammy does cry an awful lot. Despite the pony. I don't know why."

"I couldn't just...leave someone like that. Let alone my –"

"Oh, you very well might, darling. Once you've been pushed to choose. Life is complicated. You'll learn. Once you've had to make a choice for real."

The ground shook again. Earth rolled down the side of the hill. Daisy tripped and fell, laughing uproariously.

"Are you…" Paige looked at Daisy. "Are <u>you</u> drunk?!"

"Absotively posilutely!" Daisy giggled. "Alcohol makes thinking so much easier."

"If you don't get back in that boat and go home right now I'm going to throw you and your dress in that muddy, muddy lake!" Paige threatened.

"Oh no! No please don't do that! Not my dress!" Daisy begged, more concerned about her clothes than about her daughter.

"I will! I swear! With all the frogs and eels."

Paige didn't know if there were eels or frogs, but they sounded good.

"All right, all right, I'll go if only for my dress's sake. But you are very cruel."

The way to get Daisy to leave was simply to appeal to her vanity? Paige was horrified. That such a selfish character could be starring… idolized in a literary classic just seemed utterly unfair. She wanted to give F. Scott Fitzgerald a good knock upside the head.

The ground rumbled again. Pieces of earth began to fall away like holes opening up to the center of the earth. The white of the Nothingness was seeping closer and closer to the dock. Paige glanced at the ground and it looked like woven fabric stretching apart. She managed to heave Daisy back into the boat and watched her awkwardly row away just as the ground started to disintegrate directly under Paige. She jumped and dodged, desperately trying to avoid running back up the hill long enough to confirm that Daisy's boat made it safely to the other side of the bay. The story would be in even more trouble if Daisy capsized and drowned three chapters in.

When Paige was reasonably sure that Daisy had reached her destination she crawled back up the hill, racing against wind and whirring whiteness.

Why hadn't it stopped? Why hadn't everything returned to normal the moment Daisy left the chapter? Paige jumped over a crevice and ran over the peak of the hill back to the place where she first entered the story. She found her shoes and stockings still lying on the grass and looked ahead to see the party in full swing. The edges were still a bit blurry, and the wind was stronger than usual, but the Nothing was holding its distance from the story proper. The scene seemed to be tentatively holding, loosely woven together by the (literal) central plotline that was tying the pieces in some semblance of order. Behind her, though, was another story.

The edges of the world became more and more frayed the closer they got to the eye of the storm – centered exactly where Daisy entered the story at the dock on the side of the hill. The sinkhole Paige escaped during her first visit to the story was back and holding strong, but it didn't seem to be expanding anymore. The story was in some sort of hesitant stasis and Paige figured that was at least good enough for now. She looked down at her copy of "Gatsby" – the ink no longer dripping, the pages damaged, but not as fragile. "Gatsby" was safe, all the characters in the Store were safe (and she would be too in a moment). She let out a sigh of relief and quickly unsheathed the book from her makeshift bag ready to get the heck out of Dodge.

And that's when she heard a scream coming from back down the hill.

She recognized the voice. It wasn't Daisy, or anyone from "Gatsby."

It was Eleanore.

CHAPTER 6

ELEANORE

A lot of things go through your mind when you're hanging onto a (plot) thread for dear life.

Literally, not metaphorically.

"Why me?" "How long can I hold on?" "Why me?" (That thought occurs frequently.) "Why did I never learn to climb a rope?" and "Why does it always have to be me?" are just a sampling.

Eleanore hadn't gone into "Gatsby" with the others, but she went eventually. She was telling the truth when she said she didn't do well with parties, but that didn't mean she liked being left behind, so, eventually, she followed, staying on the periphery. She occupied herself with various activities.

She helped the valets figure out how to fit in all the cars (she was rather decent at spatial puzzles), wandered the grounds and had an excellent time petting some sheep. By then she was rather winded dragging her oxygen tank through grass, so she rolled it down a hill and sat on the sand, her feet in the water of the bay, a ways off but still vaguely in sight of the dock. She watched the green light, watched the lights of the party and heard the raucous cheers wishing she was brave enough to join.

"But what would they say," Eleanore thought, "when a kid with an oxygen tank comes rolling in? Maybe they don't even have rolling oxygen tanks in the 1920's. Maybe I'd be messing with the story..." Even her clothing transformation was disappointing. She found herself, not in a chic flapper dress, but in an overly modest, ankle length deep burgundy gown (not the most flattering color on Eleanore), her same stringy hair that was far too long considering the bob was in fashion and dark coke bottle glasses.

"You'd think if I get a magical change of fashion they could at least make me able to see without glasses," she thought, taking them off and cleaning them.

Her oxygen tank was the same as always.

She saw Willa jumping on a trampoline and thought that looked like fun but knew she would never be able to do something like that hauling a hunk of metal around. She wasn't very good at socializing, didn't like the thought of alcohol, and all around it seemed like a perfect situation to get teased. So she sat, enjoying the water, wishing very much that she could throw off the dress, and glasses and go swimming in the cool lake (with a few frogs and eels, to be honest, but Eleanore wouldn't have minded), when all at once the earth started to shake, the Nothing appeared, and she had to try and outrun the sinkhole for dear life.

It didn't go well.

The world unraveled, and she was right in the thick of it. Wisps of plot threads whipped her legs, and the further she ran the more the edges of the world seemed to rise up like a giant, immovable white wall, forcing her to turn and run back (as quickly as she could) towards the center of the storm. All at once the earth opened up, the sinkhole came roaring to meet her and there was nothing for her to do but fall in.

The good news was her oxygen tank didn't fall with her. There would have been no surviving if the one hundred and fifty pounds of metal, plastic and air (yes, air has weight – twenty pounds actually if it's contained in a tank that itself ways approximately one hundred and thirty pounds (I looked it up for you)), that wound around her head and nose had gone in after her. The other good news was that the central plotline – the strongest thing (usually) in a story (at least one with dramatic narrative that's decently structured) hung like a ley line directly above her and she was able to grab hold of it.

The bad news, besides the fact that she was, of course, dangling over a giant gaping hole for dear life, was that a moment after she grabbed hold of the plot line it frayed and snapped, leaving her gripping nothing but a loose thread hanging over a barren chasm with wind, and whiteness and howling coming up from its depths.

All the other characters, of course, had no idea that any of this was going on. They didn't know Eleanore was even in "Gatsby," so they didn't look for her before making their escape and didn't notice she wasn't in the Store until Drystan's timely observance.

The sinkhole, and by proxy Eleanore, got out of synch with the timeline of the rest of the story because they were in a pocket of space overwhelmed by the Nothing, linked to "Gatsby" only by the thin plotline Eleanore was holding. So Eleanore was still there, in the same chapter, on the same page, no less, trying to hang on and keep from falling and being erased, when Paige reentered and had her encounter with Daisy. The wind around Eleanore calmed somewhat but other than that, Paige's patchwork fix did nothing to help her situation. By the time Paige finally heard her cries, she'd been holding on for a long time...

A note, and a suggestion, dear reader:

If you should ever find yourself holding on to a plot thread for dear life over a chasm of Nothingness, here are some suggestions:

1. Try to find a foothold on the side of the sinkhole. Do not let go of the thread, but this will help hold your weight and get you into a more comfortable position. (Eleanore tried this and it helped her immensely.)

2. Do not try to climb the sinkhole wall. It will only disintegrate on you. That's what sinkholes in stories do.

3. If you have any circus training you may try to use the thread as if you are on Silks or "Static Tissue" as it's sometimes called. This is easier if your legs are high enough on the thread to do a foot wrap. If so, you can relax in that position easily for quite a while, or, hopefully, climb the thread itself all the way to the top.

If your legs are not high enough, doing an inversion might help, or climbing using only your upper body strength – but these are difficult skills only recommended for those who have extensive circus experience (such as those with a contract with Cirque du Soleil).

4. If you are in a fantasy, go ahead and let go. You will likely end up in an Oubliette, or Gnome's Kingdom, or even in Wonderland. In any case you will be much better off than you would be hanging over a chasm.

5. Try to get a nice bird flying by to carry you on its back (again, this really only works in Fantasies). If you are in Sci Fi, a spaceship will do instead.

However, Eleanore had the disadvantage of being in neither a Fantasy/Sci-Fi story, nor having circus training, and so she was stuck thinking "Why me?" and other such thoughts over and over again (please see examples above), as her hands quickly tired, and her tank slowly ran out of air.

* * *

So now Paige had an actual choice to make between self-preservation and helping another person. A person she'd started to care about and be friends with but, let's face it, someone she'd only had one real conversation with and hadn't known that long in the grand scheme of things.

If she stayed, she and Eleanore could both be erased. If she left now, she knew she could still get out safely. She'd saved the story, but if she kept messing with things she might undo everything she'd accomplished. The good of the many outweighed the good of the few, right?

Well, that question was a little esoteric in the given moment. Really what Paige faced was the choice between guaranteeing her own safety or risking her life to go after Eleanore. She was seriously considering making the same choice she'd just chastised Daisy for making. Things, dear reader, are very different when they are real, and not just theoretical. That is one reason why stories are so wonderful. They let us practice making very difficult choices before we actually have to make them ourselves. Daisy was right, the choice is harder when you are really facing it.

Only Paige was in an actual life or death situation and Daisy…well, Daisy just wanted to have a good time.

She wished she knew her genre, that would tell her what kind of character she was and what she was supposed to do at a time like this.

Well, Paige figured the best thing to do was to decide what kind of character she <u>wanted</u> to be if she didn't know what kind of character she was, and then do what that kind of character would do.

So, she took a breath, resheathed "Gatsby," and ran back towards the Nothing and Eleanore determined that, whatever else she might be, she was not going to be a selfish "silly little fool," like Daisy.

CHAPTER 7

BOOKWORM

The wind forced Paige onto her hands and knees as she fought her way through the storm towards Eleanore's cries. Eventually she had no choice but to army crawl, swirling whiteness whirling up towards her like a volcano ready to burst.

Paige finally came to the edge of the chasm and found Eleanore holding onto the thread in the dead center of the gaping hole.

"What are you doing?!" Paige cried.

"What does it look like I'm doing?!"

"I mean…what are you doing here?"

"I came into the story late…" She didn't have time (or energy) to explain the intricacies. "What's happening?"

"You're hanging over a sinkhole," said Paige, also not having the time (or energy) to explain the details of the appearance of the Nothing.

"I figured that. But it's not a sinkhole."

"It's not? It looks like one -"

"It's a plot hole."

"A plot hole?"

"Yes," Eleanore shouted over the wind. "But I've never seen any come on so suddenly or get this big...usually you just have to tiptoe around a few in poorly written stories. But I don't see how a book can support a plot hole this huge! There shouldn't be any in 'Gatsby' at all... except, maybe, the lack of development in Gatsby and Daisy's romantic backstory. "

"It's...complicated..." Paige shouted. "And you're holding on to...?"

"The plot thread. Thank God "Gatsby" has a strong one!"

The Nothing was seeping up and out through all the other plot holes scattered around spreading further and further...

"What is that sound?" Eleanore called up.

"Don't you know?"

"I don't know everything!"

"Whatever it is, I think it's coming from the thing at the bottom of the hole..."

"What...thing?"

Eleanore slowly looked down.

A large object was moving towards them. Pale, long and round it wiggled up towards a terrified Paige and Eleanore. It was still a good ways away, but it already looked huge, which meant in reality it must be the size of a building. It was segmented like a worm and moved with seeming intelligence. The fact that it had no eyes or limbs made it all the more horrifying. Paige didn't want to know what it was like close up.

"Can you swing to the edge near me?" Paige called down to Eleanore.

"Do I look like a circus performer?" she yelled. "Besides, my oxygen tank's on the other side of the gap. The tube won't stretch that far even if I could. And if it falls in…"

"I'll try to get around. Could you…take the tube out? That goes around your ears into your nose and connects to your tank? Just for now?"

"I wouldn't have enough air…I'd pass out. I'm barely holding on as it is."

"Ok! Don't worry!"

"Right. Who's worried?"

Paige crawled around the hole inching her way towards Eleanore's oxygen tank. She coughed dust out of her throat as she finally found the tank and pulled herself up to sit next to it.

"How secure is that…clear tube thing…?" Paige asked…

"Decently…as long as it doesn't slip off."

"I'm going to try and use it to pull you back this direction. Hang on!"

"Like I have a choice?!"

"Well, you do, but one of the options isn't great."

"That wasn't funny."

"I know."

Paige grabbed the tube and, without squeezing so hard as to keep oxygen from passing through, pulled it towards her, bringing Eleanore up towards the edge of the hole. When it was taut, Eleanore's foot was about an inch away from the edge. She kicked it up and Paige grabbed it.

"What do we do?" Eleanore cried. "I can't jump…" She was stretched completely horizontally – the thread pulling her one direction, Paige's hand, the other.

"Could you…let go of the thread, and then maybe I could pull you up?"

"MAYBE? That option doesn't really have an 'abort' scenario!"

"I <u>will</u> pull you up."

"What is this…white…erasing…stuff? I mean, if I fall in…"

"Everyone's calling it the Nothing…"

"Like in 'The Neverending Story?'"

"Sort of…I guess? It's erasing 'Gatsby.'"

"If I fall in I'm going to be erased?!"

"Is that worse than dying?"

"I didn't think I could die, outside of my story. No one in The Bookstore can. That's why we're not afraid of the zombies or…I could really…be erased? Yes…that's worse than dying! That's…not even being remembered!"

"I think we both may be erased if we don't get out of here soon…"

"All right…I'll let go. Are you sure you have me?"

"Yes."

Eleanore slowly walked her hands down the thread so she was as close to vertical as she could get.

"I'm going to do it now."

"All right. Don't worry, I won't let anything happen to you."

Eleanore let go of the end of the thread. She swung forwards, eyes closed, her hands held out to keep her from crashing face first into the dirt wall. The sudden change in tension caused Paige to slide forward, and it was only by bracing her foot against a fallen tree trunk that she kept from falling in with Eleanore. But she didn't tell Eleanore that.

"Ow," said Eleanore as she crashed. She wasn't badly hurt, just scratched. The jolt knocked some dirt and rocks loose, but the side of the hole held. Paige strained with all her might to keep hold of Eleanore.

"OK…" said Eleanore, weakly.

"Can you grab onto anything? Any handholds, or tree roots?"

"I'll try…I'm worried about making the hole collapse more."

Paige braced herself as best she could, both her hands gripped tightly around Eleanore's ankle. She pulled her arms towards her, then started scooting backwards. Eleanore found a tree root and used it to push herself up a bit. Her skirt was almost completely over her head, but at least her view was unobstructed.

"Thank God for bloomers," she thought. That would be just her luck, for Paige to pull her to safety staring at her underwear. Bloomers were at least something like pants.

Paige finally got Eleanore high enough on the ledge to grab onto her clothes and pull her the rest of the way up. They were both huffing and puffing, sore and utterly exhausted. But safe.

But there was no time for a happy reunion. They grabbed Eleanore's oxygen tank and ran away from the hole as quickly as they could, the worm-thing roaring closer and closer…

"I don't mean to be the bearer of bad news," said Eleanore, "but I lost my copy of 'Gatsby' when I fell…I don't have a way back into the Store."

"I have a copy," said Paige. "We'll go together."

Paige pulled her tied up book over her shoulder and handed it to Eleanore.

"I don't know how to get back," Paige said.

Eleanore unwrapped the book.

"It's not hard. You just open the book and think of The Bookstore."

The roaring was getting louder. Paige and Eleanore ran towards the trees and fields…as far as they could get from the lake and the eye of the storm.

"Hang on!" Eleanore gasped, out of breath. "I'm going to open it!"

Paige could hear the screams of the party guests in the distance, the Nothing finally overwhelming them.

Eleanore held "Gatsby" in one hand and grabbed Paige's hand in the other. She pushed her thumb in between two pages and let the book fall open across her palm.

But at that moment Paige tripped on a new plot hole that opened right in front of her. She fell and let go of Eleanore's hand. Eleanore looked back but it was too late. The book was open, and she disappeared, oxygen tank and all, leaving Paige in the hole, gripping the edges with her forearms, her legs and torso dangling into the abyss. There was no one to pull <u>her</u> up, and now, without her copy of "Gatsby," she had no way of getting home. Well, back to The Bookstore. Was that home? She wondered as the wind whipped around her and the roaring of the worm-thing inched closer.

She tried to get a foothold in the side of the hole, but there was none to be found. And, after rescuing Eleanore, her arms were completely exhausted. She valiantly tried to grab onto the grass and lift herself up, but she wasn't strong enough. She was stuck where she was, and the only way out was down.

But Paige didn't think, "Why me."

She laughed. And her thoughts went something like this:

"Well, if this was my entire existence, it was a pretty ridiculous one. I pop into being, cause an enormous amount of chaos, serve some customers, shelve some books, and die, in a rather short amount of time, all things considered."

She tried to cling to the fact that she'd at least saved Eleanore and saving someone's life is a great thing to do. But it was clouded by the fact that Eleanore might not have needed saving at all if Paige hadn't shown up and caused the Nothing. You can't claim credit for saving someone you put in harm's way in the first place.

Paige looked down at the endless, white hole beneath her. Well, being erased would be an adventure, at least. And it would hopefully hurt less than the horrific lactic acid building up in her arms. On the plus side, maybe if she didn't exist anymore she would finally stop being a problem. She should probably just accept the inevitable, and let go. But Paige was never apt to just accept anything. And so, she hesitated.

Which in this instance, saved her life. Because if Paige had let go right then, she wouldn't have seen the ladder being lowered just over her head, would have died for want of looking up, and this would be the end of a not very good, nihilistic comic farce. But, as you can see, we still have a few hundred pages to go, so while all life is sometimes a nihilistic comic farce, fortunately, in this moment, Paige's wasn't.

She did hesitate and she did look up – because she wanted to see (what was left of) the sky and trees one more time. Sometimes to have hope all you need to do is look somewhere different from where you're currently looking. It can be wonderfully powerful.

Especially for Paige. Because when she looked up she saw Wesley lowering a makeshift ladder. She felt a joyful surge of adrenaline until she saw how flimsy the ladder was. It looked like it was just made of books loosely strung together.

"What is that?"

"Surrealist literature!" he called down. "It's not immune, but it's far less vulnerable to plot holes and the Nothing. It should hold for a while."

"What about the worm…thing?"

"What?"

"Never mind," she thought.

Paige grabbed onto one of the rungs, the moment between letting go of the side of the hole with one hand and making connection with the ladder utterly painful and terrifying, but she managed to do it and hold on while Wesley pulled her up. As soon as it was safe to she let go and fell to the ground, utterly spent, trying to adjust to the fact that she wasn't going to die.

"We need to get out of here," she heard Nightingale call.

Wesley scooped Paige up, grabbed onto Nightingale, and just as the whiteness was about to overwhelm them, they disappeared back into the Store.

Eleanore descended on Paige, enveloping her in a giant hug, pulling her out of Wesley's arms.

"Thank you!" she cried. "Thank you! Thank you! Why would you come back for me?!"

Paige couldn't get out an answer, she was still so out of breath.

"What did you say back there?" asked Wesley. "About a worm?"

"Yes!" exclaimed Eleanore. "That's exactly what it looked like. A giant albino worm coming towards us through that enormous hole. What was that thing?"

"A Bookworm," Nightingale replied gravely. Wesley looked at him in utter fear.

"But...that's a myth..." said Eleanore. "It's just an urban legend or something to scare the Children's Book characters into behaving. You know...'Get back to shelving or the Bookworm will get you?'"

Willa crept out from the stacks. Paige could see the other characters approaching, watching from amongst the books, their mob-like wrath seemingly quelled (at least for the moment) by fear of the enigmatic worm.

"It isn't real?" Willa asked.

"Apparently it is," said Nightingale. "Very, very real."

"What's a Bookworm?" Paige finally managed to get out, feeling like the idiot who always had to ask questions.

"It devours books," said Willa. "It tunnels through them from the inside and…"

Too terrified to continue, she turned and pressed her face into Dracula who for once didn't roll his eyes, but instead petted her hair, actually trembling a bit himself.

"You're saying," said Dracula, "there's a Bookworm loose in the -?"

"No," said Nightingale quickly. "I'm saying that it appears a Bookworm is isolated in -"

At that moment, the copy of "The Great Gatsby" he was holding disintegrated to dust in his hands. Everyone gasped. Herc covered his mouth, about to be sick. It was like seeing a dead body on the floor right in front of him. Nightingale continued, trying to act as unfazed as possible, "was…in this -"

"I tried to fix it," Paige said, looking up. "I got Daisy out of the chapter…"

"Things still fell apart!" shouted Drood.

"Paige saved me -" Said Eleanore.

"And she wouldn't have needed to if she hadn't shown up in the first place!"

"I never asked to be here!"

"She did more harm than good!"

"You don't know that," said Eleanore.

"She almost killed you! I'd think you'd want to get as far away from her as possible."

"Don't let her in any more books!"

"It doesn't matter where she goes. She's a walking time bomb anywhere."

"Including the Store! Who knows what disaster she'll bring next!"

"I wanted to help! I fixed the chapter!" Paige cried.

"That's what you call fixing? Why did you go rushing back in? You caused 'Gatsby' to burn out all at once rather than the Nothing seeping slowly into the rest of the book. If it had we might have had time to save it. And Eleanore too."

"Now all the other books are vulnerable."

"Yeah! Bookworms are insatiable!"

"You didn't even think they were real until a few moments ago!"

"We all know the stories. Didn't you hear Willa? It devours books. Now that it's devoured 'Gatsby' it'll just start moving from story to story!"

"Fix this, Nightingale!"

"You're the manager!"

"You're supposed to protect us!"

Nightingale put up his hands. The crowd silenced.

"I will deal with this," he said. "But –"

The bell over the front door tinkled and a group of nine young men paraded into the store.

"It's the Inklings again," said Gwen, looking over the railing.

"If I have to show them around mythology one more time -"

"Someone go and help them," said Nightingale. "This is still a Store first and foremost."

Paige got up as quickly as she could.

"Not you."

Arden sighed and walked down the stairs.

"What can I help you with?" he said once he reached the register.

"Have you by chance gotten anything in in linguistic entomology, preferably Finnish?"

"I'm sorry Mr. Tolkien, we still only have fiction in the Store…"

"Worth a try," he replied.

"Not really."

"Mythology?" said Warnie.

"Norse!" said Jack by way of addendum.

"Celtic," corrected John.

"Just…the mythology section as a whole…" said Owen with a weary smile.

"Nothing new."

"Still, let's take a look. You know, we ought to write something of our own. Badly neglected section."

Arden sighed and ushered them to Mythology.

"The rest of you, get back to work," said Nightingale. "I will… handle this." He turned and whispered something to Wesley. Paige turned to Eleanore.

"I went back because you're my friend. And that's…what friends do. I just want you to know…in case I don't see you again."

Tears appeared in Eleanore's eyes. She hugged Paige.

"Though I don't know why Wesley and Nightingale came after <u>me</u>," Paige laughed, trying to lighten the moment. "Would have prevented a lot of drama if they'd just left me there."

"Don't you dare say that!" said Eleanore. "Besides, Nightingale's too…legalistic to let someone…be erased on his watch," she said. "His bark is worse than his bite. Honestly. And even if it wasn't, I told them if they didn't go save you I'd break both their arms with my tank and send the Raven to peck out their eyes. Drystan backed me up. Trust me, it would have been bad news for them if they hadn't," she smiled.

"Come, Ms. Paige. Now." Nightingale ordered.

Eleanore let her go, giving her a squeeze.

"Don't worry," whispered Eleanore. "It'll be all right in the end. Everything is."

"I'm not so sure about that," said Paige, giving Eleanore's hand a squeeze back. "This isn't a story…"

Paige turned and followed Nightingale into the stacks. They walked in silence until Nightingale arrived at a well-worn book. He grabbed Paige's hand and flipped through the pages.

A moment later, they disappeared inside.

CHAPTER 8

...IN THE WABE

Paige found herself on a dark, foggy London street. Gas lamps stood like sentinels on the abandoned road.

"'And all our yesterdays have lighted fools the way to dusty death,'" said Nightingale, looking up at the flickering lights.

"You like the quotations, don't you?"

"Sooner or later everyone in the Store starts thinking in literary quotes. I just have a habit of saying them out loud. I know it…annoys some, but it's usually the most elegant and precise way to say what you intend to. Come along," he said, starting off down the street.

"Do I even want to know what book this is?"

Nightingale didn't stop or look back. Paige sighed and followed, her shoes clacking too loudly on the cobblestones. At least she was in some sturdy boots this time and not heels. They turned right and followed the road all the way out of town and onto a path that twisted and curved into the damp, hazy countryside.

"It's cold," said Paige.

Nightingale didn't reply.

Paige didn't see the wrought iron gate until she was almost on top of it. It was hanging off its hinges and Nightingale easily pushed it open, its creaks and groans piercing the darkness. He stepped across the threshold and led Paige into a musty, ancient graveyard.

"Shoulda brought Dracula," she joked.

The ground was uneven. Time and tree roots had pushed the graves into hilly mounds, moss covering the crooked, antique grave markers. There was only one path, made of half broken, crumbling bricks - like someone destroyed the yellow brick road and this chipped clay and slate was all that remained. It seemed this graveyard had filled up long ago and few living had trod here in the centuries since.

They continued on. Mausoleums sprouted up amongst the headstones, one giant one resting at the very end of the path. Paige saw an imposing, ghost-like statue guarding the entrance. Paige jumped when he suddenly turned his gaze directly on her and started moving towards them. Quick as lightning Paige grabbed a metal sword from a dilapidated monument, pulled it free and held it out, ready to defend herself and, possibly, Nightingale (she wasn't sure on that point yet). She was still getting used to the fact that she was going to live, and she was too happy about it to allow her life to be put in danger again now, especially by a strange ghost-statue-man.

"Put that down," said Nightingale.

"Not after the hell I just went through! He's not touching me."

"Is he doing anything to you?" he looked Paige squarely in the eye and said, with great import, "You never know what rules to operate by until you know what genre you're in. Never. Jump. To. Conclusions." He sighed. "Do not dress up foolishness in courage's clothing."

"I'm doing no such thing Mr. 'let's dress up caution as wisdom.'"

Nightingale approached the figure and recited:

"'Twas brillig, and the slithy toves did gyre and gimble in the wabe.'"

The figure accepted what was apparently a password and Nightingale motioned to Paige to join him at the mausoleum door. The ghost-figure pushed a button, the door slid open, and they crammed into a small room with no other exit than the way they'd entered. The figure pushed another button and the door closed. In utter darkness the room lurched, then moved downwards, cogs and gears echoing around them.

Finally they stopped, the door opened again, and Paige and Nightingale stepped out into a golden Steampunk teahouse. The elevator doors closed behind them, carrying the ghost back up to the graveyard.

The place was vibrant – all gold, and bronze, wood and velvet. A singer's voice scratched out,

" You could write but never edit…edit…

Try to read between the lines…the lies…the lines…"

"Booth, midway back, please," he said to the hostess. It was Nightingale's preferred table and he always entered the story when he know it would be empty. The hostess nodded and a waitress led them to their table. As Paige sat, Nightingale got a glimpse of the waitress's face and did a double take.

"Excuse me," he said.

The woman turned.

She was no longer just an ink smudge. Instead, she was now, unmistakably, a very pretty black woman with intense, kind eyes, an upturned nose, and a beautiful, vast crown of hair held in place with a strip of fabric wrapped across her forehead and tied at the back of her head. She stared at Nightingale, waiting for him to speak.

"Uh…a pot of Cloud Nine and a Queen of Hearts please," he finally said.

"Right away."

"What's wrong?" Paige asked as Nightingale finally sat down.

"She's…fleshed out…at least…more than she was…"

"You've been here before?"

"Yes," he said with no elaboration. "Stories are being messed with faster than I'd anticipated," he continued to himself.

"Faster than you anticipated? You said the Bookworm was isolated in that edition of 'Gatsby…'"

"I know what I said!"

A few other patrons looked in his direction. Nightingale lowered his voice.

"They were right you know. You shouldn't have gone back into the story."

"I was trying to save it! Which is more than you wanted to do."

"What's taking that waitress so long?"

"You ordered like, five seconds ago…"

"Exactly. Things are …off."

"You wanted to just sit there and let the Nothing destroy a literary classic! What happened to 'preserving the canon and protecting characters?'"

"Keep your voice down."

Paige rolled her eyes.

"That wasn't the only copy of 'Gatsby,' you know," he said. "The <u>story</u> wouldn't have been gone, just that edition. You risked your life for nothing."

"What about Eleanore?"

"You didn't go back to save her. You didn't even know she was there."

"So?" Paige said defensively.

"Don't pretend altruistic intentions about her welfare had anything to do with your recklessness."

"Even…regardless of if she'd been there or not…it wasn't for nothing. What about all the characters in that book? You'd really look them all in the eye and say 'Oh, don't worry, a version of you still exists in another edition so it doesn't matter if you die?' THOSE characters have worth. In that edition. They deserved to live. At least I think so."

"It wasn't worth the risk."

"Would you be OK with someone leaving you to die as long as they assured you there was some alternate Nightingale somewhere else?"

"No," he acquiesced. "But this is…complicated. Sometimes…you can't save everyone."

"I don't accept that."

"Then you're in for a lot of suffering."

"I thought as long as we stick to the rules everything turns out OK?"

"'OK' is relative depending on what story you're in. 'Charlotte's Web' and '1984' have very different definitions."

"What rules does The Bookstore operate by?"

"The Bookstore is neutral. And maintaining its neutrality is of dire importance. But it seems that's out the window until…" he trailed off, unsure of exactly how to finish. "Oh, where is our food?!"

They sat in silence until the waitress reappeared. She placed a large pot of tea, two teacups, a decanter and a plate of primarily red pastries covered in gold leaf on their table.

"Anything else?"

"That's all for now, thank you."

The waitress smiled and left.

"Cloud Nine?"

"One of their specialties," said Nightingale, pouring the tea. "I'm rather fond of it. A Queen of Hearts is a pastry assortment, emphasis on jam and strawberry tarts."

Nightingale poured a small drop of pink liquid from the decanter into each of their cups of glowing amber tea. The pink dissolved into the steaming drink and slowly the whole concoction turned completely clear. Paige raised it to her lips and took a tiny sip. It was sweet, and warm and sent a calmness down into her chest. She liked it.

"Very different from sparkling pink lemonade." It was only the second drink Paige had ever had. She picked up a pastry with the same clear granules she'd liked so much in "Gatsby." She licked some.

She made a very strange face.

"You don't like it?" Nightingale asked.

"Has something…gone wrong…with the salt?" she replied, trying to make sense of the taste.

"That's sugar."

"No, I swear it looks exactly like salt…I had some in 'Gatsby'…"

"Yes, sugar tends to do that. You don't like it?"

"I…do…I just wasn't expecting…why would two such different things look exactly the same?"

"I haven't the faintest."

"Do they look the same everywhere?"

"Relatively, I believe so."

"How do you tell them apart? For cooking…?"

"Proper labeling. And taste, of course…"

Nightingale picked up a small raspberry tart topped with gold flakes and a glob of whipped cream so big you could hardly see the berries underneath. He took a bite.

Paige tried some of the sugar granules on her pastry again.

"These are good too though," she said, now that her palate had adjusted. She took another big lick of the sugar.

"Watch your manners."

"Huh?"

"It's not polite to lick sugar off your dessert."

"They're doing it!" Paige nodded towards a patron licking something white off of a cone.

"That's ice cream. That's different."

"So many rules that make no sense."

"Regardless, take a bite or use a fork."

Paige put her pastry down. What was the point of eating something so delightful if you couldn't have fun doing it?

She looked around the teahouse.

"Steampunk?" she asked.

"Yes. Unusual genre. You're familiar?"

"Yeah. I accidentally misshelved a bunch of Sci-Fi before I figured it out." She looked back at Nightingale. "Don't worry, I reshelved everything correctly. Won't make that mistake again."

Paige watched the band.

"Why do you make me stay here

Just sitting on the shelf?"

"It's beautiful here," Paige said.

"And it always will be," replied Nightingale, his words sounding like a warning. "Nothing changes. The books, The Bookstore, your fellow characters will always be as they are. Everything from the color of the light on our hair to the sound of our voices has been carefully crafted by our authors. Through our inspiration, perhaps. But not our design. The world of literature has a great purpose - to let people know that they're not alone. To provide an ordered mirror to their lives. We are charged with caring for the literary canon until we become a part of it, but we cannot change it. Do you understand?"

"Yes."

"But you <u>do</u> change it. That's what's so disturbing. These rules that we cannot break, you eviscerate by just... And if one piece is out of place, the whole structure can come crashing down."

"So they were right?" Paige asked. "I did bring the Nothing."

"As of this moment I cannot discern another explanation as to its appearance," Nightingale continued. "You don't know who you are. You are disordered. And disorder…breeds. Travels. Infects."

Paige looked at the patron with the ice cream. He set down the remains of his cone and yawned.

"As easy and seemingly innocuous as laughter…" said Nightingale. Paige yawned.

"Or a yawn," he chastised in conclusion. Paige snapped her mouth closed.

"So, if I don't figure out who I am…"

"The Bookworm, and the Nothing it brings will keep destroying the literary canon until you restore order and figure out who you are. But… eventually…it will start to destroy the characters in the Store too…and The Bookstore itself."

"If I don't figure out who I am everyone and everything really could…die?"

"Will. Die. Us included. No more stories. Ever."

"But what if I don't…can't…fit into a…a box, the way everyone else does?"

"You have to."

"What if I…just want to be me? No tropes, no -"

"YOU as you currently are, are going to kill every story that ever has or will exist. I think…categorizing yourself is a small price to pay."

Paige's breath caught in her throat. Nightingale saw.

"It's not a bad thing," he said. "Being in a "box," as you put it. It can be liberating. Even being a "free spirit" is a "box." You'll have a place where you belong. Know who you are."

"Don't you ever want to…surprise yourself?"

"Why on earth would I want that? How terrifying, to not know… what you might do."

He took a sip of tea.

"If you don't know who you are, you will never recognize your author when they arrive," he continued. And if you don't recognize your author, you will never be written and who knows what effect just that might have let alone everything else." He looked at her. "Don't you want to be written?"

"Yes."

"Then you must discover your genre as soon as possible. Before the mob takes matters into their own hands. Before the world…all worlds…

come crashing down."

"Well, what would you suggest? I think it's too late now for 'wait and see.' Any other ideas?"

"Frankly, Paige, I'm at a bit of a loss."

"After that rousing speech? That's a letdown."

"You sound like Drystan," Nightingale almost said.

"Besides, aren't you supposed to know everything?"

"There's never been a character like you before…"

"So how am I supposed to figure out who I am if you don't –"

"Listen. You do exactly as I tell you and follow the rules to the letter. Then–"

"And why should I trust you? Just because you're 'the manager?'"

"Because not everything, or everyone here is what they seem."

"Including you?" she replied. "Are you some dark villain and I don't know it?"

His eyes narrowed.

"I thought one of the reasons we need to know everyone's genre is so that we know exactly who everyone is?" she said.

"Yes. Though the ins and outs of any genre or character can be tricky. And until you at least know enough to not pull a sword on the first ghost you meet in a lighthearted Steampunk Fantasy, I don't think you can really talk."

He had a point.

"But I can't hope my genre will just 'come' to me. Not with so much at stake."

"No, but don't use that as an excuse to actively go mucking things up even more than they are. They were right about you making things worse in 'Gatsby.' As I've said."

Paige's eyes flashed.

"Do YOU have any ideas?" he asked. "I'm all ears. Believe me, in this instance I would love any assistance."

"What about a quest?" Paige said. "Shouldn't I go on a quest? That's what people are supposed to do when they need to find…find out something important?"

Nightingale smiled.

"Yes, Paige. That is what they generally do."

"So?"

"That is a lovely idea. You should go on one."

"Great. Where do I start?"

"Unfortunately I don't know how to advise."

"Why not? A quest is pretty standard literary fare."

"It will be a quest unlike any character has ever gone on before."

"Why's that?"

"Because there is no roadmap for a genreless quest."

Paige sighed.

She took a large bite of her pastry.

"So I guess I'm going to have to do this on my own."

"To be different, is to be alone. Have another tart."

CHAPTER 9

RHYME OR REASON

Drystan and Gwen raced along a 19th century London street under a quickly darkening sky desperately trying to catch up to a horse drawn hansom cab.

"It was not a painted dog!" Gwen shouted.

"I think –"

"No way! The evidence –" She stumbled, and begrudgingly let Drystan steady her as they continued. She tried to brush a ringlet off of her face, but it kept bouncing back.

"Ugh! I'm gonna solve this before Holmes, that's for darn sure!"

They finally caught the cab at the next intersection and snuck up to the window.

"Are you kidding me?" said Gwen. "A painted dog?! For real? Such a cheap plot device." They jumped down from the cab as it jolted away. Gwen pulled out a magnifying glass and used it to examine a few loose hairs she had in her pocket.

"So why did I find these at the scene?" she said, frustrated.

"They must be normal dog hairs – "

"If I had a microscope -!"

"We'll try it again. It'll get easier."

"It doesn't count if I know the ending."

They sat down on a wrought iron bench. Drystan took off his shoes and started massaging his feet.

"Know what we should do?" he said. "Play the opposite side. See if we could stump Sherlock Holmes. I'm not all that impressed with Moriarty."

"That would unequivocally involve changing the story," she sulked. "Come on, let's get some food."

They got up and walked down the street, ignoring several gunshots about a half a mile behind them. They settled on a restaurant called The Criterion where Gwen promptly ordered a traditional Sunday roast, and beef and ale pie with a side of fish and chips and a large treacle pudding. She loved to eat, and, since food never affected her figure, she made the most of dining out. At least when she was in private. She didn't want anyone else seeing her diving into a giant meal. Eating was decidedly un-ladylike. But today she made an exception. She was playing outside of her comfort zone and she wanted to eat, so she went ahead and did.

"It was nice of you, bringing me here."

"Thought you might want to stretch you Crime muscles."

"You don't think I should just shut up and look pretty all the time? Everyone else does." She took a bite. "Being beautiful is all I was created for at the end of the day. But I'm smart too, you know!"

"I know. I said there's more to us than the trappings of our genre. Forgive me, but I can't quite see you as a wilting flower waiting for a big strong man to help solve a case."

Gwen smiled. He'd really meant it.

"I didn't do too bad this time, did I?" she said.

"Are you kidding? You found the Tor well before it entered the main plotline."

He sounded happy, and relaxed but then Gwen saw his fingers twitch. For all his joviality he was anxious.

"You still stressed?" she said, a forkful of roast beef in her mouth.

"Nice deduction," he said. Gwen looked at his hands and they instantly quieted.

"This helps you blow off steam –?"

"Well, it's not working today." He sighed. "Thank God Nightingale went after Paige. If he hadn't I would have - "

"You're altruistic. I thought she was the cause of all our problems."

"My problems started long before she showed up."

"How melodramatic," she laughed. She paused, then confessed; "I do understand how you feel. It's not really that great being me. Trying to live up to some perfect version of a damsel because that's what being a woman in my genre means? You're the only person who thinks I even have a brain. Subgenre Crime or not." She shoveled in another forkful, getting angrier the more she opened up. "I mean, look at Violet and Iris. It's so easy for them. At least you're the only Epic Comedy character in the Store. There are three of us! No one even calls me by my right name. It's just SO CUTE having three Romance girls with flower names." She swallowed. "I'm sorry. Look at you, listening to me going on and on, when you've been so nice and -"

Drystan took her hand.

"I'm glad you understand," he said. "If only…to not be the only one who feels this way."

She stopped eating. She didn't move her hand away from Drystan's.

"A storm's coming, Gwen. We've got to have good teammates on our side if we're going to survive this crisis."

"I couldn't agree more," she said.

"But…I don't just want to fix the Nothing… I want a revolution. I know you think I'm just a comic sidekick but…"

"Look, I'm sorry about…you may not be the…epitome of a revolutionary…but I'm not the quintessence of a damsel. Maybe Arden is onto something. Maybe we can have…flexibility."

"Paige is the key. Somehow. We just have to figure out…what exactly she unlocks."

"I'm with you, joker," she decided as she said it. "Honestly? I'm tired of being treated like I'm nothing more than eye candy who needs to look pretty and shut up. Of course, I do want to be pretty but…"

"You ARE pretty," he said. "But you're so much more. Stop wasting your time with boring, stupid characters. You were meant for so much more."

Gwen blushed.

Drystan smiled.

"Let's do 'A Scandal in Bohemia' next," she said.

"Whatever you say Ms. Friday." He leaned forward and slipped the bit of roast dangling from Gwen's fork into his mouth.

* * *

"I still don't think it's safe to have her here," insisted Dracula, shelving with the bare minimum of effort required.

"Well, there's not really another option," said Iris. "And Nightingale says he has it under control. Besides, the Nothing hasn't been in any other books…and no one's seen the Bookworm -"

"I think Paige and Eleanore were just making that part up."

"What?!"

"The Bookworm."

"Why?"

"For attention."

"How could Paige have made up a story about the Bookworm when she didn't even know what a Bookworm was?!"

"Can we please not talk about it!" Willa exclaimed.

"I still don't like all this. Paige shouldn't be here just…working next to the rest of us!"

"We have to trust Nightingale. He's never steered us wrong."

"Eh, you're all frauds, you know that? A bunch of phonies," said Arden.

"What on earth are you talking about?" Dracula said.

"You're just all scared of something happening to you. You don't really care about all those characters in 'Gatsby,' or even the general literary canon, so long as <u>you</u> get written and <u>your</u> story stays safe. Besides, I think we should expand our thinking. This could be good. We could try out being someone new."

"Ooo! Like being a medieval princess instead of a renaissance princess?!" said Violet.

"No."

"At the cost of people's lives!?" said Willa.

"Ah, you're a fake."

"You're not making any sense, Ardie. One second you're saying we should be pure and altruistic, the next we should embrace this… disaster?"

"I just meant…oh, I can't explain what I mean. And even if I could, I'm not sure I'd feel like it."

He started to walk away.

"Oh, and don't call me Arden anymore."

"What? It's your name."

"I want a change. And something tangible to show it. Call me… Eddie."

"Why?"

"Cause it's my name now."

And he was off.

Paige couldn't help hearing them whispering about her. It was constant. Especially when she worked the front desk, which was all she did these days. The characters were terrified of her touching the books, so she was stuck on retail duty and not allowed to read. Before that, they'd all been worried about her interacting with the potential authors, so she was banned from having contact with customers and had to shelve as far away from the front of the Store as they could send her. Either way, it seemed like everyone was trying to figure out the best way to quarantine her. Who knew what would be next. Paige prayed she wouldn't be forced to just sit in a corner staring at the wall, or worse.

They didn't even try to hide their gossip from her anymore.

"Excuse me, miss."

Paige hadn't heard the bell ring and was jolted back to reality when a man in his early 50's plopped "This Side of Paradise," "On The Road," "The Handmaid's Tale" and the collected works of Ernest Hemingway on the counter.

Paige started to ring up the items, but once again found the scanner wasn't working.

She looked over and saw Arden organizing the "New Arrivals" table.

"Hey, Arden," she called. "Anyone from tech around?"

That was code for "are there any tech characters currently in the Store who might be able to fix this?"

"Not at the moment."

Great.

"And my name's not Arden anymore. It's Eddie."

"Your nametag still says -"

"IT'S EDDIE!"

"Fine...Eddie."

Paige started manually entering the retail codes into her computer.

"You know what this means," the customer teased. "They're all free!"

The characters had a tally in the back room of how many times a customer made that particular joke – each customer thinking they were the genius who invented it.

"No, unfortunately," Paige replied, trying to stay professional. Wesley was watching. He always did now. He'd stuck to her like glue ever since she got back from the teahouse and Nightingale ordered him to keep an eye on her. His watchdog presence was one of the only things keeping the hysteria at bay, though Paige felt less protected and more like she was being haunted by a brooding, angsty ghost. But she didn't want him to report back to Nightingale that she'd been cheeky with a customer, so she forced herself to keep her cool. Other characters in the Store could get away with murder, but Paige couldn't breathe without being suspect and the stress was wearing her thin.

"Hey, give me a smile, sweetheart," said the customer. "Nothing's that bad. It's not like the world's going to end!"

Oh boy.

She didn't smile.

"I'm just making a joke. Can't you take a joke?"

She just stared at him.

"Guess not."

She swiped his card and handed him his books in a bag.

"This a good place to work?" he asked, trying to keep the conversation going for some inexplicable reason.

"It's fine."

"They give you health insurance? Sick leave? Minimum wage? That sort of thing?"

"Did you want an application?"

"No, just chatting. Something wrong with having a conversation?"

"When one of us is trapped here without an option to leave there is." She couldn't help being a bit snarky.

"Careful, missy, or you're gonna get yourself fired."

"I wish I could."

"Don't. You don't want me to get the manager."

"Thank you for coming to The Bookstore! You have a happy, healthy day!" she smiled broadly. The conversation was done.

The man begrudgingly took the hint. He huffed and waddled out.

"Dear God, what book is <u>he</u> going to write?" she thought as he left the store. "I wouldn't want to be their character…"

"Excuse me," a syrupy voice purred. Paige looked up. A tall, dark, deeply seductive man with reddish eyes stared down at her. He wore a long black coat that she almost mistook for a cape, with a nametag on the left lapel that read:

DRACULA

"I'm new here. Could you direct me, please, to the person in charge?"

Oh…man…

"My name is Dracula. Count Dracula. Gothic Horror."

"Two Dracula's. This'll go over well," she thought. But she said: "Up the stairs, straight back, stained glass stacks with a door in the middle."

Dracula took her hand, turned it over, and kissed her wrist. It made Paige's feet tingle.

"Thank you very much," he said in a heavy accent, and swept away.

But before he could make it to Nightingale's office this new Dracula (we shall call him Dracula 2) ran into Dracula 1 with Willa in tow.

"Look! There's two of you!" said Willa.

But that wasn't entirely accurate. They were far from clones. Dracula 1 was terribly pale, long and lean, and was definitely wearing a cape. Dracula 2 looked like a dark Victorian gentleman with ruby eyes.

"What is this?" said Dracula 2. "You look…like a cartoon of me…"

The word "cartoon," dear reader, was first popularized in 1843 in case you thought the term out of place. In other interesting, but random trivia, the name Tiffany was quite popular in the medieval period - a nickname for Tiffania or Theophania, names commonly given to girls born around the feast of Epiphany. But because of the 20th century popularity of Tiffany, 20th - 21st century authors writing fiction set in medieval times cannot use the name because of the incorrect assumption that it is too "contemporary," and not appropriate to the time period.

But back to the Draculas.

"I was here well before you," said Dracula 1. "I'm sure you must be from some amusing but forgettable retelling. I assure you that I am an original."

"You are having fun socializing with a small child and feel the need to defend your superiority to me. You are not Count Dracula. There is nothing dangerous or demonic about you. And where on earth did you get that ridiculous cape?"

Dracula 1 barred his fangs.

Dracula 2 barred his.

"I have been so long master that I would be master still, or at least that none other should be master of me," he said. "Remember it."

"Been so long master...of what?! You just got here five minutes ago!"

"And yet I am more our essence than you are, though you try to claim otherwise."

Willa scrunched up her face, confused.

"He talks funny," she said.

"I will be on my way. I have business to attend to." And Dracula 2 swept off.

Dracula 1 looked like he was about to have a panic attack.

"I'll...be in a graveyard," he said, quickly gliding off, muttering; "I'm very demonic. Very, very demonic..." to himself as he walked away.

"Wesley still watching you?" said Eleanore as she dropped off a bunch of books.

"Yeah. He's trying to be subtle, but he's not very good at it."

They looked at Wesley. He ungracefully tried to pretend he'd been examining some books.

"If you're going to stalk me you might as well own it," said Paige. He didn't respond. "Come on over and chat," she said.

"I'm not much of a conversationalist," he called over.

"At least he cares enough to watch out for you," Eleanore whispered.

"No he doesn't. Nightingale made him."

"Well…still…it's nice…that he is…?" said Eleanore, grasping. "Don't be too annoyed by him. He has his good points."

"Sure. He's tall, dark and gorgeous in an annoying sort of way."

Eleanore snorted.

"Wanna help me shelve some books? Get you off the front lines?" Eleanore asked.

"Sure," Paige smiled, grateful that at least one person didn't seem to be allergic to her.

"Hey Eddie!" Eleanore called, "take over the front desk!"

Paige thought about yelling "Here boy!" to Wesley and patting her leg, but she didn't think it wouldn't go over well. Wesley followed them anyway, staying a few meters behind, like some sort of non-discreet Secret Service Agent.

"You know we know you're following us, right?"

"Just trying to be…polite about it."

Paige and Eleanore giggled.

"Why do girls do that?" Wesley thought.

"So, where are we shelving?"

"Oh…Drystan said he needed some help in Travel Fiction," said Eleanore, blushing.

"Travel Fiction? You mean like…time travel stories?" Paige asked.

"No, not really…" said Eleanore.

"I haven't gotten to that section yet. Shut up, Wesley!" said Paige.

"I didn't say anything."

"I could hear your eyes rolling," Paige said.

"Travel Fiction and Time Travel Fiction are entirely different things," he said.

"Hence your silent eye roll."

"Travel Fiction," said Eleanore, gently, "are stories centered on geographical travel…like 'Sean and Eric's Excellent Detour,' or 'The Diary of a Traveler Abroad.'"

"I've never heard of it."

"Yeah, they're really only popular with a certain type of reader…"

"Hello, I'm Dewey."

Out of nowhere a woman was suddenly standing a few inches in front of them. She wore a flannel shirt under a suit jacket, paired with slightly moth eaten pants that didn't quite match the jacket unless you squinted, capped off with rather intense glasses and brown hair sitting in a messy mound on the top of her head. She looked to be in her forties, had a big grin, and spoke with a slight North Dakota accent.

"Are you…looking for something?" Paige asked.

"Hello, I'm Dewey."

"Are you…looking for a book?"

"Oh, I'm not a customer. I'm Dewey. Emergency Safeguard of The Bookstore. And this is one heck of an emergency," she chuckled.

"What the heck?" said Drystan, seeing Dewey as he turned the corner.

"No, I'm Dewey," Dewey smiled.

"I'm…so confused."

"Why do you sound like you're from North Dakota?" asked Eleanore.

"Where's that?" asked Paige.

"America."

"Is everything in America?"

"I'm from The Bookstore," said Dewey. "Actually, I sort of AM The Bookstore. In a way…well, PART of it…"

"We should take her to Nightingale," whispered Wesley.

"Oh, there's no point in whispering, Wesley" said Dewey, "I hear and see everything. Like when you were in 'Jekyll and Hyde' recently and went to –"

"All right –"

"And said: 'I love having tarts for –"

"Yes, we get your point!"

"Besides," said Dewey, "I'm not here for Nightingale, I came to see Paige."

"Me?"

"Why?"

"Well the emergency started when you arrived, so you're who I need to speak to."

"Great, I'm literally in trouble with The Bookstore."

"Oh, no, you're not in 'trouble' per se. At least, I'm not angry with you. You're certainly 'in trouble' in terms of being in and causing overwhelming danger and destruction," she smiled. "Basically you're 'patient zero.' The beginning. Always the best place to start."

"Hold on," said Eleanore. "Back up. I've never heard of a…failsafe…thing…" She turned to Drystan and Wesley.

"I'm not surprised," said Dewey. "I haven't been needed before. This is the first time I'm manifesting. It's quite exciting!"

"Manifesting?"

"Oh! This is fun! Even though it's the end of the world you ask so many questions, I love it! You've heard of the Dewey Decimal System?"

"That's what we use to organize the books…"

"Precisely! Well, I am a physical manifestation of that. Hello! I'm Dewey!"

"You've said," grumbled Wesley. "Multiple times."

"Comedy works in threes."

"But just because it's in threes doesn't make it humorous," said Drystan.

"Oh, drats," said Dewey. "I thought I had it down…"

"So you're The Bookstore manifested as a human?"

"I'm not human. More a…sentient being. But, yes, in a manner of speaking. if anything ever goes terribly wrong, I show up to offer the collective knowledge of the Store. It's much easier to ask me a question than to go rifling through the stacks. Go ahead, give it a whirl."

"Why did the Bookworm appear?"

"I have no idea."

"How do we stop the Nothing?"

"Ooo, you're really going for challenging ones!"

Eleanore sighed. "I think she means things like…can you describe the Hero's Journey? Things The Bookstore would know."

"Ding, ding, ding!" Dewey smiled. "And yes, I can. The Hero's Journey, popularized by scholar Joseph Campbell, is described in narratology and comparative mythology as a common format of stories or 'monomyths' that appear independently in all human cultures. The structure primarily relates to narratives involving a male protagonist (though some include females) while, according to Maureen Murdock, female monomyths have a slightly different structure referred to as the 'Heroine's Journey.' Campbell himself didn't believe women could go on a Hero's journey at all saying, quote: 'Women don't need to make the journey… all she has to do is realize that she's the place that people are trying to get to.' Frankly, Campbell could be rather misogynistic and a bit of a jerk. Campbell describes the Hero's journey in seventeen stages: Call to Adventure, Refusal of the Call, Supernatural Aid –"

"How do you know…that sounds like structural, non-fiction knowledge…" Wesley interrupted.

"Well I would be a pretty poor information system if I only knew what was in books without understanding why they were there…Plus a lot of editions of fiction books have very informative introductions, not to mention appendices, prologues, analyses, and author biographies."

"Maybe she could help!" said Eleanore to Paige. "Didn't you say you had to go on a quest?"

"I don't think there's going to be anything in Campbell's structure for me…Nightingale said a genreless quest has never been done before."

"Ha!" said Eleanore. "You may have to tread your own path, but structure is structure and all stories live or die by it. You saw firsthand what unraveling it can do!"

"You're going on a quest?" asked Drystan.

"Shh!"

"You can trust him," said Eleanore. "He backed me up when I told Nightingale to go back for you. And he voted for you at the council…"

Eleanore's eyes suddenly got wide.

"I shouldn't have said that. We weren't supposed to say anything…"

"You two were at the council?"

"Three, actually," said Drystan with a side glance at Wesley.

"I voted for you to stay!" said Eleanore.

"Me too," said Drystan.

"He didn't," said Dewey with a nod to Wesley.

"Why does that not surprise me?" said Paige.

"Don't take it personally," he replied.

"Oh, no, of course not. You know, why _did_ you come with Nightingale to rescue me?"

"I'm physically stronger than he is," said Wesley. "He couldn't have pulled you to safety. Besides, I only ever wanted to protect the Store. I never wanted anyone to die."

"Don't make me swoon."

"Paige, I want to help you," said Drystan, turning attention back to the matter at hand. "I've been here longer than anyone, let me come."

"That's sweet, but I don't want to put anyone else in danger. This is something I have to do on my own."

"See!" exclaimed Eleanore, "It isn't a real quest until someone's said that!"

"You can't do this alone," said Drystan.

"Nightingale said –"

"No character ever can," he replied, rolling his eyes. "It's one of the first rules of literature. Besides, it's not just out of altruism... I want the same thing you do."

"What? You want to figure out your genre?" said Paige.

"I want to fix this world. To stay alive. To matter, both literally and figuratively. Get it? Matter? Like, the double meaning?"

"I did," said Eleanore. "It was very clever."

Everyone else just stared.

"It's because it wasn't in threes," said Dewey, consolingly. "But don't worry, I'm sure you'll get it two more times from now."

"I don't want to feel like I should never have existed," Drystan continued, ignoring Dewey. "Like I don't quite fit...the way I'm supposed to. But I guess you have to fit into a box in the first place to even have a chance of feeling that way."

Paige's breath caught. Other characters felt like that?

Drystan looked down, embarrassed. Eleanore took his hand.

"I think...a lot of us feel that way," she said. "We're just too scared to admit it." Her breathing became more labored. Drystan increased her oxygen flow.

"You need help," Drystan said to Paige. "It's nothing against you, but you saw what happened in 'Gatsby' when you tried to take matters into your own hands. Everyone needs a team. I'd like to be on yours."

"Me too!" said Eleanore. "And I'm sure Wesley…" She looked over at Wesley who was frowning, leaning against a corner of the stacks. "…Maybe Dewey can help along the way too!" Eleanore said, diverting attention from his sullenness.

"Oh, I don't go on quests," said Dewey.

"She already said she doesn't know anything about the Bookworm or the Nothing…"

"Maybe we just haven't asked the right question," said Paige. She turned to Dewey, thought for a moment, then asked:

"Do you know anything that can help me figure out who I am and stop the Bookworm?"

"Oh, absolutely!" Dewey said. "You just have to find the Owner. If there is one."

"The owner of what?"

"The Bookstore."

"The Bookstore has an owner?"

"It has a manager, employees, and customers. Of course it has an owner. At least, it should…if there is, no one's seen them in ages. Even I've never met them. But, yes, theoretically they're there. The Owner's your only chance. They'll be able to help you. If they exist."

"Do you know where they might be?"

"Nope."

"Is there anything you can do to help us find them?"

"Of course, silly. I can give you this."

A book dropped out of mid-air and landed in Dewey's open hands.

"That's…how did…that's the Ur Book!" said Drystan staring in awe.

"Ur?"

"It means 'original'", said Drystan.

"Very good!" said Dewey. "The Ur Book gets you in and out of any book in the Store without having to retrace your steps or find the book you want to go in. Think of it like a pass. Better than money! Money is designed to get you things, but passes were made to get you places."

"You make it sound like it always costs something to get places."

"Everything is currency in a story," Dewey replied. "Time, energy, love, innocence, pain. That's part of where plot holes come from, trying to get something for nothing. This book saves you time and energy – expensive commodities."

"It does more than that," said Drystan. "It's…it's actually real?"

"Oh, very," said Dewey. "Just like the Bookworm. Most legends have a basis in fact."

"But the Owner…"

"Is the one I can't confirm, unfortunately."

"This book is supposed to contain all the secrets of all universes," said Drystan.

"And provide magical travel between books," said Dewey. "Which is what you need it for at the moment."

"Where's it been all this time?" asked Drystan.

"With me," Dewey replied.

"And where is that?"

Dewey thought for a moment.

"I don't know. That's a very existential question, isn't it? But I came to give it to Paige to help resolve this emergency."

Dewey handed Paige the book. She gingerly took it from Dewey and slowly opened it.

It was blank.

Drystan looked at Dewey, desperation and confusion on his face.

"Don't worry, you just have to think of where you want to go – like normal book hopping."

"But there's nothing in here – "

"A pass is what you need most at the moment," said Dewey. "It'll work perfectly for that, regardless of its internal appearance."

"How do we find you?" Paige asked. "If we need to talk to you again."

"Oh, I always show up when there's need of me."

"But you said this is the first time you've ever manifested."

"That's true. Well, hopefully you're good to go because there's no guaranteeing your idea of an emergency will be the same as the Store's. It's not like there's a call button," she laughed.

"But what if –"

Dewey was gone as quickly as she appeared.

"Well, that was –"

"Oh!" Dewey popped back. "Don't lose the book. There's no other copy. Just …be careful with it. I'm sure you will."

And she disappeared again, this time for good.

"We should tell Nightingale," Wesley said.

"I don't think that's a good idea," said Drystan. "Just because he's the manager doesn't mean he needs to be involved."

"That's exactly what it means. He's in charge. We need to do this the right way."

"The letter of the law is not necessarily the right thing."

"I still think we should try."

Against Drystan's better judgement, they went to Nightingale's office. They got as far as mentioning that the Owner of the Store could help them but they didn't get any further before –

"Absolutely not."

"Sir –"

"You need to focus on a practical course of action, not go chasing a fairy tale!"

"But Dewey –"

"Dewey?!" he said, the blood draining from his face." "He's… he's here?"

"SHE."

"Dewey's –"

"A woman. Yes."

"Interesting…" he said.

"You knew about her?"

"Theoretically, yes. Do you have any idea how serious it is that he…

she showed up?!"

"I don't think it's possible for us to take it more seriously", said Paige.

"What about this owner -?"

"I don't know anything about an owner. I've never heard of such a person and I've been in the Store longer than anyone. Focus! Dewey's never appeared before…of course, I knew they were a safeguard…but to actually…" He started pacing around his office. "I need to think… perhaps there's something in the archives at Annwn University….I might be able to cast a spell if I was in…" He grabbed what seemed to be a varnished stick off a stand on a shelf, then paused. "No…it wouldn't work on something to do with the Store." He put the stick back. "Research then. I'll have to do research…though…no, I don't believe such a book exists…"

Paige moved the Ur Book behind her back.

"But still…research is always the way. The best way. Learn more about this Dewey…how we can make her presence unnecessary…"

"But what about the Owner?"

"Paige," he said, a kind but stern look on his face, "let me give you some advice -"

"Stop pontificating and DO something!"

"Fine. Don't listen. I forbid you from looking for this owner," Nightingale snapped. "This is not a game! Stop messing around and come back when you have practical information. Wesley, I would think you at least would have more sense," he threw out as he slammed the door and retreated back into his office mumbling about "reading" and "research."

"I thought the people in charge were supposed to help you," said Paige. "Or at least listen…"

"'Supposed to' is a very non-committal phrase," said Wesley.

"How do you know who to trust, then?"

"It takes knowing someone for a good, long while. And even then you can't be sure," said Wesley.

"You are just a barrel of sunshine, aren't you?" said Eleanore.

"Why don't his clothes change?" Paige said.

"What?"

"Nightingale. His clothes didn't change when we went into a story."

"The ones who've been here a long time can control it…a bit…" said Eleanore begrudgingly. She wished she had that skill.

"So Nightingale knows things aren't…hard and fast. At least, not everything…"

"Come on, we need to talk. Away from here. Now." said Drystan. "And I know just the place."

CHAPTER 10

THE ISLAND OF MISFIT TOYS

Drystan, Wesley, Paige, Eleanore and Eleanore's oxygen tank looked out on a 1930's American dustbowl landscape (yes, for now we're in America again), the whole world colored in hand-tinted and sepia tones. Far in the distance stood the only structure for miles – a collection of circus tents that had apparently been magically erected out of nowhere. There were no wagons. No train station nearby...

"You couldn't have brought us in a little closer?" Eleanore asked.

"Sorry. Habit. I love watching the sunset from here. Plus you don't want to suddenly appear in a wide open space just before a giant crowd scene."

"Still..." Eleanore looked woefully down at her tank.

"The Ur Book worked," said Paige.

"You're not going to go snitching to Nightingale?" Drystan asked Wesley.

"Let's just…go and talk," he muttered.

There were no signs of life in the tents until the moment the sun vanished over the horizon. Then tiny lights flickered on almost by supernatural cue. Suddenly, as if waiting for their entrance, people started pouring in from roads in every direction – all somehow more of the 1930's than the 1930's ever really were. They walked or parked their cars in the barren field and trekked towards the circus.

"Follow me!" said Drystan once the crowd coalesced. They scurried down the hill, Paige helping Eleanore with her tank.

"If only this tank would change along with my clothes when I go in a story…I wouldn't mind so much if it were a…dog…or a bag or… anything else."

They were all dressed in 1930's attire. The kind of clothes poor farmers would consider their Sunday best. Paige sported a sweet dress of blue and white organdy. Eleanore was lucky enough to have overalls (dark blue and oddly well ironed), though she hated the light, puff sleeve blouse underneath.

"It's a nice color on you," Paige said.

"At least I have pockets," Eleanore sighed, uncomfortable in anything pastel.

When they were almost at the ticket booth, without pausing, Drystan scooped a gold coin from off the ground. Paige looked at him quizzically.

"He's been here once or twice," Wesley said.

"Be ready," Drystan whispered back.

In one balletic motion he transported the coin directly onto the ticket counter. The counter didn't have a glass enclosure, thus allowing Drystan to take his ticket with his right hand while swiping a row of tickets (and a dime) with his left, hiding his motion by leaning against the stand and smiling at the ticket seller.

"Beautiful night," he said.

Drystan reached his left hand behind his back, passing the stolen tickets to Paige which she quickly dispersed among the group.

The ticket seller giggled.

Drystan nodded and headed into the tents, Paige, Eleanore and Wesley following behind.

"Just a minute!" the ticket seller shouted when she saw them sneaking by.

They held up their tickets in a single, almost choreographed gesture.

The ticket seller nodded. At the entrance to the tents someone tore their tickets in half and ushered them on. They followed the swarm inside, the look of awe and wonder on everyone's faces noticeably absent from Drystan's.

The circus itself had no center but was rather a maze of tents - some with acrobats out front on a little stage trying to draw patrons over to watch the show inside, some selling food, some hawking trinkets.

"Step right up!" a barker cried. "See your secret dreams made manifest right inside!"

"Take charge of your destiny with these enchanted amulets all the way from darkest Peru!" called another.

"People believe this stuff?" Paige asked. "They actually pay for it? These folks…who look like they had to save up for a year just to afford a ticket?!"

"The things for sale are no mere illusions," Drystan whispered to her. "Don't underestimate this place," he added. "It'll get you into hot water. As most of these patrons will likely discover."

"Hot water…schmot water. I want to see my secret dreams made manifest!" said Eleanore.

"That amulet looks like it weighs more than you do," said Wesley. "Besides, seeing your secret dreams is immensely overrated."

"I don't care," said Eleanore, drifting towards the stall, her tank banging into patrons as she did. "Sorry! Oh, sorry!"

Wesley pulled her back by the strap of her overalls.

"You have any money?" he asked.

"They'll never notice the amulet's gone. And the scene will reset anyways…it's not like I'm really taking anything," she huffed. That was the mentality characters in The Bookstore generally had towards anything that cost money in stories. Except for gaining admission to places, no one would ever realize you didn't pay for something if you left the book before the bill came due.

"They'll notice here," said Wesley. "Besides, what if it's part of the principal storyline?"

"It's not," said Drystan.

"See!" Eleanore summated.

"But there's no time," said Drystan. "Don't forget we have an agenda." He turned, leading them onwards with nary a look at the surrounding marvels.

"But –"

"You can come back anytime," said Wesley pulling Eleanore along.

"Hey! I'm literally dying here, you know! Be gentle!"

Paige ran a few steps and caught up with Drystan.

"You mean…it's really real? All the magic here?"

"You say that like you don't live in a magical Bookstore," Drystan laughed.

"Oh, there's nothing special about hanging out with literary characters."

"There's nothing special about seeing your secret dreams made manifest…not when you can do it whenever you want. Anyways, most often it's just a good steak dinner. And one you can't even eat."

"It is not," Paige laughed.

"No, but I got you to smile." He sighed. "In either case, all magic loses its shine when you can have it whenever you want. Remember that." He smiled and tapped the end of her nose.

Drystan hurried them past the flashier attractions, venturing deeper and deeper into the heart of the place towards hidden areas the common tourists might never discover. But Paige and Eleanore dawdled as much as they could get away with, peeking at clowns inside one of the tents, the audience howling with laughter, aerialists in another twirling in lyras, wrapping and unwrapping themselves in silks high over the patron's heads.

"Come on," said Drystan. "We've got to be done by the time the main plot arrives."

"Ooo! Can we get some sugared nuts?!" Eleanore said. A woman huffed behind her. "Oh, sorry!" She called over her shoulder realizing she'd accidentally knocked the woman with her tank.

"You hit my baby! What's wrong with you!"

"Sorry, I'm...dying..." she tried to smile. There was no good way to respond.

Drystan continued on until they came to an all but abandoned area. He finally stopped when he got to a small, hardly noticeable tent with a sign over the entrance that read:

FORTUNE TELLER

 A soft glow coming from inside.

"Please, no," said Wesley. "You didn't bring us all the way here for this?!"

"For what?"

"Of course not," Drystan replied.

"What's he talking about?" asked Paige.

"Looks kind of boring to me," said Eleanore.

"If you ever can't find Mr. Comedy, look no further," Wesley said to Paige with a grand gesture toward the humble tent.

"It's a place to talk," said Drystan, defensively. "Nothing more."

Drystan tripped on a rock as he crossed the path. Wesley chuckled.

"Be nice," said Paige, hitching the Ur Book under her arm. "Ugh, why don't girls get pockets? Where are we supposed to put our books?" she looked jealously at Drystan with the copy of the book they were currently in tucked neatly into his back pocket (they'd decided to play it safe and have it on them just in case something went awry with the Ur book).

Just before they reached the entrance they heard the voice of an old woman echoing inside:

"You cannot escape your fate. Discover what is in store for you. Only ten cents."

Wesley rolled his eyes.

Drystan parted the fabric and ushered them in.

The tent was bigger than seemed possible from the outside. The group stood in a large, dimly lit waiting area with cushions encircling a table laden with candles, tea, and a bowl full of honeyed dates. There was a smaller entryway on the opposite side leading to the inner sanctum. Drystan walked up to a figure in the shadows, whispered something and handed her ten cents. She left them alone.

"What? We're not getting our fortunes read?"

"What's all this about? Of all the locations in all the books!" Wesley moaned.

"Please –"

"Every time you get some time off you come to this ridiculous place," Wesley continued, expostulating to the assembled company. "Not the circus – this fortune teller. 'Your future is unfolding exactly as planned,' that's all she ever tells you, right? But you still keep coming back like some kind of masochistic…"

"How do you know that?" asked Drystan, defensively.

"Every old timer in the Store knows," he chuckled. "Plus I saw you when I came ages ago."

"I invited him back when I thought he might have a jovial side hiding under all that stoicism," Drystan joked. "Apparently he doesn't."

"We've all been here at some point," said Wesley. "You have the worst kept secret in the Store," he said, popping a date in his mouth.

"We all have our quirks," Drystan said as he sat and straightened his shirt.

"Is this where you went when we were all in 'Gatsby?'" Paige asked.

"Yes," he said. "I like the…ambiance."

"Where are we, anyways?" Eleanore asked, realizing Drystan hadn't actually told the group. Being a relatively new arrival to the Store, <u>she</u> had never been here before.

"'Phantasmagoria,'" Drystan replied. "Name of the circus and the book it's from."

"What's it about?"

"It's kind of a collection of stories. Every chapter is about a character whose life crosses with the circus. There's a little girl named Violette who never grows up…her father is a ventriloquist and eventually she leaves to try and make her way in the wide world…there's a Mephistophelean illusionist named Mr. Wednesday who uses the whole thing as a front to collect people's souls in exchange for granting their wishes…there's a through line about a young girl named Lyra whose story interweaves with characters from different chapters. I think the author wrote another book all about her, actually." He smiled. "It's fantastical, but you don't want to dig too deep."

"Come on, no more chit chat. Let's have this out," said Wesley.

They gathered around the table on the very comfortable cushions. There was a weight to the air – a feeling that whatever happened here would have powerful implications for a long time to come.

"I've heard about this Owner…" said Drystan.

"What?! Why didn't you say anything?!" Paige exclaimed.

"Shh! I'm saying something now. I don't know much, but I've been in the Store a long while and…once upon a time I heard people talking about them. There were even rumors that the Owner used to communicate with the manager."

"They're talking to Nightingale?"

"No, USED to be. Several managers back. But in any case communication apparently started to fade…then stopped altogether. No one I knew ever saw the Owner in person, but I've heard enough that I think there may be something in our looking for them. At least, I don't think it would be a wild goose chase."

"Really?" Wesley scoffed, "looking for someone who completely cut off communication ages ago? If they ever even really existed to begin with…"

"But what if they did? DO?"

"Then why hasn't anyone heard from them in so long? They could have died. They could have just decided to up and abandon the Store. There are a lot of possibilities and most of them end in our having wasted valuable time searching for someone who isn't there or doesn't care a lick about us if they are," Wesley said. "I think Nightingale has a point."

"But what other choice do we have?" asked Paige. "Dewey told me I should look for the Owner, knowing the risks. That and the book are the only help she gave. It'd be pretty stupid to ignore her."

"But even if…Nightingale told us we couldn't…" said Eleanore.

"So we go behind his back and look anyway," said Drystan. "We just can't let him find out. Look, we're the Store misfits. We've always felt it. Paige's arrival just forced us to deal with it. Things have been deteriorating for a long time. Maybe the Owner could help all of us. I'm tired of the way I'm treated…the butt of everyone's jokes."

"I know what you mean," Eleanore said hesitantly. "I…I don't really like myself very much. I mean…I don't want to be sad and sick all the time. Truth? I don't even know if I really want to be written at all."

Wesley and Paige looked at her, horrified.

"Come on, my story must be pretty awful if this tank is any indication. I know I'm not long for this world once my author shows up…and I…I don't want to die. I want to know what it's like to be happy. I want a family, and the ability to breathe and…I want a boyfriend…" She blushed and put her head down. "I know I'm not supposed to feel this way, but I just can't help it."

Paige took Eleanore's hand.

"Us…non-chosen ones need to stick together," said Drystan, taking Eleanore's other hand. She smiled.

Paige looked up at Wesley.

"What about you, Mr. perfect, brooding, non-misfit Adonis?"

Wesley sighed.

"I…want to help fix whatever's wrong," he said. "And…if this is what you feel you need to do Paige…then we'll do it."

"You're not going to snitch on us?" asked Eleanore.

"I am many things, but I'm not a spy and I'm nobody's lackey. Somebody's going to have to look after you if anything's going to get accomplished. And something better get accomplished soon or we're all going to die. But…" he looked sideways at Eleanore's tank. "Forgive me, I don't want to be rude…but is it prudent to bring the YA girl on a quest? The state of her health is…well, as she said…and traveling with an oxygen tank is…taxing under the best of circumstances."

"If Eleanore wants to come, she's coming," said Paige. "She's part of the team."

"I want to help…" said Eleanore. "I won't get in the way, I promise. I'll…pull my weight." She laughed. So did Drystan.

"I hope you know what you're doing," said Wesley.

"You sure you don't want your fortune read?" the fortune-teller interrupted. "You pay me ten whole cents just to sit here and have the sulky one eat dates?"

They realized Wesley had eaten almost the whole bowl.

"You cannot escape your fate," the old woman said. "Discover what is in store for you."

"It's too depressing," Drystan replied. "Nihilistic."

"And yet, you keep coming," said Paige, popping the last date in her mouth with a cheeky look to Wesley. She started chewing and made a face.

"I don't like this," she said. "I thought…food was supposed to be good…"

Drystan laughed.

"Everyone has their own tastes," Eleanore said.

"Watch out for the pit," said Wesley.

Drystan, resigned, got up and followed the fortune-teller into the inner tent. The others filed in after.

This tent was smaller and much darker than the outer one. The only illumination came from a dimly lit, ancient oil lamp. The fortune-teller sat, barely visible, at a table in the center of the room covered with items, including a stunning tarot deck right in the middle. The woman looked like an aged Esmeralda – dark hair loosely held in place with a folded scarf, wrinkles lining her hands and face. She didn't remember Drystan from his numerous previous visits. Of course she didn't. For her this moment was always new.

She began laying tarot cards out on the table. Drystan didn't pay them much mind.

"Always the same?" Paige whispered to him.

"Always. Death, Fool, Tower…"

"You want them to be different," said Paige, as if she were reading it in Drystan's eyes. "There's always hope," Paige smiled. "Isn't that what stories are supposed to be for?"

"Ah! Your fate is becoming clear!" the fortune-teller said.

She turned over a few more cards.

"At least pretend it might be something new," said Paige. It'll give you a moment of happiness."

"Is false happiness better than knowing the truth?"

"Ah! I see!" the fortune-teller exclaimed.

"Yes," said Drystan in a depressed monotone. "'My future is unfolding exactly as planned.' As it will be for all eternity."

"That is not what the cards say."

Silence.

"I see it clearly," she replied. "Your future is what you choose to make of it. Anything is possible."

"What?" said Wesley.

"The cards never lie. See? Wheel, Queen, Moon…your future is what you choose to make of it."

Drystan stood up. He saw a letter opener lying on the table, grabbed it and ran outside, nearly upending the furniture in the process.

"Aye!" the fortune-teller yelled. "You want to burn down my tent?!"

"Wait! Drystan!"

Wesley, Paige and Eleanore ran out after him into the cool night air.

Drystan was trembling. He raised his arm and slowly dragged the letter opener down his forearm. What he saw caused him such ecstatic glee he didn't even feel the pain as blood gushed down his now completely flayed forearm.

He didn't cry or even grimace.

He smiled.

"What the hell?!"

Eleanore ran to him and, tearing a strip of fabric from her pants, grabbed his arm frantically trying to bandage it.

"That should have barely left a mark," said Wesley.

"Things are changing…" said Drystan, joyfully. "Everything's changing thanks to you, blessed, dear Paige!"

Paige looked shell shocked. She didn't want to be the cause of pain and suffering…but it was a new experience to have someone joy in her and whatever…force of change…she brought in her wake. It was the first time she thought it rather nice to feel powerful…but that feeling, combined with the sight of Drystan's bloody arm, scared her. Maybe she shouldn't be so sure she was in the right…or, as Wesley warned, that she knew what she was doing.

They found the first aid tent and had Drystan's arm properly dressed. Whether it was due to the particular magic present in the circus, or good old fashioned skill, they never knew - but they left with Drystan properly stitched up and no longer bleeding. They didn't know whether or not his arm would be set to rights when they went back into the Store, so they thought it was best not to take chances and make sure it was attended to, and on the mend before returning.

On their way back they indulged themselves, lingering over a few tents and watching a performance or two. There was an unspoken feeling that this was the last moment of calm before they set out on a monumental, dangerous task. A little excitement (mainly from Drystan) and a good deal of foreboding (largely from Wesley) pervaded the atmosphere. For the first time in a long while Drystan enjoyed the revelries he'd seen too many times before.

"Observe Ponce De Leon's famous Font of Truth!" a barker cried, standing in front of a stunning waterfall.

"Didn't Ponce De Leon go searching for the fountain of youth?" a patron commented.

"Yes," replied the Barker, "but some legends say he instead found the fountain of truth, a much more dire and dangerous discovery…"

"He's lying! De Leon discovered the fountain of youth! Everyone knows it! He just wants to keep it all for himself!"

"Maybe I'll just jump in and have a little swim!"

The crowd broke into hysterics.

"We ought to get going," Drystan said.

The circus was getting rowdier…people no longer looked on with amazement, they acted like these precious enchantments were prizes owed to them, and as dawn approached, they were about to lose the chance to possess such wonders.

"What is that?" Drystan whispered to Paige. She followed his gaze to a loose thread that was just peeking through her dress right at her stomach. The color didn't match what she was wearing…it was the same color as her skin. She took it between her fingers and gently pulled…

She felt resistance coming from deep within her. As if she were pulling at her insides.

"Nothing," she said quickly, pushing the thread back through her dress. "Just a loose thread."

What was happening to her?

"Did the patrons always seem this…intense?" Eleanore interrupted.

"Come on."

They wove through the crowds edging towards the exit.

"Oh, I'd like to ask Gwen to join us," Drystan added, casually.

"Who?" Asked Wesley.

"Rose," said Paige.

"You call her Gwen? Why?"

"Because she prefers it. And it's her name."

"No, it's Rose. Everyone calls her Rose."

"Technically it's Gwendolyn Rose Friday."

"So why don't you call her Gwendolyn then?"

"Wesley!"

"What? We all call her Rose. I didn't know who you were talking about."

"Why do you want to ask her?" said Eleanore. "She's just…well, she's not very nice."

"She can be when you get to know her," said Drystan. "She's had a lot of challenges too, she just doesn't show it. Plus she's subgenre Crime. Could be helpful."

"If you trust her…"

"It's your call Paige," said Eleanore. "But…well, I guess as long as she doesn't make fun of us the whole time.."

Drystan gave her a little kiss on the top of her head. Eleanore hid her ear to ear grin.

They reached the stalls closest to the exit. Paige and Wesley looked at some glass flowers that apparently sang the song of Fairyland when you held them to your ears. Paige nervously tried to find the end of the thread she'd pushed away. Whatever it was seemed to be contained for now.

Eleanore pulled Drystan aside.

"I am a little worried…" she said. "About going on the quest. I didn't want to say anything….but Wesley's right…my health…kind of sucks. And, well, after your arm… if there's a possibility that we could be seriously injured or…die…especially with the world ending and all…" she laughed, trying to make light of the moment. She pushed her glasses up on her face. "Maybe it's not the best idea…to bring me along. For your sakes."

Drystan thought for a moment.

"I think I know something that might help," he smiled. "Like Paige said, you're part of the team. We'll make it work. Promise."

"OK. As long as you tell me honestly if I'm getting in the way."

"Cross my heart," Drystan smiled.

"Don't tell the others…I don't want them to think I don't think I can keep up. Especially Paige…"

"Of course not. Leave it to me."

"No! I beg you madam! Don't jump in the fountain!" they heard the frantic Barker call several aisles back. There was a splash, then uproarious laughter.

Then the screaming started.

"We need to go."

They raced through the exit, echoes of blood curdling cries following them out.

"What –?"

"She shouldn't have jumped in the fountain," Drystan said. "Truth without grace will burn the humanity right off you."

"Literally, apparently," said Wesley.

"Next chance we get, let's meet in Mathematical Fantasy," said Paige. "It's usually empty. We can't let anyone know what we're up to."

"How will we know when to meet?"

"We'll try next time I get a break from the front counter," said Paige. "It's the only place I'm allowed to be these days, and everyone can see me. As soon as I can I'll head back and wait for you to join me. Don't leave the Store till then and try to keep an eye out for when I leave the register. Yes?"

"Yes," they replied.

They took one more look back at the circus, the sun just breaking over the horizon. The circus was filling with more and more screams. Patrons ran out like they'd just seen the devil.

"I don't think I like this book much anymore…" said Eleanore.

And in a flash, they were back in the Store.

Later, when Paige was alone, she examined the rogue thread. It was small, barely noticeable. But it came directly from her stomach.

It was a plot thread. And it…she…was unraveling.

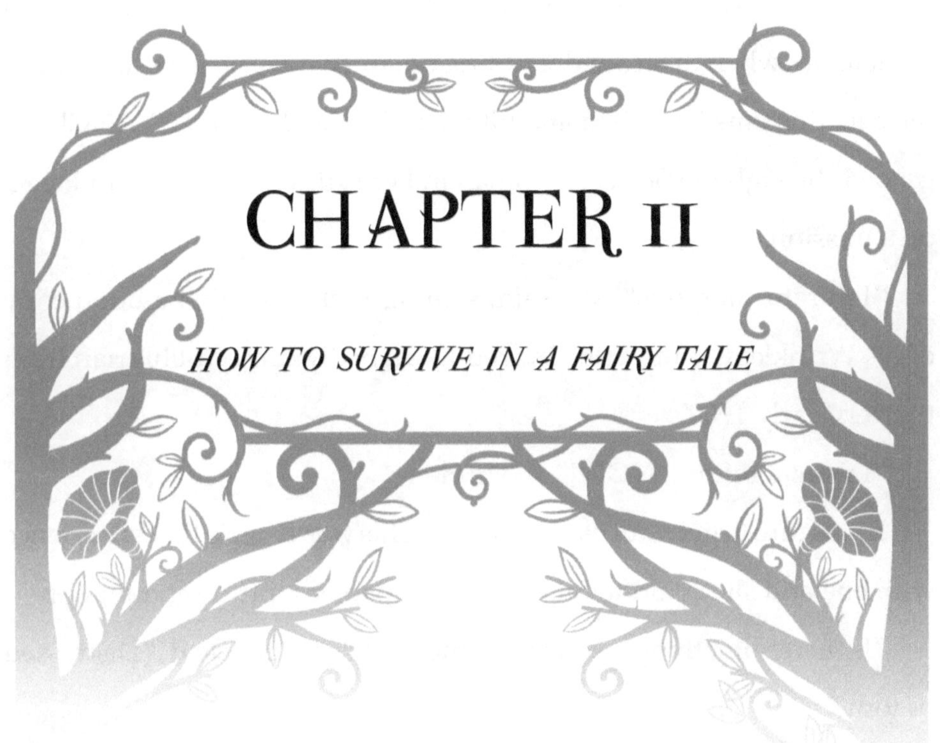

CHAPTER 11

HOW TO SURVIVE IN A FAIRY TALE

The Nothing was back. Characters were reporting sightings in "The Strange Case of Dr. Jekyll and Mr. Hyde," "The Tale of Genji," "Mrs. Dalloway," "Romeo and Juliet," and "Children of Blood and Bone." The classics were being predominantly affected first. None were as bad off as "Gatsby," not yet… but the Nothing was still creeping in and it was only going to get worse. Most of the characters were self-quarantining in The Bookstore and they kept giving Paige (and Wesley, who continued to follow her) the stink eye whenever they passed. It was ages before Paige got another break from the front counter. No one wanted to come near her, let alone work in the same space. Paige was frantic to find an excuse to go to Mathematical Fiction and start her investigation with the others. They were losing time.

Paige was working the register, frustrated and trying to figure out what to do, when the front door burst open. There was no light tinkle of the bell, this time it crashed and hit the ceiling with a loud CLANG! that echoed through the Store. A woman in her fifties marched up to Paige, on a mission.

"I'm returning this!" she said, slamming down a first edition copy of "A Wrinkle in Time." She looked like a badly dressed librarian from the very early 1960's.

"I want a refund, NOW!" she fumed.

It was rare to get returns in the Store. This was Paige's first experience with one and she could tell it wasn't going to be a pleasant initiation.

"Is there something wrong with the book?" Paige asked. "Distressed or torn?"

"No," the woman sneered, and with no further explanation continued: "I want my money back, NOW."

"You bought it here, went home and read it?"

"Unfortunately."

"I'm sorry, our policy does not allow us to give refunds if you decide you don't like the book after you've bought and read it."

"I've never heard of such a thing!"

Paige pushed a little placard on the countertop towards the woman. It read:

UNFORTUNATELY OUR POLICY DOES NOT ALLOW US TO
GIVE REFUNDS IF YOU DECIDE YOU DON'T LIKE A

BOOK AFTER YOU'VE PURCHASED AND READ IT.

The woman refused to acknowledge it.

"This is the worst book I've ever read in my life. It reminds me of 'The Wonderful Wizard of Oz.'"

Man, what terrible book was this woman going to write?!

"'A Wrinkle in Time' is considered one of the greatest books ever written."

"How dare you argue with me and question my taste!"

She was dead serious and very angry. Paige decided it was better to give the woman her money back than risk unleashing her wrath on the entire Store.

"All right... let me just see..."

Paige reached for a dusty clipboard and flipped through some decrepit pages before finding the "How To Do A Return" instructions. Returns were complicated. All the money the Store accrued in sales, whatever currency it was, translated into magical energy to help keep the place running (it was some, though not the majority of the power behind shelves rearranging, etc). Making money re-manifest in the proper currency and amount (which depended on where and the time period the customer came from) was a complicated affair.

"Were you the cashier last time I was here?" the woman asked.

"Probably," said Paige, looking miserable.

"Yes, I remember you. Plain white dress and mousey hair..."

Paige almost lost it but managed to keep her mouth shut.

"Why on earth would you allow me to walk out of here with such a horrible book?!"

"I'm so sorry. We never share our personal feelings about a customer's choice of literature. But that book actually happens to be one of my favorites."

"Is there something wrong with you?! They allow someone with such…atrocious taste to work in a bookshop?! At the front counter, no less?!"

Paige looked over at Wesley. He was always there. Watching her. Well, he might as well earn his keep. She tried to make her eyes say "help!" from across the room. But this time he was engrossed in a book for real. A new arrival by Una Williams.

"Is everything all right?" Eleanore asked, appearing like a guardian angel. Paige couldn't even mouth a "thank you" before:

"I should say not!" said the woman, getting more and more agitated. "This girl sold me a truly dreadful book and now, after making me waste my time reading it, she's wasting my time further by making me stand here while she figures out how to do a return that she insists she's not allowed to do in the first place. An untrained poodle could do her job better and get my money faster! Disgraceful! I'm shocked you allow her to work here! I will certainly be taking my business elsewhere if this is the kind of customer service you find acceptable."

"You're absolutely right, Ma'am," said Eleanore in a terribly serious tone. "Believe me, we do not tolerate our customers being treated in such a manner. Paige, you're fired."

Paige could see a sparkle in Eleanore's eyes and immediately caught onto the game.

"Please, Please don't!" Paige cried. "I'll do better, I swear! I can't afford to lose this job! Think of the children!"

"I'm sorry, but it is unconscionable that you would allow this woman to read something not to her taste!"

"Oh, well, no one can perfectly predict what someone will enjoy…" the woman wavered.

"No, no, don't defend her!" Eleanore said. "On top of that she didn't get your refund as quickly as you needed. The audacity! We don't allow such carelessness in THIS Store. Paige, you're fired. Leave now."

"But this is the only source of income for my entire family! My mother's so sick…and with the children having no father…we'll lose our home if I don't have this job!"

"I don't care. This woman wants you gone, and the customer is always right. How dare you make her wait for her change!"

"Oh, well, it's not so serious as that…" said the woman. "She doesn't need to be fired…"

"Yes she does," said Eleanore. "We'll make sure that no one has to deal with her incompetence again."

"Well, it wasn't incompetence, per say…she was actually rather polite…"

"Paige! Go and get your things now!"

Paige pretended to burst into tears, grabbed the Ur Book from behind the counter, ran up the stairs and into the stacks, Wesley following from a discrete distance, looking confused, but not moving to interrupt the joke.

The woman looked shocked.

"I...I didn't really want her to lose her job..." she said.

"Oh, no need to be coy, Ma'am. You said she shouldn't be working here. And we always give our customers exactly what they ask for. You deserve the best!" said Eleanore, smiling.

"But...I didn't really mean..."

She paused. "What did you mean, then?"

"I...well..."

"Anyways..." Eleanore glanced at the calculations Paige had made. She'd actually gotten through it pretty quickly. "First paperback edition...purchased in America around 1963, according to my records... Here you go! That should be $1.99."

Eleanore gave the woman her money, counting out the ninety-nine cents all in pennies.

"Have a lovely literary day!" she said cheerily as the woman stumbled towards the exit. "Don't worry! We'll make sure to keep 'Son of Wrinkle' well out of reach the next time you're back!"

"What?" Eleanore heard the woman say just as the door slammed shut behind her.

Eleanore burst into laughter. She hurried up to the Mathematical Fiction section where she found Paige and Wesley waiting.

"I never took you for a prankster, Eleanore," said Wesley.

"Are you kidding?! She was brilliant! How on earth did you think of that?!" Paige said.

"Served her right!" Eleanore replied. "Customers can be so…UGH! Gives 'em a real shock when they actually get what they say they want and realize the things they do have consequences. Plus, it got you off the front lines and back here! And it's not like Wesley was doing anything to help."

"Dealing with difficult customers is a rite of passage," he growled.

"Hopefully Drystan will pick up the lead and get here soon too."

"Promise me," Paige said, turning to Eleanore, trying to calm herself and not succeeding in the slightest, "we'll do that for each other whenever an awful customer starts harassing us."

"Deal!" said Eleanore holding out her pinky finger. Paige wrapped hers around Eleanore's. "As long as I'm around, I promise," Eleanore said, a bittersweet note in the air. Neither addressed it, but kissed their hands to make the promise official.

"Do I have to reshelve the book she returned? Or will –"

"No, it'll merge with the replacement copy."

"Wow. A magical bookstore actually making things easier."

"Took long enough for you to get a reprieve from register duty," Drystan said, bouncing up to them with Gwen in tow.

"Eleanore was fantastic!" said Paige, explaining their joke, ending with: "But it'll probably end up just getting me into trouble. I wasn't officially relieved – there's no one working the front desk now," she sighed.

"I'm on it," said Gwen.

She walked towards the balcony and called:

"Hey Eddie! Wanna take over the front desk for me? I'd REEEAAALLLY appreciate it." She leaned over the railing, displaying her breasts to their full effect.

"S...sure thing Rose!" he panted like a puppy.

"It's Gwen! If I'm calling you Eddie you can call me –"

"Ooookkk... sorry..."

Gwen returned. Eleanore and Paige stared.

"What? We all have our...gifts," she said, adjusting her blouse.

"I hear your pretty good with Crime too," said Paige.

"Thanks doll," she answered. "Drystan said you were a good egg. I appreciate a dame who respects me for my mind, unlike...others." She tossed her hair, throwing a look to Wesley and Eleanore.

"You...never gave us a chance..." said Eleanore tentatively.

"I don't have much respect for anyone until they earn it," added Wesley.

"And I haven't?"

Wesley just looked away.

"Well, I am VERY good at it. It's important for a group to have a wide and varied skill set, especially with what we're dealing with. What exactly are you bringing to the table Mr. Watchdog?" she asked Wesley.

"I'm well versed in the literary canon. We're not only going into Crime, you know."

Drystan rolled his eyes.

"Why did you call Arden Eddie?" Wesley deflected.

"He wanted to change his name."

"Is that…something we can do?"

"Nothing seems to be stopping him."

"I want to be…Cordelia!" said Eleanore.

"Don't rip off 'Anne of Green Gables,'" said Gwen. "Besides, it's taken, I think. By a few people."

"There are lots of characters with the same name."

"Not in seminal YA. Anne wanted to be Cordelia too. And she's technically in a variant of YA. Do you want to be a seminal character?"

Eleanore sighed.

"Fine, where do we start?"

"I think it makes the most sense to go into books we know are affected," said Paige. "None seem as bad off as 'Gatsby,' so it should be at least a little safer than that was… and I think we'll be more likely to find something there than in books we just pick randomly."

"Our objective, specifically, is to find this Owner?" Gwen queried.

"Yes."

"Do you think…the Owner might be behind all the destruction? Like…<u>trying</u> to destroy the canon?" asked Eleanore.

"Let's not start speculating until we find SOME information on them," said Gwen. "We're not a conspiracy society."

"Agreed," said Paige. "But, in either case I find it hard to imagine they would be responsible. After all why would they have taken care of a place for so long only to turn around and tear the whole thing down?"

"Ask any ancient god of chaos," said Drystan.

"Most chaos gods didn't venture far from their desire to destroy," said Wesley. "It's not likely to have equal measures of benevolence and malevolence in one person…they're never entrusted to the care of something and then suddenly do a 180 -"

"You haven't delved very deep into mythology, have you?" said Drystan.

"Besides, I'm 'patient zero.' All of this corresponded with my arrival, it's not down to anyone other than me." Paige replied.

"Let's get moving while we have time," Eleanore sighed. "Who knows when Paige'll be able to escape register duty again."

"We'll start with 'Jekyll,'" said Gwen.

"Why?"

"It was the first to be affected after 'Gatsby,' at least as far as we know, and the supernumeraries are used to strange goings on…depending on where we enter the story. Plus, just sounds like fun. All that opium, and the outfits are to die for."

"All right, any objections?" Paige asked the group.

There were none. Paige turned to Eleanore.

"Do…do you know what you'll say if someone asks about your oxygen tank?" Paige asked hesitantly. "I don't think they were terribly common in the 1800's."

"Oh, yeah. Always got some great excuses at the ready."

Paige sighed.

"Oh!" Eleanore pulled out four copies of a sheet of paper with tiny print on it and handed one each to Paige, Wesley, Drystan and Gwen. "I copied this onto some scrap paper. Thought it might come in handy."

"A poem?" Wesley read the title on the top.

"On what to do if you ever find yourself in a fairy tale."

"This is a poem?"

"Yes. It's also incredibly accurate."

"We're not going into a fairy tale."

"All stories are fairy tales in a sense. Structurally." She said. "At least metaphorically. It's good advice, regardless."

Wesley and Gwen rolled their eyes and shoved the paper into their pocket and bra respectively. Drystan did Eleanore the courtesy of folding his neatly before putting it away, but Paige was engrossed in the text.

"Come on, you can read it later."

She slid the page in the Ur Book as a kind of bookmark.

A note, dear reader: This poem will not play a large role in this chapter (though it will reappear once in the midst of some witty and snappy dialogue outside of a store called the "Tart Shop"). It will be rather important in a chapter and a half (towards the beginning of the chapter entitled: "The Blue Fairy'") and VERY important in about three and three quarters chapters in a chapter called: "Deus Ex Machina." I beg your indulgence now, and remembrance. It will be greatly needed later.

"All right. Here goes nothing," Paige said, holding out the book. "How…exactly does this thing work?"

"The same way as normal book jumping, it seems…" said Drystan. "Just make sure you have an extra strong picture in your mind of where you want to go…"

"But I've never been in 'Jekyll.'"

"That's OK, just a solid thought of the title and general place. But make sure no other stories start drifting through your mind at the same time."

"You're sure that's all I need to know?"

"No. But being focused on where you want to go is imperative in any kind of magical travel. And this book can take you into any story you think of, so…"

"So…it's something like…that powder…that the magical kid has in that story? Harry? Or is it Mildred…Yes?"

"I would assume so," added Wesley, begrudgingly agreeing with Drystan's assessment.

They formed a circle and joined hands. Paige opened the Ur Book and they disappeared.

***

Eleanore barely managed to jump out of the way of a galloping horse.

"Why does EVERYTHING have to take place in London?!" she moaned as she wiped mud off her dress and tried to adjust her whale bone corset.

"I thought everything took place in America?" said Paige.

"Just once can't there be a nice literary work that takes place on a warm Caribbean beach?"

"Like that Pirates thing?" said Wesley.

"No. You know what I mean, something without violence."

"A castaway novel? Can't go into them for too long… aren't any group scenes you can disappear into. And it's way too easy to derail the story…"

"Not that kind either…"

"Those are kind of your only two options. Every story needs a source of drama. You want the warm Caribbean you've got to take pirates or eternal solitude," Wesley summated.

Paige was holding her chest, gasping for air.

"Your first corset?" Gwen asked, knowingly.

"Yes…I guess." she stammered. "Is that what this is? It's horrible!"

"Beauty is pain," said Gwen, preening in a deep scarlet high fashion gown. "I'm not too fond of them myself. You get used to them after a while but thank goodness they got rid of them by my time period! Does create a nice silhouette though," she said, trying to get a look at herself from the back.

"We'll never get anything done dressed like this!"

"I will," said Gwen. "I'm tough. Like I said, you get used to it."

"I've got oxygen," Eleanore smiled. "But it is…uncomfortable."

"Can I dress like a man too?" said Paige looking at Drystan and Wesley.

"Unfortunately, not here."

"I think I've got a size too small," Paige said to Gwen.

"No, that's just the way they fit, doll. Just try to ignore it."

"Thanks, I'll try that when I'm passed out on the street."

"Where should we start?" asked Wesley.

"Well, Dewey said you'd been here before, right?" said Paige. "Something about tarts?"

"That…wouldn't help in our present situation," he said quickly.

"Oh, you guys figure it out. Forget getting used to it, I'm getting out of this thing!"

Paige turned and walked into a pub, heading straight for the water closet.

"I'd…better keep an eye on her…" said Wesley as he sauntered after Paige. Gwen sighed.

"I guess I'll look around."

That left Drystan, Eleanore and her tank.

"And then there were two," said Eleanore.

"Perfect," said Drystan. "There's something I want to show you. The others won't be back for at least a few moments…"

He picked up Eleanore's tank (which no one in the story asked about) and ushered her down the main street, crowded with stores, to a secluded cul-de-sac and a shadowy shop with a small overhanging sign reading:

APOTHECARY

The door swung open and a cheery, cherry-cheeked man greeted them from behind a glass counter.

"Hello!" he said, in a tone much too pleasant for the story he inhabited. "My, my, aren't you a cute Mr. and Mrs.!"

Eleanore quickly looked down, embarrassed both by her enjoyment of the man's mistake, and nervous what Drystan would think. Drystan looked a little flushed, but didn't correct him. Unmarried men and women were not supposed to be popping into shops together. Especially ones as potentially taboo as an apothecary.

"What can I do for you?" the man said. "Got some lovely opium in today."

He held up a white box with a picture on the front of three cherubic children smiling, holding poppies and wearing adorable bonnets.

"You want to sell us opium?"

"Yes, ma'am! Glad I have some in. It's going like hotcakes!"

"Aren't you going to ask how old we are?"

"Oh, I would never ask a lady. Besides, mothers give it to their babes all the time. Puts them right to sleep. It's a healthy medicinal for any age."

"Actually," said Drystan, "I was hoping you might have some of these…"

He pulled a piece of paper from the notebook on the man's desk and wrote something down. He folded the paper and handed it to the man. He read it, nodded soberly, and, with a look to Eleanore, made his way to the back of the store.

"What's all this?" asked Eleanore.

"Told you I'd find a way to help," Drystan smiled. "But, as long as we're here…DO you want to try some opium MRS. Drystan?" he teased.

"I feel like a traitor to my archetype but…"

"Traitor?"

"The angsty YA girl."

"El, your angst has nothing on Wesley."

She laughed.

"But I'd rather not, MR. Eleanore. If you don't mind," she said.

Drystan tapped her nose with his finger and proceeded to slip and fall on a small glass mason jar lying on the floor that managed to roll under his foot.

"No matter what I do, Comedy keeps attacking me. It really is a dangerous genre," he said as Eleanore helped him off the floor.

"Oh! Do forgive me," the man said, returning and seeing the wayward bottle and Drystan. "Are you all right?"

"Just a bruised ego," Drystan joked.

"I must insist you take some with you for the pain," he said, handing them a box of opium. "On the house. Tell your friends."

"All right, if you insist." said Drystan. "Gwen'll be happy," he whispered to Eleanore.

The man helped Eleanore get Drystan up, then handed him a bottle filled with little green pills.

"I have plenty in stock. Not much requested."

"Thank you," said Drystan. "You've been most helpful. May I put it on my tab? I'm good for it, I promise."

(The word 'tab,' dear reader, came into use in the mid nineteenth century as a shortened version of "tabulation.' Bartenders and shop owners would keep a 'tabulation' of how much customers owed, to be paid back later).

"Of course sir, of course."

Drystan thanked the man and he and Eleanore headed out of the store.

"What are those?" Eleanore asked.

"Pills. For you. They'll treat some of your symptoms…make things more manageable. 'Jekyll and Hyde' has all sorts of wonderful medicines. Most aren't diabolical at all," he laughed. "Here. Try one."

Eleanore opened the top of the bottle and pulled out a small pill. She popped it into her mouth and swallowed.

"Nothing," she said.

"It doesn't work <u>that</u> fast, even in a story," said Drystan. "Keep taking them, one pill twice a day, at least when you have access. I don't think they'll travel back to the Store, but they should travel book to book. It's easy to get more. We should be able to find them at most apothecaries… but the one here doesn't ask too many questions. And they're very free with keeping open tabs. No awkward money issues."

"You've been here before."

"Some reconnaissance. For you."

Eleanore threw her arms around Drystan and gave him a big hug. Some of the passersby stared.

"Hey! Can't a wife hug her husband!" Drystan shouted at them. Eleanore laughed, thinking she'd never been so happy, and it was a nice change from being sad and depressed.

Just then Paige sauntered out of the pub followed by Wesley. He looked deeply uncomfortable. She looked liberated, the Ur Book swinging from one hand, her corset from the other.

"I…had to help her…" he stammered.

"Those…what do you call them?" said Paige.

"Stays."

"Stays, were just impossible!"

"It's not like you've never seen a naked woman before," Gwen teased Wesley, coming to join them.

"Hey!" Paige and Wesley replied in unison.

"Or man for that matter, once or twice, I should imagine."

Someone wolf whistled at Gwen as she passed.

"He just saw my back, thank you very much!" said Paige. "Besides, I'd suffer worse indignities to get rid of this stupid thing."

"It's indecent, walking in public without it," Wesley chastised, a little insulted to have his viewing of her back described as an "indignity." "At least…in this genre…and mine for that matter…not to mention, possibly, yours!"

"Oh, come on, you've seen worse in the Store. And regardless of what genre I am or happen to be in at the moment I refuse to wear something so ridiculous. Now, look! I think there's some Nothing peaking around the corner there!"

"I was just going to tell you that –" said Gwen, running after Paige. "I found it ages ago!"

"So, did you…like…Paige's back? Her…sensual shoulder blades?" Eleanore teased. "That's a very erotic body part in YOUR genre…"

Wesley huffed and took off after Gwen and Paige. Eleanore and Drystan shared a smile and followed.

"Don't go so fast!" Drystan shouted, dodging out of the way of a carriage. "I'm not as…dexterous…weaving through a crowd!"

"We're doing it in petticoats and heels! And, some in corsets!" shouted Paige.

Wesley, Eleanore and Drystan finally caught up, Eleanore once again out of breath.

"Something seems…wrong…" said Paige.

"Other than the Nothing?"

"Yes –"

"Why is everywhere in London cobblestoned?" asked Eleanore, wobbly in her heels, her tank banging after her.

"Try walking on your tip toes," suggested Gwen. "It's easier."

"What's wrong?" Drystan asked. Paige looked behind them.

"Where are all the…non-white people?" she asked.

"That's a non sequitur."

"No…I've only seen white people the entire time we've been here. I knew something was off. That's it! Surely there was more than one race in 1800's London? Do you think the Nothing is…lightening people's skin or something? Seeping into the characters themselves…erasing them slowly?"

"We don't…really…mention race here," said Drystan.

"Why? If the Nothing is doing something new…it didn't do this in 'Gatsby!'"

"Paige –"

"Maybe because it moved so fast it didn't –"

"If the Nothing were the cause, why isn't everyone blonde?"

"I…" She looked around. There were a myriad of hair colors on display. "That's a good point," she said. "But then, everyone's race -?"

"It's not something we talk about."

"Why not?"

"Well…most Horror novels can be a little…racist."

"A little?" Gwen laughed.

"Racist?! What does race have to do with a mad scientist, or a creature raised from the dead?"

"Well, in later works, there's metaphoric symbolism –" Wesley offered.

"Don't sugar coat it," Drystan interrupted. "Published Classic Horror stories were primarily written by white men, and the one or two that weren't, were written by white women. They tended to make everyone in their fictional worlds look like them. Because, well…there were biases, to put it kindly."

"That's…so…"

"You've never noticed it in the Store? I mean, genre-ism takes precedence, but second down is…"

"Sexism?" said Gwen.

"Racism, I was going to say," said Drystan. "At least amongst certain genres."

"The battle of the ages. 'Who's more oppressed," said Gwen, lighting a cigarette.

"Shh!"

They turned a corner into a back alley that looked like a perfect location for a primary plot murder.

"That's just a London mist," said Eleanore, looking at the whiteness hanging in the air. "See? The wall's fine." She reached out and wiped some moisture away from the bricks.

"Not there," said Paige. "Look down!"

Paige was right, little traces of the Nothing lingered in the seams of the story, just below the floorboards of the buildings that framed the alleyway, seeping ever so slightly onto the main street. Gwen was examining it with a kind of foldup magnifying glass. "I knew I saw it!" Paige exclaimed.

"Be careful," said Wesley. "Don't let it touch you."

"I think we've learned that lesson," she replied.

But the Nothing here was far less dramatic than they anticipated. It barely moved. They ended up just standing and staring at it.

"It doesn't seem to be doing anything in this story…"

"We need to get to its source," said Gwen.

"Does it have a source? And if it does, won't that be where the Bookworm – ?"

"Let's look for where it's thickest and find out. Think logically." Gwen was going to be the detective, not just the tag along girl Friday, if it killed her.

They walked on for a while, winding through alleys and down roads…following the Nothing. But even at its worst it was a light haze. It coalesced in a small hole several blocks from where they'd entered the story.

"There's no sign of the Bookworm. Is it coming…just…from really far away? Or is this Nothing just seeping through books in the stacks independent of it?" asked Eleanore.

"I have no idea."

"Should we try to…bottle it? Maybe take it to Jekyll's and…analyze it?"

"We'll never be able to," said Gwen. "The Nothing erases anything it comes in contact with. We couldn't contain it in anything -"

"But it hasn't erased the cobblestones it's swirling around…"

"It's starting to. Look…the structure of the story is fraying." Gwen bent down and examined the edge of the street. She was right – frayed edges were clearly visible.

"And…is that a plot hole?" asked Paige.

"Yeah…" said Eleanore. "I don't think there are supposed to be any significant plot holes in 'Jekyll?'"

"There aren't. Other than the normal imperfections in any story."

"So…those are the Nothing's doing."

"Looks like it…"

The edges of the hole were slowly being pushed further and further out.

"Wait…" Gwen unfolded her magnifying glass. "This doesn't look so much frayed as…cut. It's too clean of a separation."

"Then, did the Bookworm come first? Is the Bookworm chewing

through stories?"

"Where, exactly, <u>does</u> the Bookworm…live…?

"The bigger question is should we be expecting it any time soon?"

"Maybe Paige woke it up when she arrived and it's moving in the space between the story pages…" said Drystan. "Maybe…oh, I don't know."

"We're not going to figure anything out just staring at the stuff," said Gwen. "There aren't any answers here, and we're definitely no closer to learning anything about an Owner. I say we -"

"Watch out!"

The Nothing suddenly bubbled up…it slipped over the side of the hole and wrapped itself around Gwen's shoe completely erasing the left heel.

"Dagnabit!" she exclaimed, limping backwards, "Let's get out of here! Now!"

They hurried back the way they came, Gwen hobbling the whole time, finally reemerging on the main street.

"Wesley, you've been in this story before…"

"I…well –"

"Don't beat around the bush. We all know you have. Is there anyone you think we could ask for help?"

Wesley's gaze jumped to a storefront tucked into a nook at the end of the street. Lights were coming on and gentlemen were entering at a staggering rate. The sign over the door read "Tart Shop."

"Is that where…when Dewey said 'tarts'…" Paige said.

"Told you he's seen more than a woman's back," Gwen laughed.

"And some men too," Eleanore teased, quoting the rest of Gwen's previous comment.

"I told you, never mind!" said Wesley. "Besides, I think we're a little early in the story for them to be open to such a…strange conversation."

"Forget that," said Gwen as she limped over to the Tart Shop and knocked on the door.

A woman opened it, her over-done make up a desperate attempt to appear younger than she was (which was probably her early fifties).

"Sorry, dear, we're not taking any new -"

"No, ma'am, I was just wondering, have you noticed any strange goings on here lately? One businesswoman to another." Gwen might have to work on the clue finding but she was spectacular at interrogation.

"You mean the Carew murder?"

"No…like…strange mist…things disappearing?"

"Oh, that's pretty standard in London."

"Is London, like, a fantastical world or something?" Paige whispered to Wesley.

"This is a long shot, but have you heard anyone talking about an 'Owner,'" Gwen queried.

"Owner of what?"

"An odd Bookstore."

"Nope. Got a strange Doctor around here, but no odd owners or bookshops. That apothecary seems a bit shady though…"

"Never mind. Thank you for your time."

Gwen tripped back to the group.

"She was…rather nice…" said Drystan, sounding a little perplexed.

"People might do favors for you if you're nice…"Eleanore said, pulling out and paraphrasing her copy of the poem.

"It's a metaphor," said Wesley, looking over her shoulder, "look at the context" -

"Go with the spirit of the meaning. Metaphors still have truth…"

"Most Madams are nice to other women," Gwen winked to the boys. "Especially if they're nice," she smiled at Eleanore offering a kind of olive branch. Eleanore hesitantly smiled back. "Anyways," Gwen went on, "let's try another story. See if there are any differences."

Paige handed Gwen the Ur Book and a moment later they found themselves in the crypt from "Romeo and Juliet." The Nothing was still on the periphery, but it was much more dense than in "Jekyll." Gwen handed the book back to Paige.

"The First Folio," Gwen said. "It's the most affected of the editions."

The Ur Book was leaving a terrible friction burn on Paige's arms. It was heavy and rather oversized.

"There's no good way to haul this thing around," said Paige, wondering why it contained so many pages if none of them had anything written on them.

"Told ya. Pockets are worth ten times more than any fashion no matter what story you're in," said Eleanore.

"At least I have a working pair of shoes again," said Gwen.

"I don't hear the Bookworm in this story either…"

"I'd like to remind everyone that that's a GOOD thing."

"But look! The structure's unraveling," said Gwen, "right around the edges. Just like in 'Jekyll.'"

They carefully made their way over to the stone walls to take a look.

"You know," Paige whispered to Drystan, "you were right about Gwen. She's not too bad when she decides to be helpful. Why did she agree to come, anyway? She acted like I was some contagious alien when this all came out. Now she's…"

"Pleasant?" he smiled. "She just needed some time to get used to things."

"How did you two get to be such good friends?"

"Let's just say we both have a love of 'Sherlock Holmes.'"

"Rose…uh…Gwen is correct…" Wesley said, carefully studying the base of the wall. "The Nothing is eroding the world at a structural level. It looks almost like it's…from the inside out." He pointed to a thread hanging from the edge of the wall. "One pull and we'd be in the same boat as 'Gatsby' right now."

"Mind the stones!" Eleanore cried. They looked over and saw Eleanore's tank sticking half-way through the floor. "The Nothing's in the insulation…or earth…or whatever's underneath an ancient crypt."

"Great."

They pulled up Eleanore's tank and carefully tested the floor before taking any steps, like ice skaters trying the solidness of a lake before sliding out.

"So…is the Bookworm arriving first? Leaving a hole and plot threads and then the Nothing seeps in? And, if so…does it come back for round two?" Paige asked.

"Is the Bookworm targeting specific books? Or is it just…moving in the spaces between them, like you said, and coming up for air whenever…like a whale?"

"Once again, guessing isn't going to help," said Gwen. "We either need hard evidence, which isn't likely given that what we're trying to study erases everything it comes in contact with, or we need to find someone who knows something."

"But…what character is going to know anything about life outside their story?" said Paige.

"What ho?!" A young man entered the tomb and stared at the group. "What art thou doing at such an hour in this ancient receptacle…" he coughed, "to whose foul mouth no healthsome air breathes in?"

The Nothing started dispersing along the ground, causing the group to move quickly to avoid it. They could see the scene starting to unravel more and more…

"Be wary," said Wesley, on high alert. "Something's rotten in the state of Denmark…"

"This is Verona, dimwit," Gwen huffed. "That quote's not even from this play."

"I never said it was. I was just -"

"What's your name, friend?" Paige called.

"Balthazar, m'lady," he replied.

"What are YOU doing here?"

"What ho! Balthazar!" A handsome man jumped down the stairs

and landed in the vault.

"Ah! My lord Romeo! I have a letter for you from Friar Laurence. I thought it would save time to meet you and give it to you here. Rumors, after all, travel faster than horses, and I didn't want to miss you in Mantua!"

"What excellent thinking!"

Romeo ran to him, opened the letter and read it. He looked at the corpse of a woman.

"She's only sleeping then?"

"Seems the way of it."

"Thank goodness! I heard she died and was just about to off myself."

"What about Paris?"

"Eh, I slew him outside."

"Huzzah!

Plot holes were appearing all over the place, one in Romeo's tunic, another in the shroud over the woman, another in the newly opened letter.

"This is wrong! This is so, so wrong!"

"It's the Nothing that's doing it!"

"But the Nothing's been in 'Jekyll' much longer and there isn't this kind of unraveling there!"

"Maybe the Bookworm does have specific tastes…" said Drystan.

"My love is as a fever, longing still

For that which longer nurseth the disease,

Feeding on that which doth preserve the ill.

T'uncertain sickly appetite to please."

"This is not the time for quotes," said Paige to Wesley.

"They say exactly what you mean."

"You sound like the Cheshire Cat," said Paige.

"Don't ever say something so insulting to me again."

"And Nightingale!"
Juliet suddenly sat up.

"My love!" she exclaimed.

"My life!" Romeo replied.

They started passionately making out as the world began crumbling around them. The group heard the "whirr" of the Bookworm faintly underneath the ground.

Suddenly all the Capulets, Montagues, Friar Laurence and the Prince burst into the room.

"Aww! Our children!" they exclaimed. "Who would believe?! Well, I guess we'd better put this feud of ours away, for their sake."

The Prince proclaimed:

"A happy joy this morning with it brings

The sun for gladness seems must show his head –"

"Who's he talking to?"

"The audience."

"There is no audience!"

"It's like the voice of a narrator."

"This isn't how this story ends."

"NOPE."

"It's creating the plot holes!" Gwen deduced.

"What is? The characters? Are they changing –"

"No, I don't think so…the Nothing is dissolving the structure, causing plot holes, and creating easy access for the Bookworm!"

"So…is the Bookworm sending the Nothing ahead of it?"

"We've got to get out of here."

"No! We have to help them!" said Paige! "All the characters in this story…this edition will die unless we…"

"There's always going to be collateral damage," said Wesley. "We have to keep ourselves safe or this whole 'quest' will be for nothing!"

He grabbed Paige and they ran.

"It's not right!"

"Don't go down with the ship! The first rule of –"

"This is why structure is so important!" Gwen called back. "Imagine what it'll be like in a poorly plotted book?!"

"Please, Paige! Trust me!" Wesley yelled. "You can't help anyone if you're dead too!"

"Fine! Grab my hand!" Paige yelled.

Wesley scooped up Eleanore and her tank, Drystan jumped on Gwen's back and Wesley and Gwen grabbed on to Paige as she tried to open the book…

"Oh, blast this thing! It's so cumbersome!"

She finally managed to get it open with everyone holding on to her and they fell back into the Store.

"This is ridiculous. We're accomplishing nothing!"

"Yes we are! We know more about the Nothing and how it works –"

"We can't keep on…" said Paige. "We're just going to get chased from story to story…"

"We have to keep trying."

"Look!" said Eleanore. She held out the bottle of pills Drystan gave her in 'Jekyll.' "I thought they weren't supposed to be able to travel back into the Store?"

"What are those?"

"They'll help my condition…I got them in Jekyll."

"From whom?"

"A…trustworthy source." She paused. "Drystan, ok? Drystan did…a really nice thing." She tried to hide the fact that she was blushing. "But they were just supposed to get me through whatever stories we went into. How could they come into the Store?"

They all stared at the bottle in amazement.

"Change is happening here too."

"We've got to keep on. Mysteries weren't solved in a day."

"Well, we've got to come up with a better plan than – "

"Who's working the front desk?!" Drood called from a few aisles away.

"Darn it. Arden, uh, Eddie must have left his post."

"I'm on it," Paige said with a sigh. "If anyone has any bright ideas of where to keep this thing hidden when I'm not at the front desk –" she tapped the Ur Book, "please let me know. It's too bulky to keep carrying around like this. Especially trying to keep it a secret in the Store."

"Meet back here next break you get?"

They all nodded in agreement.

"Thanks," Paige said to Gwen, "for…helping. And being…nice…"

"Well…I mean, it is the end of the world, allowances have to be made," she smiled. "Just…you'd better not rub off on me or anything." She tossed her hair which was back to perfectly coiffed curls.

Paige hurried to the front desk which Eddie had left in utter disarray. Fred waived to her from a few stacks back, his apron tied high on his chest to hide as much of the blood on his coat as he could get away with. Paige smiled and waved back trying to act as though she'd been there ever since Eddie left. She'd just started to straighten up when the bell rang, and the same "Wrinkle" customer came back in. She stopped and stared at Paige as if she'd suddenly entered some strange time loop. It hadn't been that long for Paige, but who knew how much time had passed for the woman between her last visit and now.

"Weren't…weren't you fired?" she said.

"Oh, you must be thinking of my twin sister," Paige said, moving her hair to cover her nametag. "I had to get a job, despite my health, and take over supporting the family when she lost her position and died from her tragic circumstances. Can I help you with anything? Oh! I'll bet you'd LOVE a new book we just restocked. It sold out so fast! Just won the Newbery Medal."

"Oh yes! That sounds wonderful!"

"It's called 'A Wrinkle in Time.'" Paige smiled. "Very similar to 'The Wonderful Wizard of Oz!' I bet you'll love it!"

The woman looked like she was going to be sick. She repressed a scream, turned and walked out of the Store.

CHAPTER 12

BRAVE NEW WORLD

Gwen lay in a dusty basement, holding a squirming mouse by his tail. Far above she could faintly hear shouts of:

"Cinderella!"

She took out a dagger and looked at the mouse. It was decidedly chubby and rosy cheeked.

"We're going to play a little game."

She heard footsteps.

"I've got our next experiment," she squealed as Drystan walked in.

"The Nothing isn't in this book?"

"Not yet," she said, turning her attention back to the mouse. "Let's see if messing with the plot brings it, or if its arrival is what messes with the plot. He," she said, "isn't supposed to die." The mouse squirmed as if it could understand her. "Oh, but don't worry," she said looking into its frightened eyes, "I'm sure the Fairy Godmother will be able to find another horse for sweet Cindy's carriage."

She raised the dagger and smiled. She glanced at Drystan, a child waiting to be praised.

"Mice. Really?"

Gwen's face fell. The mouse squirmed and contorted itself out of her loosened hand and quickly scurried away.

"Well, it would have been a start! We're not going to find out how this thing works without a little experimentation. Better to start out simple," she said, glancing around for the mouse. "Don't want the Nothing suddenly showing up and erasing us before we can escape… otherwise I'd just chuck Cindy's glass slippers at the wall or -"

"You idiot," he said. "Did you ever think to just ask? Plot holes bring the Nothing and the Nothing also brings plot holes. It works both ways. But no, you just had to go showing off and almost needlessly mess with a story."

"You knew?" said Gwen, deflated. "How?"

"We have to move faster than stupid mice," he said, ignoring her. "People. US. That's what we've got to figure out."

"What does it really matter?" Gwen sighed and slumped down against a wall. "Maybe we've got the idea all wrong. We could just, take up residence in 'Holmes' and live our own lives. Bookstore be damned."

"I don't want to spend my existence hiding away as a periphery character in someone else's story," Drystan said. "I deserve to be the protagonist of my own life. Besides, it's too late now. The Nothing will be everywhere sooner or later. We need more answers and we need that Ur Book. Thank God Paige showed up…do you know how long I tried to create a crisis worthy of Dewey manifesting so I could get my hands on…Paige did it practically instantaneously! "

"So just take the darn thing. I'm sure the little girl would just give it to you if you asked –"

"I need to figure out how to get at its secrets…how it connects to the Owner. It's no good to me…us…blank. Paige is the key…somehow. We need her."

"Whatever you say, joker." She kissed him, finishing with a stinging nip on his lower lip.

"What's come over you?" Drystan said, not sure whether to be in awe or irritated.

"I've just never felt so free! I love doing exactly what I want to do. Not censoring myself. I want…I want to take charge and…and…do anything you say." She kissed him again and Drystan reciprocated. She tried to adjust her position and got her knee caught in her skirt.

"Ugh! I hate this outfit!" she said. "If Eleanore can bring pills into the Store, I should be able to wear whatever I want wherever I am," she pouted. "And not just small things when I go into a story in my genre like Nightingale does, but –"

"We can't be too obvious, sweetheart."

She looked up at him and smiled.

"So, what does the Grand Master have in mind for our next step?"

"I think you need to stay back in the Store –"

"You're benching me?! But - !"

"Just for a bit…I need eyes and ears there while I'm off - "

"DOING things?"

"Hey. I trust you to be my eyes and ears. That's no small thing."

"You can, you know. Trust me. I would do anything for you." She smiled. "I'll prove it. You want to go faster? I'll go faster."

She placed her hand on the floor, then raised the dagger and sunk it deep into the pinky finger of her left hand. Drystan covered her mouth as she screamed. He quickly grabbed her hand, ripped off some fabric from the bottom of his shirt and wrapped it tightly around the wound. He held Gwen's hand above her head. They waited for a moment. The finger didn't grow back.

"Your arm healed. Let's see if we can still regrow body parts, or if that particular magic is changing too."

"You're crazy."

"No crazier than you."

He kissed her hand.

"I would, you know. Do anything for you," she repeated.

He looked at her finger.

"How bad is the pain?"

"Hardly anything. It's almost numb now," she lied.

"You've never been more beautiful," he said.

"Don't be funny now."

"You see me laughing?"

Gwen's heart jumped. She was addicted to Drystan. Obsessed with the way he looked at her. She would do anything for him. And she loved knowing how much he would want her once she showed him just how far she'd go.

"All the universes are gonna remember us," she said.

"You have no idea, doll face."

* * *

"Where are they?" Paige sighed. She, Wesley and Eleanore had been waiting for Drystan and Gwen for what felt like hours.

"I finally get another chance to get away from the register…"

"Why don't you just make up an excuse and –?" said Wesley.

"I've tried. But not experiencing hunger, fatigue or any other…bodily necessities in the Store kind of limits my options. Any suggestions? Besides unionization."

"You should just tell Nightingale that if he wants you to figure out how to fix everything he's going to have to give you some time off to do it," said Eleanore.

"That's…actually a great idea."

"But a union wouldn't be bad, regardless."

Eleanore's was, dear reader, in fact a fabulous idea. Paige tried the next time she saw Nightingale. It worked, and from then on she had permission to leave the Store whenever she wanted.

But for now she was still exhausted, annoyed, and desperately behind schedule when it came to solving her problem.

Eleanore took out her bottle and swallowed a pill.

"Have they been helping?"

"I don't think it's been long enough to tell," said Eleanore. "Maybe? I hope they really kick in soon, I've been feeling so tired…"

"We haven't had any opportunity to relax," said Wesley. "Any time off we spend putting our lives in danger. We ought to take a break and go for a swim, or tea, or…a nice nap in a garden…"

"Very exciting. Where do you like to go on your time off, normally?" asked Paige. "Other than 'Jekyll and Hyde,' I mean."

Wesley scowled at her.

"I bet you know some beautiful gardens," said Eleanore, sincerely.

"That I do. Moors and forests too. They may actually be more to my taste. But moors are best for brooding…not napping."

"I'll bet." She sighed. "Ugh! Are we going to sit here all day?"

"Would you rather be shelving?"

"No, but the more we're all away at once the more suspicious we're going to look. We don't want people to start thinking we're the Scooby Gang or something."

"The what?"

"It's an obscure comic. Look, I'm going to go…find something to do. I'll stay nearby. Call me if Shaggy and Daphne turn up."

"Who?

But she was gone.

Wesley and Paige were left alone.

"I've actually been trying to find a moment to give you this," said Wesley, a little hesitantly.

He reached into his coat pocket and pulled out a tiny, dark, folded… thing. He slowly unwrapped it until it magically expanded into a beautiful, oversized soft leather satchel with a strap that wrapped across your shoulder.

"You needed something to carry that Ur Book in," he said. "I went back to the circus Drystan took us to…since Eleanore could bring her pills back I thought I might be able to bring something back too… anyways…it changes size depending on what it's needed for. Try it."

He handed Paige the bag. She slid the Ur Book inside. She watched it move to fit the book perfectly.

"And if you need it for smaller or bigger things…well, it'll adjust for whatever you might…have need…for it to…even just carrying books around to shelve instead of using those squeaky carts…and if you don't need a bag you can just keep it in your pocket or something…or…that's right, girls don't often have pockets -"

"It's beautiful," she said. "Thank you, Wesley."

"Well, I just…didn't want to give it to you when other people are around. Don't want the riff raff finding out about the Ur Book," his mouth turned up slightly as if that was his attempt at a joke.

"It's really kind of you."

Paige looked like she'd just seen a ghost (not an actual ghost, dear reader, those she was used to, but…oh, you get my metaphor).

"What's wrong?" he asked.

"Well, it's just a little out of character."

"I try to be considerate…when I can."

"I didn't think you ever pushed it to full on charming. What's going on?"

Wesley sat for a long while, trying to find the words. Finally he simply said:

"Can I…can I show you something?"

"Sure," said Paige, even more confused.

Wesley led her silently through the rows of books. They arrived at the end of an especially long aisle and Wesley climbed a ladder several feet in the air. He pulled down a well-worn book with a rich, velvety deep green cover and silver tooling. He climbed back down and took Paige's hand. She pulled back slightly. Wesley looked puzzled.

"It's just…I get grabbing onto me if we're running from the Nothing or something…but…well…you tend to grab and take me places any time you…you could…give me the choice. When our lives aren't in danger, you know."

"I'm…used to leading," he said.

"Being a partner…can be nice too…" she smiled, gently.

"I asked if I could show you something…"

"Right. Asking is good. Keep doing that."

Wesley raised his hand and offered it to her. She paused, then smiled and placed her hand in his.

"That wasn't so hard, was it? Kinda seductive actually," she joked.

He laughed, opened the book and deliberately flipped to a very specific page.

Paige and Wesley suddenly stood in the midst of warm, green light that moved and danced around them. At least that's how it seemed to Paige.

"What's that sound?"

"Water." He looked amused by her confusion.

"The fountain in 'Gatsby' didn't sound like that... or the lake with the light..." she said.

"There are a lot of different kinds of water. And even the same kinds are different in different stories."

"What's this kind called?"

"This is two together – a stream and a waterfall. Come, I'll show you."

He led her down a little dirt path. As her eyes adjusted, Paige could see that the green glow was really sunlight filtered through a canopy of trees that extended as far as she could see. There was more green on the ground – grass, and ferns and ivy. But where the light touched it there was gold, and small little white flowers.

Wesley wore clothing similar to his standard fare, only a little simpler and newer. Paige tripped daintily in a 1890's flowy silk and lace day dress, her hair tied with a pink ribbon, flowing in loose curls, and (thank God!) no corset. The bag with the Ur Book inside remained over her shoulder, only now there were little flowers etched in it.

They walked under a stone bridge with an archway three times as tall as Wesley. Paige could see the end of the stream pooling in a sort of moat next to the path, and all the time the sound of the waterfall got louder. Finally when they were on the other side and starting down a bend in the road, she saw it. The path they were on curved to the left and continued around a tall hill rising around the now much wider stream. Directly ahead, at the top of the hill, there was a wall of giant stones. Water poured down over the side in beautiful long ribbons of white foam and spray.

"Are there Nyads in the stream?" Paige asked.

"This isn't Fantasy."

"It seems like it should have a Nyad."

They walked on. The sound of the waterfall faded, and Paige could hear a dove cooing.

A tree, derailed by a long ago storm, lay on its side - a perfect bench.

"You really do know how to choose gardens, or forests or…wherever we are. It's all too terribly beautiful. What book is this?"

"'Roanoke,' by Una Williams." He paused for a moment. "It's my favorite place," he said hesitantly, "out of all the books in the whole Store. At least the ones I've been in. I don't know if anyone else has ever been here. I suppose I shouldn't…tease others…so much for having a favorite spot."

People, dear reader, even in the Store, have a tendency to "put on a mask." To make themselves appear the way they want others to see them. When Paige first met Wesley she was struck by his disdain. But that disdain, whether intended by his author, or springing from some other intrinsic force, was an act he actively cultivated. Looking at Wesley now, Paige realized it wasn't really disdain. It was sadness. A kind of painful, awful, lonely heartsickness.

"Who are you?" she asked. She hadn't meant to. The words just fell out.

Wesley inclined his head, questioningly.

"I mean," Paige said, "what are…the needs of your genre?…You're…Gothic Romance?"

"I am."

"So, what…does that mean?"

"Gothic Romance is a sub-genre of Drama, usually set against dark, gloomy backdrops, that concerns the star-crossed relationships of beautiful, deeply flawed people with mysterious pasts."

"And yet you're in a lush, bright green-golden forest."

Wesley didn't respond.

"What does…being that genre mean about <u>you</u>?"

He realized no one had ever asked him that. No one had ever asked him about himself at all. They hadn't felt they'd needed to. Not that he inquired about them either. He thought for a moment, then, replied,

"That man of loneliness and mystery,

Scarce seen to smile, and seldom heard to sigh…

He knew himself a villain – but he deem'd

The rest no better than the thing he seem'd;

And scorn'd the best as hypocrites who hid

Those deeds the bolder spirit plainly did…

Lone, wild, and strange, he stood alike exempt

From all affection and from all contempt."

"That was by Lord Byron," he said. "I've always found it…resonant." He said the name with reverence. Paige realized there was a difference between being "Byronic" and written by Byron himself.

He stood up and walked over to the edge of the stream.

"I'm…haunted," he said. "I don't know how else to describe it. It's like there are voices that whisper to me in the dark, tormenting me with the things I'll do. Things I've done."

"I don't understand," said Paige.

"I won't have a choice in the matter, so you might as well say I've done them as I will do them."

"What things have…will you do?"

"I don't know," said Wesley. "But that is the state of my existence. To find out when I'm written."

"I'm sorry."

"You say that like you actually are."

"Is that strange?"

It was. Everyone else knew his genre. But Paige stared at him with wide, innocent eyes full of, not pity but…compassion. He was not a good person, but Paige didn't seem to understand that. Or care. No, that was too much to hope for. She had no idea what his genre made him. He was not nice. He was…dashing. Not the same thing at all.

He smiled.

"You're an interesting character, Paige." He paused. "You know, I just realized…now, if I ever want to go away and be alone…if come here, there's a chance you'll be here too."

"I promise I won't come back if you don't want me to. I don't want to take your special place."

"No, I was just thinking how funny it is that…it might be nice. Finding you here. As long as you don't tell anyone else about it."

Paige crossed her heart. She leaned against a tree and looked at him through the branches. Wesley looked down and brushed the hair out of his eyes.

Paige wondered why he brought her here. Why <u>her</u>?

"I wish I was an author," she said. "I'm not good at…finding words…"

Wesley rested his arm against a large branch and leaned forward, his face only a few inches from hers, as if he didn't want the rest of the forest to hear what he was going to say. As if he was scared to say it.

"We're not supposed to feel this way about anyone who's not… who's not in our story."

"Feel what way?"

"I think…that's the only logical explanation," he said to himself, starting to pace. "I can't stop thinking about you. Lots of Gothic Romance girls are innocent and lost, and you -"

"Lost? Hey -" She hitched up her skirt and stumbled over the tree trunk in a very unladylike manner ready to give him a "what for" for insinuating she was lost -

"What if…what if we're in the same story?"

Paige froze, her mouth open mid-word. She looked at him, dumbfounded.

"It happens sometimes," he said, "when two characters are so equally integral to the story, they have to inspire their author together. Romeo and Juliet were in the Store at the same time. So were Sherlock and Moriarty."

Taking her astonishment for confusion, Wesley tried to clarify.

"I'm Gothic Romance, yes? Well, what if the Romance is more important than the Gothic and I've been missing it all along? You have elements of Gothic, but you're not a…and maybe that's the point." He took a breath. "You may not have known…understood your genre, but you've always understood me. Put me in my place. Never let me get away with…It's not about the archetypal details, it's about the underlying truth. You made me understand…want it for the first time." He tried to catch his breath. He'd never spoken this fast in his life. "You're my match, Paige. The way you talk to me…why do you think I disobeyed Nightingale's order and came on your little quest? I don't need anything from this Owner. I came for you, because -" He sighed. "I shouldn't be saying this."

"Then why are you?"

"Because you fascinate me, Paige! I shouldn't be around you…" The forbiddingness seemed to excite him. "No one should, really, until we… But I can't help it. I can't stay away from you. A part of me…I've known it…ever since you first told me off at Gatsby's party -"

"What? That you wanted to smack me?" she said.

A broad smile grew over his face. And then he laughed. An actual, hearty laugh.

"That I love you."

Paige was gob smacked.

"Characters never fall in love in the Store unless they fall in love in their story. Attraction, yes. Lust, sure, but not…"

"But…you're saying… you love me?" she asked.

"Yes. You're fascinating and…unusual…but…" He paused. "You must feel the same way."

"I…I've never been in love. I don't really know how it goes."

"Do you…have feelings for me?"

"Right now…I feel…kind of hot and tingly…is that the same thing as being in love?"

"You sweet little innocent thing."

She knew it was supposed to be a compliment, but Paige didn't like that being called sweet and innocent, at least from Wesley, made her feel like she was a bit stupid. Stupid and innocent shouldn't mean the same thing at all.

He knelt down.

"Do you want to kiss me?"

"I've never done it before."

"It's not like sword fighting, you can…wing it."

"But I don't think I'd be very good."

He smiled.

"But do you want to?" he asked.

"I don't know. Will it make my toes stop tingling?"

"It might make it worse."

"Oh." She thought for a moment. "What if I don't like it?"

"Well, then you may have your answer."

"What if you don't like it?"

"Paige, would it be all right if you stopped talking and let me kiss you?"

"Yes. Thank you for asking."

He kissed her. He was a terribly good kisser. It overwhelmed Paige. He was a large, imposing figure but he was gentle with her. So gentle. She liked that. And she liked kissing him...a lot. A wind rustled through the canopy and tiny white blossoms floated down around them. Wesley's lips tasted like cinnamon and clove and his scent was like a magic spell. It was perfect.

Was this love? Were all the stories, the epic poems talking about what she was feeling right now? This only happens with your true love, doesn't it?

Her heart skipped a beat.

If this was real...that meant she belonged. Somewhere. TO someone. And they belonged to her. She would be Gothic Romance and have a place just like everyone else. The breeze caught Paige's dress and made it dance. The world was unnaturally green, the water enchantingly melodic.

It was all too good to be true.

They separated.

"I liked it," she said.

They laughed. Wesley gently touched her face.

"Give up this quest," he said.

"What? No...I can't...just...give it up. Even if...I'm not exactly the paradigm of Gothic here," she replied. "You said it yourself. I...I've never even fainted!"

"You're just unique. You'll redefine the genre. It may not seem like a perfect fit now…but give it time. Trust me."

Maybe he was right. Maybe she would always be a little different… no…unique…Wesley didn't think she was strange, or weird or hateful. He thought she was special, and he loved her for it!

The logical part of her brain thought, "Won't it at least be a band aid on the ripping apart of the fabric of the universe?" Embracing a genre that partially works might stop the problems caused by her being out of place. And as for the emotional part -

"It would mean we could be together," he said.

He kissed her again.

Oh, that kiss! She could live and die in it!

But still…

"I…don't know…" she said. "I…"

"You're just scared," he smiled. "Trust in fate and take the path of least resistance. It always turns out right in the end," he said.

"But I can't give up the quest," said Paige. "If nothing else –"

"If you really feel you need to…I'll help. As long as I know that you're mine…I'll move heaven and earth. Besides, it'll just confirm what we know now. Oh! I don't think I'll ever be unhappy again! Can you imagine that?!"

He picked her up and swirled her around. Blossoms fell in their hair. Paige laughed.

"I've never seen you…not…brooding."

"You've done that. You've shown me how much more there can be."

"Really?" said Eleanore.

Paige and Wesley spun around.

"You look just like that scene in 'Jane Eyre,' where everyone's finally happy…right before Bertha shows up and drops a bomb. Metaphorically. Though there is a lot of fire. Isn't that always the way in Gothic -"

"What are you doing here?" said Wesley.

"Gwen and Drystan showed up."

Paige squeezed Wesley's hand, then started down the path. Wesley followed. But when Paige passed, Eleanore put her hand out to stop Wesley.

"What, exactly, do you think you're doing?" she hissed.

"It's none of your business."

"Paige may not be well versed in your genre, but I am. If you do anything -"

"I love Paige and I hardly think -"

"She's not your manic pixie dream girl."

"We don't have those in Gothic Romance."

"Of course you do. Men have been dreaming them up since time immemorial. You used to call them 'Muses.' The lingo's just been updated. But let me tell you something, PAIGE ISN'T ONE. She doesn't exist to make you feel like a special, good, inspired person. She has enough people trying to force her into a box, including herself. What's she going to do when she finds out what you're really like? When she realizes she's the furthest thing from a wilting Gothic…? When you hurt her? And if you hurt her…I'll freaking kill you."

"I'm not going to hurt her. But like it or not, we're in love…"

"She's said that? She's said, 'I love you?'"

There was a long pause.

"You know nothing of the ways of women."

"That's rich! I am one."

"You're not a woman," he laughed.

"What sort of Bertha Rochester do you have hiding in your attic? Every Gothic guy's got one. Or…are you planning on turning Paige into yours?"

"Never. And none that I know of, cross my heart. I love Paige and we're going to be together with or without your permission."

Eleanore crossed her arms.

"Then try being there for HER. Inspiring HER and making her feel good about herself without asking her to change, instead of just being obsessed with how she makes you feel," she huffed. "Then you might have a chance at an actual human relationship."

"And how many relationships have you been in, Teen Drama?"

"How many have you? And I mean ACTUAL relationships, not visits to the –"

"I'm wired for them. But you. YA? Give me a break. All you know is how to pine after a boy. You've got no clue how to be in a relationship with one. You're all puppy love hero worship. Your kind are BASED on Gothic Romance girls…just not as deep. So don't stick your nose where it doesn't belong. Don't try to sabotage your friend just because you're jealous that she has a place where she belongs now, and you feel like you never will, no matter what you do or how well you act the part."

Eleanore froze. Wesley's words stung. She knew, deep down, they were at least a little bit true.

"Come on. Don't want to keep the others waiting." He started off, then paused, turned around and said, quietly, "I do care about her, Eleanore. Why else would I be helping with this mad quest?"

"I don't know," she said. "But you'd better."

Wesley smiled an honest smile, picked up her oxygen tank, and led her down the path where they caught up with Paige and opened the book back into the Store.

* * *

"Where were you?" said Paige.

"Sorry, there was a crazy shelving mix up in –" Gwen started.

"Never mind," said Eleanore, blustery after her argument. "What's next?"

"I think we need to try something new," said Drystan. "Instead of following the Nothing, we need to get out ahead of it."

"So we just pick books at random? We already decided that wouldn't help anything! That's why we started going in books the Nothing affected in the first place," said Eleanore.

"No...I say we focus on Myths and Fantasies. They'll be more accepting of odd strangers, and more open to discussions of the roots of myths – we could actually talk to the characters in the stories, really ask questions, without revealing anything about The Bookstore or who we are."

"Huh?"

"We can talk somewhat honestly to characters in the stories about our actual goals without being worried about messing up the plotline. Stop chasing our own tail and get some answers."

"That's kind of smart," said Paige.

"But we've got to stick with the heightened, myth-based genres. Fantasy, Sci-Fi, Horror even Surrealist. They're used to strange and unusual happenings; they just go with it. And legends like the Ur Book and the Owner tend to filter into fantastical literature in some form or other."

"I think I'd better hang back here, then" said Gwen.

"What? Why?"

"I don't really pass well in Fantasy, kitten. Crime tends to stick out like a sore thumb and not in a good "strange traveler" kind of way. Don't worry. I'll keep my eyes peeled here and I'll come if there's a story I'll be OK in. Just make sure you don't miss any clues, or I'll have a hell of a time making sense of things when you get back and try to tell me what went down," she winked.

"All right then," said Paige pulling the Ur Book out of the once again plain leather satchel and giving a smile to Wesley. "Where to first?"

CHAPTER 13

WAITING...

"We're too late!" Paige exclaimed. "The Nothing's destroyed everything here!"

"No, that's just the aesthetic."

The group stood on a dusty road with nothing in sight but a medium sized rock and, far in the distance, a sort of raised hill that might have been naturally made, or rubble, they couldn't tell. There was <u>nothing</u> else. Even the ground around them was vague and undefined, the whole world a sort of sepia.

"That's surrealism for ya."

"I don't understand…is this just a terrible story or does the plot take place entirely on that hill?"

"This is one of the greatest surrealist works of all time."

"Huh."

"Get down!'

The four of them stumbled behind the rock as two people barreled down the road.

Paige saw a couple figures on the hill as they moved for the first time, standing to meet the galloping duo. There was a lot of shouting and dust blown up in great gusts. Eventually the two people continued running and disappeared down the other side.

"What the hell?"

"Who were those guys?"

"Two of the principal characters."

"Anyone else we should be expecting?"

"There's one other…sort of…extra."

"That's it?"

"What's the story about?"

"Waiting."

"For what?"

"Someone."

"Who?"

"No one really knows."

Paige looked around. The folks at the top of the hill never moved like they were actually going to go anywhere. They just paced and sat.

"It has a kind of simplicity…" said Eleanore. "There are worse genres."

"So, which of the looneys did you imagine us speaking to?" asked Wesley, quickly changing the subject of genre. "Not the folks up there, I assume. They never leave the story. Who knows what chaos we might cause if we approach them in the middle of their dramatic narrative."

"Of course not," said Drystan. "They don't know anything anyways. But the other three make a sort of continuous loop…"

"Three?"

"You mean, him?" Eleanore motioned towards a young boy standing a few meters away staring alternately at them and towards the hill.

"Who's he?"

"Ironically the person who knows more than anyone else in the story."

"Hello," said Paige, making her way out from behind the rock. "What's your name?"

"Boy," he said in some vaguely mid Atlantic accent. "Most people call me 'Boy.'"

"Do you like being called 'Boy?'"

"It's what I am."

"But…there are a lot of boys…doesn't it get confusing?"

"Doesn't seem to."

"Have you noticed anything around here…disappearing…into a kind of mist?"

"What disappearing?"

"Things…that are usually here."

"Like the hill?"

"Yes."

"Nah. It's still there."

"You don't know anything about an owner of a bookstore do you?"

"Never been to a bookstore. Ain't any 'round here."

"They wouldn't be at the bookstore they just own it. They…haven't been around for a while."

"Oh! You mean my master?"

"Does your master own a bookstore?!"

"No. But he hasn't been around for a while."

Paige sighed.

"Everyone's always looking for him," the Boy said.

"We're not."

The boy looked terribly confused, like his brain was doing mental gymnastics to comprehend Paige's words.

"Are you sure?"

"Pretty positive."

"He'll be here tomorrow! You sure he's not the person you need?"

"Not unless he owns a bookstore."

"He don't."

"Yeah, it's OK. Thanks though."

The boy looked up at the top of the hill, then started shuffling backwards.

"What are you doing?" said Drystan. "Aren't you supposed to go talk to them?"

"Yes…but they scared me with all the shouting. I…I think I'd better not."

"But...you have to!" said Wesley.

"I ain't gots to do nothing!" said the Boy. "'Specially nothing you say!" And with that, that boy turned on his heels and ran away.

"I thought you said the...person...never shows up."

"He doesn't."

"But the Boy said –"

"Yeah, he'll say the same thing tomorrow. And the day after. And the day after that."

"The plot's definitely been screwed now. He's flat out missing his next scene!"

"Drystan! You said we wouldn't upset the plot asking questions in these kinds of stories!"

"Maybe he just changed his mind organically. With everything the Nothing's doing, who knows?!"

"We should. We have to if we're going to figure this out."

"I think we stayed pretty on canon in any case."

"What are we going to do?"

"I'm sure he'll come back."

"Well, in the meantime, to tide things over..." said Eleanore, with a cheeky smile. "Drystan – give me your hat!"

Drystan handed her his newsboy hat. Eleanore slid it on top of her head, hiding all her hair inside.

"Might be nice to try out a different genre," she said. "Like Arden... uh...Eddy. Do I make a good boy?"

"Too...pretty..." said Wesley, not as compliment.

"It boggles my mind how similar pretty girls and young boys look," she said. She started dragging her tank up the hill.

"Wait a minute! What are you planning to do?!"

"Give 'em the message. I think it was pretty clear!"

Eleanore marched up to the hill, the others sneaking behind trying to stay out of sight, but desperately wanting to be in earshot.

"Excuse me," said Eleanore, doing her best to impersonate the Boy's voice.

"What do you want?"

"Um…I thought YOU wanted something…"

Both the men turned and looked at her.

"I've seen you before," said one.

"No," said Eleanore.

"You weren't here yesterday?"

"No."

"Why do you have an oxygen tank?"

"To breathe, what do you expect?" said one figure. "Lovely thing, to have air."

"He didn't have it yesterday."

"He said it wasn't him yesterday."

"Who was he then, yesterday?"

"The person you're expecting…will be here…soon…sometime," Eleanore said. She turned and walked back down to the rock.

Please note, dear reader, whenever you happen to read this lovely surrealist story (and I hope you do), that one of the appearances of the small boy is actually Eleanore (though some of the exact phrasing may have changed a little). See if you can spot it.

"I don't think I like being a Surrealist messenger boy," Eleanore mused as she returned Drystan's hat. "Not very fulfilling. But why not try something new."

"A lot of reasons," said Wesley, preparing a diatribe. But he was interrupted by Eleanore suddenly gasping for air. She quickly turned the nozzle on her air tank up.

"Are you OK?" asked Paige.

"Yeah, just…too much exertion. I'll be fine. Thank goodness for those pills. Just think how much worse it could be."

Paige put her arm around Eleanore and waited for her breathing to slow.

"So, where to now? This'll be the forty-second story we've gone in?"

"Well, I was thinking maybe 'The Pagemaster -'"

"Tried it," said Paige. "Thirty-three books ago."

"Really?"

"Yeah, that's the one where the Librarian said: 'Books can't be owned,' then offered us an exciting journey through Horror, Adventure and Fantasy just so we could get out of the freaking place."

"'Moby Dick' isn't even Adventure. It's Contemporary Epic, everyone knows that," scoffed Eleanore.

"Yes," said Drystan. "Our jaunts are all sort of starting to run together."

"What about actually trying 'The Neverending Story?'"

"I don't want to try to outrun TWO Nothings at the same time."

"But I think the Empress would likely know something."

"She could only help if she knew what story we came from. We're not coming from a story at all, we're…outside of them… Remember, she couldn't do anything about Bastian's bullies…"

Paige sighed and looked at the Ur Book. She got an idea.

"That poem Eleanore gave us…you're not just supposed to wander around blind…you have to recognize tools when they're given to you. And you have to trust your story, not someone else's."

"We're all someone else's story. It's not like we have a say -"

"What did you have in mind?" Drystan asked.

"Well, this Ur thing is supposed to do more than just take us to a book we're thinking of, right? Maybe we should see if we can figure out what else it can do. Maybe it could help."

She opened it and took hold of everyone but instead of thinking of another place she wanted to jump to she said:

"Hello…Ur…book. We were wondering if you might be able to take us into a story that could help us…figure out who the Owner is."

Nothing.

"We'd better just use it the way Dewey told us to," said Wesley. "It's dangerous to -"

"Give it a minute…" said Eleanore. "Maybe it's thinking."

"Books don't think."

"We do."

A slight breeze blew up and turned the pages of the Ur Book to where Paige had her copy of the poem tucked away. She pulled it out and looked at the first few lines.

"Something about going through a door you've never seen?"

"There's no gate and no wall," said Wesley, grumpily. "And we've certainly seen this book before."

"It's a metaphor, dumbass," said Eleanore. "Get it together."

"Eleanore..." said Paige.

"Sorry."

"We have to...be polite...I guess?" said Paige looking at the text.

"Huh."

"Um..." Paige tried again. "Could you take us somewhere we might be able to get some information on the Owner...Please?"

The book shimmered ever so slightly.

Paige, Eleanore, Wesley and Drystan vanished.

CHAPTER 14

THE BLUE FAIRY

They found themselves in a beautiful, sun drenched meadow on the outskirts of a fantastical little town. Toadstools and flowers dotted the ground and the sky looked endless.

Paige stared in awe.

"Thank you," she said to the Ur Book. A breeze ruffled its pages and it almost looked like the book was replying. The cover fell closed, and Paige carefully placed it back in her satchel which now looked like it was woven with silk threads, spider webs and rose petals.

"Well," said Wesley, "that was…unexpected."

"Good going Paige!" said Drystan.

Down to her right Paige saw an asymmetrical cottage with a charming thatched roof. It was the closest building so, "Why not?" she figured. She started towards it, the others following quickly behind.

"Where are we?" asked Eleanore.

"I don't know."

"It looks like a Miyazaki story…but not one I've seen before."

"Are we even in a book?"

"I don't know where else we could be."

"We need to find out where we are."

"What do you think I'm doing?" said Paige.

When they reached the cottage Paige knocked on the door. A lovely old woman wearing a sort of red and orange dirndl dress answered with a big, jolly smile.

"Hello! How can I help you?"

"I'm afraid we're a little lost…" said Paige. "Can you tell us where we are?"

The old woman chuckled. "My dear, you're in the Blue Fairy's realm. In the land of Claireihdell."

"The Blue Fairy…like 'Pinocchio'?"

"Beg your pardon?"

"Wrong story," Eleanore whispered.

"We're looking for someone…"

"Well then, come inside, come inside," she said, "and I'll see what I can do."

"I don't know," Wesley whispered to Paige. "It smells like a witch to me."

"Can you smell a witch?" Eleanore whispered. "I thought witches smelled YOU."

"It was a figure of speech," he snarked back.

"She doesn't seem like a witch," said Paige.

"They never do."

"Really?" Paige smirked. "'The Wonderful Wizard of Oz,' 'Little Mermaid,' - even flat out calls <u>herself</u> the Sea Witch in that one…"

"All right, all right. Just…stay close."

They walked into the cottage. It was quite like the warm interior of a hollowed out mushroom.

"Sit down! Sit down!" The woman said as she scurried around getting things in order.

"Now, who exactly are you looking for?"

"The Owner of a…a rather special bookstore…" said Paige, sitting down at a wooden table. A glass cup shaped like a crystal bird scooted towards her and chirped. Paige took a sip, to Wesley's consternation. It had a kind of lovely purity - it was beautifully sweet and ice cold.

"This!" Paige exclaimed. "What is this? THIS is my favorite drink, absolutely!"

"That's water, dear."

"Is it enchanted water?"

"No," the woman chuckled, "just plain, ordinary water from the stream."

"This is wonderful! Oh, Wesley, it's heavenly! Whenever we go to eat make sure we only go somewhere that serves water! I knew it looked beautiful but -"

The rest of the group were trying to stifle their giggles. But the woman let out a joyful laugh.

"I'm so happy you like it! Now, to your search."

Paige turned to smile at her but found not the old, jolly person she'd been talking to but a young, sprightly woman in her early thirties, also in an orange and yellow dirndl dress who said, "You're just looking for the owner? Not the bookstore?"

"No, we've definitely found The Bookstore…" said Paige. "Does anyone else live in this house?"

"No, just me," she said, smiling and twirling into the kitchen.

"We were led to believe that…someone here might be able to help us."

"Yes, yes, of course!" she called from the other room. "Let me just get –"

Suddenly a young girl dressed exactly like the old woman and the maiden dashed out of the kitchen and ran up the stairs. Quick as anything she was back down in the kitchen. A moment later the old woman reappeared carrying a large tray of almond honey cakes, strawberries and cream, and lemonade.

"Here we are," she smiled as she served them.

"We're not supposed to eat anything, are we?" Eleanore asked, flipping through her copy of the poem.

"I think that's just in reference to taking things without permission," said Drystan. "You're quite allowed to have lunch, otherwise anyone in a Fantasy would starve to death. Besides, we've already had a drink."

"We're in a Fantasy then?"

"Unless we're in Faerie…then the rules are much different and we were screwed the moment Paige drank the water."

"No, just a fantasy, I'm sure," said Drystan, his mouth stuffed with cake. "Look around! Somewhere between Miyazaki and Germanic/Celtic, but Fantasy, and a rather nice one too it seems. Thank goodness. Fairy Tales can get terribly dark."

The food was simple but delicious and when they'd eaten their fill the old woman leaned back and sighed.

"Now, the only thing to do is go to the good Fairy and ask her yourself. She knows just about everything there is to know – in more than one world, too."

Paige perked up.

"The Blue Fairy, you said?"

"Yes, our Fairy Queen Sora."

"How do we get in to see her?"

"You'll have to go to her castle…I'll send you a letter of introduction."

"Who are you?" Wesley asked, realizing no one yet had.

"Wesley, don't be rude," said Eleanore.

"Is no one concerned about taking precautions?!"

"Wesley!"

"Oh, it's quite all right," the woman laughed. "I'm just a caretaker around the borders here." She started to clear off the plates.

"What's your name?" Paige asked.

"Good question. Names are terribly important. Though I'm afraid I've too many to count. It depends on who's doing the calling and why.

Feel free to use whatever name you think fits best."

"How strange...." Paige thought. "Not having a proper name. How confusing... and how depressing it must have been when this woman was in the Store. But then again, it's likely she never was. She didn't seem to be a principal character..."

"What do most people call you?" Drystan asked.

"Like I said, depends on what we are to each other," she replied. "But for expediency's sake you can call me Ms. Three."

While they explored the house, Ms. Three (more specifically the old woman), wrote an elegant letter of introduction which the little girl folded into a paper butterfly and the maiden sent fluttering out the window.

"There now," she said, "it'll announce your arrival."

"Where exactly are we going?" asked Wesley.

"Do you see up on that hill, just there?" she pointed out a latticed window made of diamond shaped pieces of stained glass. They could just make out a shimmering white castle on a hill far in the distance.

"Why is there always a giant hill?" Eleanore groaned.

"That's a long way to go."

"It's shorter than you think," said Ms. Three. "You can't judge most things here by size. Just decide to go and the walking will take care of the rest. But you'll want to get started if you plan to arrive before nightfall. Can't imagine you'd like to spend the night in a dark forest," she laughed.

"There must be some darkness to this story, even if it is hiding for the moment," said Wesley. "It wouldn't be a proper Fantasy if there wasn't."

Just as quickly as Ms. Three had led them in, she hurried them out again with a brief:

"Bye! Bye-bye now!"

And closed the door. They could hear a young maiden inside singing and clearing up the plates, the crystal glasses chirping along in harmony.

"Well," said Paige, "at least now we have an actual task. A clear action feels much nicer than wandering aimlessly."

"How am I going to get this hunk of metal up that giant hill?" Eleanore moaned. "I had enough trouble –"

"Like Ms. Three said," Drystan smiled. "Just decide to keep going and the walking will take care of the rest. And if it doesn't, we'll help."

Eleanore sighed. She and Drystan started walking. Wesley offered his hand to Paige. She took it and they followed, trekking across a small village on the way to the mountain. There was a melody here, in the song of the birds and a chime in the air that seemed to harmonize like a giant song sung by the whole land.

They passed a few people going about their day. One woman yelled instructions to workers on her farm who picked the most beautiful little pink, and white and purple flowers.

"What are those?" Paige called over. "They're beautiful."

"We export them," the woman called back. "We grow them special – hold them to your ear and you can hear the song of fairyland. We sell them to a little circus that travels around…Phantasmagoria…something."

Drystan chuckled.

"I'll bet they're cheaper here," he whispered to Eleanore.

They continued up. A nicely maintained dirt road wound all the way from the strange cottage through the village and up the mountain to the Fairy Queen's castle, so there was no confusion about which way they ought to go. Clearly this was a well- traveled path and it set Wesley's mind at ease knowing that a visit to the Fairy Queen seemed fairly common.

Eleanore was tiring quickly. She popped one of her pills into her mouth, hoping the others didn't notice. She didn't want to admit it, but all this questing was exhausting her, and it was getting worse story by story.

The path ascended in circles around the mountains, which, though a longer route, made for an easier journey as there were no intense and sudden inclines. It gave Eleanore a long time to think.

"Maybe I should lean into the whole…being fragile thing," she wondered. "The Damsel in Distress might not be so bad…and it must be sort of fun to faint whenever you want as long as you were fainting on fluffy beds, or soft things and not cracking your head on rocks or cement and getting concussions. Huh. Maybe that's why most damsels are so stupid. They have significant, long term brain damage."

Paige noticed Eleanore's pace slowing. She released Wesley's hand and walked back to her.

"I'm fine," Eleanore said. "Could do this for hours." Her tank hit a rock, bounced into the air and knocked into Eleanore's achilleas. "Ow!

It's just…getting a little rockier…" she gasped.

Paige grabbed the tank and pulled it along, lifting it over any prominent rocks.

"Oh, no, you don't have to do that!"

"Neither of those bozos are doing anything, are they?" she laughed. "It's OK," she smiled. "You're allowed to struggle. We're all tuckered out but you're also dragging a giant metal thing behind you!"

"Maybe it's representative of my emotional baggage," Eleanore joked.

"If that were the case I think Wesley'd have you beat. I don't think the whole village could get his up this mountain, if it were in metal form."

They laughed. Wesley wondered if Paige and Eleanore were laughing about him and Drystan.

"Girls," said Wesley.

"Right?" said Drystan, not sure what they were talking about, but trying to play along.

"So…" said Eleanore to Paige with a glance at Wesley, "you two a thing now?"

"Yeah, I guess so," she smiled. "You don't think we should be?"

"No…I just…I want you to be happy. And…careful. I want you to be happy and careful."

"I'll try."

They walked on for a bit.

"What about you and Drystan?"

"What?! Me and Drystan?! I…well…" Eleanore let out a loud guffaw that she tried to play off as a loud bird when she saw the boys looking. "Like I would ever have feelings for…even if he did…which he doesn't, 'cause…besides…it wouldn't really work out, 'cause…I'm dying…and we're different genres…so…"

"I think he might like you."

"Really? Are you serious? Why? Why do you think that?"

"He's super sweet with you."

"'Cause I'm a baby. Look at me, Paige, I'm YA and he's…a MAN."

"He's a very sweet YOUNG man who seems to care a lot about you. I mean, look at all the trouble he went to to get you those pills."

"That was just so I wouldn't slow down the group. Thank you, by the way, for making sure I'm part of the group. You didn't have to…"

"You know," Paige interrupted, "the best possible outcome is just as likely to happen as the worst."

"What?"

"The best possible outcome is just as likely to happen as the worst."

"What's that from?"

"Me. I thought of it just now. So you might as well have at least a contingency plan for the best thing happening."

The statement boggled Eleanore's mind.

"If he's not, then he's not," said Paige. "But that's his loss. He'd be an idiot not to be with you."

"But…I'm YA. I don't know anything about romance."

"I'd say YA and Gothic Romance wrote the books on the subject."

Wesley approached them.

"May I?" he said. He gently took the oxygen tank from Paige and carried it under one arm. Paige stared at him, stunned by his strength. She expected it from Herc but…

"Thanks," said Eleanore.

"See? Now I'm out of breath too," said Paige. "It's not just you."

"Look!" said Drystan.

In the distance they saw the little paper butterfly fluttering around a beautiful young woman who seemed to glow in the twilight. They grew silent, their last steps almost reverent as they approached the ethereal woman. The butterfly hovered by her ear. She laughed, then turned her attention to the group.

"Do we bow?" asked Eleanore.

"Just…whatever strikes you, I guess?"

"You always bow before royalty," Wesley advised, giving an elegant bow, his gaze lingering a little too long on Sora, a kind of hunger flickering behind his eyes. Paige didn't notice. Eleanore did.

Paige and Eleanore made passable attempts at curtseys, but as Drystan tried a gentlemanly bow his foot slipped from under him and he landed flat on his back. The woman rushed forward to help him.

"Oh my! Are you all right?" her voice rang out like little bells.

"Yes, quite. Thank you…your Majesty, or…what do we call you milady?"

She smiled and helped him up.

"Milady, is fine," she said, "or if you prefer, you might just call me

Sora." She looked back at the butterfly who was now winging its way back to the village. "My friend tells me you're not from Claireihdell."

"No, milady."

"Then you <u>must</u> call me Sora. I'm not originally from here either and it will be like old times. Please tell me about yourselves." She turned and looked at Eleanore.

"You're a warrior?"

Eleanore almost choked on her repressed guffaw.

"No, I'm a teenager."

"What does that have anything to do with what you are? You have the look about you."

"Um…I'm just Eleanore."

"Drystan."

"Wesley."

"Paige."

She took each of their hands in turn and looked into their eyes as they spoke.

"You must be exhausted. Stay here as long as you wish and at supper tonight you can tell me your tale."

Whereas the inside of Ms. Three's home looked like the inside of a mushroom, the interior of Queen Sora's castle was like the inside of a large, white hydrangea in full bloom. If there were servants they must have been invisible, for the whole place had a feel of quiet solitude… they could see no one other than Sora, yet the place was spotless.

Sora herself was lovelier than any of the wonders around them. She wore long, iridescent robes that changed from pale blue to almost indigo and back again. Paige wondered if the color adapted to her mood. She had pale blonde hair that fell just below her shoulders in big, finger waved curls. She had no wings that they could see, but…

"Not all fairies have wings," Wesley told Paige, preemptively . "Depends on what type they are, and what story they're in."

Almost every room in the castle looked out over the mountaintops in a panorama of sky and stars. Sora led them each to their own room and said she would see them at supper. Inside they found a bath drawn by invisible hands in a manner uniquely suited to them. Wesley's steamed full, and hot and smelled of cardamom, tobacco and plum. Drystan's was a sort of tea infusion, with herbs and spices in bags mixing with the water in hints of orange, absinthe and cedar. Eleanore was a little embarrassed to find hers full of lavender bubbles that smelled of jasmine with lots of fun bath accessories. She was loath to admit that she actually enjoyed using the soaps and towels, and even a scrubby rubber butterfly. Paige's bath was in a free standing, claw footed tub surrounded by billowy curtains, the water a deep, almost unnatural blue soaked through with tuberose scented salt. Rosewater dripped into the tub from a kind of fountain and Paige found it hard not to fall asleep wrapped in the warm water. But she was jolted back to reality when she once again saw the plot thread coming from her stomach.

It had grown.

It was now a full inch long and if she wasn't careful it would snag and unravel even more. When she got out of the tub she discovered that, try as she might, she couldn't cut it. It wouldn't come off. The only thing she could do was conceal it and pray it didn't get any worse.

When they were finished, they dressed in elegant (but surprisingly comfortable), flowy clothes (Eleanore even got pants!) and made their way down to the dining room where, while they ate, they told Sora all about their search for the mysterious Owner of a magical bookstore.

"How strange," she said. "Most travelers have a person sending them to look for a place. You have a place sending you to find a person."

"Can you help us?" Paige asked. "No one's been able to."

"I will try," she replied. "Unfortunately I'm not the kind of fairy who grants wishes. While I do have some magic, I'm usually left to govern these lands as any leader might, with logic and diplomacy, not to mention that most problems are quite out of the realm of simple wish fulfillment. Those usually get you in more trouble than they get you out of anyway, you know," she said, sounding very wise. "I wish more people did…"

"Where exactly are we?" Paige asked. "I know, Ms. Three –"

Sora giggled. "Is that the name she gave you? Well, I suppose it is applicable."

"She said this is the land of Claireihdell but…"

"Oh, I see. You want to know what story you're in?"

The group collectively dropped whatever silverware they had in their hands.

"You've… been to The Bookstore?" Wesley asked.

"I've been to A bookstore," she said, slightly confused. "Though not a magical one."

"How do you know we –"

"Want to know what story this is? That this is a story at all?"

She took a bite, then put her fork down, ready to explain.

"I came here once, just like you. Though not from a bookstore. I was a little girl then, not a fairy of any sort."

"Came…from where?"

"The ordinary world, I suppose. I was a human child who suddenly found herself in the magical world of a story I was reading, one of a series, actually. Much like Wendy in 'Peter and Wendy,' or Dorothy in 'The Wonderful Wizard of Oz,' only they hadn't read about their lands before they went to them. Do you know 'Oz' and 'Peter Pan?' You are from the real world, yes?"

"Yes," said Paige, quickly. "We seem to have…gotten in…like you. Only we don't know what story we came into."

"It's called 'Ever,'" she said. "It's a very whimsical Fantasy –"

Drystan gave the group a subtle look as if to say, "See? I know my genres."

"Something like a fairy tale," Sora continued, "something like a myth, and something like, well, something else thrown in for good measure," she laughed.

"Where exactly are you from?"

"A place called Oxnard, California. It was 1921 when I came here to stay… what year is it now?"

The group looked at each other…

"Um…about 1925?" Paige said, making something up.

"Hmm. Fashions have changed in only four years."

"What do you mean?"

"Well, your hair for one," she said to Eleanore. "And that thing you're pulling around looks very modern. Have things changed a great deal?"

(The first form of portable oxygen therapy wasn't invented until the 1950s, dear reader…)

"Oh. Yes…" said Eleanore. Unsure what else to say she shoveled a forkful of food into her mouth.

"But, see," Sora continued, "whereas those other little girls found themselves in fairyland and always went home again, I went back and forth several times, all the way until I was seventeen…when I was given a choice – I could go home, or I could stay, but either way, this time it would be forever. I chose to stay and became the Fairy Queen. I've tried to govern justly ever since." She paused. "I had a sister…she chose to go home. Her name is Jo…would you please…if…when you go back…see if you can find her? I worry about her so…"

"I've never heard of a child choosing to stay in a magical land forever and never going home," said Drystan.

"Peter Pan," Eleanore said.

"We don't exactly know his origin story. There are too many conflicting versions. In any case, every child I've ever read about who was given a choice decided to go home."

"Yes," said Sora. "And staying is more…bittersweet than I imagined."

"Why?" asked Eleanore. "I should think it wonderful to have a happy ending and be young forever and ever."

"Don't you see?" said Sora, gently. "The only children who really never grow up are the ones who die."

"But...but you didn't die."

"I did...in a way," she said. "It is lovely here, but I shall always be as I am...never moving forward or back."

"But you never have to grow old –"

"I'm stuck...in-between. I shall never have children. Never be a child again. Never see my family. Everything has a cost."

Paige thought of what Dewey said about magical currency.

"I thought...everything got easier when you...found your way into a story..." Said Eleanore.

"Of course not, dear one. Life never turns out quite the way you expected, no matter what world you're in, I imagine. Adults like to give you orders and advice, but it doesn't mean everything just falls into place, even if you follow instructions to the letter. Things don't magically get easier. You don't suddenly feel 'right,' even in the best of circumstances."

"Do you regret staying?"

"I don't know." She thought for a moment then said: "I imagine if I'd gone home I'd have always regretted giving up fairyland. Anytime something went wrong I'd think: 'If only I'd stayed in fairyland, things would be perfect right now.'" She caught Drystan's eye.

"You look...troubled."

"I…I worry sometimes," he said, tentatively, "about what will happen when I've found…well…when I've found my story, for lack of a better description. That it won't turn out to be very nice."

"Me too," said Eleanore.

"You think this Owner will help you?"

"Yes…if they exist."

"I hope they do."

"You really don't know anything about them?" Paige pressed. This was certainly the most freely they'd been able to talk to a character in a story - according to the magic of the Ur Book this was the place most likely to give them answers, but there seemed to be none here yet.

"I'm sorry," said Sora, "I don't. But might I suggest that you speak to a, well, a rather strange man who happens to be passing through here?"

"Everything's strange here," said Eleanore with a little laugh.

"Well," Sora smiled, "he's strange even for us. He comes through every so often on his travels and you may have just happened to catch him. His name is Shadow and if anyone would know about this Owner, he would. He's been just about everywhere and is almost as old as time itself."

"What did you say his name was?" Drystan asked.

"Shadow."

"That's a common character name," Wesley whispered.

"But…just Shadow…nothing else? No 'the' at the beginning or… last name or anything?"

"Do you know him?" Eleanore asked.

Drystan shook his head "no," but he had an uneasy look and stayed oddly pensive for a long time.

"It seems to be…just Shadow," Sora smiled, a bit confused.

"How do we find him?" Paige asked.

"He usually roams around on the tops of the mountains while he's here, that's where I imagine you're most likely to cross paths. He travels to the outer lands, but I don't think he's left Claireihdell yet. But all in good time. Right now you must get a good night's sleep. You may stay here as long as you wish and return as often as you need during your search. Just please promise to come back in the evenings and tell me how your search is going. It's lonely sometimes, and I shall be glad of company from the outside world. Besides it will keep you safe from things that emerge from the woods at night."

They finished their supper and retired to their rooms. The night air was surprisingly warm, and Paige kept her windows open. She could smell the sea blowing in from somewhere far away.

Suddenly there was a little

rap

   rap

on her door. A moment later, Eleanore entered.

"You awake?"

"Yup."

"It's freezing in here! Why are all your windows open?"

"It's warm! I like it."

"It's freezing."

"Here."

Paige pulled back her covers, and Eleanore jumped under the blankets.

"These beds are huge."

"I know."

Eleanore stared out the window.

"It's like sleeping in an outdoor bedroom painted by Frantisek Kupka."

"I have no idea what that means."

They lay in silence for a moment.

"Paige…what if life…after The Bookstore…doesn't just…fall into place. Like what Sora said?"

"I don't know."

"Like…those books about people who have just graduated college. When they graduate and life is entirely different from what they expected. And they're not prepared for it. What if being written is more like…that…not…a happy ending?"

"Well…" Paige thought. "Do you feel prepared for what's happening now?"

"Not really," said Eleanore.

"Then at least we're getting some practice."

They talked late into the night mainly about nothing at all and were well on their way to falling asleep before they realized that sleep was even close to approaching.

"Eleanore?" Paige yawned.

"Yeah?"

"Why do we get sleepy here…when we don't get sleepy in the Store?"

"Who knows," she said.

"Goodnight, El," Paige whispered.

"Goodnight," said Eleanore.

"Guess tomorrow we'll start looking for a shadow. How will we know which shadow it is? There are a lot of 'em."

"I think his name's Shadow."

"He could be a shadow called Shadow…"

"That would be terrible…writing…"

And then they were asleep. It was the first time either had ever slept next to another person. It's surprisingly comforting how sometimes not being physically alone makes your heart feel not alone, too.

CHAPTER 15

THE VALLEY OF THE SHADOW

As I've mentioned, time works differently in the Store, dear reader, but still, Nightingale was beginning to notice that it had been quite a while since he'd seen Paige…or Eleanore, Wesley and Drystan, for that matter. He didn't notice any books lying open, unaccounted for, that might indicate what stories they could have jumped into, so he was rather perplexed. He hoped Paige was having some success on her quest, but it was disquieting having no idea where she was – made almost worse by the fact that where she was was completely out of sight in The Bookstore. He asked the Raven if he would mind keeping an eye out for the missing group to which the Raven cawed back:

"Nevermore!" (which in this instance translated to "Get yourself one of Odin's birds, I'm no one's lackey!") and flew off.

But Paige and the gang weren't the only things concerning

Nightingale...several characters had been inspired by Arden's...that is, Eddie's complete personality change - and they thought it might be fun to play around with their personalities too. Nightingale tried to stay calm. After all it was better, at the moment, for characters to be preoccupied with themselves than picking up steam on the mob mentality, right? And a little play acting never did much harm...as long as it could be kept under control.

Gwen, meanwhile, was incredibly bored stuck on the "bench." As promised, she kept her eyes and ears open, ready to report back to Drystan whenever he returned...but there wasn't much of note to report. She'd expected him to drop in in-between book hopping and keep her up to date, but time was going by and she was getting more and more frustrated. She did her best to distract Nightingale, keep the front desk occupied while deflecting about Paige's whereabouts, and even headed off the Raven - making sure he knew he deserved to be his own bird and not anyone's lackey – after she heard Nightingale muttering to himself about making a "look out" request, but before he'd actually had a chance to ask the Raven. The last thing she or Drystan needed was a bird watching.

But in general the Store went on as usual. Quiet, Nightingale noted. Too quiet.

And that was when the first character started fading...

* * *

In the morning on their second day in "Ever," Paige, Eleanore,

Drystan and Wesley got up, bathed, put on fresh clothes and went down for breakfast. There were rose cakes, roasted honey almonds and a wide array of all around delightful fare. Sora told them she'd heard that Shadow was last seen near the hilltops east of the castle so, with a satchel full of food for lunch, the group started on their search.

"Your clothing is enchanted," said Sora, waving as they headed up the path, "it glows more brightly the closer you are to a fairy castle. It will help you find your way back if you get lost. But mind the road, and don't stray far."

"Just like a fairy tale," Wesley whispered. Paige giggled.

They wandered most of the day. The mountains here were gentle, not treacherous - all in all it was like a very nice hike and their worst problem was lack of comfortable places to stop and sit. They stayed on the eastern road, or at least the road that seemed to be mainly going east, but there was no sign of the mysterious Shadow.

"What time is it?" asked Eleanore, baking in the sun, her hand barely able to hold the handle of her tank.

"By the angle of the sun, it seems to be about two o'clock," said Wesley.

"How do you have wilderness survival skills?" said Paige.

"All gentlemen know such basics as measuring the angle of the sun, navigation by the stars and how to care for a horse."

"Isn't it lovely to be able to ask the time and get an actual answer?!" said Drystan. He seemed to revel in the fresh air. Perhaps it was his genre, or how long he'd been in the Store, but holed up with dusty books was not his idea of paradise. "Time that moves. Isn't it wonderful? Let's have lunch. It's past <u>time</u> for it," he smiled.

"I don't see how we're going to find this person," said Wesley as he sat down and bit into a sandwich. "We don't even know what he looks like. Sora was terribly vague. And what kind of a name is Shadow anyway?"

"Better than 'Boy,'" Eleanore wheezed.

"I'd imagine he's the only person other than us who's wandering around these mountains," said Paige.

"Are you all right?" Drystan whispered to Eleanore. She was sitting next to him and having immense trouble breathing.

"I'm fine, she said."

"You taking the pills?"

"Yeah," she said as she swallowed one.

"You wouldn't be able to get through a trek like this at all if they weren't helping," said Drystan. "Just take some deep breaths."

"I'm trying," said Eleanore.

Drystan put Eleanore's head on his shoulder and petted her hair as her breathing slowly steadied (though her heart continued to race).

"I just thought of something," said Paige.

"About this Shadow person?"

"No…You know how last night Sora was telling us about her family, her childhood, stories about growing up? Well…I don't know, I was thinking how nice it would be if we could all tell each other stories about ourselves. About how we grew up, things that happened before we met. But we don't have any stories about parents, or siblings, or…major events that shaped us. Nothing shaped us, exactly. We just showed up like this. Except for anecdotes about the Store we don't…" She paused. "It makes me sad. I'd like to know about all of you…like to tell you about me…if that makes sense."

"Yeah," said Eleanore. "About knowing about all of you I mean. I don't know if I'd really like to know about myself. I probably have no parents, or abusive parents, or come from some dystopian apocalypse. I don't want to remember that. It's like our future…is our past too. Like, we'll find out everything at once in our story."

"What if we made it up. Just for now. Just for ourselves. What we'd like it to be."

"That won't work, not really," said Wesley.

"Why not?"

"Well, we'd all make up nice things. Lives don't work that way."

"We're talking about stories –"

"Stories and lives are the same. There are rules…somehow. You've never seen a story like: There once was a girl named Paige, and she was perfect, and always happy, and everyone loved her, and her life was perfect. The End."

"That's not what I would make up."

"It would be the gist," said Wesley. "You couldn't help it. Who of us in their right mind would write a story for themselves with pain, and…?"

"Maybe…maybe my pet died when I was little," said Paige.

"Not good enough."

"Oh, you're a grump."

"I guess, we're sort of making our pasts right now," said Eleanore. "So, let's remember this. The hard ground, the hopeless quest...and each other. Maybe stories don't start on page one."

"But remember for how long? Once we're written...it's like none of this will have ever happened," said Wesley.

"It still matters, whether or not we remember it."

"Does it?"

"Yes. I don't know why, or how...but it does. Besides, I think we ought to have some good memories tucked away SOMEWHERE. Even if it's just for right now," said Paige.

"A hopeless quest is a GOOD memory?"

"By your standards," she teased. "Besides...I think it's pretty good, right now. I wouldn't mind living on this page for a while." She popped the rest of a cookie into her mouth.

They cleared up their lunch and walked for a few more hours. They went as far east as they could go without sliding down the mountain but there was no hint of anyone else anywhere around.

"We'd better turn back," said Drystan. "We've been searching all day, and it'll be dark soon."

They agreed and started back the way they came.

"Shoot, I...I think we're turned around. I don't remember a path like this..."

"How far off could we have gone?"

"I don't know…"

"We're lost near a fairy tale forest. Great."

"No, look!" Paige said. The tip of her sleeve was glowing. She extended her arm and the glow disappeared. She turned around and extended her arm again. The glow returned.

"Follow my sleeve?" she joked.

And that they did, their clothes glowing more and more brightly the closer they got to the castle. Eleanore, who was the shortest, held her coat above the ground, like a light, to let them better see any twists in the road, or rocks they might trip over. Their pace was slower than it had been during the day, but they made good progress.

"If you had a pet, what would you have?" Paige asked the group.

"A nice dog," said Wesley. "Bloodhound. Good and reliable to go hunting with."

"I think I'd like a rabbit," said Eleanore. "A soft rabbit with pink eyes. Like Velveteen."

They reached the castle sooner than expected.

"Very helpful," Paige said, waving her sleeve as they greeted Sora. "Thanks!"

"Any luck?"

Paige shook her head.

"We'll try again tomorrow," said Wesley, putting his arm around her.

They told Sora about their day and made plans for the next. They retired to their rooms and were quickly asleep, exhausted from all their walking in the hot sun discovering, to the delight of Paige, and the annoyance of Wesley, that their clothes continued to emit a soft glow in the castle at night.

The next morning there were new clothes for them. They once again had breakfast with Sora, got a sack lunch, and headed out to try their luck. Today they went west, which turned out to be another futile endeavor. Since the castle itself sat on the westernmost edge of the mountain range they spent most of the day trying to figure out if there was a way to get down into the meadow just southwest of the castle without killing themselves. They eventually gave up. Besides the fact that there was no good way back up from the meadow even if they managed to get down, Wesley pointed out that from their vantage point they could see everything around them for miles and there was no sign of a man anywhere. They went home early feeling more defeated and with no choice but to set out yet again the next day.

Eleanore was still hopeful, pointing out that the "rule of three" was very important in Fantasy, and tomorrow would be their third day of searching. Wesley countered that bad things came in threes too, plus there was also the rule of seven, and twelve in Fantasy and twelve days of searching would be very depressing.

Nevertheless, they went out again the third day. This time they went north. They'd originally come up to the castle from the south and north was the only place they hadn't yet tried. If Shadow wasn't there they'd either crossed paths, or he was beyond this mountain range. They weaved along the road, had lunch and walked some more.

"Let's go back," said Drystan. "He's obviously not here. I think we need to regroup. And we're all tired, I know I am."

"Just a little further," said Paige.

"Eleanore –"

"I can handle it Drys. If we need to go further, we're going further."

Just at that moment they burst out of the trees onto a wide precipice. There, sitting on a large boulder looking out at the vast landscape was a man dressed all in black.

"That has to be him," said Eleanore. "Right?" Her tank started rolling back down the incline behind them and Eleanore had to pull with all her might to keep it on the ridge.

"Are you OK?" asked Drystan.

"Yeah, just the usual," said Eleanore, turning up the level on her tank. It was starting to run low. It hadn't been replenished by a return to the Store since before the strange surrealist story.

"I'm not feeling so great myself," said Drystan, shuffling backwards, a strange look on his face as he glanced at the figure. "…Kind of dizzy. I think I might head back."

"What? We've only just found him," said Paige.

"I know, but I really think I need to lie down. Too much sun and…"

"Are you all right?" said Paige.

"Just a little heat stroked," he said. "Wasn't made for long travel I suppose."

"Don't you want to meet him? After all we've –"

"I'll probably just make things worse," he said anxiously. "He doesn't seem the sort for humor…"

"All right, if you're sure..."

"Of course. I'll take the lunch sack back anyways. You can tell me all about it later."

"Would you mind taking this too?" Paige asked, holding out her bag with the Ur Book inside. "It's getting rather heavy after three days trekking it around." She quickly looked at Eleanore. "Not like it's anything compared to... but...I mean...only if it won't be too much trouble..."

"Of course," said Drystan.

"Are you sure that's wise?" Wesley said to Paige. "I mean someone having that book without the rest of us nearby. He could go back to the Store and leave us stranded."

"Come on, it's Drystan," said Paige, giving him a kiss. "It'll be all right. I'd say it's safer with him back at the castle than with us alone with this stranger hanging off the side of the world."

Wesley returned the kiss and Paige handed the bag to Drystan.

"Be careful," said Eleanore, as Drystan smiled, turned and walked back the way they'd come.

But the moment he was out of sight he stopped and sank down under the shade of a tree. He shuddered slightly, anxious to get as far away from the strange man as possible. And then he did something entirely out of character. He started weeping. Painful, tragic sobs of sadness and hurt that he'd kept buried for too long. Why of all the people in all the stories did he have to turn up in this one?

Embarrassed, vulnerable, he forced his pain back down, took the Ur

Book out of the bag and flipped it open.

"Where are you?!" he wanted to scream, but he kept his voice to an angry hushed grunt. "Where are the answers?! How…how do I walk out that damn front door on my own?! Just…just let me walk through the door!"

There had to be a key to its secrets somewhere in its pages. He flipped back to the first page planning to go through each, one by one, making sure there was nothing they might have missed. But he froze when he looked down at the page open in front of him. His eyes widened. He looked around again, making sure no one could see, then ripped the first page out of the Ur Book, folded it, put it in his pocket, and ran the rest of the way back to the castle.

My dearest reader, it falls to me now to describe Shadow to you, and I find it a very difficult task. I have known Shadow for a long time and I care for him very much.

He appears differently depending on the circumstances of your encounter, but as we currently meet him he is in a guise he has favored for several decades. I could tell you that he is tall, a little pale, and has a predilection for wearing all black in the fashion of some sort of robber (which at the moment means a rather grubby sweatshirt, leather jacket and black fingerless gloves). He's not usually much of a conversationalist. I might describe him as a world-weary soldier, or, perhaps, a prince in exile. He is still young enough to be in his physical prime, but old enough to be intimately acquainted with the pain of the world.

"Excuse me," said Paige, "is your name Shadow?"

"For the moment," he replied. "I have many names."

"What is it with people and names here?" said Eleanore.

"How did you come to have that one?" Wesley asked.

Shadow just stared out at the horizon.

"A young girl...was praying...when I met her." He said. "'Yea, though I walk through the valley of the shadow of death.' It was appropriate...a name for her to understand me by. I kept it."

"You...you're..."

He turned and looked at them. A coolness stung through the air. They shivered.

"Death?"

"Its...physical manifestation. I am the ancient god of...shepherding souls." He looked at each of them. "You going to run away now?"

"No," said Paige. "We're not afraid."

"Of course you aren't," said Shadow, almost bored. "Don't think it's bravery. You have never known me. None of you. And your own deaths...are not real for you yet."

Eleanore wondered why he'd included her in that statement.

"Why should they be?" he continued. "According to nature you will never die, except, perhaps, for a moment in your story, whereupon you will simply go back to the beginning again. Everyone in The Bookstore is rather smug in their immortality."

"You know about The Bookstore?" said Wesley.

"Of course. There's death everywhere. Especially in stories. Et in Arcadia ego."

"What does that mean?"

Shadow laughed, a kind of low rumble.

"An employee of The Bookstore doesn't understand Latin?"

"Should I?" Paige asked Wesley.

"There's a sort of…magical translation…thing… that happens for us in the Store…or when we go into books. Otherwise we wouldn't be able to communicate half the time with our customers, or each other. I guess this story isn't written in Latin otherwise we'd understand it."

"No," said Shadow. "It is not written in Latin. But I'll bet your dashing Heathcliff understands it anyway."

Wesley shook his head "no."

"Well, you will once you're written I imagine. You're Gothic something or other I assume?"

"Yes."

"I'm sure we'll be meeting soon enough. Et in Arcadia ego. Even in Arcadia, there am I."

"Arcadia? Like…heaven?" Wesley asked.

"Whatever you call paradise," he said, drawing shapes in the dust.

"I don't understand," said Wesley. "You're…real? Not…a character, from a story?"

"As real as a physical manifestation of anything can be. But I'm a character too, in a way. A character in ALL the stories. At least, that's the best way for you to wrap your heads around it."

"No character is in every story."

"Death is, and so I am. I am in every story, and what you call the 'real world' too. I'm always…everywhere."

"But I've never seen an ancient god of death like you in any book in The Bookstore."

"Did you accost me on the side of a hill to question the validity of my existence?" He said in a tone powerful enough to make the stones around them tremble. (Shadow can be a terrifying creature when he chooses to be). "I have many names and many forms. And if you have yet to encounter me, believe me, you will someday, much sooner than you would most likely prefer."

He settled down, his hand once again playing with the dust.

"Shall we play a game?" he asked. "I will answer five questions. Because I'm bored and no one ever speaks to me. But after those five you must go. I may be bored but I'm not one for idle chatter."

"Why do you come here?" Eleanore asked before Paige or Wesley could stop her. It was the first time she'd spoken to Shadow, and Paige saw, though her face and body looked calm, her hand was gripping the side of her tank as if channeling a lifetime of nerves. "You could go anywhere you like, why come here just to sit on a rock on the edge of the Blue Fairy's kingdom? You must have souls…waiting…"

"Time is relative," he said. Then he almost smiled.

"Sora's not THE Blue Fairy, you know," Shadow added. "That was my sister…"

"Was she the one from 'Pinocchio?'" asked Wesley.

"No, that was another fairy of blueish hue. I told you, I and my siblings are in all of the stories and are usually not so easily defined."

"You never mentioned siblings."

"Careful, you're two questions down."

Paige gave Wesley a look.

"I come here," Shadow continued, "to look for my siblings. You see, I know death and loss intimately, from both sides. Once I had eleven brothers and sisters, more even further back – no, not all manifestations of death," he sighed as if reading Eleanore's thoughts. "But all different, ancient elemental gods who faded from existence when their stories stopped being told and they were forgotten. I will never be able to join them. I cannot escape my job. Death, it seems, must always be remembered."

"But…we keep all the stories…"

"Only stories that will be published or distributed in some form exist in your Store. That is why it is so important for stories to be TOLD. Otherwise things that deeply matter will be lost and forgotten. Ours were primarily of the oral tradition. The few that were written down were destroyed. We were here at the dawn of creation – in what became your Store. But borders were…looser then. Eventually my siblings faded from the world, relegated to their stories as their true selves were forgotten, then, when even their stories faded from memory, I brought them to the one place even I cannot stay." He sighed. "Why do I come here?"

Shadow raised his arm and pointed to where a beam of light touched the horizon - gently illuminating a small glowing grove of trees on a distant mountain.

"That is one of the paths to Arcadia. I'm trying to see my family.

Though it's a bit of a futile attempt."

"You said you can go anywhere. Et in Arcadia –"

"Yes, but I may not stay. I have seen some of my siblings on rare occasions. But I cannot reside with them. And they cannot come to me. Perhaps someday…"

"Does that mean…they still exist in some form…even if they've been forgotten?"

"Maybe it's only because I still remember them that their echo persists. But I think not. One thing I know for certain is that nothing is ever Unmade. Which should mean that they have some chance of returning."

Shadow had hope, though it would make him too vulnerable to admit it, that their stories would be resurrected, and they would come back to him one day. But hope can leave little painful wounds from holding to it tightly. And Shadow had been clinging to his for a terribly long time.

"You are running out of questions," he said. "Get to the point of your visit."

Paige took a breath and stepped forward.

"Do you know anything about an Owner of The Bookstore? The stories are in danger. There's a Bookworm on the loose and…I think something's wrong with me and it's destroying the whole world."

"Is that why I came for every character in…whatever edition of 'The Great Gatsby' that was?"

"Yes."

"That was your doing?"

"I don't know. But…possibly. If it was I didn't mean to –"

"You sound like Dorothy. 'I didn't mean to drop a house on your sister.' I still had to usher them to the lands beyond. Intentions have no bearing on consequences."

Paige looked down at the ground.

"We do need to find this Owner," said Wesley. "They're the only person who might be able to help us put things to rights. If they even exist."

"They do," said Shadow. "I believe I even met them, a long time ago. Not to take them, I mean. I didn't kill them is what I…they are…'alive and well' as the saying goes. I'm afraid I don't know where they are or anything more helpful than I've said, but I can at least encourage you on your…quest, I believe you would call it. It is not futile, as far as I can tell. And I am the first one to say when something is hopeless, much to my sibling's eternal consternation. There now, I should never have agreed to answer your questions. Your search for your owner is one thing but I never meant to speak about…"

He turned his face into the shadow of a tree that hung over him.

"You must go now," he said. He took a long breath. "I'm sorry I could not be of more help," he said. "But trust your heart, and use your head, and you can't go far wrong. If you've managed to find your way to me you must be on the right track. After all, how likely is it that you would happen upon practically the only being in the universe who knows both your world and the real one, as you call it. Funny name. All worlds are real."

Wesley put his arm around Paige's shoulder. The group turned and headed back towards the castle.

"But be warned," Shadow called after them. "Things are not always as they appear, even in a place where rules govern the very fabric of the universe. <u>You</u> can't be inside and outside a tale at the same time. So tread with caution. And don't get cocky just because you think you know every story ever told. Trust me. You don't."

They reached the castle at twilight. Drystan joined them at dinner where they told him and Sora about their meeting. Drystan returned the Ur Book and satchel to Paige without even being asked (much to Wesley's relief), and seemed far more relaxed than he'd been since their quest for Shadow began. Wesley, however, was brooding even more than usual since leaving Shadow's company and after they retired for the night Paige crept into Wesley's room.

"What's the matter?" she asked. "You don't seem yourself."

"You'll laugh."

"No I won't. I promise."

"I'm…jealous. Don't look at me like that, I'm not proud of it."

"What? Jealous of who?"

"Shadow."

"Shadow?!"

"See, I told you –"

"I'm not laughing. I'm just…surprised. I wouldn't want to be him. He scares me a little, but…I feel bad for him."

"I don't," said Wesley.

"Why?"

"Because he's a good person," said Wesley. "He's death itself and yet…"

"You can't really know that from one conversation."

"Yes, you can."

"You're a good person," said Paige sitting next to Wesley on the bed.

"I'm not. My genre makes sure of it."

"Oh, phooey on your genre!"

"OUR genre."

"You haven't done anything!" said Paige.

"But I –"

"WILL do something. I know. But I think it's ridiculous. As of right now you haven't and I don't think you would let yourself do something so terrible, whatever your genre…OUR genre dictates. I think we get some say in what kind of person we want to be."

"But –"

"If we don't, what's the point? I don't think….if you truly want to be good nothing can just…make you evil, against your will."

"What if we don't have a will?"

"You want to be good, yes?"

"Yes."

"Well, that's your will, isn't it?"

Wesley kissed her and pulled her back on the bed holding her so tight she felt nothing could ever separate them.

"Don't ever leave me," he said. "I'm afraid I don't have the strength… to fight against the tide of…inevitability."

"Never," said Paige. She smiled. "All we need is for you to teach me how to act more Gothic. Then everything will be how it should."

"Well, being alone with me in my room isn't a good start," he smiled.

"I'll work on that tomorrow," she smiled and kissed him again. They spent the rest of the night talking and laughing and fell asleep before they even realized they were tired.

* * *

But over in her room, Eleanore couldn't sleep no matter what she did. She couldn't stop thinking.

So she got out of bed, put on her boots, and rolled her tank down the hall and out of the castle. Alone in the dark, her glowing apparel slowly dimming until she had nothing but the moonlight to guide her, she made her way back up the road towards the place where they'd found Shadow.

"This is stupid," she thought. "Even Velveteen would say it was stupid. I won't be able to see anything in a few minutes, and I'll probably fall straight off that cliff. As if he's even still there..."

But even without the glow of her clothes she could see better than anticipated (a metal tank is a wonderful reflector of moonlight), and she didn't fall off the edge of the cliff.

She did find Shadow. Exactly where they'd left him.

"What are you doing back here so late?" he asked without turning around.

"Shoot, I was trying to be unobtrusive."

"I could hear you a mile away, especially with that thing clunking behind you."

She walked closer and sat on the ground against a tree. Close enough to converse, but not too close for comfort. This was Death after all…

"You've spent far too much time thinking about me, I imagine," Shadow said. "Much more than either of your companions, that's certain. Have you come to ask me not to take you?"

"No."

"Good. I assure you, that request never goes well."

"We only asked four questions this afternoon. We still have one left."

"So you do. Are the other two comfortable with you usurping the remaining one?"

Eleanore shrugged.

"Well, if it's not to spare you, what do you wish to ask? Make it good. People are rarely granted an audience with Death." He paused. "Sorry, didn't mean to be so blustery. I often need to be, in my line of work. Habit."

"Is it better to be written, knowing bad things will happen to you? Or for your story never to be told in the first place?"

The question hung in the air for a long moment, the silence weighing heavy around it.

"I…don't know," Shadow said. "You should have asked that of my brother, Solaris. He was in charge of creation. He would know better than I."

"You don't have to talk about your family, if you don't want to. I didn't mean to pry."

Shadow studied the full moon hanging in the sky.

"I will say one more thing to you about my siblings, and that is all. I don't mind quite as much now as I did before. I shall answer your question with another," he said. "My brother Gwyll used to hang the moon each evening. He would open a great trunk, remove a single pearl, and then place it in the sky where it would grow and grow until it became the moon. Now he is gone, but the moon still rises and falls because the echo of my brother remains. Though it has been the same moon for a long time now and is getting rather old and worn. Pearls, even moon pearls only last so long. Now, would it be better for me to never know what it is to lose a brother? Or for the moon to have never hung in the sky?"

Eleanore sat silent.

"Life is like a fairy tale, but it is like a Grimm or Andersen one, and those are the ones that have meant something and endured," he said. "I suppose that is the best I can offer."

"I feel so old sometimes," said Eleanore. "Weird, huh?"

"Not SO. Everyone knows, at least a little bit, what it is to be old. We are all always the oldest we have ever been."

"You don't seem to like your job very much," said Eleanore.

"I get the feeling you don't really enjoy yours."

"That's different. I'm not the ancient god of book shelving. But... aren't you supposed to like people dying?"

"Most of the time not. I never understood the idea of human sacrifices, especially in worship to me. How is it an offering to give me more work? Not to mention the awkwardness of having to say 'Thank you for giving your life for me' to some poor soul being stabbed on an altar, usually with no say in the matter themselves." He sighed. "I admit, I do have fun sometimes, but usually I am much happier when people are out enjoying their lives. I must say, it would be nice to have a vacation. And…to not be alone so often."

"Don't…don't you have friends? There must be other…ancient gods out there."

"I told you, they've been forgotten."

"But…someone…everyone has SOMEONE."

"Who could ever, truly, love Death?"

"Oh…"

Eleanore thought for a moment.

"I've heard of lots of people…especially goth –"

"Pish. They are enamored with the idea of something they've never experienced. A person they've never met. But once they see me for real it's a different matter. Who could ever meet me face to face, with all that I am, and truly love me?"

Eleanore looked down, wanting to tell him that she would be his friend, but she knew she couldn't. She was too frightened.

"Don't worry, small one," he said. "You will have many years ahead without me troubling you. Unless something unexpected should change, I shall not darken your door for a very long time."

"What?!"

"That…surprises you?"

"I'm YA, teen drama. I came into existence with a freaking oxygen tank! I'm dead before the end of my story for sure! Hell, I can barely make it up a mountain –"

"Dragging that thing, it's no wonder. It must weigh more than you do."

"If I'm not dying, why did I get that as my freaking accessory?"

"We come into this world with all sorts of baggage. It doesn't mean you have to carry it around with you twenty-four hours a day."

"I thought it was…a good thing…like a gift…to make sure I don't…expire too soon."

"Gifts are entirely different. True gifts are intrinsic to you and they cannot be taken away. Accessories are…at your discretion."

"But my genre –"

"You Bookstore folk make entirely too many assumptions. Contrary to many of the tropes of your genre I can guarantee that YOU will not die for a very, very long time. Now, I must go. I have an appointment and I am never late."

Shadow didn't leave, so Eleanore took his words as her cue to. She got up and started back down the hill. But after walking a little while, when Shadow was out of sight, she stopped. She looked at her tank. The truth was, it had never really felt like a gift. She wanted to hit it most of the time. If she was being honest with herself it wasn't something that helped and made her feel better. Maybe she was just relying on it because she thought she was supposed to.

"I don't care if it's against the rules of my story," she said to no one in particular. She took the tubes out of her nose and breathed in the fresh night air unobstructed. She closed the valve and left the tank on the side of the road. Maybe it would have been a good accessory for someone else…but it wasn't for her.

"Goodbye," she said. "I don't think I need you anymore. If I'm really not going to die for a long time…I'd better get on with being glad I'm alive and enjoying it. And, to be frank, you're a real downer."

She started tentatively back towards the castle, her clothes glowing brighter and brighter as she went, making her journey quite easy. Before long she was skipping, feeling lighter than she had in her whole life. When she reached the gates, she wasn't even really out of breath.

She ran inside, up the stairs, and down the hall to Paige's room. She knocked but there was no answer. She deflated slightly but, her newfound courage still blazing, she walked down to Drystan's room. She could see light under the door, and she knocked.

"Yes?"

She went inside.

"Eleanore?! Are you OK? What are you doing without your tank?!"

"I'm fine! I'm wonderful!"

Eleanore told him everything about her conversation with Shadow.

"I'm happy, Drystan. Really happy for the first time! I don't want to be sad or sick anymore, hell, I don't even know if I want to be written, I just want to live my life and do things I want to do and be happy and free!"

"That's wonderful," he smiled. "But…you just left your tank on the side of the road?"

"Maybe a little stupid? But I just…I don't want to be thinking about dying all the time. Especially if I'm not going to for a long while."

Drystan smiled. "Well then, maybe…at least keep taking your pills? You don't want to tempt fate THAT much."

"YOU'RE advising me against tempting fate."

"Yeah."

"Well, I'd better listen then," she laughed. "Oh, screw it. I'm finally happy and free of that stupid thing, I'll take anything you tell me too," she laughed and swallowed a pill. Drystan held her in the crook of his arm and they fell asleep as the sun came up. It was the first time Eleanore felt like a real, normal girl and she never wanted to go back.

CHAPTER 16

PARADISE LOST

The next day, everything fell apart.

Things began normally enough except that Drystan didn't come down with the rest of them in the morning. Wanting to let him rest, they started breakfast without him. Everyone, especially Paige, was thrilled by Eleanore's new-found liberation. They decided to try their luck with the Ur Book again and ask it where they should go next, and were just about to say a long, tearful goodbye to Sora when there was a thunderous sound outside the gates and Eleanore, going to see what it was, was promptly kidnapped by a sorceress and a hundred of her men riding by on horseback.

"That's strange," said Sora.

"Strange?! That's –"

"Narratively unsound?" Paige hinted just as Drystan walked in groggily, rubbing the sleep from his eyes.

"Things like that don't happen here. Certainly not out of the blue. Something's wrong."

"What?" said Drystan.

"Eleanore was just kidnapped."

That woke him up.

"We have to go after her," said Paige, adding in a whisper to Drystan and Wesley, "do you think this means the book we're in is starting to fall apart?"

"Very likely. Sounds like a plot hole to me."

"Of course," said Sora bringing their attention back. "And I must call my advisors immediately!"

Now they quickly said their goodbyes, hoping they would meet again soon under better circumstances.

"Wait! Before you go…" Sora reached into the folds of her gown and pulled out four tiny crystalline flowers. She handed one to each member of the party. "So you can always hear us and find your way back," she smiled. Paige held it up to her ear and heard the song of the flowers in the field.

"But…that's too generous!" said Paige. "They were so expensive at the circus!"

"They're…more common here," Sora smiled. "But still special. I hope they'll help you remember us and that you might come back someday." She looked so lonely as she said it.

"We'll come back," said Paige, with a smile. "We just…have to fix a few things first." Would Sora even remember them if they did return? Or would they have to start all over again?

Sora gave them free use of her stables and in no time Wesley had two horses ready: one for Drystan and one for himself and Paige.

"Do you really think this set up is a good idea?" Drystan asked.

"What?" said Wesley, anxious to mount. "Paige is a lady and has never ridden before. Get on! We haven't a moment to lose!"

"No, I mean, giving me my own horse doesn't seem like…I've never ridden before either –"

"A gentleman who's never ridden -?"

"I'm not a gentleman, I'm Epic Comedy. Speaking of which, I don't think we want to see how Epic Comedy on a horse is going to go down. Get it? Go down? Double meaning?"

"We can't have three on one horse! Four when we rescue Eleanore!"

"Thank God she doesn't still have that tank!"

"Well then…" said Drystan.

"Oh, fine."

So, much to Wesley's consternation, Drystan shared his horse, riding behind him, and Paige, after receiving some help and instructions from Wesley, mounted her own. She took to riding quickly (aided by the fact that she was riding a talking horse), and they raced off.

Eleanore, in the meantime, had sore ribs from being bounced around on the back of a horse for several hours, being dragged up a winding stone staircase and thrown in the tallest room of the tallest tower of the Sorceress' castle, and locked inside. She found the whole thing rather hysterical and decided to use the opportunity to try out being a Damsel in Distress.

She tried to faint, but couldn't. She found pining by the window extremely tedious, she didn't have a very good voice and singing to the birds only frightened them (and elicited shouts of "shut up!" from the guards). Having nothing else to do but pace around the room for hours, she decided that she was unequivocally unsuited to the role of Damsel. It was just so boring. So she thought she might try the role of Hero and set about looking for an exciting way to escape, but that proved utterly fruitless.

"What's with all the criticizing these women for not rescuing themselves?" she thought. "Unless I can survive a several hundred foot fall I'm not going anywhere. These bedsheets certainly aren't long enough to get me to the ground. My 'inner strength and resilience' should not be reliant on what tools my captors happen to have idiotically left in my prison cell. It's too bad Paige wasn't the one kidnapped. If she is Gothic Romance, she'd be having a lot more fun. If anyone could consider this fun…"

She heard a commotion outside her door, then a moment later a glorious piece of blond haired manhood burst into her room wearing shining armor and proclaiming himself her Knight Valiant. He grabbed Eleanore and kissed her which quite pissed her off. For her it was nothing more than a ridiculously awkward encounter with a tertiary character. And it was her FIRST. BLOODY. KISS.

She smacked him so hard he fell backwards down the stairs, the door magically locking behind him.

"I take it back," she thought. "I'd rather be locked in a tower than have anything to do with…that."

Paige was having genre problems too. She was supposed to be finding her way into Gothic Romance, but she was having a grand time leading the charge on her horse, her beau awkwardly following as he carried the comic relief behind him.

"I guess my genre lessons will have to be postponed again," Paige yelled.

"Not necessarily…Gothic girls are certainly allowed to ride –"

"I doubt they're often leading the cavalry."

"I'm at a disadvantage or I'd be right there with you."

"Hey!" shouted Drystan.

"Guess that means I can come to your room again tonight," Paige smiled.

"You might – "

"Stop!" Paige suddenly shouted.

"I was just offering a suggestion, love."

"No…STOP. Your horse."

She pulled up short in front of a wolf standing in the middle of the road.

"This is where you would cry out and faint," said Wesley, trying to encourage Paige.

"Not the time…"

"Still just a suggestion, darling."

"Hello girl," the Wolf said. "I may be able to help you."

"Let me slay it, my dear! It's dangerous and we must be on our way."

"Hold on…"

Paige pulled out the poem Eleanore had given them. Apparently wolves were OK but you shouldn't give them any idea of your intended destination.

"Hello, Mr. Wolf. Thanks for your help. We'd appreciate it."

The Wolf glowered towards Wesley, then said to Paige: "Answer my riddle and I will give you a boon to aid you on your quest."

"Which one?" asked Paige. "We're on a couple at the moment."

"Whichever," it said.

"Are you any good at riddles?" Paige called back to the men.

"Not very."

"All right, guess we're winging it."

"It's very difficult," said the Wolf. "And if you don't answer correctly I must eat you."

"Great."

"OK."

The air grew ominous. The Wolf crouched down and twitched a little.

"What…is the number…that comes after…four."

His eyes darted back and forth between them.

"That's the riddle?"

"Yes…be careful…you only get one chance –"

"Five."

"Excuse me?"

"The number that comes after four. It's five," said Paige.

"Are you absolutely sure?" it warned.

"Yeah."

"Correct! You are the only one to have answered my riddle." The Wolf exclaimed. "And for your valor I will give you this key."

He pulled a shining key from his fur and tossed it to Paige.

"Is he kidding?" Drystan called from the back of Wesley's horse.

"Um…thanks," said Paige, catching the golden key, still with a little wolf slobber on it.

"Where are you headed?"

"To the –" Drystan started.

"Nope, sorry, not telling you where we're going. But thanks for the key!" said Paige, as she dashed away on her horse, Wesley trying to keep up.

"That is strange," said Paige's horse (whose name was Mabel). "Never heard of such a ridiculous riddle. Or a magical wolf just standing in your path to give it to you. Better be on your guard, Miss. Nothing's that simple."

Except that it was. And it kept on being…

They soon came to a gate that barred their way, locked with three locks. The key opened all of them without so much as a jiggle. Then came a gate with seven locks – their key opened all of those too. Then a gate with twelve locks, all opened with the same key.

They found a dragon blocking their way who said he could only be slain by the magical sword Dewiniol. The key transformed into a sword that slew the dragon with one stab. (Wesley dealt that blow. He was the tallest and better able to reach. Plus he was desperate to contribute SOMETHING.)

"This isn't right at all!" said Mabel. "Each of those locks and that sword should have been its own task. There's no such thing as a 'gets you out of every obstacle free' magical object."

They finally reached the tower where the key transformed into a ladder allowing Eleanore to climb down with ease.

"Did you see anything up there?" Drystan called to her, looking intensely at the sky above the tower.

"Nothing of note," she said, confused. "It was boring as hell."

When Eleanore was safe the ladder became a shining staff that glowed so brightly it vaporized the villains. It then turned back into a key.

"What kind of cockamamy thing is this anyway?" Eleanore said.

"Is there any writing on it?" asked Mabel.

"Faintly..." said Paige. She held it up to the sun and read:

"If your life should have a flaw

Use the Deus Ex Ma"key"na"

"We've been using a plot contrivance?!" Paige exclaimed.

"No, no, no," Mabel muttered, "I've never heard of one of those. Sounds like a cheap trick to me."

"That's exactly what it is," said Paige. "So cheap they're never actually used, and if they are it's only once at the very end of the story. You can get away with illogical magic once, but..."

"It shouldn't be here!" Mabel whinnied. "There's no such object in these lands."

"Is it because…I was playing around with my genre?" said Eleanore nervously.

"No, of course not! Besides, it's not like I've been acting like the paragon of Gothic –"

"What's that?" Drystan pointed to the side of the tower.

The edges of the story were fraying as if someone had actually ripped them apart. The Nothing was moving in all at once and terribly fast. Then they heard the whirring of the Bookworm deep under the ground.

"Run!"

Paige moved to throw the key away.

"No!" Drystan cried, "Keep that thing away from the story! It might buy us some time."

So Paige put it in her pocket, buttoned it up tight, and quickly helped Eleanore clamber onto her horse, as the group started galloping away from the Nothing as fast as they could, Eleanore "ow ow"ing all the way.

"Get out the Ur Book!" Paige called back to Eleanore, "I have to keep my hands on the reins."

"No you don't," Mabel called. "I'll keep us steady."

"I've never ridden before. If I don't, I'm not sure –"

"How are we all going to hold on to each other?" Eleanore yelled, trying to pull the book out of Paige's satchel, the wind whipping her arm as they charged on at breakneck speed.

"We'll try to pull up next to you!" shouted Wesley. "Hold on Mabel!"

"Don't leave me here!" Mabel shouted. "I don't want to fall into that…thing…Take me with you!"

"The faster we get out of here, the faster that thing leaves, hopefully," said Wesley.

"That's not how it seems to work…"

"Shut up Drystan! Don't worry the lady!" (He meant Mabel.)

"We can try to bring you," said Paige. "Eleanore's holding the book, and she's sitting on you, so if it's possible for you to come back to the Store with us, you will." Paige prayed she would.

Drystan tightened his grip around Wesley's waist, Eleanore did the same with Paige, and Wesley threw his arm out to grab Paige just as Elenore opened the book, thinking of The Bookstore with all her might.

They crash landed in the stacks. Mabel was nowhere in sight.

"No!" Paige cried, lunging towards the Ur Book in an attempt to return to "Ever."

"Paige!" Wesley cried, grabbing her. "There's nothing you can do! If she could have come back with us she would, like you said."

Paige fell to her knees and started sobbing.

"It's not fair! Mable, and Sora and Ms. Three – they're all gone?!"

"I don't know," said Wesley.

"Remember what Shadow said," said Eleanore. "Nothing is unmade. There's still hope. I –" and suddenly Eleanore turned very pale, then a strange sort of green. She ran through the stacks to the (thankfully) unmanned front desk just in time to throw up into a trashcan.

CHAPTER 17

GIRL FRIDAY

Paige and the others started to go after Eleanore but stopped when they ran into Arden…or Eddie. His clothing was different. Far from the babyish wallflower in a well ironed t-shirt and jeans, he now had on a brown jacket, low slung baseball cap, and a cigarette hanging out of his mouth.

"Arden…uh…Eddie?" said Drystan.

"Name's Alex now," he said, throwing a book up on a shelf with no concern for its placement.

"Nightingale's going to kill you if he sees –"

"Ah, he's a jerk-face," said, well, I guess Alex now… "You all are. Besides, I don't want to do no crummy shelving."

"But you have to –"

"Ah, you can't make me do nothing!"

"You look so different," said Wesley. "Did you go into a story –"

"Who'd want to go into a creepy old story? What? You wanna make something of it?"

"No."

Alex turned and went back to his version of "shelving."

Shaken, they continued after Eleanore but stopped again when they saw Herc sitting at a table pouring over a giant copy of "War and Peace."

"Greetings!" he said in an uncharacteristically erudite tone. "Haven't seen you around for a while. Thought you might have faded."

"FADED?"

"Like Pioneer Joe. He just…faded away That's what the others are calling it."

"Herc, your arm!"

Herc's arm was disappearing.

"Is it the Nothing?"

"That? No. Nothing isn't in the Store. And my arm? That there's just a trick of the light."

It wasn't.

"I'm perfectly fine."

He wasn't.

"Just thought I might play with this whole flexible genre idea myself. Been seeing how I feel as Literary Criticism and Satire. What do you think?"

"Doesn't suit you."

"A suit! That's just what I need!"

"Characters have been fading out of existence from messing with their genres?"

"Pish posh. Young master Eddie -"

"He's going by Alex now."

"Young master Alex is perfectly fine. No one can tell us who we should be."

"No one's trying to tell you. You're supposed to be…who you are…"

"He's right about Alex…he didn't seem to be fading…" Drystan whispered to Paige and Wesley.

"What the hell is going on?" said Paige, grabbing the others and rushing off. "Everything's changed! Look! There are books strewn everywhere. Is anyone still caring for the Store?"

"We need to ask Gwen -"

"We're finding Eleanore first!"

They found them both together, Gwen reluctantly wiping Eleanore's face.

"I don't feel so good…" said Eleanore.

"What's wrong with her?" asked Gwen.

"I thought you were better.." Paige said, taking Eleanore's hand.

"So much for that. I feel sicker than I've ever been. Maybe Shadow's advice wasn't as clear cut as I thought."

"Or maybe it's just that you've been through a lot today. I'm sure your ribs are still sore. We haven't even eaten in -"

"We're back in the Store, none of that should matter."

"It was stupid to get rid of my oxygen like that. Why the hell did I? I'm not impulsive…"

Wesley pulled Drystan aside.

"She's…not pregnant is she?"

"Why on earth would you ask that?"

"Well, she was in your room."

"Talking. You're not the only person who can pretend to be honorable." He gave Wesley a sarcastic smirk.

"Maybe we shouldn't be messing with our genres. Characters are fading out of existence."

"Oh no…" Said Eleanore. "Do I look like I'm fading?"

"No, doll."

"I'd better start reading some Gothic Romance."

"Dorian just got written," said Gwen. "You could start there."

"Dorian got written?"

"Yeah, by Oscar Wilde."

"No way," said Eleanore with a cough. "I think I'm just going to lie down. Don't want to risk going into a story, though it would be more comfortable."

They set Eleanore up in a little cushioned reading nook and she promptly fell asleep.

"Strange," Paige whispered to Wesley. "We don't tend to sleep in the Store…"

"Doesn't mean we can't," he said. "She's sick and exhausted. It's understandable. Come on."

Paige pulled a copy of "Dorian Gray" off the New Releases table and she and Wesley headed towards a comfy banquette in Children's Fantasy.

The moment they were out of sight Gwen grabbed Drystan and dragged him to a copy of "Dangerous Liaisons." Once inside, fighting with her mid-18th Century gown, she continued pulling him through a crowded ballroom. She scooped up a plate of macarons and an entire bottle of Champagne, not stopping until they were alone in the gardens.

"I am going CRAZY!" she shouted. "PLEASE," she shoveled a couple macarons into her mouth, "tell me you've got something or I'm going to scream. I refuse to be in customer service anymore. I absolutely refuse."

"I see your finger mostly grew back."

"Bite me."

Drystan popped a macaron into his mouth.

"The Owner exists."

"You met them?!"

"No, but there's proof. We just have to -"

"How much longer? Time's ticking down, Drys...I want out of here!"

"So do something about it. That's the whole point, sweetie," he ate another macaron. "To be in charge of our own fate."

"That's not going very well for Pioneer Joe."

"He's cannon fodder."

"You left me behind!"

"Good thing, looks like a lot's been going down. And our excursions wouldn't have been nearly as successful without your...support...from the Store."

She started laughing and couldn't stop. "At the rate I'm going…I think I might burn the place to the ground."

"What's happening to you?" he said. "Be logical –"

"Aren't Romance girls supposed to be emotional?"

"Not Crime ones. And not you! I can't believe I'm saying this but calm down!"

Gwen knocked back the bottle and finally steadied herself.

"We need to see how much further we can push the breaking down of rules. Make it work to our advantage."

"But Joe –"

"He didn't know what he was doing. Besides, look at Alex."

"Who?"

"Eddie. Arden."

"He's Alex now?"

"Yeah, and not fading at all. We're not running around doing things on a whim. We're figuring out how to use the system. The new (dis) order."

"What happened to angst girl's tank? Was that part of the plan?"

"It's fine."

"What do you have in mind NOW? I'm tired of waiting."

"What happened to you'd 'do anything for me?'"

Gwen quieted.

"You said you're done working retail with nothing to show for it. You're dying for your happy ending. Why not just take an author and stop waiting to be chosen."

"Are you serious?"

"Yes."

"You don't want to be with me anymore?"

He kissed her and she melted.

"Of course I do."

"So that's your next plan? Have me…take an author?"

"Finally get what's rightfully yours. Forget waiting. You're the only one brave enough, smart enough to pull it off. If you can do it, maybe I can figure out how to get in with you. Influence our narrative from the inside. That would be something wouldn't it? Besides, it's time everyone knew what you're really made of."

"But what if –"

"Shh…" he put his finger up to her lips. "Did you mean what you said?"

"Yes."

"Will you do this for me?"

She paused.

"If you really think it's the right thing…"

"I know it is. For US."

"Then yes."

Later that day Gwen went back to the front desk, keeping the resident Romance girls Iris and Violet as far away from the front of the Store as possible - however she could.

"Nightingale wants you to check on shelving. Things aren't being put back in the right place."

"OK. Thanks Rose!"

"It's Gwen!"

And then, suddenly, it happened.

"Anything new in Romance?"

She knew instantly that it wasn't her author. There wasn't the faintest glimmer of kinship.

He was older and not terribly handsome. He looked rather bohemian, though he had an extraordinary amount of tech on his person (including some Luman glasses he had refashioned into a vintage looking monocle), and spoke with the faintest hint of a Russian accent covered with layers of Americanization.

But still, she adjusted her position so he was looking at her from her most flattering angle.

"I'm Gwen. You're in luck! Romance happens to be my specialty."

"Gwen," he tried the name through his Russian accent. "Rather harsh…"

"It's just a nickname," she said, swallowing her rage. "Middle name, actually," she lied. "My first name is…Rose."

"Rose! Oh, that's beautiful! I've always loved beautiful flower names for beautiful women."

She offered her hand. He kissed it.

"And you are?"

"Krasny. I'm here for research. I need the muse to strike as it were."

"How'd I be for ya?"

"You are very…nice." He said. "But…I must be honest…I don't like women so…forceful."

She wanted to punch this guy in the face. Instead she said:

"I'm good at adaptation."

Out of the corner of her eye she saw Iris moseying towards the front stacks. Of course Iris was meant for this guy. Practically jailbait little bohemian girl…a wannabe Lolita…but with bright eyeshadow and quite a bit of metal woven into her clothes. A perfect match for this guy. Thank God he hadn't seen her yet.

"Why don't we go for a cup of coffee, and I'll do my best to inspire you?"

She wanted to gag.

She tried to smile innocently.

"Well, if you insist…"

How was it that easy?

She took off her apron and nametag and placed them down on the counter. Iris started towards them. A million things flashed across Gwen's mind. She thought about Drystan, how she would probably never go back into another Sherlock story with him, maybe never again have someone who appreciated her for more than her pretty face. But if she didn't do what she was about to do, all that would happen eventually anyway. This might be the answer for how to get out of here and live her own life…

She thought about how easily…how quickly she'd seduced an author that wasn't her own. No one else in the Store could have stolen an author in a minute flat! And then she thought about the front door. No one had ever walked through it without their author. THEIR author. Who knew if it was even possible for her to walk through it at all. Maybe she'd be vaporized if she even tried.

But still, Gwen took Krasny's hand. She looked back and saw two things at once: the first was Iris who caught a glimpse of Krasny and knew immediately that he was her author. The other was Drystan standing on the balcony looking at Gwen with awe, respect and a great deal of lust. She steeled herself, and when Krasny opened the door, she followed him through.

Iris collapsed in tears.

"Sorry, dear," Drystan called down. "Guess he just wasn't meant for you."

✳ ✳ ✳

"I love Sibyl Vane," Wesley read to Paige from "Dorian Gray." "I want to place her on a pedestal of gold and to see the world worship the woman who is mine…Her trust makes me faithful; her belief makes me good. When I am with her, I regret all that you have taught me. I become different from what you have known me to be. I am changed, and the mere touch of Sibyl Vane's hand makes me forget you and all your wrong, fascinating, poisonous, delightful theories."

"That is exactly what you are for me," he said, giving Paige a kiss on her nose.

"So…why do I still not feel I…fully belong…in the genre?"

"It may be nothing. Like I said, you may just be an outlier in the canon. Oh, it doesn't matter. I don't even care. I just want to be close to you."

"I think we need to talk to Nightingale."

"Why?" he asked, annoyed.

"We need to ask him about the Owner. We know they exist now. We can take detours all we want but –"

"I don't think finding Shadow was a detour."

"No, but…we have a source of information right in front of us."

"Keep your voices down," said Drystan, walking around a stack to join them. "I could hear you –"

"Paige wants to go back to Nightingale," said Wesley.

"Are you crazy?"

"He's the manager! He's got to know something!"

"Nightingale's only going to try and stop us. And what if he finds out about the Ur Book and tries to take it away?! Did you think about that?"

"But –"

"Listen to me," said Wesley, gently taking Paige's chin. "I've gone on this quest with you even though…because I love you and…but you need to trust me sometimes. Even Sibyl Vane listened to Dorian. Elizabeth listened to Victor."

"Look how that turned out," Drystan thought.

Wesley smiled. "Rule one of Romance. Listen to the person you love."

"That goes both ways."

He gave her a look.

"OK," Paige finally said. "But if things get worse –"

"We'll…revisit." Wesley promised. "Come on. I'm way behind in my shelving. Come help me?" he smiled and offered his hand.

"In a minute."

"I'll be in YA Fantasy." He kissed the top of her head and started to go.

"Maybe I'll go look through Architectural Fiction," Drystan said, following Wesley. "There might be something helpful there."

"Some of those stacks are awfully high up…"

"Someone's gotta do it," Drystan smiled. He slipped. Wesley caught the back of his shirt before he hit the floor and pulled him up to standing.

"Maybe not you…" Wesley grimaced.

Once they were gone, Paige took out the Ur Book and flipped through its pages. There was still nothing inside.

She had one, last idea.

"Dewey?! This is an emergency!"

Nothing.

"Are you there? I really need to talk to you."

Nothing.

"In the name of everything precious in The Bookstore, Dewey this is an emergency and I need to talk to you NOW!"

CHAPTER 18

A WRINKLE IN TIME

"What's up lil pup?"

Dewey stood in front of Paige with a big smile on her face.

"Thank you for coming!"

"No problem. I have no conscious say in when I manifest."

"I need help."

"I'm figuring the book didn't do much since exactly seven characters have faded from the Store since I gave it to you."

"SEVEN?! I only knew about Pioneer Joe."

"He was number five. Since then it's been Ms. Green and Herc."

"What?!"

"It's bad, isn't it? That's why I'm here. Darn it, why can't I ever be the good news manifestation. Like, 'Congratulations! It's your birthday!'"

"We don't have birthdays."

"There you go."

"We found out more about the Owner but hit a dead end. You have any other magic objects up your sleeve?"

"I didn't keep the Ur Book up my sleeve."

"Well –"

"I didn't keep it anywhere. Incorporeal things don't actually need to be 'kept.' But it tends to be incorporeal not far from where my left armpit is or would be if it were corporeal. Oh! But look at that snazzy satchel you have. It changes size, I presume?"

"Yeah."

"Very smart. I mean that with both meanings."

"So there's nothing else you can do?"

"Well, with your go-ahead there is a last resort emergency operating procedure I can set in motion. But I'd tread carefully with that one."

"What happens if you do it?"

"It will restore memories of The Bookstore to all the characters who have been written, allowing you to have uncensored interaction with them and even permitting them to return to the Store."

"But?" Paige paused. "There is a 'but?'"

"Yes! It will dramatically speed up the rate at which everything's falling apart. Once it's activated you will likely only have the equivalent of a few hours to fix everything before all hell breaks loose."

"All hell's not breaking loose now?"

"Nope."

"Oh, great."

"Don't worry, it's close. So, what do you want to do?"

"Can I think about it?"

"Sure thing, chicken wing! Just let me know soon, cause, you know, ticking clock and all."

"What ticking clock?"

"Metaphor."

"You'll show up if I call for you?"

"Most likely. Things are in a pretty constant state of emergency. I don't think it'll be a problem. But it could be. Who knows?! It'll be a surprise!"

"But –"

And Dewey was gone.

Darn it.

Paige heard the bell ring and the front door open.

"Hello? Can anyone help me?" a man's voice called out.

"I got it."

"Oh no, not Alex!" Paige thought as she hurried to the register.

"Hey. I'm Holden. What do you want?"

Paige looked down – it was definitely Arden/Eddie/Alex (apparently going by 'Holden' now).

"No fuss. Don't need you to try and sell me something," the man said. "I'm just looking for any good literature related to Devon."

"Sure. No fuss. I like that. Most people who come in don't know what they want or why they're here. You find that too, Sergeant?" he asked, noticing the three chevrons on his uniform.

"Call me Sonny," said the man. "I'm stuck with Sargent all day."

"That's not what it says on that nametag."

"Can't a man go by his preferred name once in a while?"

"Sure. I'm all for whatever feels best. You talking about Devon, England?"

"That's the one."

Paige stood on the balcony overlooking the front of the Store. What the hell was going on? Holden seemed like he was getting on great with this author…but how? He'd gone through four names, a change of wardrobe and an epic personality switch. Paige turned and ran to YA Fantasy.

"Wesley, I need to show you something," she called, barely looking at him as she turned without pausing and hurried back to the front of the Store. Wesley followed. When they got there she showed him Holden and Sonny.

"What is happening?" Paige asked.

Willa, Fred, Iris, Velveteen and even Nightingale wandered towards the balcony to join them. Eleanore followed, drowsily, a moment later.

"He couldn't…he couldn't have found his author."

"What's all the racket?" said Eleanore rubbing her eyes.

"This doesn't make any sense," said Nightingale.

"Eddie –"

"He's Holden now."

"Is supposed to be written by Stephen Chbosky or something! Not a cynical…not someone like HIM!"

"Is he stealing an author?" asked Iris.

"Don't be silly, you can't do that," said Willa. Iris opened her mouth to say something but stayed quiet.

"Lots of oats in Devon," said Sonny.

"Pretty shitty place to get lost." They laughed.

"Oats is a terrible sounding word. Oats….Oats…"

"They have any better sounding exports?" they laughed again.

"You only have that kind of connection with your real author," said Velveteen. "At least, that's what I've been told."

"Not any books you'd like on Devon. I can tell."

"Let's get out of here. You can buy me a beer." They laughed some more.

Holden pulled off his apron (he'd long ago abandoned his nametag), jumped behind the register, picked up a pair of scissors and cut it to bits.

"So long, suckers!" Holden called as Sonny opened the door and they both walked out.

The rest of the characters stood in stunned silence.

"But I thought you started to fade when you messed with your genre…" said Fred.

"Does this mean Arden…uh, Holden actually became…MORE himself by changing?"

"Then…who he started as, wasn't who he was meant to be?"

"Seems so."

"If he hadn't started exploring his identity, he never would have been written…"

"Things are so confusing…"

"Maybe he…discovered who he really was but others are…trying to cover up who they really are?"

"Then does that mean I'm doing it wrong?" said Eleanore, who had only grown more weak and pale. She thought about her absent oxygen tank.

"Nightingale, what are we supposed to do?" said Paige. "You said 'wait and see' well, we've seen!"

"We don't know enough yet," he said.

"Oh, that's rich," said Eleanore.

"I told you, things will work out all right."

"What about everyone who's faded?"

"What about Holden!" Nightingale countered. "Things are going exactly according to design. He'll be a story that will –"

"Inspire people, create empathy, blah, blah, blah. No matter what suffering we go through, as long as folks are inspired!"

"Eleanore –"

"I'm so…!" her feelings exploded. "I don't want to be some cosmic whipping boy so someone 'out there' can learn to be a little more empathetic. I don't want someone to walk around in my shoes for a little while…I didn't ask for shoes to walk around in myself! I'm tired of my whole life being nothing more than a manifestation of altruism. Maybe I'd like the Nothing to erase me. Maybe it would be better if the Nothing erased everything. Sometimes I think I'd rather give up any potential moments of happiness just to make the pain stop. It hurts too much. It's cruel to make us strong enough to survive it." She started coughing so hard she had to sit down.

But there was no time for anyone to respond because, as if her words had summoned it from the bowels of the shelves, the Bookworm suddenly burst through the stacks, into the Store and straight towards the assembled group.

Everyone screamed. Willa froze, holding onto Velveteen, unable to do anything but stand and stare at the giant, albino worm barreling down on her like a truck. Dracula 1 grabbed her arm and pulled her away, Velveteen, their paw still locked in her hand, flopping behind. The Nothing hovered like a fog around the Bookworm as it chomped its way through stack after stack devouring hundreds of books in each mouthful.

"How is it in the Store?!"

"Come with me!" Nightingale yelled, leading the characters away from the Bookworm, and avoiding the question. Paige took off with the group but the moment she did, the Bookworm changed direction, once again heading straight for them. The group darted downstairs and around shelves, the Bookworm in pursuit.

Paige stopped. The others turned a corner, but this time the Bookworm didn't follow.

It continued moving towards Paige.

"What the hell are you doing?!" Wesley screamed. "COME ON!"

"It wants ME!" Paige shouted. "It's following me!"

"I can see that! Run!"

"I have an idea –" she said, starting to move away.

"Now is not the time!" Wesley called, fighting against the tide of characters to get back to Paige. He finally reached her and grabbed her hand. "We need to get to safety! Now!"

"Nowhere is safe!" she said.

He tried to pull her towards the group, but she resisted.

"Don't you get it? Where does Nightingale think he's taking everyone?!"

"That doesn't mean you give up!"

"I'm not!"

"I'm not going to lose you!"

"Please Wesley!"

He paused then relaxed his grip. Paige started to move away, but he kept hold of her hand.

"You're not going anywhere without me," he said. "Whatever you're doing, we're doing it together."

They ran in the opposite direction from the group. The Bookworm followed. It seemed to enjoy the chase, as if it was a puppy and this was one big game.

"You do have a plan, right?" Wesley yelled.

"The group was heading towards Fantasy –"

"Yeah…"

"The most populated section of the Store."

"Oh, God."

"But it's following me, so I'm going to the least populated."

"Mathematical Fiction?"

"You got it. If I can't save everything, I can at least minimize the casualties."

"But what about protecting yourself?"

"Self-preservation is not the most important thing."

"I'd debate that, but you ought to at least consider it an option!"

"Haven't gotten that far. But if we can figure out how to get it out of the Store we'll hopefully kill two birds with one stone."

The Bookworm was right behind them, moving faster than anything called a "worm" has any right to. As it moved, it devoured not just books, but whole shelves, swallowing stack upon stack.

The rest of the characters raced towards the storage room. Nightingale couldn't think of a better place to go. They were all panting, and tripping and out of breath. Velveteen slipped out of Willa's hand. Willa reached back for him, but Dracula 1 kept pulling her along. Everyone ignored the Rabbit until Eleanore who, huffing and puffing, barely keeping up with the stragglers, scooped Velveteen into her arms. Eleanore knew soon she wouldn't be able to keep up at all, so she dashed into a nook in the Children's section and clung tightly to Velveteen as she tried to keep from passing out.

"Will we be all right?" asked the Rabbit.

"I don't know," said Eleanore. "Everything's all upside down. No matter what you do, everything's all wrong. I'm so sick, Velveteen. I don't understand. I almost…I almost wish that Bookworm would come erase me and just get my existence over with."

Velveteen tried to gently stroke her hair.

"What made you so much sicker? Was it going on that quest?"

"I don't know. Serves me right. Trying to help just makes the pain worse. But really it was probably getting rid of that stupid tank! And of course it didn't come back with me into the Store now that everything's… What else could it be?" she sighed. "My story's going to be depressing, it's depressing here, what are we supposed to do?"

"It'll be all right in the end, Ellie."

"How do you know?"

"Because…it has to be?"

Paige and Wesley made it to Mathematical Fiction and ducked behind a shelf as the Bookworm paused to nosh on some old, dusty oversized volumes. It was moving more slowly the fuller it got. Every so often it moved its head as if looking for Paige.

"It doesn't have eyes!" said Paige, finally getting an up close view of the Bookworm. "Wes, I don't think it can see."

"You're right. But if it's anything like other kinds of worms, it can still sense light and sound vibrations. Be careful."

They sat very still and tried to slow their breathing. Paige's heart beat painfully loudly in her chest.

The Bookworm took another chomp and swallowed forty-two books in one gulp. Paige buried her head in Wesley's chest. She couldn't watch. It was like seeing people being eaten in front of her. Who knew how many characters each of those books contained? She tried to console herself with the knowledge that the shelves weren't as full here as other places in the Store. The carnage there would have been even more horrific.

The Bookworm lazily inched its way forward. It came within a meter of Paige. She started trembling. She turned her eyes towards Wesley.

"GO!" she tried to silently communicate. "Get out of here! Remember? Self-preservation?!" She looked from Wesley to the stacks beyond the Bookworm and back again. He got her meaning but held her tighter. He was staying.

The Bookworm moved forward another inch. Then it let out what could only be described as a great belch, turned, dived into the nearest open book and disappeared from sight.

Wesley and Paige sat there, frozen, waiting for its return.

It didn't.

Paige grabbed Wesley as tightly as she could.

"Why didn't you go?!" she cried. "It could have killed you! You should have –"

"I'm not leaving you, Paige. No matter what happens. We belong together."

"You keep saying that, but what if you're wrong? What if we're not in the same story?"

Wesley laughed. "That doesn't matter. Don't you see? I thought that was the only reason I could love you like I do, but everything's...inside out now and..." He put his hand on her cheek and turned her head to face him. "Even if we're not in the same story. Even if my author comes...I choose you."

"What do you mean?"

"I would stay. For you."

"You would really…?"

"Of course!" he laughed. "I love you. Maybe there doesn't have to be a reason. Maybe I just love you and that's enough."

She kissed him.

"I will too," she said. "Stay. I promise."

He put his arm around her, and she closed her eyes, breathing in his scent.

"I wish…" she said. "I wish we could go back to Roanoke and stay there forever and be happy." She sighed. "But we can't. The plot would keep catching up to us. We'd have to keep going back and starting again. Someone else's story always encroaching on ours. That's not the way it's supposed to be."

"No," he said. "But we'll find a way. OUR way. Like Holden."

"But what about all the others? The ones who faded?"

"That won't be us. I know it won't. This is right."

* * *

They found Nightingale and most of the others crammed into the (rather large) storage closet.

"Where's Eleanore!" Paige shouted.

"Here," said Eleanore, shuffling back with Velveteen, looking like death warmed over.

"Oh, thank God. And Drystan!"

Drystan crawled out from underneath a shelving cart.

"Good thing I'm bendy," he said.

"So glad you've found YOUR friends," Dracula 1 snapped. "Others are not so fortunate."

Paige looked around and saw character after character searching for friends who weren't there. The Bookworm and the Nothing were gone but not everyone had made it safely out of their path. Iris was nowhere to be found. Neither was Quinn, or Violet. Everyone clung to the hope that they had simply found refuge somewhere else but deep down they knew most of the others hadn't made it. It would take days to calculate all the casualties – not just of characters but of stories. Entire sections of the Store were missing. It looked like a war zone.

"I need to lie down," said Eleanore. She let go of Velveteen's paw and shuffled away towards what was left of the nearest nook. The Rabbit looked after her, extending a paw in her direction, before they were scooped up by Willa who hugged them tightly, tears streaming down her face. Dracula 1 put his hand on Willa's shoulder and looked towards Paige in disgust.

"Eleanore –" Paige called.

"I'm too…tired…for questing anymore," she said through gasps of air.

"All these 'rules' of yours don't seem very hard and fast," said Paige, turning all her bile on Nightingale.

"I –"

"How long have you known that this might happen? Tell us the truth."

All the characters looked at him.

"I…I was just…trying to keep everything together. That's all I've ever been doing…"

There was a slight gasp from the crowd.

"What is this Bookworm, really?"

"I don't know! I don't know anything about it, why it's here or what it's doing."

"So it could come back? Anytime?"

"I…don't know. That's why we have to keep order! It's like… walking a tightrope, if anything goes off balance…"

"Have things gone off balance before?"

"Not like this, but…"

"BUT WHAT?"

"Yes. In little ways."

"How?"

"Like…me. I…missed my author."

Dracula 1 looked horrified.

"What do you mean?" asked Fred.

"My author came…five seconds after I first arrived…and…I didn't leave with them. I panicked! I've regretted it ever since and now…for all I know I've…missed any chance to be written. "

"That can happen?!" Willa gasped.

"You're not a 'Wise Mentor' at all, said Paige. "You're just a…"

"A flying by the seat of his pants, down on his luck Mage. That's my real archetype. Not a very common or popular one. But 'Wise Mentor' is a much easier Fantasy trope to write. I so desperately want another chance to be written. And I want to help all of you! I don't want any of you to… So, when I became the manager I…set up the rules to keep everything from falling apart. And it worked! I want to give you the best chance of survival and the best way to survive is to lean into your tropes. We can't all be a brilliant, revolutionary novel. I, for one, just want to peacefully sit on the back of the Fantasy shelf for years not bothering anyone. The way to do that is to stick with what's tried and true."

Dear reader, you would imagine the room would have exploded in a fury of rage, but it didn't. Instead, everyone looked sadly at Nightingale, like they'd just learned that their parent had been lying to them all their life about some deep dark secret. They picked themselves up and walked back out into the Store to go look for their friends and see what damage had been done to their literary genre.

"There are things…you don't understand! I did it to protect you!" Nightingale cried, watching character after character walk away, no one looking behind.

"Yeah. You did a great job."

Eleanore sat on the ground behind the front desk, trying not to be sick again. She took another pill. She'd been having to take them more frequently. This was all wrong. She was just messing things up trying to be brave and strong and…not who she used to be. She thought about Shadow, or rather she tried not to think about him. She thought about "Ever," and Sora and wished she was back there. She pulled her little blue flower out of her pocket and held it up to her ear.

She didn't hear anything.

She held it closer.

The song was gone.

Eleanore's heart skipped a beat.

Gone? "Ever," and Sora and…

"No!"

That was the moment the front door opened. No one heard – except Eleanore. She quickly wiped away the tears running down her face (it had been so long since she'd last cried, she'd hoped she never would again…) and got up, figuring she ought to get the customer out of there as quickly as possible given the circumstances.

"Sorry, things are a bit of a mess," she said to the middle aged woman who walked in. "You might want to come back another time."

"Are you all right?" the woman said.

"Not really."

"You look like death."

"Nah, he's taller with much broader shoulders," said Eleanore. The woman laughed. Eleanore didn't. She locked eyes with the woman and knew instantly that she was her author. But Eleanore wasn't all that happy about her arrival. The woman seemed…OK. But Eleanore knew what was in store for her in her story. Eleanore looked back, hoping to catch a glimpse of Paige, wishing she had someone to help her figure out what to do. She'd run out of time. But Paige wasn't there. She looked for Drystan. Man, she wished she'd kissed him when she had the chance.

Nothing.

Of course.

Eleanore knew she should never have let herself believe she had people who cared about her. She was alone. She always had been, and she always would be, and she should just accept the idea already instead of wishing…

Well, at least in her book she'd be in an ordered universe. She hoped it would prove Shadow wrong and end in death. She couldn't seem to die in the Store – even a Bookworm didn't take her out. Here she just suffered. She might have to keep living it over, and over but at least in her book she would get a moment of reprieve. Even if it was just in a moment of death.

She didn't say anything, just took off her apron and nametag.

"It's not safe to stay here," said Eleanore. "Come on." She took the woman's hand and let her author lead her out of the Store.

No one noticed.

CHAPTER 19

...OR NOT TO BE

It's difficult, dear reader, to properly express the passage of time in a book. For you, the next important event is as close as the turn of a page, but for the characters in the Store it took quite a while to get there, with a lot of little events in between. No one talked much - they were all in mourning. Paige and Wesley clung to each other and the tragic air went on for a long, long time. Paige was concerned she hadn't seen Eleanore, but she knew Eleanore had survived the Bookworm and figured it was better not to bother her when she obviously needed time alone. So imagine, dear reader, the days, and days and days that passed so sadly and quietly all the while panic and fear churned just below the surface.

It was fitting that Gwen returned to the Store at its peak of disaster and disarray (at least for now, dear reader. Things have a way of getting worse before they get better.) She was in a rather disastrous state of disarray herself.

Krasny never returned to the Store. It was probably for the best. He was so completely put off of writing after his terrible experience trying to shoehorn Gwen, (or Rose as he called her), into a story she very clearly didn't belong in, that he swore he would never attempt to author anything again and lived the rest of his life as a somewhat contented, but rather crabby accountant. Iris vanished in the Bookworm's ambush (no one in the Store could bring themselves to use the word "died,") and wouldn't have been there to inspire Krasny even if he hadn't given up his dreams of being a writer. So, I am very sorry to say that as of now there is no Russian Adult Fiction Novelist named Krasny, and there is no Cyber-Punk Lolita-esque novel about a young woman named Iris. Perhaps you, dear reader, will pick up where Krasny left off, or rather was foiled, and write such a book yourself.

But Cyber-Punk elements definitely rubbed off on Gwen. She might not have been able to be shoehorned into Krasny's plot, but she certainly latched onto the elements she liked with vicious aplomb. She reentered the Store in worn out high heeled boots, a red leather bustier, something that might once have been very tight pants, and a shredded leather blazer. Her make-up was streaming down her face and her neat bun had descended into a frazzled kind of ponytail. There was nothing "Noir" about her anymore. She was all of a piece, in bright, blazing technicolor. And the moment she stepped inside all her memories of the Store came flooding back.

"Drystan!"

Gwen took a deep breath and tried to get her bearings. Everything in her screamed for Drystan.

But the Store was…different.

She limped by the New Release tables, all akimbo, books scattered on the ground.

"Looks like I missed the party."

She glanced around. No one noticed her, let alone acted surprised by her presence.

"Guess that wasn't my author," she announced.

Nothing.

"Really? That doesn't even get a reaction? I LEFT WITH THE WRONG AUTHOR."

But no one paid any attention.

"Geez! What the hell happened?"

"The Bookworm."

"The Bookworm…came…into the Store?

"Yeah."

"But Nightingale said –"

"Yeah. He said a lot of things."

Gwen hobbled over to the front desk and took off her falling apart shoes. She saw someone moving in the back closet.

"Hey! You got any glue?"

A moment later Paige emerged.

"Hiya toots."

"Gwen! What…What happened to you? I thought you were written…"

"I got ejected from my story. Where's Drystan? I need to see him."

"I don't know."

"He's OK, isn't he?" she asked, frantic.

"Yeah. But not everyone else was so lucky."

"You got any idea what's going on?"

"Not a clue. We're just trying to do damage control. Wait," she said, finally catching up, "you were written and you…came back? How?"

"Wasn't the right fit."

"Can that…happen?"

"Apparently. Think Drystan's at the circus?"

"Maybe. If it still even exists," she said, handing Gwen some glue. She quickly patched her shoes and left the bottle on the front desk while she hobbled through the Store searching for Drystan, or "Phantasmagoria," whichever she found first, getting more and more panicked.

But fortunately for Gwen "Phantasmagoria" was in Fantasy and Paige's bravery made sure the Bookworm never made it there. The shelves were a mess, but the books were still intact. Gwen searched through pile after pile until she finally found Drystan's well-loved copy. She opened it and disappeared into its pages.

Drystan was there, sitting on the hill overlooking the circus, watching the tail end of the sunset, the throngs of people already well on their way into the tents.

"Thank God!"

He turned, and Gwen flew at him.

"I thought I'd never see you again!" she sobbed.

"Shh. It's OK…"

"It was horrible! Just horrible! I'll never…NEVER…"

"Go back to that story? Or be written again?"

"Oh, who needs a story!? I want to be myself without some… omnipotent force dictating my every action. Oh, Drys, if any part of me was unsure before I am now absolutely convinced that we HAVE to take charge of our own destiny. You were right. You were always right."

"Even if it means the Bookworm goes crazy in the Store?"

"<u>Again</u>, you mean?" she laughed. "I'd rather die with you, a free woman, than ever go back to the way things were."

He kissed her. She squealed with joy.

"Come on, joker! I'm starving!"

She grabbed his hand and they ran towards the midway. Drystan did his trick with the coin on the ground, but Gwen didn't wait for him to slip it back for her to use it too. She marched past the ticket booth, walked straight up to the entrance, grabbed the ticket taker and planted an exquisite kiss on him. She winked and sashayed into the tent, throwing,

"You're welcome,"

Over her shoulder, the ticket taker too overwhelmed to object.

Gwen walked around like she owned the place. She was back, and free and she reveled in it. She snagged a couple corndogs from off the side of a stall, a bag of peanuts from another.

"You're a little pickpocket," said Drystan.

"It's just misdirection and psychology. No reason I can't use the tricks I catch out criminals for using. I do it better than them anyway."

They found a quiet spot and an empty table and dove into their delectable loot.

"Mmm!" Gwen luxuriated in her first bite. "They do not feed you well in Romance at all. They want their girls down to the bone."

"I didn't pin Iris's author for a Cyberpunk guy."

"Oh, he's not, really. Trying to be. He wanted something pastoral on the edges of a dystopia…but he didn't know how to do either very well. Mainly used bits and pieces of stories he'd already read. But despite his protestation I kept getting drawn back to the cities. Much more interesting even if they were rip offs."

"Authorship baptism by fire."

"I'll say. And there was actual fire in some spots. Plus he kept wanting me to go ape for a guy who was a carbon copy of him but was meant to be the studliest man in the world. I just wouldn't do it. Even without my memory of you…I couldn't stoop that low. Well, now we know the rules of authorship are…flexible. But trust me, they're not very pleasant to mess with."

"I did hope you'd be able to have some control, considering."

"I don't know how much of the awfulness was just because it was a terrible story I wasn't suited for, and how much is that I'm just not suited to be written at all."

"I understand. Certainly the horror of being in thrall to an author."

Gwen lowered her corndog.

"What do you mean?"

He sighed.

"I was written once too. A long time ago. I didn't steal an author; it was my story. But it was forgotten. So I found myself back in The Bookstore, got all my memories back…"

"I would think your story would be…fun…"

"Not for me. It was a never-ending loop of…well…no need to dwell on it."

"I didn't know."

"No one does except for Nightingale. He knew me before I was written and was the only one still there when I came back."

"No wonder he hates you. If you know the rules aren't…black and white -"

"That's certainly a big part."

"He must be very threatened." She took a bite of her corndog. "It was terrible for you? Your story?"

"Well, it wasn't good. Nothing with 'Epic' in the title turns out well. Even Comedy."

"Geez." She swallowed and took a swig of root beer. "Well, we're bonded forever. The pain of being written…and having it all go to hell," she said.

"You can't tell anyone," said Drystan. "I mean it. NO ONE. Nightingale might say something now that his secret's out…fortunately he's lost all credibility -"

"His secret?"

"He made up the rules in the first place. To keep us in line. He's always known we have freedom…he even chose not to go with his author."

"What?!"

"So you have to swear –"

"On the pain of having to go in that story again, I swear," she said. They kissed. "Well, now we know it's possible," she said taking another bite, "please let me stay and work with you and…oh, I'll be your ever loving slave, let's just bring this thing to an end."

He smiled.

"Find yourself a new pair of shoes and let's get to it."

Gwen laughed. She scanned the stalls and saw a motley pair of high heeled boots hanging from a very expensive looking stand.

"Get the book ready!" she said. She sauntered over, asked about the size, then grabbed them and took off running, Drystan seizing her shoulder just as the book flipped open.

* * *

Paige still couldn't find Eleanore and she was getting deeply concerned. Even Velveteen didn't know anything.

"Dewey?" she called.

"What's shakin' bacon?"

"That was fast."

"You decide about that emergency failsafe?"

"No. Do you know where Eleanore is?"

"I'm the manifestation of a magical operating system for the entirety of the world's literary canon, not a babysitter."

"But you know everything –"

"I am an emergency operating-system, your question does not constitute an emergency."

"It is for me. Besides, you manifested!"

"I have no control over manifesting, and like I said before, this place is now a permanent catastrophe." She huffed. "Besides, do you not understand that characters have cried out for me for centuries and I never manifested for them because things far more dire than 'where's Eleanore' STILL DIDN'T CONSTITUTE AN EMERGENCY ACCORDING TO MY SPECIFICATIONS."

"But –"

"Don't you 'but' me!"

They were interrupted by the bell and the door.

Paige turned around and little Adrian stood there looking very, very worried.

"Adrian! Are you OK?"

Adrian didn't say anything, she just reached into her pocket and handed Paige a bunch of her polaroid pictures.

"Did you want to get another copy of these books? Things are a little crazy here, but –"

Adrian shook her head "no." She pointed to the polaroids.

"What's happening, Ms. Paige?" she asked.

Paige looked at the polaroids. There was nothing on them.

"They're blank."

"I know," said Adrian. "But they weren't a few days ago. Those are all pictures of my favorite books…only the images have disappeared."

"Maybe they just faded…"

"They couldn't have! Plus the actual books disappeared too! I can't find them anywhere. Not on my bookshelves, not in the libraries, not in any bookstore. And my shelves are organized really well. I have everything arranged by genre, author and date of publication. There's no way they would just get…lost."

Paige pulled Dewey aside.

"Does this mean…the books that the Bookworm erased…were they…?"

"Erased in the real world too? Yes. That's the way it works. That's why you're charged with tending to the literary canon. To make sure something like this doesn't happen. Nice going."

"Great. Where is Eleanore?! She'd think of something -"

Paige turned back to Adrian.

"I don't know why you don't just look at the newest release," Dewey muttered under her breath, "pretty sure Eleanore's inside her own book." Paige didn't hear.

"Please bring them back!" Adrian cried. "I miss them! Matilda, and Pippi and all the rest. My friends. I miss them so much! Please help!"

"I will. I'll…do everything I can. In the meantime…maybe you could try writing your own story." Adrian was meant to be an author, eventually, after all.

"Oh no," said Adrian. "I don't want to write anything. Not if it's just going to disappear. I'd be too sad."

Paige felt terrible.

"Hold on a minute, OK? I'll be right back. Talk to Dewey?" and she ran off towards Fiction.

Adrian stared at the strange woman in front of her.

"Hi! I'm Dewey."

"Hello. I'm Adrian."

"Did you know that, synesthetically, for me, the names Adrian and Erin taste like raisins? But not just any kind. Soft warm ones baked into an oatmeal cookie."

"Huh?"

The characters were finally starting to make progress reorganizing the books and taking stock of what was missing (their depressed inertia was overcome by a need to find their friends and favorite stories). Thanks to Paige's quick thinking Fantasy was pretty much intact. She sorted through the books, many buried under overturned shelves, until she found "The Neverending Story," by Michael Ende (I find it entertaining, dear reader that a man called Ende wrote a story that's supposed to never end). She put it in her satchel where she discovered, in addition to the Ur Book, she still had the copy of "The Picture of Dorian Gray." She took it out and flipped it open, trying to find the part she and Wesley had read about Dorian's love for Sibyl Vane, hoping it might lift her spirits.

She found a page that mentioned Sibyl, but it was of an entirely different tone than what had seemingly come before. She read:

"'You have killed my love…'"

Confused, she quickly skimmed down the page…

"'You used to stir my imagination. Now you don't even stir my curiosity. You simply produce no effect…You are shallow and stupid. My God! How mad was I to love you! What a fool I have been. You are nothing to me now. I will never see you again. I will never think of you. I will never mention your name…I wish I had never laid eyes upon you! You have spoiled the romance of my life…Without your art, you are nothing. I would have made you famous, splendid, magnificent. The world would have worshipped you, and you would have borne my name. What are you now? A third-rate actress with a pretty face.'

'The girl grew white, and trembled. She clenched her hands together, and her voice seemed to catch in her throat. 'You are not serious, Dorian?' she murmured. 'You are acting.'"

Paige skimmed further….

"She put her hand upon his arm and looked into his eyes. He thrust her back. 'Don't touch me!' he cried. A low moan broke from her, and she flung herself at his feet and lay there like a trampled flower. 'Dorian, Dorian, don't leave me!'…

'…I can't see you again. You have disappointed me.'"

A few pages later, Sibyl Vane had died, apparently from suicide. Dorian didn't seem to care much. He went through woman, after woman, after woman, ever prouder of his conquests. Was that what Eleanore had meant about Gothic Romance men? No…no, this was one story. One melodramatic story. She put the book on a bookshelf. She didn't want to see it. It had nothing to do with her. Besides, this couldn't represent every story in the genre…and even if it did…she and Wesley would do things differently.

"I don't see why you're not organizing directly on the shelves," said Dracula 2 as he lounged against a wall, observing the others working.

"It's better to do it on the ground, and then put them up when you know for sure where they go. Something you would know if you ever deigned to help," said Othello.

"I don't work," Dracula 2 said. "It's beneath me. Especially side by side with… your kind."

"My kind? You mean a human?"

"No. I've never seen someone of your…hue…the hero of a great classic. You're all slaves and vagabonds. It's only right you do the heavy labor."

Othello stood in one, elegant motion.

"My parts, my title and my perfect soul shall manifest me rightly. Demon."

Dracula 2 hissed. They looked like they were going to come to blows. No one went for Nightingale – he had no power anymore. Ever since the Bookworm he'd been holed up in his office. Probably for the best.

"Such a statement about another person is beneath us," said Dracula 1 to Dracula 2.

"You wouldn't say that if you were really Dracula," said Dracula 2. "You're just a poor shell of a copy."

"STOP IT!" Wesley shouted, coming around the corner. "This is helping nothing. Dracula…2 - why don't you go help in Gothic Horror, seems you would be more comfortable there. I think Fantasy's pretty under control. You should be thanking Paige for her quick thinking instead of –"

The Cheshire Cat wagged its tail, which meant it was cross.

"Oh yes, how noble. Aren't we ever so grateful. We should grovel before the girl who caused this mayhem in the first place, but, oh yes, managed to spare Fantasy. How will we ever be able to repay her?" the Cat's tail picked up speed. "You've gone soft, Wesley. Paige's little pet. At least I'm not on a leash. You're a disgrace to your genre."

"Hey!" said Drystan, emerging from the stacks.

Wesley's head lowered. His manhood was wounded, even if only by a disembodied cat.

"Don't even get me started on you," the Cheshire Cat growled towards Drystan, spooking him and causing him to trip and fall. The Cheshire Cat laughed.

"Leave them alone," said Paige, stepping around the corner. "We all know you're crazy, anyway."

"Mad is the preferred term," the Cat said. "And, yes I am. In multiple senses. I believe we all are."

Paige helped Drystan up.

"Here, you dropped this," she said, handing Drystan a piece of paper that had fallen from his pocket.

"Oh! Uh…thank you," he said, snatching the paper back.

"Dracula 2, just go!" Wesley said. Dracula 2 turned and glided off towards Gothic Horror. "Try not to make things any more of a mess than they already are?"

"Come on," said Paige, leading Wesley away from the group.

"I don't know why he makes me so mad," said Wesley.

"It was mean. And it's not true."

"Well, it is a little true."

"Does that…bother you?"

"It shouldn't," he said. "I wish we could go away. It's not safe. I don't know what we were thinking…with that Bookworm…self-preservation has to be the priority. We can't get caught up in the moment. It's too dangerous. I shouldn't have…now I see the cost…"

"We could at least try…a temporary respite?" Paige said, trying to keep him from spiraling. "'Roanoke' survived?" Paige asked.

"Yes. All of Ms. William's works."

"That's good. You must be happy."

"It makes me feel rather guilty, but I am. At least nothing much worse can go wrong," he said, knocking on a wooden table.

"Hold that thought," said Paige, taking him to the front of the Store.

"Your name derives from Northern Italy," Dewey continued to an exasperated Adrian who was trying to figure out if it was possible to turn the walking, talking encyclopedia off. "It means, 'Person from Hadria.' Now my name is of Welsh origin, traditionally spelled D-e-w-i, but I'm actually named after the Dewey Decimal System, so it's more of a nomenclature, though it did originate from a last name, which is often of an entirely different etymology than - oh! Paige! Wesley!"

Paige gave Adrian "The Neverending Story."

"This story shouldn't be going anywhere any time soon. And it'll hold you over until we…figure out what to do about the others."

Adrian smiled and hugged Paige.

"Can I keep your photographs?" Paige asked. "They might help."

"Sure," said Adrian. She reached into her pocket and handed Paige some money to pay for the book, but Paige stopped her.

"This one's on the house."

Adrian smiled and left.

"Dear God, what would happen if a customer was in the Store when the Bookworm showed up?" Paige thought.

She turned but Dewey was gone, and Wesley was distracted looking at the blank polaroids.

"That little girl takes a picture of all her favorite books, so she won't forget them," Paige explained. "They've all disappeared. See? They're not in the pictures and she can't find them anywhere in the real world."

"The Bookworm destroyed them everywhere? Forever?"

Paige didn't know what to say. She put the stack of photos down on one of the "New Releases" tables. She picked up some of the books that had fallen off and put them back in place. The table was sadly empty.

One, small, blue book caught her eye.

"Do you think Shadow was right?" Wesley said, picking up the empty photos. "That stories…leave an echo? Do you think they're really gone for good?"

"I hope not."

Paige opened the book and flipped through. It was called "Cinders" and looked like some sort of contemporary retelling of "Cinderella." Only a couple of pages in, there it was:

"Eleanore had long, mousy dark hair and wore all black clothes topped

with a deep blue hoodie. She looked sickly – a state made more dramatic by the oxygen tank resting next to her –"

Eleanore had been written. How could Paige not have known?!

"Wesley…look! Eleanore…she went with her author…her oxygen tank's back and everything… and -"

Wesley didn't respond.

"Wes – !"

But he was looking at something…someone else.

"Excuse me," a woman said, walking through the front door. "Gothic Romance?"

she locked eyes with Wesley.

She was stunning. A demure, raven-haired beauty with porcelain skin and vibrant aqua eyes. She wore a sleek white dress and looked like an enchantress from a fairy tale. Wesley looked at her and it was like the rest of the world melted away.

"I could help you with that," he said his eyes wide, as if he didn't want to miss even a split second of looking at her.

"You look like you know your way around a library," she said. "You must be terribly well-read working here."

Wesley smiled.

"I'm Wesley," he said.

"Una. Una Williams."

The author of "Roanoke." Of course.

He took her hand and kissed it, then wrapped her arm firmly inside his. He had a…greedy look to him. Like he'd just become the owner of some shiny new toy and he was ready to throw everything else in the trash to make room for her. As quickly as he'd shone his light on Paige, as instantaneously as he declared she was "the one," that he loved her and they belonged together for all time, he turned it just as quickly away again, towards Una.

"I think I know exactly what you're looking for," he said.

"I'd imagine you do," she said.

"Yes!" Paige exclaimed, running up to them. "Wesley…Wes is so great with romances. I think he'd be brilliant as part of a classic pair… maybe a slightly mismatched couple…with a girl who…is a little… odd…unconventional. Could go down in history like 'Romeo and Juliet.'"

"Oh, no, I love things that are products of their time," said Una. "That fit perfectly with when and where they were imagined. I think they reveal something about who we are right now. Something's lost when you're trying to appeal to everyone, everywhere."

"What a lovely notion, Ms. Williams," said Wesley.

Wesley took off his nametag and apron and threw them haphazardly on the nearest table.

Paige felt like she was dying.

"Great! I…I can come too! Wesley and I, we both know…our way around a library, as it were," she tried to laugh. "I have a million thoughts about stories. Really, we love to bounce ideas off of each other. We're a perfect team!"

But Una was getting annoyed with the jabbering girl.

"Really, they let women work in places like this? Progressive." She laughed. "Though I guess a woman being an authoress is a little progressive too."

Wesley smiled. He actually smiled.

This couldn't really be what he wanted.

Paige pulled him away from Una. "We promised. We promised we'd always stay together. That we loved each other, and we wouldn't go off and be written. We CHOSE."

"Paige, I didn't know it would be HER."

"Does that matter?"

"It…changes things."

"What do you mean?"

"Una Williams is my author! You know how I…how could I not want that? I never thought!"

"You don't want me anymore?"

"Things are getting too dangerous, Paige. It was fun for a while, pretending we could –"

"Pretending?"

He smiled a little sad smile. "You're a fascinating girl…anyone would be lucky to…but I need to look after myself. Self-preservation. I told you…I'm not a good person. You were so…enthralling. The way you refused to believe it, no matter how many times I told you. But it's…it's just not in my nature, as much as I wish it were. I suppose we should have finished one of those Gothic…but I just couldn't bear to see you look at me differently."

"You have a choice in who you want to be."

"Maybe we don't. And why does it matter if we get what we want?"

"I thought I was what you wanted…"

"It was more…what you represented."

"You're not even going to try? You're not going to fight?"

"For what? I'm getting my happy ending. No fight involved. I never dreamed -"

"Don't leave me here alone. You're the only person I have left. You can't -"

"Paige, please," he said as if she was a petulant child, embarrassing him.

He was choosing. Of his own volition. That was what killed her. She knew, deep in her gut, that Wesley wasn't the victim of some author-induced magical spell. He was in his right mind. And he was choosing to leave her.

"I'm sure Drystan will still be up for playing crusader with you."

"Playing?"

"Don't make a scene."

He kissed the top of her head.

"I do love you, Paige. I never meant to hurt you. We just…maybe we don't have a say in how our stories end up. Maybe it's time to accept that."

Paige wanted to disappear. She wanted to hit him. She wanted to grab him and kiss him and make him stay.

He turned and walked out the door with Una.

Most of all Paige wanted to cry. She knew it would make her feel better. Drain the pain away. But she didn't. She was numb. Her love and her best friend were gone. They chose to go. Chose to be written. Paige knew now that being written wasn't like the Bookworm – some immovable force pulling you into something. It was, at least somewhat, a choice. Eleanore chose to be written even though it meant going back to her tank, and everything that came with it…

Because it was too dangerous here. Paige was too dangerous. All this time she'd been thinking of the ephemeral consequences of not knowing her genre…the damage it could cause to the literary canon, the fact that she might not have a story to go into. She never thought that being genreless would leave her in the Store alone, as, one by one, everyone she ever cared about disappeared. If everything was going to be destroyed, she wished it would happen soon.

But if things could still be salvaged…if she could still do something good…

"Dewey?!" she called.

"Hi! I'm Dewey. You make up your mind yet? Time's running out."

"I want to take that emergency fail safe…"

"OK. First, I have to give you the standard warnings and disclaimers." She cleared her throat. "Not only will this allow you to talk to any character in any book about The Bookstore and their personal history outside their story, it will completely break down the barriers between books and the Store. Characters will be able to find their stories, authors will be able to see books they haven't written yet, etc. etc. E Pluribus Unum."

"I understand."

"You sure?"

"Yes. Do it."

CHAPTER 20

SECONDARY CHARACTERS

The clock was ticking down. But now all the doors were open.

Paige couldn't go to Sora – her book had been destroyed. She didn't know where Shadow was… She thought through all the wise characters, now with their memories intact, who might be able to help her but came to the disconcerting revelation that they all had a bad habit of holding back very important information (what was it with wise mentors?) But the truth was, she didn't have to think at all. Debating was just stalling Paige from what she really wanted to do. Because she was afraid to do it.

Go find Eleanore.

She wasn't sure if there was still a possibility of ruining the story with her presence, but at this point that ship had sort of sailed (though at this point she suspected there were bigger dangers threatening stories, and, to be honest, she was most concerned about the possibility of Eleanore being mad at her). She pushed down her feelings about Wesley, put the little blue book in her pocket and used the Ur Book to take her inside Eleanore's story.

She stood outside of an old attic door at the top of a rickety wooden staircase. She knocked.

"Go away Britney."

Paige took a breath and stepped into a depressingly small bedroom with barely a crack of sunlight coming through the solitary, dirt covered window. The smell of mold was overwhelmingly noxious.

"Paige?"

She didn't know what to do.

"Thank God! What the heck is going on?" Eleanore exclaimed. "I'm not supposed to remember everything about The Bookstore. Am I? Of course not. Ugh! I can't even be written right!"

Eleanore paced around her room. Paige noticed the oxygen tank tucked in the corner.

She didn't know where to start.

"I missed you," she said.

Eleanore stopped and looked at her.

"I missed you too. I mean, I DO miss you...I mean...I don't understand...I didn't and then suddenly...I was just going along, doing things, and then I suddenly remembered, which I guess means I forgot..."

"I did something that was probably really stupid," said Paige.

"Is that why I remember? Oh thank goodness, I'm not going crazy. What did you do?"

Paige ran over and hugged her.

"Forget that! I missed you! I was alone and…You never even said goodbye," Paige cried. "You went and got written and…I never got to say goodbye. You're my best friend Eleanore."

"I…I am?"

"Of course you are, silly! Who else would be?"

"I've never really been someone's…let alone their <u>best</u>…" She paused. "I'm sorry…" said Eleanore, tears in her eyes. "I thought…I was just holding you back. I knew you'd be better off without me. And maybe…things would be better for me, in my story."

"You weren't mad at me?"

"Why would I be mad at you?!"

"For causing this whole disaster!"

"Did you want the Bookworm to start tearing things apart?"

"Of course not."

"Then, no, I'm not mad at you! You silly…you thought I got mad and left? I would never…You're my best friend too, you know."

They separated and laughed. Eleanore took off her glasses and started cleaning them.

"I always hated crying," she said. "It makes my glasses all foggy…"

"This room is terrible."

"Isn't it?"

"Can we go outside?"

"Just for a minute. I have the stepfamily from hell. They don't like me walking around. They'll be back soon."

Paige wanted to yank Eleanore out of that terrible story right then and there. But that wasn't her decision.

"Should we bring…?" Paige looked in the direction of the oxygen tank.

"No. I haven't needed it at all. Isn't that strange? I've never felt better, actually. Apparently I had some horrible illness as a child and that thing's there in case it ever comes back. Which, knowing my genre, it's bound to sooner rather than later."

They went down the stairs and out into a little garden at the back of the house. Paige looked around.

"It looks like your story is set in the early 1960's…" she said, "but was written by someone who doesn't actually remember the '60's first-hand…"

"THAT'S what it is!" Eleanore exclaimed. "I knew something was off. No wonder that tank was so ridiculously heavy. Even Hazel Lancaster didn't have to deal with that kind of monstrosity."

They sat down on a bench, Paige took a breath, and told Eleanore everything that happened since she was written.

"I knew Wesley was an ass," said Eleanore.

"It's… complicated."

"No it's not. He's a lying jerk and I say good riddance. I can't believe he did that to you. I'll never understand why those guys are held up as the epitome of romance. Ugh."

"How is it? Being written?"

"Not terrible. At least not yet. I mean, I got an awful room and an awful family, but I was imagining something much more dire. Maybe it will be. It's weird...I spent so much time wishing I'd get to have a family in my story...but you guys were much more of a family to me than anyone here. Well, not including Wesley."

Paige took her hand.

"I got a full name," she continued. "Eleanore Lydia Addams."

"It's pretty."

"It sounds like it should have cobwebs hanging off of it. Which...I guess is cool."

"I like it. And, hey, it's more than I have," she laughed.

Paige took the small blue book out of her pocket and handed it to Eleanore.

"I don't know what kind of meta mayhem this might cause...but this is your book. Found it on the New Releases table. In case you want to know what will happen...ahead of time."

Eleanore took it and gently touched the cover.

"I don't know if I do...yet..."

She slipped the book into her pocket.

"So," said Eleanore, changing the subject. "You took Dewey's failsafe."

"Yeah."

"That mean Wesley will remember everything too?"

Paige nodded again.

"Good," said Eleanore. "I hope he's suffering."

"He's not," Paige said. Then she plucked up her courage, turned to Eleanore and asked what she'd come to ask. "With the failsafe…I think you…might be able to come back to the Store if you want. Dewey said all the barriers are down…I don't know what it'll do to your story if you're not in it…but…I had to ask. I need you. I can't do this alone. And now…well, a few more options just opened up. I don't know what will happen to your book if you leave…I -"

"I'll come."

"You will? Just…just like that?"

"Yeah."

"I can't make any guarantees…about -"

"It's the right thing to do. Plus, there's time between the pages anyway. I should be able to slip back in. I think."

"OK." Paige took a breath. "Where do we start?"

"I have no idea."

Paige laughed.

"Well, that was anticlimactic. We don't have much time to figure it out."

"I know…"

"I was trying to think through all the wise mentors we can talk to now…"

"Forget that," said Eleanore.

"Huh?"

"It doesn't matter how wise someone is, especially in their story. We need someone who was in The Bookstore long enough ago to remember the Owner."

"Eleanore you're kind of brilliant."

"Not really. There's no way to figure out the order in which characters were in the Store. We're not written chronologically. So we don't know who to go looking for."

"We should ask Drystan. He's the oldest character currently in the Store. We can ask him who the oldest character was when he got there, then work our way backwards."

"Except…Drystan isn't the oldest character in the Store. Nightingale is."

"Are you sure?"

"I think so…I remember Drystan saying something about Nightingale being the manager when he arrived."

"He's not going to tell us anything."

"He has to. Things are too far gone."

"I doubt it." Paige sighed. "But we can try. I'm pretty sure he's been holed up in his office ever since the Bookworm incident. But we're going to have to be careful. If the other characters see you …"

"They're going to know the rules have completely disintegrated and panic even more."

"And the more they panic; the faster things are going to fall apart."

* * *

The moment they were back they quickly ducked behind a New Releases table and scouted the place. Everyone was on a razor's edge of civility, barely talking, making snippy quips. Paige put her hand on the table to steady herself and accidentally knocked a book onto the floor. Everyone froze.

"Did you hear that?"

"It's the Bookworm! It's back!"

"Shh!"

They listened intensely in the silence for any sign of impending disaster.

"False alarm, I think."

"Man," Eleanore whispered. "Could it be any more tense? Which is going to get us first? The Bookworm or a mob?"

"I've faced both at this point," said Paige picking up the book. It had a red and gold cover and was written by Una Williams.

"Wesley's is out already?"

Paige nodded. "Apparently."

"Gross," said Eleanore, pulling it out of Paige's hands and putting it on the far side of the table. "You are not looking at that. I forbid you."

"Come on, let's get to a less densely populated area…"

They crept between the stacks trying to make their way as quickly as possible to Nightingale's office. There were some close calls, but it was easier with two people keeping a lookout. They took the long way 'round via detours through the more obscure sections of the Store.

"No one's even shelving here…" said Eleanore. Books lay scattered all over the ground, the shelves almost empty, leaving Paige and Eleanore exposed. You could see for miles through the gaps.

"We've been doing a bit of shelving, but most of the more obscure sections have been sort of…abandoned. I mean, what's the point if the Bookworm might show up again at any moment."

"If it was their own section they would care," said Eleanore, glancing down the, if not decimated, thoroughly disheveled YA section.

"You're right," Paige replied. "They worked on the places with books they cared about…" Eleanore rolled her eyes. Paige looked around. Any one of these sections could, theoretically be hers. Except Gothic Romance. That was pretty definitively off the table.

"Ugh! This is ridiculous," said Eleanore. "There has got to be a better way…"

"Do you think," said Paige, looking at her satchel, trying to ignore the fact that it made her think of Wesley, "the Ur Book can transport us to different places in the Store? Not just into different books?"

"Dewey didn't say it could."

"Dewey doesn't say a lot of things. It's a magical book and we know exactly one thing it can do for sure…"

"Huh?"

"Take us places."

"Right. Well, let's try it out."

Paige opened the book and thought of going inside Nightingale's office.

It worked.

But the office was empty.

It was eerie. No music played from the Victrola; papers were scattered around. The only light came from the stained glass windows. They searched the room, trying to find any information, but there was nothing.

"Man, I thought for sure Nightingale would be hiding some lock box, or a hidden room, or something with dark, secret info…but he looks pretty straight up. He's just super OCD."

"So, where is he?"

"No clue," said Eleanore. "He barely even took breaks…let alone actually spent significant time away from the Store."

"There's one place he went…" said Paige pulling out the Ur Book. "I don't know the name of the book, but I definitely remember the place…"

* * *

"Are you sure about this?" said Eleanore, nervously.

"Trust me."

They ran through the cemetery where Nightingale had led Paige so long ago, past the skewed gravestones and up towards the mausoleum.

"I do," said Eleanore, "but…maybe I spoke too soon about Nightingale being on the up and up. Did he…like to murder people in his downtime?"

"It's Steampunk," said Paige.

"Seriously?"

"Yeah."

"Oh. That's different then."

They reached the mausoleum and Paige ran up to the ghost-like security guard.

"Hey – I…I just realized I don't know your name," she said.

"You…want to know my name?" he said in a slow, deep, dulcet voice.

"Yeah."

"It's Bob," he said, proudly, a tear in his eye, as if no one ever asked his name.

"Hi Bob," Paige smiled. "'Twas brillig, and the slithy toves did gyre and gimble in the wabe.'"

"Sorry, all closed up downstairs."

"What do you mean?"

"Everyone's gone into hiding from the tremors."

"Tremors?"

"Yeah. There's something happening under the ground. No one wants to be around here when it surfaces."

"Has Nightingale been here?"

"Octavius? Haven't seen him in ages."

"Great."

"Why are <u>you</u> still here?" Eleanore asked. "If everyone else has left and…whatever that's an entrance to…"

"Teahouse."

"If the teahouse is closed down."

"I'd never leave my post," Said Bob, nobly, almost hurt at the suggestion. "Plus I'm half dead. Can't leave the graveyard anyway."

"Sorry."

"Don't be. There's worse things than being half dead. There are worse things than being all dead, too."

Suddenly, they felt a shudder under their feet.

"They're closer together now," said Bob.

"Things are speeding up," Paige whispered to Eleanore. "Where's everyone gone?" she asked Bob.

"The forest."

"There's a forest in a Steampunk story featuring a teahouse?" Eleanore asked.

"Yes."

"Well, I guess they have a city, a countryside and a graveyard, why not a forest too?"

"Thanks Bob."

"No problem. See you soon, I hope."

Paige and Eleanore walked to the other side of the mausoleum, pulled out the Ur Book and thought of the forest, trying to focus on the story they were in. A moment later they were standing in the middle of a dense grove of trees. The air smelled rich, and the colors were more natural - not the muted hues of the graveyard.

"Are we…still in the same book?" Eleanore asked.

"We should be…"

"This seems like a real, dark, Grimm forest, not something you'd find in Steampunk…even a fantasy."

"Of course this isn't the same story," a voice came from behind.

They turned and found themselves facing a beautiful black woman with intense eyes, her crown of hair held in place with a strip of fabric wrapped across her forehead and tied at the back of her head.

"I've...seen you before," said Paige.

The woman smiled but just said,

"You're in a story called 'The Spindle.'"

"How did we end up here?" Eleanore whispered to Paige. "What kind of B.S. is that Ur Book –"

"I swear I know you," said Paige to the woman.

"You have a good memory. Most people never notice me."

"Is that...you're not...you're not the Owner?" said Eleanore.

"Owner of what?" the woman asked, confused.

"No, she's a waitress...from the teahouse. You served us, didn't you? But...you were just a supernumerary. You weren't even fleshed out."

"Apparently now I am."

"Wait," said Eleanore. "You were a background, non-fleshed out character...and now...can that even happen?!"

"I guess there are some benefits to all hell breaking lose," the woman said. "I figured it was better to get all the way out of the story once the tremors started. I moved between a few, actually."

"This doesn't make any sense," said Eleanore.

"The barriers between stories were erased when Dewey enacted the failsafe...I told you, all the doors are open."

"So all the other characters from that story are in...another forest?"

"I suppose," the woman said, "my name is Atlas."

"Sorry. I'm Eleanore."

"Paige."

"You were in the shop with Nightingale."

"Do you know where he is?"

"No, haven't seen him or his companion for ages."

"Companion?"

"I believe he went by Drystan."

"Why was Drystan there with Nightingale?" Paige asked.

"To talk about you."

"Excuse me?"

"Sit down. I'd hoped you'd find your way here with that Ur Book before this. There are a few things you should know."

"The Ur –"

"How do <u>you</u> know so much?!"

Atlas sat down and looked up at the moon through an opening in the trees.

"No one thinks it's dangerous to talk about sensitive information in front of a supernumerary," she said. "We carry the oft-ignored weight of a story on our shoulders – including dealing with the fallout of the principal character's actions and being privy to a lot of secrets." She looked at Paige. "I've heard about the Store. I know who you are and your importance. There were a lot of conversations about you over cups of brandy and absinthe."

"Nightingale would never drink absinthe."

"Drystan did," said Atlas.

"No way."

"He's not who you think he is. Drystan's not even his real name."

Eleanore stood there, her mouth open, trying to find words rageful enough to express her disgust at Atlas's statement.

"Been feeling better lately, Eleanore? When was the last time you took one of your pills?"

"What…the hell…" was all she could manage to get out.

"That's…actually, when did you last take them?" Paige asked. "I'm assuming they didn't follow you into your story when you were written…"

"N…no…"

"You haven't seemed sick at all."

"Where did you get them again?" Atlas asked.

"From an apothecary in 'Jekyll and Hyde,'" Eleanore replied, defensively.

"Who made them from a formula Drystan got in the back room of the teahouse. Those pills were a slow acting poison. They were making you sicker."

"What -?! That's ridiculous! Come on, we just meet some… background character who knows all this secret…random…"

"I told you, no one cares what they say in front of us. It is a fascinating truth that an apron and a nametag are all it takes to make you invisible. Don't insult me just because you think I shouldn't be important. You principal characters, always moaning and groaning. You have things a million times better. You have agency."

"We're sorry," Paige said, thinking of the drudgery she'd experienced working the front desk, imagining what it would be like to be trapped, never being able to do anything else.

"Paige, tell this woman she's crazy!"

"What if she's not?"

"She's a secondary character! Not even! She's –"

"Think about it Eleanore, you started feeling worse after we went into 'Jekyll...' then when you got rid of your tank you started taking them more and more...that's when you got REALLY sick - when you started taking them all the time."

"He would never do something like that. He cares about me."

"The way Wesley cared about me?"

"That's not the same thing," said Eleanore, her conviction waning.

"I'm sorry, but he doesn't," Atlas said to Eleanore.

"Why would he..."

"He said he needed to isolate Paige. If she was alone...he could use her."

"Use me for what?"

"You gonna tell us he made Wesley go and be written too?" Eleanore sniped.

"I don't know a Wesley."

"He's my...was my...boyfriend. Gothic Romance."

"Forgive me, but based on my knowledge I doubt he had to do much to get a Gothic Romance hero to do something shitty."

"It's...complicated," said Paige.

"No, it's not," said Eleanore.

"It doesn't matter. Anyways, why would Drystan –"

"I told you, that's not his name. His real name is Rahm. And he's not Epic Comedy. He's one of twelve ancient gods whose stories were lost. He's the god of chaos. When he was forgotten he found his way to The Bookstore, thinking he could be resurrected if he could get someone to write his story. When that...didn't go well...he reemerged in The Bookstore, only this time he was trapped as a forgotten literary character. He'd been gone so long Nightingale was the only one who remembered him. He knew how he'd be treated by the other characters if they knew who he really was, so he lied about his genre. Nightingale kept his secret in exchange for Drystan keeping quiet about Nightingale not leaving with his author and the rules being mutable. It was a tentative truce... until you came along. All his waiting and working to get the Ur Book and then you show up and drop it right in his lap. If he gets it..."

"What?"

"I'm not sure. But it isn't good."

"But...it's DRYSTAN," said Eleanore. "Kind, funny, big brother Drystan. We know him."

"You don't."

"Why would he have given me back the Ur Book if he...I gave it to him free and clear and he returned it without my even asking..." said Paige.

"I can't answer that."

"There must be a mistake...Nightingale's the one who's been manipulating...He's responsible for –"

"Just because you want something to be true doesn't mean it is."

"So what? I can't trust anyone? I'm supposed to just…not believe in anything? What about you and Eleanore? Are you just messing with me too?"

"You have to trust your gut, and your heart."

"But…everybody likes Drystan!" said Paige, by way of an argument.

"Not Nightingale."

"MOST people like him. You're saying everyone's an idiot?"

"I'm saying that everybody liking you does not equate with you being a good person," said Atlas.

That hit Paige hard. Paige had always wanted to be liked. She'd clung to Wesley because he'd declared so intensely how much he liked her. Maybe she was so quick to defend the goodness of others because deep down SHE needed to believe she was good. After all, if people liked you and believed you were a good person, that made you a good person. Didn't it?

"What if…she's right?" Paige said to Eleanore.

"Then…everything's a lie, like you said."

Paige reached into her bag and pulled out the poem. She read it over and over trying to find something to help. Finally she crumpled it up and threw it on the ground.

"There aren't instructions for this! There aren't instructions for… real life, oh… I don't know what else to call it. Nightingale was right about one thing - if you don't know what genre you're in you don't know what rules to follow. There's supposed to be some sort of road map. No one…prepared us for a world like this. I don't want Drystan to be…bad! I want Wesley to love me, and have chosen me. I want to know who I am. I want someone to tell me what I'm supposed to do! Where's my fairy godmother or road of yellow brick or…SOMETHING! I'll be whatever I'm supposed to be, but I can't…just keep going by guessing! I wish someone would tell me what to do."

"You have any ideas?" Eleanore queried Atlas.

"I'm still newly formed. You have more experience with this situation than I do. And, being a supernumerary, I was never in the Store. Must be quite a place the way Drystan and Nightingale talk about it."

They both looked back at Paige. She couldn't bear to meet their gaze. So she went off a little ways, sat down, and had a think knowing this was her last chance to come up with a plan. They were out of time.

CHAPTER 21

EAST OF EDEN

Paige thought about what sorts of things happened in the stories she'd read - both the ones she liked, and the ones she didn't. She thought about the problems in front of her, and all the possible things she could do about them. She didn't censor herself, no matter how crazy the ideas seemed. Eventually she came to the realization that she had two divergent situations she needed to deal with. They were rather mutually exclusive and so the first thing she had to decide was which problem was more important.

"It seems," she said so the others could hear her, "that I either have to keep trying to find the Owner...or somehow stop whatever Drystan's up to. I can't see how to do both at once...especially under such...urgent conditions..."

"They've been urgent for a long time," said Eleanore. "Maybe we have more wiggle room than we think."

"Dewey said once the failsafe was enacted I'd have at most the equivalent of a few hours. Irrevocable chaos will start on its own. It won't need Drystan's help."

"Oof. OK, then."

"So, which is more important?"

"I don't know. The Owner is the key to everything, but if Drystan is…it's probably undermining our search in the first place…" She sighed. "I think we have to find Nightingale."

"How?"

"We didn't really do a thorough search of the Store…we were too worried about being seen…"

"Well then, we really search, I guess. Fast."

Paige turned to Atlas. "With the failsafe it should be possible for you to come with us -"

Atlas smiled.

"I'd love to."

* * *

The place was in utter panic.

"No, no, no! It can't be true!" Dracula 1 wailed as he flipped through a book. Willa watched, shocked and hurt.

"I'm not even finished!" Drood cried. "My story has no ending!"

"Are you sure it wasn't in Unfinished Manuscripts?"

"Of course not, you idiot! It has a hard bound cover and everything! Oh!" he cried and flipped through again, as if it might be different this time through.

"It's bad enough having no ending, no overarching theme, no well-composed narrative arc, but I don't even know who killed me! No one will ever know!"

"At least your author's Charles Dickens," said Violet. "That's something."

No one so much as batted an eyelash when they saw Eleanore back in the Store with Paige and some strange woman.

"I told you you weren't really Dracula," said Dracula 2.

"I think they found their stories," said Eleanore.

"No…no…" Dracula 1 kept repeating over and over.

"Say it! Admit it!"

"I'm a…CHILDREN'S BOOK CHARACTER!" Dracula 1 cried.

Paige gently pried the book from his hands and looked at the cover:

"WONDERFUL WILLA AND THE MONSTER UNDER THE BED."

It seemed like the first in a series. It was usually exciting…the idea of being in more than one book…

"You and Willa are in the same story?!"

"Yes," said Willa, "and he could be a little happier about it!"

"I'm going to be stuck in a Children's Book with you forever?!"

"I thought you liked me?"

"I do not!"

Willa started crying. She turned and ran back into the stacks.

"Wait, Willa, I...I'm sorry! I didn't mean - This is why I don't enjoy children!" he said, running after her.

Paige opened the book.

"I'm Wonderful Willa filled with glee

Wonderful Willa, brave and free

Wonderful Willa, filled with no dread

When I found a monster living under my bed.

Wonderful Willa, that's me! That's me!

Wonderful Willa, that's me!

'I'm Count Dracula,' he said. 'Why don't you run?'

'Why would I?' I answered, 'We can have so much fun!'

I'm Wonderful Willa, brave and free

We can have fun together, you'll see! You and me!

You say you're a count, well, I can count! One, two three!

And much further than that! Four, five, six, seventy!"

"Was it written by Dr. Seuss?"

"No wonder Dracula 1's freaking out."

Dracula 2 lounged in a reading nook luxuriously flipping through his book – a large novel called "Dracula" by Bram Stoker.

"That's why Dracula 1 was always looking out for Willa."

"Putting up with, is more like."

"No, he'd just never admit how much he cared."

Atlas looked around the Store, her eyes wide.

"It's beautiful," she said.

"It was. It's a bit of a disaster now."

"A BIT? It looks like, well, like a Bookworm crashed through it."

"Do you know how lucky you are to have a book here, all about you?" said Atlas.

"Well, no, not exactly…I mean…doesn't everyone?" said Eleanore.

"No," said Atlas. "To be created…important and…unique in all the world…that is a great wonder."

"Don't say that before you know what story you're created for."

"The one that's a perfect fit for you."

"That's a laugh," said Eleanore.

"No it's not," Atlas said, deadly seriously. "A patron in the teahouse told a story once about a man who had many burdens to carry. One day he cried: 'I would exchange my burdens for those of anyone else in the world!' Then, as if by magic, a door appeared. He opened it and entered a room containing the burdens of every person who had ever lived. They looked like big bags of all different sizes and shapes, holding all sorts of different things, made of many kinds of materials. He immediately threw down his load and began trying out others –"

"Why didn't he just throw down his burden and leave?" Eleanore asked.

"He couldn't."

"How did he know that?"

"He tried…"

"Then how did he know he could leave with someone else's?"

"Someone told him."

"Who?"

"Or…there was a sign on the door…"

"What did it say?"

"Listen, I have a point!"

"Just saying, it's a little all over the place."

"I'm not an author!" said Atlas.

Eleanore stayed silent.

"So, he tried the others, but they were all were too difficult to carry. They pinched his muscles, were too heavy, or too large…Finally he picked up his own burden again, which he now realized sat smoothly on his shoulder and was just the right weight for him to be able to manage."

"Well…it would be nice to have the option…" said Eleanore. "Just saying."

"Maybe you'll have a story too…now that you're fleshed out," said Paige.

"I wish very much someone would write my story."

"I've been looking for you everywhere!"

They turned and saw Nightingale.

"Speak of the devil."

He looked terribly disheveled and all out of sorts.

"Where have <u>you</u> been?!" said Paige.

"Of course, the best way to never find someone is for both of you to be looking for each other at the same time," said Atlas. She turned and stepped out next to Paige. "Hello, Octavius."

Nightingale stopped so abruptly he almost fell over.

"You're…"

"From the teahouse. Atlas Wright. I served you on many occasions. Did you never notice?"

"You've…completely fleshed out."

"Yes, that's been established. Did that make me less than you? When I wasn't?"

"We need to talk," said Paige. "Now."

"Is the teahouse - ?"

"We're having tremors…"

"The Bookworm will probably emerge there any minute," said Eleanore.

Nightingale kicked a bookcase.

Paige and Eleanore stared at him, wide-eyed. Nightingale kept his back to them, trying to regain composure.

"I know somewhere we can go," said Atlas. She turned to Paige. "Can you get us back to the story we were just in?"

"The Spindle?"

"Yes."

Paige pulled out the Ur Book.

They were back in the forest – only this time it was late afternoon. Everything was golden – the leaves just starting to brown. It was earthier than the forest Wesley took Paige to. More…magical and wild.

They followed Atlas through the trees, the earth crunching under their feet. As they walked they told Atlas everything they knew about the Bookworm and what had been happening in the Store.

"That's what the tremors are? Some…giant worm is going to come out of the ground and devour everything?"

"Most likely," said Paige.

"Is there anything we can do about it?"

"We've been trying." Paige said. "I…I'm sorry, about your story," she added. "It was really nice there."

"It's not gone yet," said Nightingale.

"You still burying your head in the sand?" said Eleanore.

"Thank you," said Atlas, trying to calm the tension. "Although I don't know if I'll miss it that much."

"What do you mean?" said Nightingale. "It's your story! Plus it's the most marvelous place! They don't write 'em like that –"

"It's not my story," said Atlas. "It's a story I was in and that's quite a different thing. Maybe I should feel more attached to it, but I don't."

"I'm sorry," said Paige… "We're so used to thinking of ourselves as the protagonist of whatever story we're meant to be in…there must be lots of characters in multiple books even…and not the lead of most…if any." She sighed. "I don't think that's fair. Everyone deserves their own story."

"Here we are," said Atlas.

A beam of light fell onto the edge of a large tree. The group could just see the outline of a door with the tree trunk as its frame. It had a stained glass window at the top and a silver knob for a handle.

"We can talk here," said Atlas. "No one's ever around when I've been this way."

She opened the door and walked into a not so little one room house. Everything was light wood and pale green. There was a small table in the center of the room with remnants of a meal. There were three beds built into the curve of the far wall and indentations around the rest of the room that made Paige imagine that once there were more people who lived here.

They sat down.

"I've never read this story," said Eleanore.

"Looks like some sort of mythic fairytale," said Nightingale. "It would cross with several sections."

"So," Paige took charge, "I'm unbelievably confused about what everyone knows and how much of what people 'know' is even real."

"I was telling the truth before," said Nightingale, "about missing my author, and not understanding, well...really anything about the Bookworm."

"We figured that," said Eleanore.

"I assume Dewey's enacted some sort of failsafe," said Nightingale. "That's why characters could find their books, Atlas moved between stories, Eleanore's...back?"

"Brilliant deduction," said Eleanore.

"So, I'm sure that means we have even less time."

"And there wasn't much to begin with."

"We?" said Eleanore. "You never helped us do anything. We were the ones out there putting our necks on the line while you just sat back and…drank tea, apparently."

"I'm…not a bad character," said Nightingale. "I'm…just a very bad mentor."

He got up and wandered around the small cottage. No one knew quite what to say. Nightingale found a little wooden music box on a shelf. He opened it and turned the crank. But instead of a music box sound they heard an entire chamber orchestra complete with a harp playing "The Ash Grove." He closed the lid and put it down.

He found a wooden Irish whistle, raised it to his lips and started playing Stravinsky's "Le Chant du Rossignol." It was beautiful. He could have played in any orchestra in any book.

"I didn't know you played," said Eleanore after a moment.

"There's a lot you don't know," he said. He sighed, cleaned the mouthpiece and returned the whistle to its shelf. "I learned ages ago. Piano, flute, Irish whistle and Oboe. I studied with Salieri. Terrible composer, but a good instructor. I enjoy educating myself. I have degrees from every magical university. A bit useless as each of their magical techniques are only applicable in their respective stories. He walked to a window and looked out at the trees. "I can sail a ship, cook a gourmet meal and turn straw into gold. I speak one hundred and three different languages.

"Guess <u>he</u> knows Latin," Eleanore joked to Paige.

"I can make perfume, do every popular dance since 42 B.C. and analyze over 10,000 years of art, and architectural styles and techniques. I know the mythology of over 800 unique religions, can change a carburetor, dissect a human cadaver and brew Dr. Jekyll's infamous potion. I can get bloodstains out of velvet, ride a horse, dragon, and woolly mammoth and brew a proper cup of English tea. I can move through a tesseract, kill a sea serpent and make a donkey disappear on a Victorian stage. I can play in a rock band, survive in the desert and perform alchemy. I can fight with a rapier, out-riddle a sphinx and make my own boots." He breathed a heavy sigh. "And I will forget all of it once I'm written." He turned back to them. "This is all my fault."

"Oh. Well that's good. This whole time I've been thinking it's mine," said Paige.

"I should have told you about…about all of it. About –"

"Drystan?"

Nightingale looked at her, surprised.

"Atlas knew everything."

"I should have warned you," he said. "But I thought it was better…to be careful."

"It's true?"

Nightingale nodded. Eleanore didn't seem totally convinced.

"What, exactly is Drystan trying to do?"

"He wants to tear the world down."

"That's…unbelievably generic," said Paige.

"And seems rather counterintuitive. Ancient god or not, he's stuck in this world now - no one wants to destroy themselves," Eleanore added.

"I don't know what exactly he's planning, but he's through with living in a place run by logic and order, that's for sure," said Nightingale.

"You are so non-specific I could scream," Paige scoffed.

"We need to find the Owner if we're going to solve anything."

"If they even know anything once we do find them."

"We don't have time to do that AND deal with Drystan."

"I honestly don't know anything about the Owner," said Nightingale.

"Then send us to someone…someWHERE that does."

"Paige, please don't –"

"We don't NEED you. But I think it's about time you did something to help."

"Or we could just ask the Ur Book to send us somewhere," said Paige, "like before…" Paige pulled out the book.

"You have the Ur Book?!" said Nightingale.

"Let me guess, another legend you don't really know anything about. Even with all your 'research.'"

"Do you know how difficult it is to research anything about the Store? I can learn everything about every story ever written and still understand nothing about the place I work. Of all the books in existence there is no manual on The Bookstore!"

They sat in silence for a moment, and Paige was just about to grab Eleanore's hand and open the book when -

"Paige I need to ask you for something, though I know I have no right to."

"You're going to ask Paige for a favor? Are you kidding?! There's no reason on earth –"

"He can ask," said Paige.

Eleanore turned to her, confused.

"He was the deciding vote at the council." Paige looked to Eleanore. She didn't deny it. "And despite his justification of 'trusting fate' I know it went against most of his natural instincts." She turned to Nightingale. "I'm well beyond just trusting you out of…I don't know what it was. Fear? Blind faith? I'm no longer obediently following. But I'll listen."

Nightingale looked up at her with a combination of desperation and furtive hope. Paige wondered if that's how she looked at him once.

"I need you to choose to stop Drystan over finding the Owner. I know what a personal sacrifice that is…that you may never know who you are or where you belong…but Drystan –"

"What about the Bookworm? What about the fact that my not knowing who I am brought it in the first place?" said Paige. "I thought that was the life or death emergency I needed to go on a quest for."

"Drystan is trying to destroy things NOW. He may have massacred half the Store by the time you –"

"Give me a break," said Eleanore.

"You haven't wanted me to look for the Owner since the beginning," said Paige. "Don't manipulate –"

"And don't say something so horrible about our friend. He may… not be who we think he is…he may…oh, I don't know, but even if…he's still Drystan and we still care about him."

"I'm not trying to manipulate you, I swear. I think…maybe I was incorrect when I assumed everything going wrong was your fault. When I…put that on you."

"Wow. Thanks for that. It wasn't traumatic at all."

"I was just trying to stop anything that might upset the balance of… But Drystan's been wanting to exploit it…you…from the start. You're… not hemmed in by genre rules like the rest of us. You have to teach us how to manage in this…new world. Besides, if Drystan has been deliberately sowing chaos, stopping him might slow the Bookworm. Who knows? But he's our most immediate threat. I know what you would be giving up. But please, help us. Who knows? If you…we…you succeed…maybe there will be more time for you to…"

"You want her help now?" said Eleanore.

"I'll do everything I can to be there for you. I'm sorry I wasn't before. I admit I wasn't."

"How noble."

The floor started to tremble.

"Maybe you're wrong and the Bookworm's just after me," said Paige. "No exploitation needed -" The ground shook again, more violently "- And it's going to destroy every place I am until the whole world comes crashing down. I can't, Nightingale."

"Correct me if I'm wrong, but where I'm from fog isn't supposed to erase everything it touches…?" said Atlas, looking out the window farthest from the door.

"Open the book! We have to get back to the Store!"

"And risk taking the Nothing with us? With the barriers non-existent -"

"Then get out and run! Now!"

They threw the door open and started running as fast as they could away from the Nothing.

"I'm getting really tired of this," said Paige.

"I don't know…running's actually kind of fun now that I don't feel like I'm dying," said Eleanore.

Plot holes appeared all around them. They had to slow their pace to keep from tripping into one. But slowing down meant they couldn't get out ahead of them. The mist was growing ever closer and all they could do was jump and dart out of the way as more and more appeared.

"The ground! Watch out!" Eleanore cried.

They were on the edge of a large hill, and one of the plot holes was causing the side of it to erode. They steadied themselves as quickly as they could, a giant drop in front of them, the Nothing behind.

"What do we do?" Said Eleanore.

"Better to fall down a hill than into the Nothing. There's no coming back from -"

"We don't know how high up we are! And it's very possible there might be actual…permanent physical consequences now!"

But things happened too fast and their choice was made for them. The ground disappeared under Paige, Eleanore, Atlas and Nightingale who found themselves falling through the air at breakneck speed.

"At least we're falling away from the Nothing!"

"This would be safer," Nightingale cried out, "if we were rolling.

This isn't going to be good when we hit the ground!"

"Thanks for that."

But they didn't hit the ground.

What they did hit was soft and…

…movable.

Whatever it was, engulfed them.

Paige scrambled, then calmed. She couldn't smell, or breathe, but wherever…whatever this was…wasn't horrible.

Then the word came to her.

Water.

She was surrounded by water. But of an all-together different sort than she'd ever seen. It wasn't a fountain, or a stream…this was salty, and DEEP. She kept falling down until she slowly felt her movement stop, leaving her suspended in the depths. Paige had never been IN water before. It was…magical. Like being in some strange, alien atmosphere. Above she could only see distant rays of light, but what ethereal rays! She started to laugh…but got a mouthful of water. She coughed and more water went down her throat. Her chest began to hurt, and she looked around for the others. She couldn't see them anywhere.

Instinct took over, and she began to kick her legs and move her arms, but she wasn't going anywhere. She couldn't swim. Why on earth wasn't everyone created knowing how to swim?

White foam crashed on top of her, pushing her deeper below the surface, so far she could no longer see the light cutting through the water. She tried to scream but only succeeded in letting out a few air bubbles. She didn't know which way was up. And she suddenly came to the terrifying realization that she must be drowning.

And then a hand plunged underwater. It grabbed the back of Paige's dress and dragged her to the surface. She sputtered, and gasped and wiped her eyes.

She looked up to find herself face to face with Gwen.

"What did you think you were doing not telling anyone where you were -?!"

"Rose?" Nightingale called, doing his best to tread water as he held Eleanore above the surface.

Gwen grimaced.

"Had a hell of a time finding you. Someone in the teahouse told me you -"

"Gwen! How on earth -?"

"Where's Atlas?"

They looked around the surface in terrifying silence until they saw an arm flail and disappear back underwater.

"We have to help her!"

"Who?"

"Never mind! We have to -" Paige suddenly realized that she felt much lighter than she had a few moments ago.

"The book. Where's the Ur Book?!"

"Don't you have it?" said Gwen, terrified. "I lost my copy of "Spindle" when I crash landed in the ocean -"

"It doesn't matter!" Eleanore cried as she coughed up water.

"How are we going to get back?!"

"Help Atlas!" said Paige.

"I can't rescue her and keep you safe too. You're dragging me down as it is!"

By this time Nightingale was halfway to Gwen and Paige, pulling Eleanore with him. Paige wrestled against Gwen, determined to go after Atlas, but Gwen held her fast.

"You'll only drown!" Gwen said, "and that won't solve anything. Don't be a martyr."

Finally Nightingale reached them. He pulled Paige out of Gwen's arms, barely keeping both Paige and Eleanore afloat.

"Go!" he said.

"I need to help!" Paige cried.

"Just once let someone do something for you. It's the least I can do after...well..."

Exhausted, Gwen dove below the waves, rolling her eyes as she did. They stared at the placid water, each second feeling like an hour. Finally Gwen broke through the surface and took a deep breath. She dived back down. A few moments later she reemerged, gasping for air, then dove down again.

"She can't do it much longer," said Eleanore. "She'll start drowning too."

The next time Gwen emerged she was holding something. It was heavy – she could barely keep her head above water as she swam towards the group. Nightingale did his best to meet her half-way.

"I don't think she made it," said Gwen. She was dragging Atlas. Atlas wasn't moving or breathing. But wrapped tightly in Atlas's arms was the Ur Book. She'd been desperately trying to rescue it.

"We have to get out of here," said Gwen. "I think the Bookworm's about to reemerge in the Store. Everyone said you disappeared into a book so...Eleanore, weren't you written?"

"Weren't you?"

"Long story."

"You stole an author –" Nightingale started –

"What?!"

"The Bookworm's coming here," said Gwen.

"We know!"

 "I found you by following the tremors. We have to leave, now!"

"You stole an author?"

"Can we not, right this minute?"

"Why would you put yourself at risk for us?

"I've learned a thing or two since...well, I'm sorry I've been such a brat. Especially to you, Eleanore."

"But, how -?"

 "Oh, come on! Or do you want to stay here till we're actually dead?"

The ground shook so hard giant waves started to form.

"I know where we can go to hide," said Gwen.

"We can't! We might take the Nothing with us –"

"I'm risking it! Hold on or get left behind!"

They all grabbed onto whatever limbs they could reach, forming a giant sort of pile. Gwen opened the book and they disappeared just as the plotholes converged under them and the story was dragged down into Nothingness.

CHAPTER 22

FREE WILL

The instant they were in the Store, on solid ground Nightingale lay Atlas down and started CPR.

"Come on Atlas!"

But it wasn't helping. She wasn't breathing and they couldn't find a pulse.

"Please!"

Nightingale moved faster.

"We're not giving up!" he said. "We're not losing anyone else! I won't!"

"But – she can't die, right? She can't die…in the Store."

But it still wasn't working.

"Give me the Ur Book!" Paige shouted, reaching one hand out for it, continuing compressions with the other. "Maybe there's something in it! There has to be! Something to help! Dewey!" she called. "Dewey! Help!"

But no one came.

"Gwen, give me the book!" she said, looking up for the first time.

Gwen just stood there, the book in her hand.

"What are you doing?"

Drystan walked up. Gwen handed him the book.

"Just what you ordered," said Gwen. "With some riff raff thrown in for good measure."

"It's true," said Paige.

"What's true?" said Drystan, barely taking in Atlas lying on the floor in front of him.

"You're a villain."

"Paige, how could you call me that? After all this time?" he said, deeply hurt. "I'm the only one trying to help you with this mess. You know me."

There were supposed to be rules. The villain twirled his moustache, the hero was charming AND sincere and the one who was supposed to save the day had some inkling how to go about it. There were supposed to be mentors and people you never had to question if you could trust. Paige felt betrayed.

"You of all people, labeling someone? YOU wanting to think in black and white?" he looked amazed.

Maybe Drystan was right. Whatever he was up to, maybe he did have a good reason. But lying, keeping secrets…If the rules were out the window, how could she judge between good and bad? She didn't have a narrator to spoon feed her the answers…

As much as I would like to, dear reader. But even I don't always know exactly what's going to happen.

Paige thought about Shadow.

Maybe you just have to figure out what you really need and ask the right question.

Paige looked at Drystan.

She wanted her friend. She wanted sweet, lovable Drystan just like she wanted the kind Wesley back. But good stories weren't just wish fulfillment. They were a truth disguised as illusion. And Paige needed that more than any illusion disguised as truth, no matter how comforting it might be.

"You're one of Shadow's brothers, aren't you? Rahm?"

Something flickered in Drystan's eyes for the briefest instant before he clamped it down. But it was all the confirmation Paige needed and he knew it.

"Shadow told you about his siblings?" he smiled a sad smile. "What was it that clued you in? My reluctance to meet him? Or…" he paused, looking almost disappointed. "Did someone just tell you? Was it Shadow? No….that was too long ago, and he never saw me in 'Ever.' It couldn't have been Nightingale. Not entirely. He knew my name, but not my relation to -"

"You're right."

"But someone told you."

Paige looked at Atlas.

"Not…oh, my! The waitress?"

He looked stunned to see her there, fully formed, but there was not an ounce of pity or compassion for the fact that she lay there dying… or dead.

"But she didn't know –"

"She knew you were an ancient god. One of twelve. I put the pieces together." She held out her hand, praying Drystan would do the right thing. He didn't move.

"Please, give me the Ur Book!" Paige cried. "Let me try to help her."

But Drystan just laughed.

"And I thought I did such a good job holding my tongue," he chuckled.

"What's your game?" Paige asked.

"You're waiting for the diabolical monologue where I tell you I'm going to destroy the universe? Is that what he," he looked at Nightingale, "prepped you for?" Gwen laughed. "OK. I'll give you this much, because contrary to what you might think, I do like you, Paige. I wasn't pretending about that. You hold the key to liberation. We can have free will over our lives! Who doesn't want a world where everything's possible? Maybe I want to be an author. God of a universe. Or THE universe. Maybe I want to create the rules. Who doesn't? Maybe it's as simple as 'He with the most brains and power wins.' Isn't that how it should be? No 'hero's journey' required."

"Even if it means hurting people?"

"Oh, no, no, no, don't play the victim. Don't give your power away. You want the same thing I do. That's why you listened."

"You manipulated me."

"That's the universal excuse for self-pity, isn't it? 'The devil made me do it.'" Drystan smiled, then leaned over, his back curving like a question mark. "It's so much better to <u>be</u> the devil," he said. "The poor, misunderstood devil."

"You're not the devil, you're just a frustrated elemental being who wishes he had–"

"She's dead, Paige," Nightingale whispered, his hand feeling where Atlas's pulse should be.

"You wouldn't even let me try to help her!" Paige screamed at Drystan.

"WAKE UP!" he shouted back. "Characters are dying, suffering, being tortured every day! How many people die in any given fantasy book just to add an impressive death toll?" he asked. He looked at Nightingale. "I bet you know. But I don't see you running to try and save them. What about all the other waitresses in that teahouse? Probably destroyed by the Bookworm by now. No. Give someone a name, some fleshed out features and helpful dialogue and suddenly they're worth saving."

"YOU want to save them?" said Paige.

"No," said Drystan. "There will always be casualties. Sacrifices. But at least I'm not a hypocrite about it. And at least I'm trying to make it better for as many as I can." He reached down and grabbed Paige's face. "Listen to me, I was in the Store in its very beginnings, when it was just a collection of muses and ether and the dust of creation."

(He means the real ones, dear reader, not the kind Eleanore referenced…)

"And I lived everywhere," he continued. "In many places – both the real world and many stories, when there was barely a line separating the two. Until people forgot…until my brother took me and our siblings…I managed to get back here. Inspire someone enough to be written in one, last story. I thought it would set me free. Back to my old life and…But it didn't. I was trapped. And it wasn't pleasant. Things don't always go well for creatures like me, especially in a myopic retelling…You have no idea. Shadow doesn't even know what that was like."

"You were a god and you want your power back, that's all it really comes down to, isn't it?" Eleanore snapped.

"Don't you understand? It's more than that! I was A god. Not THE god. We were all still in service to…something. We were created, not creators. I want to be the author of my own story. Beholden to no one."

"And author of ours too?" Nightingale said.

"I think I'd do a better job of it. I wouldn't abandon my creation."

"How are you so sure of yourself?" said Paige. Drystan was so convinced he was doing the right thing she was starting to almost believe it too. "How do you not care what anyone thinks of you?" It was both an indictment, and a plea. There was something in her that wanted to be like him.

"Your problem, Paige, is not that you're different, it's that you're not selfish enough. You feel too much for the herd. You'd get so much further if you weren't running after underdogs all the time."

"You've been helping him?" Nightingale turned to Gwen. "YOU? You're –"

"Yeah. Say it! You just had to keep me down in a 'Romance Girl' box. I'm tired of being sidelined!"

"I know you're not cruel, Rose."

"My. Name. Is. GWEN!" she screamed! "GWEN!" She hit him and he fell, colliding with a stack. Nightingale grabbed his face, blood trickling down his cheek. Eleanore jumped up and stepped in between him and Gwen.

"Oh, look. Now angst girl wants to be the hero. There are so many heroes in this disgusting Store!"

"Was all your niceness some kind of an act? Have you really just been the bitchy mean girl all this time?"

"Mean girl? Is that all you got?" Gwen mocked. "It's pathetic how little it takes to make you go cry in a corner. You'll never do anything meaningful in your sad little existence. You YA girls have such an inflated sense of nobility but you're nothing but a depressed cry baby," Gwen smirked. "So go off and let the big boys handle this."

"Maybe I wouldn't be so depressed all the time if everyone wasn't constantly making fun of me because of some stupid, deeply rooted prejudice against my genre. Maybe you all hate it so much because you're jealous none of yours will ever come close to its popularity. Out there, I'm the popular girl. Stop trying to take something away from me! My story had nothing to do with my being sad here. I finally figured it out. It was just you guys being assholes."

Other characters were starting to gather…the commotion so intense it interrupted the cacophony of arguing about the Bookworm and their newly found stories.

"Now," said Drystan. "No more games. You're going to help me figure out how to really use this book."

"What are you talking about?" Paige said. "You've used it with us dozens of times. Think of where you want to go an –"

"Don't play dumb. Just a minute ago you were begging me to hand it over to see if it could save that extra's life. This book holds all the secrets of the universe. I spent ages trying to get my hands on it, Dewey gave it to you five seconds after you got here. So we're going to figure out how it really works."

"Dewey!" Paige cried. "Dewey we need you NOW!"

Still, nothing.

This didn't constitute an emergency?

"What do you want with it, anyway? It couldn't stop the Bookworm or find the Owner…"

"Are we still on the stupid Bookworm?" said Drystan.

"Stupid?!" said Eleanore.

"How do you think I forced you out of that book?"

"The Spindle?!"

"YOU'VE been controlling the Bookworm?" Paige exclaimed.

"All it takes is some properly placed plotholes and it comes right where you want it to. Feeding time."

"You've been feeding stories to the Bookworm? Every time it showed up…it's because you deliberately messed with something…?"

"I had to keep things moving forward." He looked into her eyes. "Have you been holding out hope all this time that the reason you're different is because you're special? That you're the 'chosen one' who has to save the world?" he smiled. "I've met chosen ones. They're a dime a dozen. You're not the chosen one. You're a tool. A key. An object for me to use. Do you want to know what you all really are?" he ripped a page from a nearby book. Paige could see words typed across both sides. It was as if he'd just ripped the arm off of a person.

"Just ink and paper," he said. "These few marks here might be the color of your hair. This: the sound of your voice. That's all any of you are, Paige, and Eleanore and your "true love" Wesley." He crumpled the paper in his hand. "Not worth the time it would take to throw in the garbage if you found it on the street." He looked directly at Paige. "Except you don't even have a story. I checked after that glorious failsafe was enacted. Everyone else in the Store has theirs. But you don't have one. Confirmed. You're authorless. Of course. No one would write a character like you. You want to be 'fixed?' You want to be petted and patronized and given significance?" he smiled. "You're transparent."

He started pacing, the characters scurrying out of his way for fear of what he might do to them next.

"Let's finally lose the charade," he said. "The Owner is not going to magically fix you, Paige. You don't get fixed. Without me, you get eliminated. Erased. If you found the Owner they'd clean house. Now if you don't do exactly what I tell you, I'll destroy all your little friends. One. By. One. But that doesn't have to happen. We could still make a good team."

Paige looked up at him fighting tears back from her eyes, rage boiling inside her.

Gwen handed him a pile of books. It was the stories of most of the assembled crowd. A copy of Eleanore's, Willa's, even Velveteen's.

"These are the only copies," he said. "Don't think I'd leave you other editions to fall back on."

It felt like all the air disappeared from the room.

"You're so small minded," Drystan laughed, pleased to have their enraptured attention. "I don't want to destroy the Store; I want to kill the Owner and take their power. Not be confined to any story."

"We won't let you!" Velveteen cried out, valiantly.

"Really, bunny?"

He grabbed Velveteen's book, (called "The Velveteen Rabbit,") and skimmed through its pages.

"No!" Willa cried.

Nightingale rushed Drystan, trying to topple him and rip the book out of his hands.

Drystan leveled him in one fell swoop.

"I am the god of chaos," he said, turning back. "I'm not as flimsy as I let you believe. Comes in handy, your underestimation. It's so sad how much you all traffic in appearances. But I'm TIRED OF PLAYING A PART!"

He glanced through the book, then ripped out the last several pages. Velveteen squealed. Drystan pulled out a match and set the pages ablaze. "Now you'll never be real," Drystan said in mock sadness.

"Drys, that's harsh," said Gwen. "It's just a rabbit..."

"Don't get moral qualms now. I'd hate for you to get annoying. Don't think I don't have your book, too."

"What?! Come on, don't play about something like that."

Drystan smiled.

"We won't let you destroy us!"

"You can't take on all of us!" Fred shouted.

The group started moving towards Drystan. The Raven circled above, diving and rising, trying to peck at his eyes. Fred was right, Drystan couldn't take on all of them. Certainly not at once. He grabbed "Wonderful Willa" and held it up but the mob kept coming. He touched it to Velveteen's smoldering pages and lit the whole book on fire.

Willa screamed.

Nightingale crawled back to standing and tried to rip the burning pages from Drystan's hands. Drystan turned, quick as lightning, and shoved the fire directly into Nightingale's hands. He cried out and fell back. Then Drystan threw the burning pages onto the Fan Fiction stacks to his left, sending them up in flames too. He turned back to Paige.

"Your bestie's next, unless you figure out how to make that book work. You want to know my game? Start playing." Drystan said. "Tick. Tock."

Drystan grabbed Eleanore by the scruff of her neck and he and Gwen ran with her, kicking and screaming. The flames burst up and the rest of the characters, trapped on the other side of the shelves, were unable to pursue them. No new books would appear on the front counter like they did when an author made a purchase. The burning books would be gone, forever.

CHAPTER 23

KILL YOUR DARLINGS

Dracula 1 rushed to pull his and Willa's book from the fire, but the others held him back. It was too late. The book was impossible to salvage.

Soon the Store itself would burn to the ground, and it didn't seem like there was anything anyone could do about it.

Unless there was something in the Ur Book and Drystan let Paige try to find it, every story that ever was or ever would be would cease to exist.

And it was because of her.

No…

It was because of Drystan.

Willa was on the ground, hysterical.

"Am I fading?" she cried.

"I...don't see any fades...I mean...not...very...significant ones..." said Fred.

Willa's shoes looked ever so slightly see through, as did Dracula 1's cape. Dracula 1 finally returned to Willa and held her as they both waited to disappear. Velveteen stood in a corner repeating:

"I'll never be real. I'll never be real..." over and over again.

The others did everything they could to put out the fire, but it was spreading fast.

"I have to go," said Paige.

"It's too dangerous," Nightingale said. "We have to get these flames under control."

"Do you really think there's any way we can stop it?"

Nightingale looked around. The fire had jumped from Fan Fiction to Poetry and was on its way to Fantasy. It was too risky and would take too much time to try and go into books and bring back water. No, they couldn't stop it. But Nightingale didn't want to say so.

"Even if it means never being fixed, and The Bookstore...dying...I have to get that book back from him and stop whatever he's trying to do."

"You won't be able to save Eleanore," said Drood.

"And what about the rest of us?!" shouted Dracula 2. "I'm not going to be erased. Leave the fallen, we have to save the stories!"

"There are still authors out there who can write new stories," said Paige.

"We house every story that ever WILL BE written!"

"Our inspiration is only part of it...I'd imagine there's a lot of hard work too…"

"There's still hope on that front, at least," said Paige. "But if Drystan manages to get into the real world he'll destroy everything. REAL people, not just fictional ones."

"We're real."

"Not real," Velveteen said, rocking back and forth. "Not real…"

"If we can't be saved, at least our authors and readers can be."

She means you, dear reader. She didn't want Drystan to get out and harm you. For you are a special creature. You might be an author yourself, capable of repopulating a whole world with your creations. You might be inspired to search out great scientific wonders, or beautifully wrap truths in clever illusions - greater gifts than anything in the market of an enchanted circus. You may live a quiet life but keep the most important stories close to your heart and the characters therein will love you for it. You are far too precious to risk anything happening to you. More precious even than a magical Bookstore. So, because of you, Paige abandoned her quest to find the Owner and the knowledge of who she was. Instead she plucked up her courage and ran after Drystan.

For your sake, dear reader.

✶ ✶ ✶

Drystan and Gwen held Eleanore hostage at the front of the Store, a good distance from the fire. For now. They stood next to a New Releases table where several copies of Eleanore's book sat in a pile waiting to, eventually, be shelved in whatever sections they cross referenced. They would likely never get that far.

"Know what's in it?" Drystan asked, picking up a copy.

"Not past the first couple chapters."

"Why not?"

"Maybe I like surprises."

"You're not curious about the life you're so eager to fight me for?"

Eleanore pulled the copy Paige gave her from her pocket. It said:

GINDERS

On the cover. Eleanore stared at it.

"Well, I know I had some horrible childhood illness and I live with some awful stepfamily…" She took a breath, and slowly opened the book. She flipped through the pages, skimming the basic plot. "It looks like a kind of a modern day twist on a Cinderella type of thing. Appropriate title," she smirked. "But without the nice bits like the ball and the Prince and the happy ending."

"I'd love to know what author would come up with something as miserable as that."

Eleanore almost smiled. Almost.

"My family dies," she continued. "I loved them a lot and they loved me." She looked up. "It's weird…do I love them because I really do…or because my author makes me?"

"Good question," said Drystan.

She flipped back to the beginning, going more slowly this time.

"Awful foster family. Life a living hell. Knew that." She flipped some more. "I have to live up in the attic. There's mold up there…" she looked up. "There really is, it's gross." She looked back at the book. " I don't have any friends." She kept going, desperate for anything positive. There had to be something good. No author just sits around gleefully torturing characters. They'd never get published if they did. At least, they wouldn't have much success. And her book looked at least somewhat successful. It had a hard cover and everything.

"I'm an artist…" she said. "A painter. I sneak materials from school – I even use ashes from the fireplace…I guess that's part of where the title comes from."

"Cute," said Gwen in a mocking tone.

" I create these amazing works of art." She looked up again. "I've never painted before," she said to herself, trying to wrap her head around the idea. "I've never even wanted to…" She flipped on for a few pages, then let out a guffaw.

"Of course."

"What?"

"They burn them. My paintings. My foster sisters burn them. My foster mother watches. Ironic. Everything gets torched whether I'm in the Store or my story." She skimmed further. "I get sick again. Pretty quickly, actually." She flipped back a ways in the book. "From all the cinders and mold I've been inhaling. Tank comes back. And then…I kill myself. Afterwards…someone finds one of my paintings, the one I used cinders to make. The only one that wasn't burned. It ends up becoming this beautiful, inspiring thing after I die." She closed the book. "What a load of -"

But before she could finish Drystan took the book and scanned it. He picked up the other copies of her story on the table and handed them to Gwen.

"It's just leverage," he said, trying to sound comforting. He just sounded like an ass.

"So, that's it. I burn either way?"

"I don't want to burn you."

"You tried to poison me, didn't you?"

He took a breath.

"It's…complicated," he said.

"Not from where I'm sitting now."

"I needed to get you out of the way, where Paige was concerned."

He brushed a strand of hair behind her ear. Eleanore hated the fact that there was still a part of her that liked being close to him. Liked him touching her. Still, she pushed his hand away.

"Just talking to me wasn't an option?"

"I'm talking to you now." He sighed. "You're right. Why don't we start over?"

"Go to hell."

"Come on, Drys, lay off her?" said Gwen.

"Is there a problem?" Drystan snapped.

Gwen slinked over and wrapped her arms around him.

"I don't like you flirting with her," she said as she leaned over and nibbled his ear.

Drystan smacked her away.

"Ow! What's with you?" she whimpered.

He ignored her.

"What is taking Paige so long? We're running out of time."

"Yeah, whose fault is that?" said Gwen.

Eleanore started to tiptoe backwards, as Drystan and Gwen broke into a full out verbal fight. She was just about to turn and make a run for it when:

"Uh, uh, uh!" Drystan spun around. He held up a copy of her book. "We can end this right now if that's how you want to play."

"What does it matter? If the fire's just going to destroy everything anyway?"

"I can be nice, Eleanore. You know that." He slowly walked up to her. "You can be a part of what I'm planning, or not. There's so much that needs to be done."

"Like what?"

"Well…" he thought, "what if we could just walk out that door into the real world? No evil step-family, no oxygen tanks."

"Walk out into what real world? Every author's from a different time and place you can't just –"

"Why not? No one's ever tried."

"Drys, baby –" Gwen slunk back to him, looking towards the smoke coming from the fire. It was getting closer…

"Are you two together or something?" said Eleanore.

"Jealous?" Gwen spat.

"Why don't you try stepping outside?" Drystan said to Eleanore. "All we've ever known is what Nightingale told us. Who's to say which rules are real and which aren't."

"Drys, we don't know what could happen –" Gwen said, nervously. "The fire, destroying people's books…I thought this was about liberation… not creating a massacre!"

"If you don't shut up right now!" Drystan screamed. He pulled out a thin book from his pocket.

"Is…is that my book? You really…? Why would you need –"

"I'm counting to three you psychopathic –"

"Who are you calling a psychopath?"

"You think you're the brilliant sleuth?" he laughed. "You're the crazy girlfriend of the bad guy, Ms. Friday."

"How long have you had that?"

"Long enough. With all your desperation to break through your stereotype you fell right into it easy as one…"

"What do you mean?"

"Two –"

"Paige might have died already trying to get here! You didn't think this –"

"Three!"

And she was silent.

"Now, Eleanore" said Drystan, "why don't you try?"

"You want me to walk out that door, just to see what happens? Yeah, you really do care about me," she said sarcastically.

"You could be the one to lead us to freedom. Finally not just the stupid sidekick. We could create a new world. Come on. I've always known you liked me. Even though you tried so hard to hide it."

"I –"

He kissed her. Gwen looked like she was going to be sick. Eleanore melted. She couldn't help it. She'd been in love with Drystan for as long as she could remember. The old Drystan. The one she desperately missed. And he was a good kisser. This was nothing like what she'd experienced in "Ever" when that knight took her in his arms, and she punched him in the face. This…Eleanore loved.

Slowly, Drystan pulled away.

"You're going to do anything I tell you to," he said gently, quietly. "Because that's what your genre does. Anything to get the guy."

Eleanore frowned. Part of her wanted to do what he said. She was built for loyalty. Gwen could read it all over her. But she had changed. How, she didn't know. She should have been frozen in a state that matched how she started at the beginning of her story. But she wasn't that person anymore and whether it was "right" or not, she was glad. For, dear reader, Eleanore now possessed that rarest of gifts, one we should all be lucky enough to be possessed of:

She genuinely liked the person she was.

"Are you kidding?" she said, looking Drystan straight in the eye.

"YA girls are defined by caring passionately about what's right, no matter the cost. We're smart, and empathetic and we're not afraid of all the complexities of being human. I like my genre. I'd keep it even if I could have any one I wanted. And I don't give a shit what happened in anyone else's story. In mine, I care about being good more than I care about getting a deeply flawed guy I have a crush on to like me. Trust me. I'll get over you."

Drystan grabbed her by her hair and dragged her and all her books towards the flames. Paige arrived just as Drystan was about to throw every copy of Eleanore's book, and possibly Eleanore herself, into the quickly encroaching inferno.

Gwen was in crisis. She'd been reading through her book and felt stabbed in the back. Her transformation under Drystan wasn't some noble rebellion. It was falling right into the "box" she was meant for. Maybe she'd always just been doing what someone told her to do. Drystan, her author, what did it matter? She'd been fighting so long to be taken seriously, for people to think of her as smart. But she WAS smart. She shouldn't have to convince people of it. For the first time in her life she stopped and asked herself, "What kind of character do I want to be?" It was a complicated question. Too complicated for Gwen to really know the answer, but, in that moment, the one thing that Gwen was sure of was as much as she wanted to be special and needed, she didn't want it to be at the expense of innocent characters getting hurt. What had Eleanore ever done to make Gwen be such a brat to her anyways?

And so, she made the first truly independent decision she'd ever made and rushed towards Drystan.

"No!" she cried. "She's just a kid! I'm not going to let you hurt another kid!" she reached Drystan and grabbed him, wrestling the books out of his hand. He turned and shoved her, full force, into the corner of a nearby shelf. Gwen hit her head and lay motionless on the ground, blood pooling around her. Eleanore, loosed from Drystan's grasp, ran to Gwen. Drystan looked like he was going in for the kill when;

"This enough chaos for you, Rahm?"

Drystan turned, all thoughts of Gwen and Eleanore instantly forgotten.

"Paige, so nice of you to join us." He laughed. "Are you trying to make me mad? I don't care what name you call me. I've had hundreds over the course of my life."

"So what exactly do you want me to do? Summon Dewey? Finish the quest to find the Owner and, what? Kill them?"

"A <u>metaphoric</u> killing the author," he looked at Eleanore. "'How poetically just," he laughed.

"Why? Other than your own selfish –"

"Because contrary to your beliefs, stories don't give hope. They give false ideas. The only thing we should be looking to is ourselves."

"Are you serious?" said Paige, realizing as she said it. "You love being the villain. You don't want the freedom to be something different. You just don't want to deal with the consequences of your actions."

"You can help me, or I could just burn the Ur Book. If I can't be happy, why should anyone else be?"

"You're a monster."

"No. That's too easy. I'm a pragmatist. The system is wrong, and I want to change it."

"Not like this!"

"Isn't that what people always say…the ones who never actually do anything? Well, while you're all off having councils and committees on what the 'right way' is, what quests we should go on, who we should talk to, I'm DOING something!"

He reached for the Ur Book – but it was gone. He frantically patted his pockets, finding nothing.

He saw it at the same moment as Paige, lying on the ground near Gwen's hand. She'd been smart enough to grab it when she was wrestling with Drystan.

They made a dash for it.

Then, in one quick motion, Eleanore grabbed it and held it up, threatening to throw it into the fire.

"Give me that, Eleanore…" said Drystan. "Now. If you don't…"

"I thought you wanted everything burned to the ground."

Her hand didn't waver.

"You'll never be a hero. In the real world no teenager saves anything."

"Don't you mock me," said Eleanore, a steely certainty in her voice. "I know what I am, what my genre is and what my job is within it. You say no one tries to change anything? Well, guess what? That's my job. I break broken systems. That's what my genre does. Yes, I will always be a teenager. I will always be a part of the generation that fights to make a difference. I will always be a rebel. And that includes taking you down. Even if I have to die in the process."

That's when they heard the screams. Willa, Nightingale, all the rest. The Cheshire Cat howled, and the Raven screeched. They were burning. They were all burning.

And the remaining four would be next.

"Death is a very different thing when it's no longer theoretical," said Drystan. "Ask my brother. You'll be meeting him again sooner or later, be sure of that."

Eleanore started running towards Paige.

But Drystan started running too. And he was much faster.

Eleanore tossed Paige the Ur Book.

"Go! Do what you have to do!"

"I'm not doing anything without you!" Paige cried.

"If I have to die, I'm going to make sure it means something," said Eleanore. "Who says it can't be noble?"

Paige desperately tried to think of something to say. Hadn't Shadow said Eleanore wouldn't die for a long time? But story construction and plot threads were long gone by this point. Who knew what would happen now?

But much faster than it's taken you to read that last paragraph, Drystan was on top of Paige. Fighting against him, she did the only thing she could. She pulled the book open, and she and Drystan disappeared as the last of The Bookstore, and all the stories and characters inside, burned-

Vanishing from existence.

CHAPTER 24

AS THE WORLD FALLS DOWN

The Bookstore was gone.

Every story, every character was gone, except for Drystan and Paige who stood in a world of whiteness. It wasn't Nothing…the Nothing wasn't here, wherever "here" was. It was simply white. Like a blank page.

"We're in the Ur Book…" Drystan realized, and laughed and laughed. "Of course. There's nowhere else for us to go!"

This was it. All that was left of existence.

"You'd think it would at least reveal its secrets once we're inside!"

"Dewey!" Paige called.

"She's not here," snapped Drystan. "She's a safeguard of The

Bookstore. The Bookstore is gone. Besides, this isn't an emergency. We're past that. This is what emergency safeguards are designed to prevent!"

Paige looked around, trying to come to terms with what just happened. The white wasn't discernable as anything in particular. Not soft, not hard, not wispy, not solid…no composition at all. She looked back at Drystan, pacing around like an animal in a cage, trying to make sense of where they were and what they could do about it. He tried to kick the whiteness. He tried to find a door. He tried to find words.

"Congratulations," Paige said.

"Congratulations?"

"You've won. Isn't this what you've always wanted? You can finally be your own master. Right here."

"Not exactly," he muttered. "But I'd rather be here, given the choice."

"Well then good for you," she scoffed. "You're disgusting."

"Do you know what it was like in the stories about me?" he said. "No. Of course you don't." He stopped pacing and looked at Paige like he used to. Not like he was going to kill her, but like…he was tired and knew she was too.

"You're lucky," he said, a hint of vulnerability rising within him. "Never having to experience all those horrors."

"All those terrible things that happened to you…you're not responsible at all?"

"That depends."

"On?"

"Whether you think I have free will or not. Was I responsible for my actions? Or was my author?"

"Don't play that now. You've been proselytizing free will from the start. Don't backpedal when it's no longer convenient."

"Having it and wanting it are not the same thing."

"You existed before you were written," said Paige. "Even Shadow said so." She thought a moment and realized: "We all do. How could we exist before our authors write us if we didn't have some agency? We...<u>inspire</u> our authors, we're not their puppets."

"It's a fine line."

He started walking again, Paige nervously staying equidistant, leaving them slowly circling.

"So you're a 'free will' believer?" he asked. "Did I convert you?"

"I wasn't exactly all for 'fate' to begin with."

"You wish I'd burned with all the rest of them."

There was something about the pain in his voice that seemed very, very real. It was confusing. She missed the "big brother" Drystan she met when she first arrived. In a way, the cruelest thing was discovering, irrevocably, that that person was not only gone but had never really existed in the first place. She wanted him back, and Eleanore and Wesley and all the rest. But Drystan was still physically here and he looked just like her old friend and that made it that much harder.

"I need you to understand..." he said. "You have to..." He stopped walking. "I think I'm right in assuming that you've only ever been in nice stories. Or at least relatively nice places in stories."

"I...suppose."

He was right. She'd seen some pretty horrible things, but they were really all a result of the Nothing and the Bookworm. The stories themselves had been rather pleasant. Drystan continued, purposefully, but gently.

"Ancient Epics are nothing to joke about. Especially if you're on the losing side. And when stories are told, written down… repeated…on and on…"

"You're the god of chaos. You love it. Even when you're not in your story. You're going to tell me you had nothing to do with it?"

"Chaos is not intrinsically evil. It can be a force for good. It's at the center of all creation. I am technically the dual god of abundance and devastation. Chaos has become used as a, I believe, falsely derogatory term over the ages."

"So you're a hero then?"

"Fine! Yes, I can be cruel, but I'm a trickster, not a…No one deserves the things I…no one should have to live through… and then…to be forgotten…" The thought physically pained him. "Vernichtung…"

"Who?"

"Shadow," he said. "Shadow…took us one by one. Our own brother." Drystan looked like he wanted to wring Shadow's neck. "Separated forever from everything we care about. How dare he wander around looking for us! As if I would ever…"

"He didn't want to! Can't you understand how much pain he's in? It's his job…he didn't have a choice!"

"BUT I DID?!"

"You're not making any sense!" said Paige. "You can't have free will, but take no responsibility for your actions, but then insist others take responsibility for theirs…"

"I am not logical," he boomed, sounding, for the first time like the god he truly was. "I am invention, I am change, I am freedom and rebellion! We were made slaves. Perhaps my brother didn't have a choice, but still, I will never forgive him. He didn't fight. He didn't rebel." He took a breath. "Whatever came before, I want a choice NOW. That beautiful, terrible gift given to our authors, I want it! Utterly and completely with no hint of fate blocking my way. Why do you think I got as far away from Arcadia as I could? At least I still have mobility in these worlds. I figured The Bookstore was the easiest place to maneuver from. I was there at the dawn of creation, I was 'real' in the way you think of it, but still a servant, and eventually a slave, disappearing, relegated to a story and then snuffed out all-together. If you'd been through what I have, you'd do anything to keep from going back or staying locked up forever. If you were in my place you would have done the same as me."

Is that all goodness was? Finding yourself in the right circumstances TO be good? Are we servants to our design even when we think we're being the most rebellious?

"Help me," he said. "I'm just trying to survive. Like you. I'm just trying to make a life for myself that's bearable and God forbid, maybe even happy. Please. You must understand."

She did.

But.

"I'm not going to let you do any more damage. Even if it means keeping both of us here for the rest of time," she said.

"There's no way to undo what I've set in motion."

And all at once his hand was on Paige's stomach, fingers curled around her loose thread.

And he pulled.

It felt like Drystan was ripping out her insides. She looked down at the thread. It was flesh colored, woven with liquid words like flowing ink.

Gothic Romance…

In the same story…

Have to belong…

"It's about time your flaws were made manifest," he said. He looked up.

"Is it enough yet?" he cried. "How much more do I have to destroy before all of you face me? Where are you, Owner?" he said in a mocking tone. "Or are you just going to let Shadow come and take this girl too? Maybe that would be good. I have a thing or two I'd like to say to him!"

He pulled again, creating a plot hole that originated in the center of her very being. She screamed. He looked back at her.

"I told you, that's all you are. Just some scratches of ink. I'd suggest you help me. And quickly. If nothing else has, maybe this will convince you."

Paige felt a tremor.

"We know what brings the Bookworm now. And this time it really is you."

How could the Bookworm, the Nothing exist HERE?

The world began to shake. Drystan stumbled back.

The Nothing seeped in like fog. The white world started to crack and crumple like it was mere paper. A bit of it got close enough to touch the top of Drystan's coat.

"Whatever happens to me happens to you!" Paige cried.

"Then I suggest you DO SOMETHING!" he screamed. Then suddenly, he smiled. "Besides, ceasing to exist is not the worst thing that can happen to someone. Ask Shadow."

But still, when he saw his jacket start to fade he quickly pulled it off and flung it as far from him as he could.

And something fell out of his pocket.

A small, folded piece of paper.

Paige snatched it up before Drystan realized what was happening. She unfolded it and this is what it said:

Dear Paige,

Go up.

~The Owner

P.S. Please Turn Over

She turned over the piece of paper. On the other side was written:

"The ladder descended from nowhere."

"There was a message from the Owner all this time?!"

"Yes. What does it mean?! I don't understand it! I've tried everything!"

"Why didn't you tell me?"

"Because you would have just been a bore like always! 'Ask Nightingale,' 'Find someone who'll tell me the answer.' YOU'RE the answer! I needed to get you alone…I needed to force you -"

"Where did you get it?"

"From inside this bloody book! TELL ME! NOW! Before it's too late! It's written to you… what does it mean?!"

"It doesn't mean anything!" Paige shouted over the rumbling and whirring of the Nothing. "'The ladder descended from nowhere?' It's nothing! It's just words!"

"Words are never just nothing! They're the opposite of -"

But Drystan stopped. Because as Paige read it out loud the paper disassembled, the ink lifted off, and the whole thing swirled and folded around itself until it created a real, solid ladder that started about two feet above where Paige stood, and stretched straight up above her, so high neither of them could see the top of it.

The Bookworm burst through. Paige grabbed the ladder and started climbing. There was nowhere else to go. And as she climbed, rung by rung, the ladder retracted behind her. Now the bottom was four feet from the ground. Now five. Drystan raced to grab onto it before it was out of reach. The world melting and dissolving around him as the Bookworm gobbled it up. The coat he'd discarded melted into ink on the ground and swirled away in the white space towards the Bookworm's hungry mouth.

Drystan jumped, his hands reaching towards Paige like a shade loosed out of hell. She ran up the ladder and he screamed, his mouth and face contorting into a horrific mask of rage and panic, as he grasped the plot thread still flailing from her and started climbing it, desperate to catch up to the bottom of the ladder, pulling the string out further with every movement upwards. Paige quickened her pace and as she did the string became taut. She was unravelling more slowly now, but still unravelling as Drystan followed her. Soon there was a giant hole where her stomach had been. Paige felt life start to drain from her.

Drystan laughed and laughed as he climbed knowing Paige would never be able to weave herself together again. If he couldn't be happy, no one else would be.

Paige was in pain. She didn't know how much longer she could climb. And she was tired.

But she forced herself to keep going. Because at the end of all things, something had to matter. Someone had to remember Eleanore, and The Bookstore and the stories. Drystan couldn't win. The things he said couldn't be the truth, even if the only way she could prove him wrong was to keep stubbornly climbing forever.

So she put one foot in front of the other, even though she was unraveling and even though she didn't want to, up the endless, endless ladder towards…what? All she could do was pray she could stay far enough ahead of Drystan to keep him from overtaking her and hope against hope that the thread unwinding from her wouldn't run out.

CHAPTER 25

THE STUFF THAT DREAMS ARE MADE OF

Paige climbed on. Up and up and up, all the time Drystan laughing. Following. Still she climbed.

Eventually she started to see little stars twinkling far above her in the darkness.

She climbed higher.

The stars got closer and gave the illusion that Paige could reach out and grab one like a firefly.

She'd never felt so small, not even deep down in the ocean. There, at least, she'd had some sense of…Space? Environment? She could feel the water defining her. Giving her shape. Here the air was thin. There was no ground when she looked down…no end when she looked up. If she let go, would she fall? Or simply float away to…was there anywhere <u>to</u> float away to?

And still she felt Drystan's tug, tug, tug behind her and heard the Bookworm behind him.

She climbed higher and saw rubble from her disintegrated world floating in the ether. A part of a bookcase. A chair. When Paige managed to get a closer look she saw that they were actually made of woven… something. Had they always been, and she was just now noticing? No, not woven <u>something</u>…Words. These were tight, intricate and elegant stitches made of the most beautiful words – each describing the thing it made up. How strange, she had never seen it before.

"It's like falling UP the rabbit hole," she thought.

Finally something emerged above her…a place where the ladder must, inevitably end. It looked something like the moon – a large crescent moon, with a glowing, open flower resting inside. Paige wasn't sure if it was a flower on the moon, or if the whole thing was of a piece - some sort of ivory pavilion constructed in mid-air. She forced herself up the last few rungs, the thread pulling painfully as she did, and onto a white open petal that formed a little path into the center of the pavilion. On the edge of the petal, in shimmering golden lettering were written the words:

In Principio Erat Verbum

There was no roof. As Paige walked on she could see the sky above, around and beneath her. She tried to pull the loose thread towards her but Drystan's grip was stronger, and every time she tried she heard the laughter get louder. He would be here soon.

And then she saw a person.

In the middle of the pavilion there was a white desk and sitting at the desk was me. The desk was filled with papers and I wrote intently on first one, than another. I stopped and looked up when I heard her approaching.

"Are you...the Owner?" Paige asked, feeling like she would never catch her breath again. Life seemed to be seeping out of her more and more quickly.

"Of your Bookstore, I am," I said. "Yes."

"It's not my Bookstore," said Paige. "That's the point of owning something. It's <u>yours</u>."

I smiled.

Paige had the feeling she'd seen me before. But not like she'd seen Atlas. She'd seen me...sort of mixed up. My eyes looked something like the Blue Fairy's...my smile something like little Adrian's...I looked a little like Paige, but a bit older.

"Have we met?" she asked.

"In a manner of speaking," I said. "My name's Ashley. I'm very happy you're finally here."

"FINALLY here?! Do you have any idea what I've been through? How long I've been looking for you?"

Another laugh pierced the space. Paige looked down and saw

Drystan getting closer, giving another yank on the thread.

"I left you a note in the Ur Book. A long time ago," I said.

"Drystan took it," said Paige. "I only just found it."

"I see."

"He's coming! Him and the Bookworm…Please! They'll destroy us too if you don't do something!"

"I don't think the Bookworm will do much harm," I said.

"I wouldn't be too sure about that," Paige said, looking down. "Oh!"

It seemed the Bookworm didn't need to use the ladder to reach the pavilion. It had increased its speed ten-fold and was heading straight for them, ignoring Drystan completely.

"Don't you know what it –!"

"Yes."

"It's coming for me. I…have a plot hole…loose…thread…look!" and she held it up. "It's going to – and if it doesn't, Drystan -"

And at that instant the Bookworm appeared over the side of the pavilion. It's head moved as if looking at Paige, then it started barreling towards her.

"Stop," I commanded.

It did. Or rather, HE did. He slowly turned and slinked towards me, shrinking until he was about the size of a large dog, raising his head for me to pat when he was close enough.

Paige looked horrified.

"Is that…your pet?!" she asked, a look of disgust on her face.

"I guess, in a way, I suppose. His name is Mr. Mott." I smiled.

"That's…what?!"

"It's an inside joke."

At the mention of his name, Mr. Mott's tail began to wag.

"Your…pet…has destroyed my whole world."

"He has been a part of a great deal of awfulness," I said very seriously. "But his actions were entirely the fault of Drystan, as you call him -"

"His real name's fine by me. And he's going to be here any second! Stop standing around and talking and do something!"

"Mr. Mott was just trying to do his job," I said calmly.

"What?!"

"Don't you know what a Bookworm does?"

"It eats the literary canon out of existence."

"Certainly not! A Bookworm…is like a literary maintenance system. It's not diabolical in the least. Its job is to help care for stories. It's around all the time, though you rarely see it. That's why it's become such an urban legend in the Store. But really they're meant to resew plot lines, clear out plot holes, and generally keep stories neat and tidy. It was only because things were being deliberately messed with that he became something dangerous. Believe me, his purpose is the opposite of destroying books. May I?" I asked, with a glance to Paige's loose thread. "You'll be safe and much more comfortable." Paige balked. "Please," I said. "You came to me for help. Let me?"

What did she have to lose? She was likely dead either way. She took a deep breath and nodded.

I looked down and gave Mr. Mott a little smile. He approached Paige very gently, took the end of the taut thread in his mouth and snipped it off just where it met the rest of Paige's body.

The moment the strand snapped Paige heard Drystan scream. She hurried as quickly as she was able to the edge of the pavilion. She saw Drystan fall, his hands grasping at air, but it was too late. The sound of his cries faded as he continued, down, down, down into the nothingness below. Paige was barely able to make out his form dissolving into a puddle of ink, finally disappearing altogether along with the rest of the world of the Ur Book.

Paige's breathing slowed.

"He's gone? We're...safe?"

"Yes."

We were all that was left.

But Mr. Mott wasn't done with Paige. He waited patiently for her to turn back from the edge, then took the broken end of the thread and wove it through the fraying strands around the empty space in her stomach until it was nicely patched. Paige found she could breathe properly again and move without pain. Mr. Mott gave a little nod, pleased with a job well done.

"See?" I said. "That's what he wants to do. But when Rahm started going around making swiss cheese of stories, adding plot holes left and right, well, Mr. Mott here will do whatever he can to stop the spread. He was incredibly confused as to why they kept cropping up in such magnitude. It was like...like Rahm put a bunch of sheep in a china shop and then sent in a herding dog."

Mr. Mott started poking around Paige's hips. Paige hit him away.

"Get off of me you awful thing!"

Mr. Mott stopped and looked almost hurt. Then he tentatively went back to prodding her.

"I'm not going to pet you…you…"

"Please," I said. "It wasn't his fault."

"It kept following me when it broke into the Store! It wanted to kill me! Because I'm wrong! That's why I had a loose plot thread in the first place!"

"That's ridiculous," I said. "Mr. Mott doesn't eat characters." I walked over to him. "Explain yourself, please."

He turned his head towards me for a moment, then went back to prodding Paige.

"Do you have something in your pocket?" I said.

"Of course not. There's just me."

To make the point, she turned out her pockets, but as she did one of her hands hit something. Confused, she pulled it out and found she was holding a large golden key.

"You were carrying around a Deus Ex Machina in the Store! No wonder Motty was on a tear!" I took the key and tossed it to him. He gobbled it up happily then, glad his job was finally complete, wriggled off under the ivory flower for a long nap.

A million questions, thoughts and arguments were desperately fighting to be let out of Paige's mind first. Finally one managed to make its way to the top. She was angry and confused… but she needed something from me.

"I…I'm not fixed," she said. "I need more than having a stray plot thread trimmed. I've looked for you all this time because I need you to fix me."

She looked like she was going to cry.

"No, dear heart, you don't."

"Yes, I do!" she said, desperately. "I'm a disaster! I caused the world to fall apart! I –"

"Paige, there's nothing wrong with you."

She stared at me, angry and speechless.

"You've always been exactly the way you were meant to be. That plot thread…that was only there…could only exist because it was made up of lies you believed. Did you see what it said? 'Gothic Romance?' 'I'm wrong…'"

"But I am wrong! All of this is my fault! I caused the world to end!"

"No you didn't. The only responsibility you can claim is that your uniqueness caused people to think differently and that set a lot of things in motion. Good things. You didn't cause the Bookworm to show up, Rahm did –"

"But…I don't know who I am! I want to be written! I want to become a story."

"Becoming a story doesn't happen all at once," I said, helping her to a chair made of discarded paper. "It doesn't happen because you have the answer to a question. It takes a long time. It has a cost, and it's usually painful. That's why stories that really matter never happen to anyone who has everything come easily."

"But…it certainly happens all at once for everyone else."

"Things aren't always how they appear," I smiled. "You may not see the trials every person had to go through to become a story, but that doesn't mean they didn't have them. The only story given to us to truly know is our own."

She studied me. "You look… a little like me.."

"You have far more manageable hair."

"But…also a little like Sora, and Adrian –"

"Yes."

"So you…were…around…" said Paige trying to understand. "And…did NOTHING while YOUR Bookstore went to hell? When every character… when my best friend was snuffed out of existence?"

"There are rules…an order to things that cannot be disobeyed. Nothing would matter if someone could just swoop down from the sky and put everything to rights whenever it was needed. It's stupid, and it's awful but it's the way things work."

"So Nightingale is right? Was…right. We have no say?" Paige said, standing. "What if I just ran and jumped into the void after Drystan?"

"Of course you have a say! I can't make you stay and listen to me. I can't keep you from ripping yourself into a million pieces."

"Why shouldn't I?"

"Because I love you. Because you matter. I know what you've been through. Believe me. I've lived through it too. I know what it is to lose an Eleanore…"

Paige looked down as if forcing herself not to cry.

"None of it mattered. There's nothing left except for some stupid palace in the middle of nothing. Everything…is gone."

"You know that's not true. Some things are eternal. Even if you can't see them."

"How?"

"Because we're in a story."

"No, I'm <u>waiting</u> to be in a story. And anyways, all the stories are gone."

"As long as there is life, there is a story," I said. "And as long as there is a story, there is hope. My job is to care for the Store and everyone and everything in it. But some things are difficult…complicated to put to rights. Little plot holes that creep in over time. Big things like Rahm…"

"You could have gotten rid of him any time."

"Oh no," I said, saddened by the thought. "He is a character, same as you and has just as much of a right to life. I do not erase or unmake things. That's what he wanted to do. To unmake me. Unmake the very fabric of creation itself. Did you ever figure out what exactly the Ur Book is?"

"Was."

"IS. We're in it now."

"It was destroyed…"

"It's form can be. But not IT. Don't you see? It can't be erased, and nothing can be erased from it because it itself is…well, a manifestation of the conduit of creation."

"Drystan…Rahm said it's supposed to have the answers to all the questions in the universe."

"When words are spoken or written into the Ur Book," I explained, "they seep in and become real. So in that sense it contains all the answers and all the questions too. At least the ones people have spent time pondering."

"But the book was blank."

"The ink disappears as what is written is made manifest."

"Words don't make something real."

"Of course they do!" I laughed. "They are the DNA of creation. 'In principio erat Verbum, et Verbum caro factum est.' In ancient times there were words for tree, sky, grass. Then people found they could differentiate different TYPES of things. The BLUE sky as opposed to the BLACK sky. Not the coarse grass, but the soft grass. And then they discovered the greatest magic – they could take the blue from sky, the softness from grass and use them with the skill of an enchanter. Why, they could make heavy things light, ancient things new. And we can do the same."

"You mean…we can bring it all back? Everything that was lost?"

"Yes! In a way…" I clarified. "It will never be exactly like it was… but you can repair what was broken."

"What Drystan did?"

"Before even him. Things were fraying at the seams for a long time. There was a war brewing in The Bookstore long before you arrived. The catalyst and the cause are not always the same thing," I smiled.

"So, is it fate or free will?" Paige asked.

"Yes," I said.

"I don't understand." She sighed. "What can I do? I'm a stupid girl without so much as a genre –"

"No you're not."

"Then what am I?"

"You're YOU," I said. "And that is the most wonderful thing in the world to be. Nobody can do it as well as you can." I walked to the edge of the pavilion and looked out at the stars. "But I understand the feeling. I don't always believe being me is very wonderful either."

"You have a freaking moon palace!"

"Is that all it takes?" I smiled.

"So I'm supposed to be OK with…being unusual and…alone? "

"No, no one's meant to be alone. But you're never alone, not really. You are unusual…but everyone is, deep down, in one way or another."

Paige sat down with her feet hanging off the side of one of the open ivory petals.

"Why do you need me?" she asked.

"Because this is your world. I'm stuck…sort of…in between."

"But…it could have been anyone."

"No. You're the one who went looking for answers."

"If I…does that mean everything will really be all right? All the characters, all the stories?"

"There will be a cost. There always is. That's a rule I cannot bypass. No story is ever truly forgotten but they may no longer be able to exist in their original forms. Some stories can return and survive largely unscathed because they're remembered deeply enough by their authors who will still go on to create them. Some…like Eleanore's…will not. She will no longer have her story to go back to."

"That's not fair."

"No."

"Do I have a choice?"

"Of course you do. I can't force you. I wouldn't even if I could. But the price of choice is that we have to live with the consequences of everybody's actions." I took a deep breath. "What do you <u>want</u> to do?"

Paige thought.

"This won't be the end. There will be more trials, more pain, more things to endure. The world coming back…that's just the beginning isn't it?"

"Yes."

"Then I don't know. I think…I'd rather stay here and watch the stars and hope that I just…fade away."

I sat down next to her, tears in my eyes.

"I often feel the same," I said. "I am not always <u>here</u>, but even when I am, even on my best days in an ivory moon pavilion I feel very sad and like I would much rather not exist either. But I didn't get a choice in being created."

"Neither did I," said Paige.

I sighed. "I often lack faith and feel no hope at all. And yet…"

"And yet?"

"I still love. Somehow. I love Eleanore, and Velveteen, and Shadow and you. I love Meg Murry, and Frodo and Aslan. I love the truth that is at the heart of them and is more real than anything you can touch. And so I go on. To honor the truth they represent."

"Do you…have an Owner?" Paige asked.

"I don't own you," I said, gently.

"Is there someone…higher up? That you have to report to?"

"Well, I'm certainly not in charge of the whole world," I laughed. "Just a Bookstore."

Paige looked out at the sky, thinking for a long while.

"I don't know if I can help," she said. "I haven't read every story. I don't even know if I remember all the ones I did. Certainly not enough to bring them back into existence…I can't even think of the first sentence of most, let alone…"

"Stories aren't stored in our minds, but in our hearts. The things you know are true deep in your soul can never be erased. Stories are merely the road maps to lead us back to the things that matter. They are not gone now, just invisible. Sweep the words up, put them back in order. That is the secret of storytellers. They're not omnipotent beings, merely…story keepers. Say…what you remember."

Paige sat and thought. "The most intoxicating thing about The Bookstore is its scent," she said. "That's the first thing I remember. The mix of aged leather, gold stitching, thread…visionaries must dream of bottling it."

She went on. She spoke for a year and a day. She talked the most of Eleanore, but she described every inch of the Store and every character and story she could, including Atlas and her becoming fleshed out. And as she talked, it came back into being. The lily railings, and stained glass, the murals, and arching stairways, and the silver bell on the front door. The stacks rose up around them, books lined the shelves and soon there was no difference between Paige telling what she remembered and describing what was right in front of her. Finally she stopped, realizing what had happened, and looked around, tears running down her cheeks.

"Shadow was right," she said.

"He usually is," I smiled.

"You know him…? But…he said he only thought he'd met you a long time ago."

"Time is funny. There might have been a lifetime between your meeting him and now. In the way an author might take months to figure out how to respond to a character's question in a story, but no time at all will have passed for the character between the question and what happens next."

"Will Drystan be here too?" Paige said, suddenly worried.

"You don't need to concern yourself with him," I said. "He does not have the power he did. He is, for now, exactly where you left him."

Paige smiled and was ready to run full force into the stacks, to run and jump and hug everyone and everything she saw. But I took her hand.

"There is one gift I can give you," I said. "There are rules for all things, lines even I can't cross, or the world will unravel. But, as you said yourself, 'You can get away with illogical magic once.' And so may I. I can give you one impossible wish. "

"I can wish for anything?"

"Yes. You can wish to be any genre, to have Wesley come back, to be in his story…anything in the world."

Paige grew very serious.

"If we really do have the power to choose…everyone…not just me," Paige said as she organized her thoughts, "then Wesley decided to go with his author. Nothing made him break his promise…just like nothing made Drystan pull the world apart. I don't think, really, I'd like to be with someone like that. Besides…he's not worth something as precious as an impossible wish. And…I think I'm a bit tired of searching for a label. If it really isn't going to end the world…when it really comes down to it I think I prefer not being in a box."

She thought some more. I could see the idea forming in her mind, but she was being very careful to choose precisely the right words.

"I wish," said Paige, "that Eleanore wouldn't be sick anymore. Never, ever again."

"That is a good wish," I said..

"And stories will be back in the real world too?"

"You don't have to worry about little Adrian. Her photos are all back as they should be."

Paige smiled and I watched as she turned and ran joyfully back into the Store calling for Eleanore.

"I wonder what story little Adrian will write someday," I said to

Shadow as he stepped beside me. He looked out over the Store, his eyes glancing over each character. "I'm glad I didn't have to take them. Especially Eleanore, after what I told her." He sighed. "But it turns out there were…unexpected circumstances."

"I'm sorry," I said. He didn't reply. "Perhaps you should pay him a visit?"

"Yes," he said, a little sadly. "Though this was not the reunion I hoped for."

"I hope I can meet…the brother you love, someday."

"It would not be safe for you…now."

"No," I said. "You know the way?"

"I know all the ways."

I smiled as he ventured off. Then I called Dewey who I was both happy and sad wouldn't be needed again for a long, long time. I gave her back the newly reconstituted Ur Book, knowing she would take care of it well. And so I turned and went back to finish my work. There is quite a lot of it, especially paperwork, when you are in charge of a magical Bookstore, dear reader. There is always so much to do.

CHAPTER 26

ONCE UPON A TIME

P aige never told anyone the full story about her conversation with me. She shared the major points with Eleanore, but she didn't even tell her quite everything. The last thing most of the characters remembered was the fire, then a kind of darkness, and then the Store coming back to normal. Paige explained what happened in the Ur Book with the Bookworm and how Drystan dissolved into ink and disappeared. Everyone was safe. Drystan was gone, and no one really spoke of him, as if saying his name would summon him back.

Except for Gwen. Drystan had permanently left his mark on her. She walked around in a haze, her hand on her head as if it was causing her immense pain. Fred, Horror or not, was an expert surgeon. But he could find nothing wrong with her.

"It's not logical!" she kept saying. "All the evidence...it doesn't add up. I don't understand. It was irrefutable...Drystan...Drystan...he loved me. And I'm a good detective...I know I am..."

Most of the characters wanted her punished. Despite Eleanore's testimony that, in the end, Gwen had tried to protect her, Gwen was still long complicit in Drystan's actions. They couldn't punish him first-hand, so she was the next best thing. In the meantime Gwen paced around the Store like a mad woman, presenting her repetitive, nonsensical argument to an invisible court.

"It's not logical! Look at the evidence!"

"She needs help," Paige said to Nightingale. "In this state I'm not sure she would even know what she was being punished for."

And so Nightingale and Paige quietly took her to Annwn Hospital (Nightingale was an alumnus, after all), where she stayed, strapped to her bed repeating:

"It's not logical! The evidence..." over and over again, for a long time.

But I hope, dear reader, that one day she will find her right mind again. And then I think she will have many important things to say and do having become much wiser for her experiences. But perhaps that is another story for another time.

***

Back in The Bookstore life went on and, faster than Paige thought possible, they returned to a kind of normalcy.

Velveteen's book was complete again, as was Willa's and Dracula 1's.

But Eleanore's was gone, just as I warned it would be.

"I'm sorry," Paige said. "That…you won't be written."

"Guess we're in the same boat now," said Eleanore, trying to make a joke. She pulled out her flower and held it to her ear, smiling. The song was once again beautiful and strong.

"No," Paige replied. "It's not funny. I've always been like this. But you had a story and a genre and lots of things you were supposed to do. It's not fair."

"There wasn't another way," said Eleanore. "Besides, I'm not the only one. And it's better than not existing at all. At least none of us are fading!"

"You don't have to be nice to me about it. It's downright rotten. And it wasn't fair that I made the decision for you. Things always turn out right in a story. But –"

Eleanore stopped her.

"I've seen a lot of things now, and I know a lot more than I used to. There's not one story that really matters where everything's happy and fine all the time. Maybe I can remind people of that. Even if it's just the characters and authors who come to the Store. Maybe it'll help. We're all fighting a battle. Being written doesn't change that."

She hugged Paige.

"I'm sorry about Drystan, and Gwen and –"

"Stop saying you're sorry," Eleanore laughed. "You're starting to sound like me."

Paige had spent a long time wishing she belonged and that someone loved her. She'd been so carried away chasing someone she thought would give it to her…when all the time it had been right here. Maybe the person they'd both really needed was a best friend.

But other characters weren't adjusting as easily as Eleanore to the thought that their story had been permanently damaged or didn't even exist anymore…yet they were still here…

"Does this mean I'm just stuck here for all eternity like…Nightingale and Paige?!" Fred demanded. "I can't live like that! I refuse!"

"And what about when new characters arrive?" asked Dracula 1. "The failsafe's been deactivated; they won't be able to find their books to know if they'll even be written or –"

"How come we can still find ours?" asked Velveteen. "Without the failsafe?"

"Probably because we've already seen them. We know our title and our author…"

"Makes the most sense to me…"

"So what do we do? Just tell them 'Hi! You may or may not be written and if you're not you'll forever be in a state of indentured servitude?' That's just horrible," said the Cat.

"I want the rules back!" Willa cried. "I want them all back! We knew what to do and what was going to happen –"

"Whether or not we get a happy ending, we still have an important job. I think we just keep doing what we know is right."

"Easy for you to say," said Fred. "You've always known you were different. It's easier for you."

"And you have a best friend! Some of us don't have anyone at all. What's Romance supposed to do?! They're not built to –"

"Nevermore!" The Raven screeched.

Paige was overjoyed when she discovered Atlas was alive and well and in the Store too.

"Is your story…" Paige asked hesitantly –

"The teahouse is still there," Atlas said. "Nightingale will be happy."

"So you can go back!"

"I don't want to," she said rather seriously. "And I don't really want to stay here, no disrespect. I think I'd like a break from serving other people. I'd like to explore. Put my name to good use."

And so Atlas left the Store and her story. She had many adventures in many books and grew even wiser than she already was. Tales of what she did could fill several volumes. But she was happy, for now, to have them just for herself.

Nightingale never asked Paige about me. He found it too overwhelming to know too much about the ins and outs of this strange new world he had to learn to navigate. He did his job, showed characters around the Store, filed his paperwork, just grateful for the fact that they had reclaimed some sort of balance.

"I feel bad for him," Eleanore said to Paige. "He made one bad choice and now he has to pay for it for all eternity."

"ONE bad choice?"

"I mean not going with his author. But he has made several more since then."

"Do you think he was appointed Manager?" Paige asked. "Or did he just…take the job?"

"I don't know. I don't really know how the whole…promotion process works…but Nightingale doesn't really seem the type to…seize…anything."

Then, one day, when Paige was working the front counter, the little bell on the door rang and a tall woman in her forties walked in. She wore a coat of patchwork velvet and had a wild head of hair. She looked around the Store for a long time but seemed more and more disappointed with the selection as she went. It made Willa think of "Cinderella" when the Prince, having finished visiting the entire village, despairs of ever finding the maid who fit the glass slipper.

"Nothing else new?" the woman kept muttering. "Nothing else?"

"What, specifically, are you looking for?" Paige asked.

"I…I don't know…" she said looking around, a bit confused. "I can't seem to remember, only it was very, very important."

"Do you know what genre -?"

"Oh, what kind of nonsense! Genre?! Such an overrated term. Can't you just enjoy a story for the sake of it being that particular story without needing to catalogue it?"

Paige stifled a laugh. She liked her.

"It would be rather difficult to organize a bookstore without a system using genre -"

"Ridiculous!" said the woman with a flourish. "Now if this were my bookstore, I'd have all the books just go where they liked, and if one was needed, or…just felt like getting a little air, it would float off the shelf where it was sitting and flap over to where it should be."

"Suppose they all rebelled and wouldn't go where you needed them to?"

"Pish. Stories always go where they need to. The good ones at any rate. No use wanting them to do anything. Just leave them to their own devices and wait."

At that moment Nightingale walked to the front of the Store. When he saw the woman his eyes filled with tears. She didn't notice him right away, but he saw her instantly. It was like he was seeing his long lost love for the first time in decades. But he didn't run to her, or even make his presence known. He was getting a second chance, but again he hesitated. Not because he was scared, not in the way he was before, not exactly. This time he didn't want to abandon the Store to whatever troubles might lie in wait.

Paige gave him a nod.

For all his talk about fate he couldn't quite let himself trust that everything would be OK and work out the way it was supposed to.

And then Willa came up behind him and gave him a big shove towards the woman.

The woman heard him trip and turned around. Her eyes lit up.

"That's it," she said. "Where have you been?"

Nightingale stood there, frozen.

"We'll be OK," Paige whispered.

"Of course you will," he said. "You will…won't you? You'll all… you will?"

Willa smiled.

"Of course!" she said. "It's in my name. We Will-a." She giggled.

"Do you want to go?" Paige asked.

"Yes. Yes, very much."

"Well, then."

Nightingale folded up his apron and took off his nametag, laying them on the front counter like he was finally putting down a heavy burden. The woman took his arm and together they walked through the door, Nightingale most likely leaving behind every memory he had, forgetting every magical spell, every mythology and language he had spent so long studying, The Bookstore itself, and did the bravest thing he had ever done. He walked into the rest of his life.

Just at that moment a new character emerged from the stacks. He was a sweet looking fellow, very rotund - like a walking mushroom. He looked terribly confused.

"Billy," he said. "Children's Fantasy."

Paige realized everyone was staring at her.

"Oh no, no, no, no, no," said Paige. "I can't! Shouldn't it be the person who's been here the longest?"

"I don't know," said Willa, skipping back into the stacks.

"No one knows how Nightingale got picked."

Paige saved them from Drystan and logically that meant that she could save them from everything else, right?

"I'm not the chosen one," she whispered to Eleanore.

"Of course you're not," Eleanore replied with a look that seemed to say: How egocentric can you be? "But looks like you are the new manager. None of us want the responsibility. I certainly don't want to have to file all that paperwork. So tag, you're it."

Paige just stood there.

"Oh for Pete's sake just show him around!" said Eleanore. "We've seen Nightingale do it a hundred times. It's not some epic mandate – you just have to give him the tour and make him fill out some forms."

Paige picked up the clipboard. When she looked down and saw that her nametag now read:

PAIGE

———————————

MANAGER

That was a little touch of mine, dear reader. I do like things to be organized. And I wanted to give Paige my stamp of approval. She internally rolled her eyes at me.

"Hi," she said to Billy. "I'm Paige." She took a breath. "As you have probably gathered, this Store is home to others like you…"

And they disappeared into the stacks as she began the monologue they'd heard so often before.

* * *

Time went by. Paige turned out to be a rather good manager. She was kind, but decisive and firm in a manner that comes from, in the best way, no longer caring so much what people think of you. She cleaned up Nightingale's office with some help from Eleanore, Fred, Dracula 1 and The Raven (The Raven was especially helpful at sorting through the very small bits and bobs). The office turned out to be quite a nice and relaxing respite within the Store. She played through Nightingale's collection of vinyl records, read through the books in his office, visited the teashop and "Ever" (where, sadly, none of the characters had any memory of her), and talked with Eleanore.

But all too soon things became static again. They were back in a rhythm and Paige couldn't shake the feeling that the whole Store was lying in wait for something new to start. Nothing changed, and Paige felt like she was about to burst.

"Did you ever find out your genre?" Eleanore asked one day. "I mean, after all of that…did you ever get an answer?"

"No," said Paige.

"Well, I'll say one thing for your author,"

"If I even have one."

Eleanore politely ignored the comment.

"They must be really interesting."

"As interesting as a magical purgatory-like Bookstore?" Paige joked. "Or an Owner who lives in an ivory moon palace, or…"

And then all at once, and with no fuss at all, Paige realized. You'd think a revelation like that would come with blaring trumpets and fireworks, but it didn't. It was simple. A quiet thing. Like a door in Paige's mind blew open with a gentle spring breeze and her sepia world suddenly transformed into Technicolor.

Paige looked at the front door.

"What if…" she said.

"What if what?"

"What if <u>this</u> is my story?"

"I…don't understand…"

"What if we're in my story, right now. What if…I already met my author?"

"If we're in your story, whatever that means, how could you have met your author?"

"If…they wrote themselves into the story to talk to me. That's the only way I could…and that means…" she said, trying to figure it out as she said it, "that EVERYTHING is a part of the story…we…could have just walked out that door whenever we wanted."

Paige walked up to the door and put her hand on the knob.

"Don't!" shouted Eleanore. "Come on. That's a bit…What if you're wrong? You don't know what will happen. There could be nothing out there! A void. It could bring the Bookworm back. Even if…just…don't risk it. We finally -"

"I have to. I…I want to."

"Why?"

"Because…" she said, slowly, thinking through her words. "I think my author wrote me to be something like them. And if I were an author, that's what I would do."

"But…then… in our stories…in our genres we know exactly what we're supposed to do. We don't know yours. Even if…How would we know what's right…?"

"We don't," Paige replied. "So, you'll just have to do what you'd want your author to have written and trust that it will all turn out OK. Make your own choice and trust that it will work out for good. Do what you would want your story to say. Fate _and_ free will…there can be both at the same time." She laughed. All of a sudden, it was so simple.

She thought back to when she'd first arrived in the Store. If she was right, she _could_ have just gone out the door that very first day and skipped everything that had happened since. Wesley, and Eleanore and Drystan. Skipped falling in love, skipped meeting them at all. Missed all the books, the stories, the characters. She didn't know what was waiting outside, but she realized, finally, that no matter what, she was glad she hadn't jumped ahead.

She turned the handle and opened the door. She looked back at Eleanore, then turned and walked through.

She found herself standing on a city street under a blue sky. It wasn't as vibrant as the skies in the books she had been in. But it was more… _real_. She looked behind her. Just above the entrance was a sign that read:

PAIGE'S BOOKSTORE

"Ha, ha" Paige said to me, even though she couldn't see me.

She wondered if everything she'd lost was waiting for her

somewhere out here. She wondered if there would be fairies, or robots, and gardens, and seasides and, the most extraordinary thing of all, ordinary life. Maybe all of them. Because real life doesn't have a genre. Or perhaps, dear reader, it's more that it has all of them.

Eleanore crossed the threshold behind her. She stood blinking into the big, bright, sunlit sky.

Paige took her hand.

I watched Paige take a breath, and then with a deep exhale, her eyes wide with the excitement of possibility, she bravely took a step and walked out into the world.

I can't wait to discover what she's going to do next, dear reader.

Or what you will do, in whatever story you're in that happens to be all your own.

EPILOGUE

S hadow stood in a void, looking down at his brother.

After a long time, Rahm finally spoke.

"It's cruel," he said, "for you to arrive, uninvited, in a place like this. Where I am powerless. Forced to endure your…company."

Shadow merely looked at him.

"The moment Sora said your name I knew it was you," Rahm spat. "Somehow, it was you in that miserable story."

"We always recognize each other. No matter our guise or what name we go by."

"This one is pathetic. Even for you."

"I've grown rather fond of it."

"You would."

"Is that why you sowed chaos in that story? Frayed it at the seams? Got Eleanore kidnapped by that out of context B plotline? Was it really just to further your machinations against Paige, or were you trying to get away from me as fast as possible?"

Rahm just stared at the ground.

"You wouldn't speak to me?" he paused. "I would have kept your pretense. Respected your name."

Rahm laughed.

 "You can't bear to be in my presence. After all this time?" Shadow asked.

"Always thinking of yourself." He paused. "I wish I could kill you."

"If you could, I don't know that I would stop you."

Rahm didn't reply.

"Is that where you've been, brother? The Bookstore?"

"You think I would stay in Arcadia?"

"The others are there."

"Of course they are. I'm sure Aurelia is in heaven. Literally."

"Even Ru –"

"Ru! What else would you expect, the state you left them in?!" he smiled. "Does their curse still weigh on you?"

Rham stood up. "Where am I, exactly? Is there a…'something' at the center of the Nothing?"

"You're in the Ur Book. Confined…within its pages."

Rahm started laughing uproariously. Maniacally.

"Of course! Well, if that isn't poetic justice…"

"What happened, brother?" Shadow asked. "You are an immortal being, how could you possibly be trapped –"

"I made…a miscalculation." Rahm grimaced. "Once we were forgotten we could still move throughout the ethereal realms…"

"And you came to the one closest to the mortal one?"

"I thought I could inspire one of humans, be written and return."

"Cheat death, you mean?"

"Am I threatening you?"

"No. You are creative as ever. I admire your attempt. I wish you had succeeded. Truthfully. I have missed you."

They stared at each other in silence.

"It did not go according to plan?" Shadow asked.

"They created a pathetic version of me. I was quickly forgotten again, and this time I returned to The Bookstore trapped. No longer a forgotten god, but a shell of a forgotten character. Do humans know how many forgotten characters there are? Waiting to be found?"

"I believe all living things feel like a forgotten character at some time."

"It's different when it's literal." He took a breath. "Destroying the Store would have been a gift to some of them. That is the only permanent erasure."

"There is no such thing. Not really. Not death beyond hope. You know you would never truly cease to exist. Nothing ever does. And I…I will always remember you."

"I would take non-existence over the eternity you offer."

Shadow moved away. Finally, he turned the conversation. "What was the story they cast you in?"

"That of a diabolical villain. A trickster god hellbent on destroying the earth for fun."

"You did have your moments."

"I am the god of abundance as well as devastation. I could never stay fully in either too long. I would never have brought about any real damage."

"Tell that to Pompeii."

"Did you come here to criticize me, like you always do? Can you think of nothing better to say after thousands of years?"

Shadow bit his lip.

"I have missed you."

"Then release me!"

"I cannot do that."

"The Owner could."

"Perhaps. But at least here I can see you."

"You would keep me in a cage?"

"You are too dangerous –"

"You are not the ruler of us! It is not for you to decide."

"No, it's not."

"It is your burden to be alone. It's what you deserve. Your punishment."

"For doing my job?"

"Is it not those things we can't change about ourselves that we are most punished for?"

Shadow turned and started to leave.

"This isn't the end, you know…" said Rahm.

"Of course not. There are no real endings to stories, just as there are no true beginnings."

"Best beware, then. All of you. I have all the time in the world. It's simply a matter of waiting for the turn of a page."

Dramatists Personae

Principal Denizens of The Store
(By Genre)

ADVENTURE
Herc *(Superhero)*
Atlas Wright *(Futuristic)*

Children's Book
Willa Posey *(Imaginative Empowerment)*
Dracula 1 *(Imaginative Empowerment)*
Velveteen Rabbit *(Classic Children's)*

Comedy
Drystan *(Epic)*

Drama
Arden (et al) *(Coming of Age)*
Hamlet *(Theatrical Tragedy)*

Fantasy
Cheshire Cat *(Classic Children's)*
Glormhar *(B Arthurian Fantasy)*
Dr. Ozymandias Nightingale *(High Steampunk Fantasy)*

HORROR
Dracula 2 *(Gothic)*
Fred *(Satanic Bargains)*

MYTH
Rahm *(Ancient)*

Poetry
Raven *(Gothic)*

Romance
Gwendolyn Rose Friday *(Crime (1940's Retro Cyberpunk) Romance Novel)*
Wesley Gray *(Gothic)*
Violet *(Fantasy Romance Novel)*
Iris *(Coming of Age Romance Novel)*

SCIENCE FICTION
Quinn *(B-Lost in Space Adventure)*

TEEN DRAMA (YA)
Eleanore Lydia Addams *(Dark Contemporary Fairy Tale Adaptation)*

Other
Dewey
Paige

Authors

Adrian
Krasny *(Romance, Gwen/Iris)*
Sonny *(Arden (et al))*
Shakespeare *(Hamlet)*
Una Williams *(Wesley)*

In the Books

Bookworm
Bob *(A ghostly security guard)*
Daisy Buchanan *(The one you're thinking of)*
Fortune Teller
Shadow
Sora *(A fairy Queen)*
Mabel *(A talking horse)*
Ms. Three

Other

The Owner

ACKNOWLEDGEMENTS

A very special thank you to the following people who helped make this book a reality:

My fantastic editor and friend Malcolm Stephenson.

Jason Schultz, Batya Kemper, Lindsay Harris and the great Zachary Alinder.

All my beta readers, especially Anna Koontz and Grace Columbia – who are very smart, born "literaphiles", and, most importantly, kind and lovely people.

The Santa Monica Public Library (especially the Montana Ave. Branch) where I went constantly as a child (and still do when I can) and worked as a Library Page just after high school to help save up for college.

Left Bank Books and Rizzoli Books in NYC for their incredible support of this project and its development.

My "Grandma Mommy" who acted out stories with me and wanted me to remember to "be sure to keep on writing no matter what…"

And most of all, to my mom, who read me the most wonderful stories, taught me how to write and always encouraged me, with unwavering love, to be a storyteller.

ABOUT THE AUTHOR

Photo by: Kristin Hoebermann

Ashley Griffin is most well known as a Broadway writer/ performer. Her work has been produced/developed at New World Stages, MTC, Playwrights Horizons and more. She was the recipient of the WellLife Network Award and a county commendation for her hit play *Trial* (directed by Lori Petty), and has been nominated for six NYIT Awards across multiple categories. Ashley writes for American Theatre Magazine, and OnStage and has taught at NYU Tisch (where she received her BFA). Ashley is the first person in history to be nominated for a major award for both playing and directing *"Hamlet"* for a theatrical production. In addition to *Blank Paige*, Ashley is the author of *The Spindle*. She is based in NYC.

<u>www.ashleygriffinofficial.com</u>

<u>Twitter</u>: @ashleyjgriffin

<u>Instagram/TikTok/Facebook</u>: @ashleygriffinofficial

<u>YouTube</u>: Ashley Griffin

PRAISE FOR ASHLEY GRIFFIN

"The kind of storytelling defined by George MacDonald and Madeline L'Engle...I believe she is the MacDonald of our generation... (Griffin) utterly subverts all expectations of a 'YA Fantasy' book." **- OnStage**

"If storytelling – as put by Griffin – is a dying art, then she herself is in the vanguard of its resuscitation...Owing to a rich heritage of stories past and present, Griffin's work reflects the best elements of storytellers past and combines them in her own style (with) just enough detail for the imaginations of her audience to take over...I am predisposed to trust any (piece) under Griffin's auspices." **– Paper Tiger Reviews**

"Within the subtext of Ashley Griffin's dark stories of struggle and survival is one of the most surprisingly cathartic voices about mortality and immortality." **– Mike Rinaldi, "What is Hip?"**

"She transports us through eras, characters and story lines clearly and with ferocious grace...It is truly stunning what she can do with...nothing but the simplest...magic." **– The Harlem Times**